THOSE JENSEN BOYS!
RIDE THE
SAVAGE LAND

THOSE JENSEN BOYS!
RIDE THE SAVAGE LAND

William W. Johnstone
with J. A. Johnstone

PINNACLE BOOKS
Kensington Publishing Corp.
www.kensingtonbooks.com

PINNACLE BOOKS are published by

Kensington Publishing Corp.
119 West 40th Street
New York, NY 10018

PUBLISHER'S NOTE
Following the death of William W. Johnstone, the Johnstone family is working with a carefully selected writer to organize and complete Mr. Johnstone's outlines and many unfinished manuscripts to create additional novels in all of his series like The Last Gunfighter, Mountain Man, and Eagles, among others. This novel was inspired by Mr. Johnstone's superb storytelling.

All Kensington titles, imprints, and distributed lines are available at special quantity discounts for bulk purchases for sales promotions, premiums, fund-raising, educational, or institutional use. Special book excerpts or customized printings can also be created to fit specific needs. For details, write or phone the office of the Kensington sales manager: Kensington Publishing Corp., 119 West 40th Street, New York, NY 10018; attn: Sales Department; phone 1-800-221-2647.

ISBN-13: 978-0-7860-4034-6
ISBN-10: 0-7860-4034-3

First printing: May 2018

10 9 8 7 6 5 4 3 2 1

Printed in the United States of America

First electronic edition: May 2018

ISBN-13: 978-0-7860-4035-3
ISBN-10: 0-7860-4035-1

The Jensen Family
First Family of the American Frontier

Smoke Jensen—The Mountain Man
The youngest of three children and orphaned as a young boy, Smoke Jensen is considered one of the fastest draws in the West. His quest to tame the lawless West has become the stuff of legend. Smoke owns the Sugarloaf Ranch in Colorado. Married to Sally Jensen, father to Denise ("Denny") and Louis.

Preacher—The First Mountain Man
Though not a blood relative, grizzled frontiersman Preacher became a father figure to the young Smoke Jensen, teaching him how to survive in the brutal, often deadly Rocky Mountains. Fought the battles that forged his destiny. Armed with a long gun, Preacher is as fierce as the land itself.

Matt Jensen—The Last Mountain Man
Orphaned but taken in by Smoke Jensen, Matt Jensen has become like a younger brother to Smoke and even took the Jensen name. And like Smoke, Matt has carved out his destiny on the American frontier. He lives by the gun and surrenders to no man.

Luke Jensen—*Bounty Hunter*

Mountain Man Smoke Jensen's long-lost brother Luke Jensen is scarred by war and a dead shot—the right qualities to be a bounty hunter. And he's cunning, and fierce enough, to bring down the deadliest outlaws of his day.

Ace Jensen and Chance Jensen—*Those Jensen Boys!*

Smoke Jensen's long-lost nephews, Ace and Chance, are a pair of young-gun twins as reckless and wild as the frontier itself . . . Their father is Luke Jensen, thought killed in the Civil War. Their uncle Smoke Jensen is one of the fiercest gunfighters the West has ever known. It's no surprise that the inseparable Ace and Chance Jensen have a knack for taking risks—even if they have to blast their way out of them.

CHAPTER ONE

It began with a rattlesnake in a glass jar and Chance Jensen's inability to pass up a bet he believed he could win.

A balding, beefy-faced bartender with curlicue mustaches reached under the bar, came up with the big glass jar, and set it on the hardwood with a solid thump. The top of the jar had a board sitting across it. Somebody had drilled airholes in the board so the fat diamondback rattler coiled inside the jar wouldn't suffocate.

"Five bucks says no man can tap on the glass and hold his finger there when Chauncey here strikes at it," the bartender announced.

A cowboy standing a few feet down the bar with a beer in front of him looked at the jar and its deadly occupant and said, "Step aside, boys! This here is gonna be the easiest five dollars I ever earned!"

The men along the bar shifted so the cowboy could stand in front of the jar. Chance and his brother Ace had to move a little to their left, but they could still see the show.

The cowboy leaned closer and peered through the glass at the snake, which hadn't moved when the bartender set him down. "He's alive, ain't he?"

"Tap on the glass and find out," the bartender said.

The cowboy lifted a hand covered with rope calluses. He held up his index finger and thumped it three times against the glass, lightly.

Inside the jar, the snake's head raised slightly. Its tail began to vibrate, moving so fast that it was just a blur.

The saloon was quiet as everyone looked on, and even through the glass, the men closest to the bar could hear the distinctive buzzing. That sound could strike fear into the stoutest-hearted man in Texas.

"Yeah, uh, he's alive, all right," the cowboy said. "What do I do now?"

"Show me that you actually have five bucks," the bartender said.

The cowboy reached into his pocket, pulled out a five-dollar gold piece, and slapped it down on the hardwood. Grinning, the bartender took an identical coin from the till and set it next to the cowboy's stake.

"All right. Tap on the glass a few more times to get Chauncey stirred up good and proper, and then hold your finger there. Then we wait. Shouldn't be too long."

Another man said, "Chauncey's a boy's name, ain't it?"

"Yeah, I suppose so," the bartender said with a frown. "What's your point?"

"I was just wonderin' how you know for sure that there snake is a male. Did you check?"

That brought a few hoots of laughter from the crowd.

The bartender glared. "Never you mind about that. If I say he's a boy, then he's a boy. If you want to prove different, you reach in there and show me the evidence."

"No, no," the bystander said, holding his hands up in surrender. "I'm fine with whatever you say, Dugan."

The bartender looked at the cowboy. "Well? You gonna give it a try or not? You were mighty quick to brag about how you could do it. You decide you don't want to back that up with cold, hard cash after all?"

"I'm gonna, I'm gonna," the cowboy said. "Just hang on a minute." He swallowed, then tapped three more times on the glass, harder this time.

"Hold your finger there," Dugan said.

From a few feet away, Chance watched with all his attention focused on the jar and the cowboy who was daring the snake to strike at him. Ace watched Chance and felt a stirring of concern at the expression he saw on his brother's face.

The cowboy rested his fingertip against the glass. Inside the jar, the snake's head was still up, its tiny forked tongue flickering as it darted in and out of his mouth. The buzzing from the rattles on the tip of its tail steadily grew louder.

Then, faster than the eye could follow, the snake uncoiled and struck at the glass where the cowboy's finger was pressed.

"Yeeeowww!" the cowboy yelled as he jumped back. The rattler's sudden movement startled half a dozen other people in the Lucky Panther Saloon into shouting, too.

For a couple seconds, the cowboy stared wide-eyed at the jar, where the snake had coiled up again, and then looked down at his hand. The index finger still stuck straight out, but it was nowhere near the glass anymore. Obviously disgusted, he said, "Well, hell."

Grinning, Dugan scooped up both five-dollar gold pieces and dropped them into the till. "Told you. Nobody can do it. It just ain't natural for a man to be able to hold still when a rattler's fangs are comin' at him, whether there's glass in between or not."

Ace tried to catch Chance's eye and shake his head, but it was too late. Chance stepped closer to the spot on the bar where the jar rested and said, "I can do it."

People looked around to see who had made that bold declaration. If not for what happened next, they would have seen a handsome, sandy-haired man in his early twenties, well dressed in a brown tweed suit, white shirt, and a dark brown cravat and hat.

But all their attention turned to the man who shouldered Chance aside, said, "Outta my way, kid," and stepped up to the bar. "I've never been afraid of a rattler in my life, and sure as hell not one penned up in a jar." He was tall and lean, dressed in black from head to foot, and probably ten years older than Chance and Ace, who were fraternal twins. His smile had a cocky arrogance to it.

Ace was more interested in the gun holstered on the man's hip. In keeping with the rest of his outfit, that holster was black. The revolver was the only thing flashy about him. It was nickel plated and had ivory grips.

However, the gun wasn't just for show. Those grips showed the marks of a great deal of use. Maybe the man just practiced with it a lot—or maybe he actually *was* the gunslinger he obviously fancied himself to be.

The man in black held the edge of a coin against the bar and gave it a spin. It whirled there for a long moment, so fast it was just a blur, but finally ran out of momentum and clattered on the hardwood. "I reckon my money's good, Dugan?"

"Sure, Shelby," the bartender said. "You're welcome to give it a try."

A spade-bearded man in a frock coat stepped up. He hooked his thumbs in the gold-brocaded vest he wore and said, "I have fifty dollars that says Lew can do it."

That wager was too rich for the blood of most of the patrons in that particular saloon in Fort Worth's notorious Hell's Half Acre, but the tinhorn gambler got a couple takers. Coins and greenbacks were put on the bar for Dugan to hold while Shelby made his try.

Ace nudged a bearded old-timer who stood next to him and asked, "Who are those two?"

"The gun-hung feller in black is Lew Shelby," the codger replied. "The one in the fancy vest is Henry Baylor."

"He looks like a card sharp."

"Good reason for that. He is. Or at least the rumor has it so. Nobody's ever caught him cheatin', though, as far as I know. If they have, they've had sense enough not to call him on it." The old-timer licked his lips, his tongue emerging from the shaggy white whiskers for a second. "Baylor might be even slicker at handlin' shootin' irons than he is at cards. Him and Shelby is two of a kind, and they run with a bunch just about as bad."

Ace nodded. Chance didn't look happy about Shelby pushing in ahead of him, but for the moment at least, he was keeping his annoyance under control. Ace would say something to him if necessary, to keep him calmed down. They didn't need a gunfight in the middle of the saloon—or anywhere else, for that matter. The Jensen brothers were peaceable sorts.

That was what Ace aspired to, anyway. Oftentimes fate seemed to be plotting against them, however.

Lew Shelby stood in front of the bar, feet planted solidly, hands held out in front of him and slightly spread. He rubbed his thumbs over his fingertips and took deep breaths, as if he were working himself up to slap leather against the snake, not hold his finger against a glass jar.

The crowd began to stir restlessly.

Shelby sensed that impatience, glanced over his shoulder, and sneered. "Hold your damn horses." Then he reached out and tapped the glass several times, fast and hard. He pressed his finger against the jar as the snake reacted, coiling tighter in preparation to strike.

Everybody in the place knew it was coming. Nobody should have been surprised, least of all Shelby. But when the rattler struck with the same sort of blinding speed as before, Shelby jumped back a step and yelped, "Son of a bitch!"

Several men in the crowd cursed, too. Others laughed, which made Shelby's face flush.

Dugan picked up the gold piece that was all he'd had riding on the bet, but the other men who'd placed wagers moved quickly up to the bar to claim their winnings. Shelby and Baylor looked startled and angry.

That anger deepened as Dugan smirked. "Told you so, boys. No man alive has got icy enough nerves to manage that little trick."

Ace tried to get hold of Chance's coat sleeve and pull him away, but Chance was a little too quick for him. He stepped forward and said, "I told you, I can do it."

Lew Shelby looked at him and scowled. "Run along, sonny. This business is for men, not boys."

Chance's voice held an edge as he said, "I'm full-grown, in case you hadn't noticed." He moved his coat aside a little, revealing a .38 caliber Smith & Wesson Second Model revolver with ivory grips resting in a cross-draw rig on his left hip.

Shelby's dark eyes slitted, giving him a certain resemblance to the snake. "You better walk soft, boy. I don't cotton to being challenged."

Ace stepped up next to his brother. He had been born a few minutes earlier than Chance, and he was slightly taller and heavier, too. Dark hair curled out from under a thumbed-back Stetson. He wore range clothes, denim trousers and a bib-front shirt, and his boots showed plenty of wear. He didn't take the time or trouble to polish them up, the way Chance did his. The walnut-butted Colt .45 Peacemaker leathered on Ace's right hip was strictly functional, too.

"Nobody's challenging anybody." Ace had plenty of experience trying to head off trouble when Chance was in the middle of it.

"That's not true," Chance said. "I'm challenging that rattlesnake, as well as Mr. Dugan here. I can hold my finger on the glass without budging when the snake strikes at it."

"If I can't do it, kid, you sure as hell can't," Shelby snapped.

"The two hundred dollars in my pocket says I can."

Ace bit back a groan. Actually, the two hundred bucks was in his pocket, not Chance's, but they had that much, all right. They had worked for several months on a ranch north of Fort Worth to earn it, and they were ready to take it easy and drift for a while, which was their usual pattern.

They couldn't do that if Chance's reckless stubbornness caused them to lose their stake.

Things had gone too far to stop. Chance had thrown the bet out there.

Henry Baylor stroked his beard. "I'm down a hundred dollars tonight. Winning two hundred from you would allow me to show a profit for the evening, son."

"I'm not your son," Chance said.

In truth, he and Ace didn't know whose sons they were. They had been raised by a drifting gambler named Ennis "Doc" Monday, after their mother died giving birth to them.

Once they were old enough to think about such things, they had speculated about whether Doc Monday was really their father, but there was no proof one way or the other and they had never worked up the nerve to ask him about it, since his health had grown bad over the years and he was living in a sanitarium. A big emotional upset wouldn't be good for him.

"If you actually have the money," Baylor said, "you have a wager."

"I've got it." Chance glanced around at his brother. "Ace?"

With a sigh, Ace dug out the roll of greenbacks and set it on the bar. He said to Dugan, "That's our whole poke. We don't have an extra five dollars to cover the bet with you."

The bartender laughed and waved a hand. "Hell, kid, I'll waive that for the occasion. In fact, I'm so sure your . . . brother, is it? . . . can't do it that if he does, I'll add a nice new double eagle to your payoff. How's that sound?"

Chance said, "We're obliged to you, Mr. Dugan. But get ready to pay up as soon as this fella"—he nodded toward Baylor—"proves that *he* can cover the bet."

Lew Shelby bristled at that. He tensed and started, "Why, you impudent little bas—"

"That's all right, Lew." Baylor stopped him with an easy but insincere smile. "It's fair enough for the lad to ask for proof, since I did." He took a sheaf of bills from a pocket inside the frock coat, counted out two hundred dollars, and placed the money next to the Jensen brothers' roll. "Satisfied?"

"Yes, sir, I am." Chance turned to the bar and studied the snake in the glass jar. He asked Dugan, "His name's Chauncey, you said?"

"That's what I call him," the bartender replied. "Caught him in the alley out back earlier today. I started to kill him, then realized that maybe I could use him to make some money."

"All right, Chauncey." Chance leaned closer, putting his face almost on the glass as he peered at the rattler. "Get good and mad now, you scaly little varmint."

The snake stared back, as inscrutable as ever. The buzzing from its rattles sounded angry.

Three times, Chance thumped his fingertip against the glass. With the last thump, he left his finger there, pressed hard against the jar. The snake didn't waste any time. It uncoiled and struck furiously, jaws gaping wide to display wicked fangs dripping with venom.

CHAPTER TWO

Just like the other two times, several men in the Lucky Panther let out involuntary shouts when the snake's head darted at the glass. One gaudily dressed saloon girl pressed her hands to rouged cheeks and trilled a little scream.

A few seconds of stunned silence ticked past before the place erupted in cheers.

Chance Jensen was still standing in front of the bar with his finger pressed against the glass. He hadn't budged.

He remained where he was in the middle of the excited commotion, other than turning his head and smiling at Henry Baylor. "I believe you owe me two hundred dollars, my friend.

Baylor smiled in return, but his lips were tight and his eyes hooded. "It appears that I do."

A few feet away, the bearded old-timer Ace had been talking to tugged on his sleeve. Ace had to lean down to make out what the old man was saying.

"Better collect your winnin's and get outta here in a hurry, kid! And keep your eyes open! Baylor won't like losin' that money, and Lew Shelby sure as hell will be mad about your brother showin' him up."

Based on the expressions on the faces of Baylor and Shelby, Ace agreed with the old man. He reached out, scooped up their roll from the bar, and shoved the stack of greenbacks from Baylor into his pocket, as well. Dugan grinned ruefully and handed him the double eagle he had promised as an extra payoff.

"Come on, Chance," Ace said. "Time for us to drift."

Chance still hadn't taken his finger away from the glass. He did it leisurely, mockingly, then lifted the finger to his lips and blew across the top of it as if he were blowing away a curl of smoke from a gun muzzle.

"Wait just a damn minute," Shelby rasped.

"Why? You're not going to claim that I cheated, are you? That would have been hard to do with this many people watching me the whole time."

"But *were* they watching you the whole time?" Shelby turned to the bar. "Dugan! Did you have your eye on this kid? You didn't look away any?"

"I don't think so," the bartender said.

"You didn't even blink when the snake struck?"

"Well .... I was trying to watch pretty close . . ."

Shelby glared as he jerked his gaze around the room. "I'll bet everybody in here blinked just then! Nobody was watching the kid the whole time. He could've taken his finger off the glass for a split second, and nobody would have noticed." When nobody spoke up to agree with him, he scowled even more and demanded, "Isn't that right?"

Shelby had a reputation in Fort Worth as a gunman. Nobody wanted to disagree with him. Some men shuffled their feet and looked down at the floor in obvious discomfort. Others edged toward the door, figuring it was better to leave than to wait and see how things played out.

Then one grizzled hombre spoke up. He looked like a successful cattleman, the sort who didn't take any guff from anybody. "I was watching the whole time, and I didn't blink. The kid's finger didn't move."

Emboldened by that blunt declaration, several other men muttered agreement.

"You know I didn't move my finger," Chance said to Shelby. "You're just mad because I was able to do it and you couldn't."

A feral hatred came into Shelby's eyes as he said, "I can do it! By God, double or nothing! I'll show you."

"Lew, I'm not sure that's wise," Baylor cautioned. "We've already lost enough tonight."

"I'm not gonna let this damn kid think he can get the best of me!" Shelby's jaw jutted out as he said to Chance, "How about it? You willing to bet the four hundred that I can't do it?"

"Chance . . ." Ace said.

"Relax, Ace," Chance said with a smile. "If we lose, we're no worse off than we were before."

"Yeah, we are. Two hundred bucks worse!"

"Life would be mighty dull without a little risk now and then to spice it up." Chance nodded to Shelby. "We'll take that bet, mister. Go ahead." He glanced at Baylor. "I won't even ask if you can cover it."

The gambler was grim-faced. His friend had put him in a bad position, but he jerked his head in a nod and made a little gesture with his slender, long-fingered hand. "Go ahead,"

As Shelby faced the jar, Dugan said, "I don't know about this. Chauncey's been banging his head against the glass every time he strikes. He's liable to be gettin' a little addled by now. I don't want him to hurt himself."

"You gettin' soft on a rattlesnake, Dugan?" one of the customers asked with a jeering grin.

"No, but if he bashes his brains out, he can't win me any more bets, can he?"

"Does a snake even have a brain?" another man asked.

"Got to," his companion said. "Ever'thing that's alive has got a brain. Don't it?"

"Don't know. I never studied up on snakes. Just shot 'em or chopped their heads off with a Bowie knife."

Shelby snapped, "Shut your damn yammering! A man can't hear himself think." Once again he went through the routine he had performed earlier.

Silence descended on the saloon, broken only by the sound of men breathing. Even that seemed to die away as Shelby hunched his shoulders a little. He was ready. His hand stabbed forward. His finger shoved hard against the jar. He didn't even have to tap on the glass this time. The snake was so keyed up it struck immediately.

Shelby's finger jerked back as the fangs hit the inside of the jar. He didn't flinch much, maybe half an inch, but his fingertip definitely left the glass and everybody who was watching saw that. Shelby tried to press his finger against the jar again, but it was too late.

"That'll be another four hundred dollars," Chance said into the awed hush that followed.

Shelby took a quick step back, away from the bar. A stream of obscenity poured from his mouth as his hand dropped to the fancy gun on his hip. Ace grabbed the back of his brother's coat collar and yanked Chance out of the way as he used his other hand to grab his Colt.

The gunman wasn't aiming to shoot either of the Jensen brothers, however. He was still facing the bar when his gun leaped up and spouted noise and flame.

The first bullet shattered the jar and sent glass shards flying through the air. The second swiftly triggered round whipped past Chauncey's weaving head and blew a bottle of busthead on the back bar to smithereens. The snake shot out of the wreckage, slithered across the bar, and dropped writhing to the sawdust-littered floor, the thick body landing with what must have been a thump.

Nobody could hear it, though, because the saloon still echoed from the reports of Shelby's gun. At least half the people in the Lucky Panther started yelling and screaming when they realized the big rattler was loose.

"Chauncey!" Dugan bellowed to Shelby, "You bastard. You tried to kill my snake!"

Shelby snarled and shouted, "Get outta the way! I'm gonna blast the damn thing!"

Dugan reached under the bar, came up with a bungstarter, and raised it as he leaned across the hardwood. Another second and he would have brought the bungstarter down across the wrist of Shelby's gun hand, probably breaking the bone.

Before the blow could fall another pistol cracked, this one a small weapon that Henry Baylor had grabbed from concealment under his frock coat. The slug tore through Dugan's forearm and made him drop the bungstarter and howl in pain.

The Lucky Panther had two entrances—the batwinged main one facing Throckmorton Street and a regular door on the side that faced Second Street. The customers stampeded for both. The furious gunman and the equally agitated rattlesnake had everybody scrambling to get out of there before they caught a bullet or got bit.

Everybody except Ace and Chance Jensen. They knew Shelby was liable to hurt an innocent person if he kept flinging lead around.

Ace scooped up the beer mug he had emptied a few minutes earlier and heaved it at Shelby's head. The heavy glass mug struck the gunman a good enough lick to stagger him. At the same time, Baylor swung his gun toward Ace. Acting instinctively to defend his brother, Chance tackled the gambler before he could fire.

The collision drove Baylor's back against the bar. He grunted and swiped at Chance's head with the pistol. The blow knocked off Chance's flat-crowned brown hat but missed otherwise.

Charging into the fray were two of the three men Shelby and Baylor had been sitting at a table with earlier. The third man, an Indian by the looks of him, drew a knife from his belt and stalked across the room, ignoring the rapidly developing brawl. Probably all three were the bad bunch the old-timer had warned Ace about.

Getting walloped by the beer mug had stunned Lew Shelby enough to leave him stumbling around in aimless circles. One of his friends took up the battle for him and went after Ace. The other man looped an arm around Chance's neck from behind and dragged him away from Baylor.

Ace ducked a roundhouse right that his attacker threw at him. He brushed his hat back off his head so it hung from its chin strap behind him. He crouched even lower and waded in, hooking punches to the man's soft-looking belly. That paunch was deceptive. Hitting it was like hammering his fists against the wall of a log cabin, Ace discovered.

The man hit Ace a backhanded blow with his forearm.

The impact knocked Ace halfway across the bar. He caught himself and managed not to slide all the way over. As his opponent charged in, he raised both legs and straightened them in a double kick to the chest.

That sent the man flying. He landed on a table that collapsed under him and dumped him among its shattered debris. He sat up and shook his head groggily.

Halfway along the bar, Baylor was slugging Chance in the belly while the other man hung on to him from behind. Chance was red in the face from the choking grip around his neck.

Ace swerved wide, picked up a chair, and crashed it down on the back of the man who had hold of Chance. That knocked him loose.

Chance twisted free, grabbed Baylor's arm as the gambler tried to hit him in the stomach again, and pivoted, throwing Baylor over his hip in a wrestling move he had learned during a rough-and-tumble childhood spent traveling with Doc Monday. Chance might look like a bit of a dandy, but he could handle himself just fine in a fight.

Baylor rolled across the floor, dirtying his nice frock coat. In the scuffle, he had lost the little pistol with which he had shot Dugan, but that wasn't the only weapon he carried. As Chance closed in on him, ready to continue the fight, Baylor came up slashing with a folding straight razor that he flicked open with a practiced twist of his wrist.

Chance had to jump back to avoid being cut. Baylor came after him, backing him against the bar.

Ace was being hemmed in by Shelby and the man he had kicked in the chest, both of whom had recovered their wits and appeared to be ready to beat him to death.

The Jensen brothers found themselves standing side by side, backs against the bar, with no place to run as trouble closed in on them. Sadly, it wasn't the first time they had found themselves in such a perilous position. Judging by the anger and hatred twisting the cruel faces of the men stalking toward them, they might not get out of it.

With no warning, the deafening roar of another shot slammed through the room and made everybody freeze.

CHAPTER THREE

All eyes turned toward the saloon's main entrance. A dapper man in a dark suit and vest, silk tie, and narrow-brimmed hat stood there with a smoking gun in his hand. He was rather handsome, with a full mustache and tawny hair long enough to sweep back in waves behind his ears.

What really drew the eyes, though—besides the gun—was the badge pinned to his vest.

"All right," he said quietly, "what's the trouble?"

"Baylor shot me!" Dugan said. Using his left hand to hold up his ventilated right arm, he displayed the blood staining his sleeve.

"I had to," Baylor said. "He was about to kill Lew. I've got a right to protect my friend, don't I?"

Dugan stared. "What? Kill him? I was gonna knock the gun out of his hand, that's all."

Baylor said, "It looked to me like you were about to stave his head in with that bungstarter. I couldn't take the chance."

Shelby spat disgustedly on the floor. "Hell, he just wounded you. I would've shot to kill."

The lawman came farther into the room. He didn't holster his gun but used it to gesture. "That explains one of the shots. How about all the others? And what's all that broken glass doing on the bar?"

"He tried to kill Chauncey, too, Marshal Courtright," Dugan said. "You need to arrest him!"

"Who the devil is Chauncey?"

Dugan suddenly looked a little sheepish. "My, uh, snake. He's a rattlesnake."

Courtright raised an eyebrow. "I didn't know you were keeping a pet rattlesnake in here, Dugan, or I might have locked you up for being a public menace and a damned fool."

"The snake wasn't a pet," Chance said. "He was using it to win bets and make money. He bet that a man couldn't hold his finger against the glass and keep it there while the snake struck at it." A grin spread across Chance's face. "I did, though."

"And Shelby here couldn't," Ace put in. "That's why he got so upset he shot the jar and busted it."

Coolly, the marshal asked, "And who might you boys be?"

"I'm Ace Jensen. This is my brother Chance."

That perked up the lawman's interest. "Jensen, eh?"

"Yeah, but we're not related to Smoke or Luke," Ace said, mentioning the two Jensens whose names were most likely to be known to a star packer.

Smoke Jensen was widely regarded as the West's fastest, deadliest gunfighter, despite the fact that these days he lived a mostly peaceful life as a rancher in Colorado. Anybody who had ever read a newspaper or a dime novel had heard about him.

Luke Jensen was Smoke's older brother, a bounty

hunter whose name might well be familiar to a lawman. Ace and Chance had met both men and shared adventures with them in the past.

"Not related that we know of," Chance added. "Personally, I lean toward the idea that we're actually the long-lost black sheep of the family."

Ace just rolled his eyes at that.

"Well, even if you're not blood kin to that hell-raising bunch, you seem to take after them," the marshal observed. "You two were at the center of this ruckus. Maybe I should arrest you as well while I'm locking up Shelby and Baylor and their friends." Courtright cast a baleful eye on the four men. "I've had run-ins with you before, and I'm tired of it."

"Marshal, these boys didn't do anything wrong," Dugan said. "That one there won his bet fair and square." He pointed at Chance.

"We all claim that he didn't," Baylor put in hastily. "The five of us will swear that the boy pulled away when the snake struck, so it's our word against Dugan's." A satisfied smirk appeared on the gambler's face. "I'd say that makes the count five to one in our favor."

"Five to three," Ace said. "Chance and I both know he didn't flinch."

Baylor shook his head. "Still not a winning hand."

Courtright appeared to consider that for a moment, then nodded. "Much as I hate to agree with you, Baylor, it seems that you're right." He looked at Ace and Chance. "Whatever money you won from this tinhorn, give it back. I'm declaring all bets null and void."

"You can't do that!" Chance protested. "I won!"

"We try to discourage gambling around here," Courtright said with a look of bland righteousness on his face. That statement was a blatant falsehood since Hell's Half Acre was full of gambling dens. "You're fortunate I don't lock you up for that."

Ace sighed and pulled out the bills he had picked up from the bar. He started to hand them to Baylor, but Courtright intercepted them.

He peeled off a bill and dropped it on the bar. "For the damages and for the pain of Dugan's wounded arm."

Shelby pointed at Ace and Chance. "These two little bastards ought to pay for part of the damages. They were fighting just like we were."

"Legally speaking, you may be right. But I don't like you, Shelby, and I'm still reserving judgment on these youngsters." Courtright handed the rest of the money to Baylor. "You can keep that with you while you spend the night in my lockup. Let's go." He glanced around. "Where's the Kiowa?"

"He had nothing to do with this," Baylor said. "He stayed out of the fight completely."

"That's true," Ace said. "We were just scuffling with these four."

"All right." Courtright frowned. "Something else I just thought of. What happened to the snake?"

"Over here, Marshal," said a man with a deep, calm voice.

Everyone looked around and saw the Indian who had been sitting with Shelby, Baylor, and the others before the battle erupted. He held up his knife. Skewered on the end of it was the limp, lifeless body of the big rattlesnake. "Good eatin'."

"Chauncey!" Dugan wailed.

* * *

Shelby, Baylor, and the other two men were disarmed and ushered out by Marshal Courtright. A doctor carrying a medical bag bustled in to tend to Dugan's wounded arm. Obviously someone had sent for the medico. Since Ace and Chance hadn't been arrested, they remained in the Lucky Panther and sat down at one of the tables.

Chance sighed, and Ace said. "I don't know what you're looking so glum about. We're not behind bars."

"Yeah, but I won that bet fair and square." He held up a hand to stall Ace's protest. "I know, I know. We're not any worse off than we were before, but that lawman didn't have any right to make us give our winnings back. It's the principle of the thing."

A new voice spoke up. "When Longhair Jim lays down the law, it *stays* laid down."

Ace and Chance looked up to see the whiskery old-timer Ace had been talking to earlier. Most of the saloon's customers were filtering back into the place now that the fight was over and word had spread about the rattlesnake's demise.

"That's the marshal?" Ace said.

"Yep. Longhair Jim Courtright. Fast on the draw and a dead shot. Lew Shelby may have thought about takin' him on, but with Jim's gun already drawed, Shelby knew he'd be stretched out on the floor gettin' cold iffen he tried." The old-timer looked hopeful. "You boys fixin' to have a drink?"

"I'm sure you'll want to join us if the answer is yes," Chance said.

"Weeellll . . . if you're askin' . . . reckon I don't mind if I do."

"Sit down." Ace caught the attention of the aproned

man who had taken over as bartender while Dugan was getting patched up and held up three fingers.

The old-timer sat down. "I heard you boys say your name's Jensen. Mine's Greendale. Harley Greendale. Fancy moniker for an old pelican like me, ain't it?"

"Glad to meet you, Mr. Greendale."

"Call me Harley. Mr. Greendale was my pa, damn his black heart to hell."

Ace didn't ask what that comment was about. There was a good chance Harley would tell them sooner or later anyway. The old man was the garrulous sort.

"You boys always carry this much excitement around in your back pockets?"

"That ruckus wasn't our fault," Chance said. "Nothing would have happened if Shelby and Baylor had just admitted I won that bet fair and square."

"Them two ain't the sort to take kindly to losin', like I was tellin' your brother earlier."

One of the serving girls delivered three overflowing mugs of beer on a wooden tray. Harley leaned forward eagerly, picked up one of them, and sucked the foam off the top. He sighed in satisfaction. "That bunch drifted into town a couple months ago."

The Jensen brothers hadn't asked him to fill them in on Shelby and the others, but Ace thought it might not be a bad idea to learn more about the men with whom they had clashed. Shelby especially struck him as the sort of hombre who would hold a grudge and try to act on it.

Harley took a healthy swallow of beer and wiped the back of his hand across his mouth. "Inside a week, Shelby was mixed up in a killin'. Plenty of witnesses saw the other feller reach first, so Shelby didn't go to jail for it. Nor for the other two shootin's he's been part of since then. Both of them were over card games. Fellas didn't like losin' to Baylor. Didn't come right out and accuse him of cheatin'—there wasn't no proof of that—but they pushed it hard enough that guns was drawed anyways."

"It sounds like they have a partnership," Chance said. "Baylor fleeces the lambs, and Shelby shoots the ones who object too strenuously to being shorn."

"Reckon that's about the size of it."

Ace asked, "What about the other three?"

"They just sort of hang around with Shelby and Baylor. Jack Loomis is the bald-headed one with the big belly. Feller who always looks like he just bit into somethin' sour is called Prewitt. Don't know that I've ever heard his first name." Harley paused. "Then there's the Kiowa. Nobody ever calls him anything else."

The Indian had left the saloon after Marshal Courtright herded his friends off to jail. As far as Ace and Chance knew, he had taken the dead snake with him and might be cooking it over an open fire at this very moment.

"He never says much," Harley went on. "I don't like the look in his eyes. Just as likely to scalp you as to say howdy. Probably more likely." He swallowed more suds. "All I know is that they're a bad bunch. Iffen I was you boys, I reckon I'd be ridin' out of Fort Worth tonight. First thing in the mornin' at the latest, 'fore Longhair Jim lets those varmints outta jail. Shelby is liable to come lookin' for you."

"Let him come," Chance said. "I'm not going to run away from anybody."

"That's a good attitude to have, son. But in this case, you might ought to give it some extry thought."

Chance was going to argue with the old-timer, but Ace lifted a hand from the table to forestall the wrangling. When he had Chance's attention, he tipped his head toward the saloon's main entrance.

Marshal Jim Courtright had just come in and was looking around the place. When his gaze landed on the table where the Jensen boys sat with Harley, he started across the room toward them with a stern look on his face.

Chapter Four

"I was hoping you fellows had enough sense to be on your way by now," the lawman said when he came up to the table.

"You didn't actually order us to get out of town, Marshal," Ace said.

"I advised 'em it'd probably be a good idea, though, Jim," Harley put in.

Courtright didn't sit down, but he rested his left hand on the back of the remaining empty chair, pushed his coat back a little, and hooked his right thumb in the lower pocket of the vest on that side. That pose kept his gun in easy reach. "I'd just as soon not deal with any more killings than I have to. Shelby and Baylor will come after you for what happened tonight, if you're still around."

"That's what people keep telling us," Chance said.

"If you're gone, I doubt they'll go to the trouble of tracking you down," Courtright went on. "I can get away with keeping them locked up until nine o'clock. You can be well away from Fort Worth by then."

"What about their Kiowa friend?" Ace asked. "He's still loose, isn't he?"

Courtright nodded. "I couldn't justify putting him in jail."

"So even if we leave town, what's to stop him from following us? He could ride back later and tell the others where we went. They could come after us and ambush us on the trail."

"The world is full of danger," Courtright said. "But my bailiwick is Fort Worth."

Chance said, "So you don't care what happens to us as long as it doesn't happen here."

The lawman smiled. "That's about the size of it." He straightened from his casual pose and strolled toward the bar. All the broken glass had been cleaned up, as well as the other damage from the fight.

Ace looked across the table at his brother. "We were probably going to be riding out tomorrow anyway. We might as well get an early start."

"It seems to me like running scared," Chance said. "I don't cotton to that."

"Neither do I," Ace admitted. "But that marshal's not going to give us any more breaks. If there's more trouble, we'll wind up behind bars . . . assuming we live through it."

A shudder ran through Chance. "I'm not sure but what I'd rather go out fighting than be locked up." He sighed. "All right. We'll pull out first thing in the morning. Which direction?"

"West," Ace said without even thinking about it. He was perfectly content to let his instincts and a hunch guide him.

"In the meantime," Harley Greendale said, "we could use some more drinks."

"We haven't finished these," Ace pointed out.

"Well, drink up, boys! You're fallin' behind."

After months of herding cattle, mending fence, digging post holes, and pulling calves out of the mud, Ace and Chance had been ready for some excitement and entertainment. They'd been staying at an inexpensive hotel a couple blocks closer to the Trinity River, not far from the edge of the bluff overlooking the stream, while they looked around to see what diversions Fort Worth offered.

Even without the violent encounter in the Lucky Panther, they were ready to move on. Their fiddle-footed nature never allowed them to remain in one place for very long unless it was absolutely necessary.

They left Harley Greendale happily snockered in the saloon and walked along Throckmorton toward the river.

More than thirty years earlier, an army detachment had established a garrison on the bluffs to help protect the expanding frontier from the Comanches and named it after General William Jenkins Worth, a hero of the Mexican War who'd never set foot in the post named after him. The fort had long since been abandoned and no sign of it remained, but it had given its name to the town that grew up around it and still existed.

Fort Worth had boomed since the opening of the cattle trails to the railheads in Kansas. The steel rails had arrived in Fort Worth a few years later, and now there was talk of building a large stockyards area on the north side of the river to accommodate the vast herds that poured in from all over Texas to be shipped to the rest of the country.

The town once noted for being so sleepy that a panther was spotted dozing in the middle of Main Street was now bustling with industriousness.

If Ace and Chance had been ambitious sorts, Fort Worth—or Cowtown, as some people were starting to call it—would have been the perfect place for them to settle down. Since they weren't ambitious by any stretch of the imagination . . .

Ace reached in his pocket and brought out the double eagle Dugan had paid them. "This will cover the rest of our expenses. We'll be leaving town with almost as much money as we had when we rode in. That's not bad."

"We should have been two hundred dollars richer," Chance said. "Hell, *six* hundred dollars richer because Shelby lost that last bet, too, and he said double or nothing."

"We have money for supplies and ammunition. We won't need anything else for a while. What would you do if you had eight hundred dollars? Put it in a bank?"

Chance looked at his brother with disgust on his face, thinking Ace had just made the most revolting suggestion he'd ever heard. "Banks are for people who stay in one place."

"Doc had money in several banks. Santa Fe, Denver, and San Francisco, if I remember right."

"That's different. He was raising two young'uns, and he wanted to put something away for us, for when he was gone . . . which I hope is still a long time from now."

"Me, too," Ace agreed. He couldn't imagine a world

without Doc Monday in it, although they saw him only rarely.

They were nearly to the hotel, a two-story frame structure with a balcony along the second floor front.

Ace glanced up at it and frowned as he thought he saw something move. The half moon cast silvery light down on Fort Worth, but that glow also created shadows. Maybe he'd imagined the movement, Ace told himself when he didn't see anything else.

Still, he was wary as they approached, making sure that his right hand didn't stray very far from the Colt.

Nothing happened.

The brothers went into the hotel lobby, where all the lamps had been turned low at this hour, and crossed quietly to the stairs leading to the second floor. Behind the desk, the night clerk dozed in a chair tilted back against the wall. His lips flapped as he snored.

Ace and Chance turned right at the landing and went around to their room, which was on the front of the building. Ace took the key out of his pocket, unlocked the door, and stepped into the room.

Instinct and the smell of something rancid like bear grease warned him at the last second that he had been careless.

He dived to the floor as something whipped over his head. Powering into a swift roll, he crashed into the intruder's legs. He *had* seen someone on the balcony—someone breaking into their room through its single window.

"Chance, look out!" he called as the intruder fell heavily to the floor beside him.

A small oil lamp burning in a wall sconce at the far end of the corridor provided the only light in that part of the hotel, so the room was full of shadows. Ace caught a glimpse of a man with long, dark hair lunging at him as he tried to get up.

The Kiowa.

Light glinted for a split second on something else as the two men grappled. Most likely a knife, Ace knew. He reached up blindly with his left hand, brushed the Kiowa's wrist, and caught hold of it, straining to keep the blade away from his flesh. With his right, he threw a punch where he hoped the Kiowa's head would be.

The blow missed. With muscles like bundles of steel cable, the Kiowa rolled Ace onto his back. Ace twisted to avoid the knee thrust at his groin and heaved his opponent to the side.

Over and over they rolled, which made it impossible for Chance to risk a shot from just inside the doorway . . . even if the light hadn't been so bad.

Ace and the Kiowa bumped against the bed, stopping them. Ace grabbed his opponent's wrist with both hands and slammed it against the floor. He heard the knife skitter away.

Unarmed, the Kiowa turned to wrestling. He writhed free, got behind Ace, and looped an arm around his neck. Ace felt the terrible pressure on his windpipe and desperately drove an elbow back into the Kiowa's midsection.

It took two more powerful blows before the arm pressing into his throat slipped. Ace ducked his head to keep the Kiowa from getting a hold on him again and bucked up off the floor.

At that instant, light flared in the room. Chance had flicked a match to life with his left thumbnail. His right held the Smith & Wesson .38. Ace was half-blinded by the sudden glare, but knowing it was coming, Chance had squinted his eyes against it and could see well enough to shoot. The .38 barked as the Kiowa scrambled to regain his knife. The bullet chewed splinters from the floor just ahead of the intruder's outstretched hand.

The Kiowa jerked back, abandoning the knife. He made it to hands and knees and then to his feet. A swift step carried him toward the open window as Chance fired again.

Evidently the Kiowa wasn't hit, because he never slowed down. He dived through the window just as the match burned out and the light vanished.

Charging past his brother, who was still struggling to see clearly, Chance leaned out the window and triggered again at the fleeing form. The Kiowa reached the end of the balcony, put a hand on the railing, and vaulted over it. He dropped out of sight as he fell toward the street.

"Damn it!" As far as Chance could tell, all three of his shots had missed.

Ace got to his feet and stumbled over to the window. "Did you get him?"

"I don't think so. He was still moving pretty fast the last time I saw him."

"He was going to kill us!"

"Yeah," Chance said dryly. "Seemed like that was what he had in mind. Why would he do that? He wasn't even mixed up in that fight we had with the others. He was chasing that damned snake while the ruckus was going on."

"I guess he feels some loyalty toward them. He figured that while they were locked up, he would settle the score on their behalf. Maybe he hoped Baylor and Shelby would give him some money for getting rid of us." Ace shook his head. "I don't guess there's any way to know for sure. We'll need to keep our eyes open for him until we're well away from Fort Worth."

"You think he'll try again?"

"I don't know, but we can't rule it out."

Ace found a match in his pocket, struck it, and lit the lamp that stood on the small table next to the bed. As the light washed over the room, he took a careful look around. No blood on the floor, so it seemed likely the Kiowa was unhurt.

The door still stood open. A footstep sounded from the hallway, prompting the Jensen brothers to turn in that direction. Carrying a shotgun, Marshal Jim Courtright stood there with a disgusted expression on his face.

"You two again," he said. "You're just determined to keep me from having any peace and quiet tonight, aren't you?"

"We're leaving in the morning," Ace said.

"And it's not our fault that blasted Indian decided to sneak in here and ambush us," Chance added.

Courtright raised an eyebrow. "The Kiowa was here?"

"He was waiting in our room when we got here," Ace said. "I didn't think about that until I was walking in, even though I thought I saw someone moving around on the balcony while we were still outside. I'm just lucky he didn't cut my throat before I realized what was going on."

Chance said, "Luck's got nothing to do with it. Jensens are quick."

Courtright grunted. "Jensens are trouble. If you want to swear out a complaint against the Kiowa, I'll have a look around for him. I can't guarantee that

I'll find him, mind you—there are plenty of places to hide around here—but I'll look."

Ace sighed and shook his head. "No, I don't suppose it would do much good. Anyway, he didn't get what he came after—" As he said that, something made him reach down and rest his hand against the pocket where he carried the roll of money he and Chance had earned with their months of hard labor. He caught his breath as he realized he didn't feel the familiar lump.

"What's wrong?" Chance asked, knowing his brother well enough to recognize when Ace was surprised.

Ace shoved his hand into the pocket to make sure, then checked all his others as well. He didn't find the money in any of them and realized that while he was being choked, the Kiowa had slipped his other hand in his pocket and taken the roll of greenbacks.

"It's gone," Ace said in a hollow voice. "Our money is gone. The Kiowa stole it."

CHAPTER FIVE

The loss of the stake for which they had worked so hard made things different, and Ace and Chance were willing to swear out a complaint. Of course, that didn't make it any more likely Marshal Courtright would be able to find and arrest the Kiowa. In all likelihood, that two hundred dollars was gone and the Jensen brothers would never see it again.

The night clerk, looking unhappy that his sleep had been disturbed, came upstairs to make sure the shooting hadn't done any damage to the hotel. Some of the other guests peered curiously out of their rooms as well.

As Courtright was leaving, he told them. "Go on back to bed, folks. All the excitement is over. And to tell you the truth, it wasn't all that exciting to start with."

Maybe it hadn't seemed that exciting to the marshal, Ace thought, but when he'd been battling for his life, it had been pretty doggoned pulse-pounding.

"When are you boys planning on leaving town?" the clerk asked when Courtright was gone.

"Figured we'd ride out in the morning," Ace replied.

The clerk grunted. "Probably be a good thing if you do. This is a respectable, law-abiding establishment."

"I didn't know it was against the law to defend yourself from somebody who's trying to kill you," Chance snapped.

"Some guests just seem to attract trouble," the man said, scowling. He left the room and headed back downstairs.

Chance went to close the door behind him and glared at the other guests who were still looking toward the room where the shooting had taken place. He slammed the door a little more forcefully than was absolutely necessary. "Damn buzzards," he muttered as he turned back to Ace. "Always interested in somebody else's bad luck."

"We've had our share tonight, that's for sure." Ace held up the twenty-dollar gold piece they had gotten from Dugan. "This is all the bankroll we have left, Chance. We're going to have to pay some of it to the hotel and the livery stable before we leave town, too. Not to mention we haven't stocked up on supplies yet, and we'll have to do that before we ride out."

Chance shrugged. "You're saying we'll be leaving town flat broke."

"Pretty close to it. In a few days, maybe a week, we'll have to stop somewhere else and start looking for jobs again."

Chance winced as if Ace had struck him. "We can stay around here for a few more days and see if I can run us up a better stake at the poker tables."

"If we do that, it's liable to mean a shooting scrape with Shelby and Baylor."

"I'm not afraid of those two," Chance said with a snort.

"Neither am I," Ace said.

That was true. He knew that he and his brother were fast and accurate enough with their guns to stand an even chance with most men, even the ones who were supposed to be dangerous pistoleers like Lew Shelby. Men such as Smoke Jensen, Falcon MacCallister, John Wesley Hardin, Ben Thompson, and Frank Morgan occupied a different level when it came to gun-handling, but Ace and Chance were more than good enough to get by.

Problem was, with Loomis, Prewitt, and the Kiowa backing Shelby and Baylor, it wouldn't even be close to a fair fight. The Jensen brothers might be able to shoot it out with the five hardcases and survive, but even if they did, it was likely Marshal Courtright would throw them in jail.

Chance was smart enough to know that, too. He sighed and said, "What are we going to do, then? Turn outlaw and rob a bank so we'll have enough money to ride out of here and keep going for a while?"

"We both know good and well we're not going to do that. I reckon we'll just have to wait and see how things look in the morning. Who knows, maybe Marshal Courtright will recover our money."

Chance just shook his head. Both of them knew that wasn't going to happen.

The next morning, five women dressed in traveling outfits emerged from a different, somewhat fancier hotel in Fort Worth and stood on the porch while a porter carried out their bags and stacked them. Each woman had two bags, one small and one larger. That was all they were allowed to bring with them on the journey they were about to undertake.

Four of them were quite young, a year or so on either side of twenty. The fifth woman was older, around thirty. She had honey-blond hair done up in swirls under her hat and a small beauty mark on her cheek. Her name was Lorena Hutton, and as she stood there she began to grow angry.

"Where the devil is Cyrus with that wagon?" she asked the others, even though she knew logically they wouldn't have the answer to that question any more than she would. In the time they had been together, they had learned that Lorena was the most plain-spoken among them.

"He is only a little late," Isabel Sheridan replied with a slight trace of an accent that seemed to go with her dark, sultry good looks.

"He probably overslept," Jamie Gregory added. "He's getting old, you know."

Like Lorena and Isabel, Jamie was a beauty. The youngest of the group at eighteen—almost nineteen—she had thick blond hair so pale it was almost white.

The other two young women didn't say anything because they tended to be quiet and keep to themselves.

Molly Brock wasn't as pretty as the three who had spoken up, but her red hair, green eyes, and a scattering of freckles across her face gave her a wholesome attractiveness that was more evident when she was away from Lorena, Isabel, and Jamie.

The fifth member of the group didn't have the beauty, grace, or elegance of the others. An ungainly air clung to her. Her clothes didn't fit her as well, and when she walked across the porch her heavy shoes clunked on the boards. Her best feature was her long, dark hair, but it was done up in braids and wrapped around her head at the moment. Her name was Agnes Hampel, and if ever a name fit its owner, this was one.

Lorena grew more impatient as the minutes passed. The streets of Fort Worth were getting busier.

Finally, she said, "The hell with this. I'm going down to the wagon yard to look for him. He had to go there before he came here to pick us up."

"Are you sure that's a good idea?" Jamie asked. "Mr. Keegan told us we ought to stick together."

"Nothing's going to happen to any of us in broad daylight, in the middle of town." Lorena laughed. "Believe me, darlin', I've been in plenty of worse situations than this and taken care of myself just fine."

"Yes, I can believe that you would take care of yourself," Isabel said, her voice a slightly sharp-edged purr.

Lorena frowned at her. "What do you mean by that?"

"Nothing," Isabel said, waving a slender hand. "Perhaps we should all go to the wagon yard?"

Molly spoke up for the first time since they'd come out of the hotel. "And leave our bags here?" She looked and sounded as if she didn't care for that idea at all.

"I can stay and watch them," Agnes suggested. "I won't let anybody bother them."

The others thought about that. They knew Agnes had grown up on a farm, which meant she was used to hard work and was the strongest, physically, of all of them. She would be able to protect the bags.

"All right. That's what we'll do," Lorena decided. "Come on."

"I can stay with you if you'd like," Molly offered to Agnes.

"No, that's not necessary. I'm fine. Really."

With obvious reluctance, Molly went down the steps behind Lorena, Isabel, and Jamie. The four of them turned and walked west along the street toward the livery stable and wagon yard where they were supposed to meet Cyrus Keegan, the man accompanying them on their trip.

In wetter times, the streets of Fort Worth were seas of mud churned up by horses' hooves and the wheels of countless wagons. It had been a fairly dry spring, however, so the footing wasn't too bad. In fact, the air would get dustier from the traffic as the day went on.

Patterson's Stable and Wagon Yard was on a cross street between Throckmorton and Houston, not far from the courthouse. The proprietor, a stocky man with a rust-colored beard, was standing in the open double doors of the livery barn when the four women approached. He frowned as he saw them coming.

"Keegan's in the office," Patterson said, pointing with a thumb to a smaller door beside the large ones. "I've already sent for a doctor."

"A doctor!" Jamie exclaimed. "Oh, my Lord. What happened?"

"See for yourself," the stableman said. He walked over and opened the office door.

"We intend to." Lorena strode into the office, followed by the other three women.

A man lay stretched out on a ratty old sofa on the other side of the room. It was hard to say what was more shocking about him, the odor of whiskey that filled the air around him, even early in the morning, or the way his right leg was bent at a painfully unnatural angle.

"Good Lord, Cyrus!" Lorena said. "What happened to you?"

"I think"—he stopped to hiccup—"I think my leg is broken."

"Aren't you in terrible pain?" Molly asked.

"To tell you the truth, my dear"—again he paused . . . to giggle—"I don't feel a blessed thing!"

"That's because he's drunk as a skunk." Lorena blew out a disgusted breath. "Of all the damned bad luck—" She turned to look at Patterson, who stood in the doorway with a shoulder propped against the jamb. "What happened?"

"He came in to get the wagon, and since I was busy with somebody else just then, he decided to hitch up the team himself. He was so drunk he made a bad job of it, though, and spooked the horses so much that one of 'em kicked him." Patterson shook his head. "I was on the other side of the barn, but I heard the thigh bone snap. It was that bad."

On the sofa, Keegan began to sing a bawdy song. Lorena's mouth tightened. She had heard the song before, and much worse besides, but she wasn't in the mood for it right now. "Let's get out of here."

Patterson stepped aside as she led the other three women out of the office. A block up the street, a man in a suit, carrying a black medical bag, hurried toward the stable. That would be the doctor Patterson had summoned.

"What are we going to do?" Molly asked, practically wailing.

"Can the doctor fix Mr. Keegan up well enough that he can drive the wagon?" Jamie added.

Lorena said. "Honey, with a leg busted that bad, Cyrus is going to be laid up for weeks. He's not going anywhere."

"Then neither are we," Isabel said. Her lips compressed into a thin line. "This is unacceptable."

"Just because Cyrus isn't going doesn't mean that we aren't." Lorena frowned in thought for a moment, then went on. "I'd be willing to bet a new ostrich feather for my hat that Agnes can drive a wagon."

Patterson said, "Wait a minute. You ladies ain't thinkin' you'll travel all the way from Fort Worth to San Angelo by yourselves, are you?"

"I don't see why not," Lorena said.

"Would it be safe to do something like that?" Jamie asked.

"As a matter of fact, it sure wouldn't," the stableman said. "You'd be liable to run into all kinds of trouble along the way. Bandits and other sorts of rough hombres, for sure. Comanche renegades who've jumped the reservation and gone out raiding. And this time of year there's always a chance of a tornado or a storm with hailstones big enough to bust your head open. To tell you the truth, I was worried about the five of you ladies goin' that far with just Keegan to look out for you. By yourselves"—Patterson shook his head—"I can't allow it."

Coldly, Lorena told him. "You don't have anything to say about it, Mr. Patterson. Your bill's paid up, isn't it?"

"Well, yeah, but—"

"Then there's nothing stopping us from taking that wagon, is there?"

"Just the fact that it doesn't belong to you. I could send for the marshal."

"Oh, really?" Lorena smiled. "You think I can't go in there and convince Cyrus to give me his permission, in writing if necessary, to take the wagon?"

"That wouldn't count. He's drunk!"

"As a skunk," Lorena said again. "But if he signs his name to a piece of paper, it'll hold up in court, and you know it."

Patterson's frown deepened. He was perplexed and didn't know what to do; then an idea occurred to him. "Maybe you could get somebody else to go with you and make sure you get there safe."

"And who would we get to do that?"

Patterson looked around, and his expression brightened.

CHAPTER SIX

The Kiowa hadn't come back during the night.

Ace and Chance had taken turns staying awake and standing guard over each other, but it left both young men a little more tired and out of sorts than they would have been if they'd gotten a full night's sleep.

In the morning they'd packed their gear and gone downstairs to settle up. They owed for two more nights, which cost a couple dollars out of the twenty they had.

The clerk was not the man who had been unhappy with them the night before. "I heard about all the troubles you boys had. Sorry for your misfortune, but can't say as I'm unhappy to see you go."

"We're not unhappy to leave this place, either," Chance said. "I've slept on trails that had less lumps than that mattress."

Actually, the mattress hadn't been that bad.

Ace knew his brother was just in a bad mood. "I don't suppose Marshal Courtright has been around looking for us?"

The clerk shook his head. "No, I haven't seen him.

Could be he's still asleep. The marshal's job keeps him out and about more at night, if you know what I mean."

Ace understood. There was more trouble at night for a lawman to deal with. For that matter, according to some of the things Harley Greendale had said, Jim Courtright preferred spending his time in saloons, gambling dens, dance halls, and the like.

The brothers walked out of the hotel with their saddlebags slung over their shoulders. Each carried a Winchester in his left hand.

They headed for the livery stable a block and a half away, around the corner on a cross street. It was run by a friendly hombre named Patterson. They owed him for the last two nights their horses had spent at the stable, which would account for another dollar and a half out of their dwindling funds.

By the time they bought food and ammunition, they would be lucky to be leaving Fort Worth with ten dollars to their name.

As they walked, Chance said. "Do you think there's any point in waiting around to see if Courtright caught that Indian and recovered our money?"

"If he had, he would have sent word to the hotel or come himself," Ace said. "We're just going to have to accept that those two hundred dollars are gone."

Chance cursed bitterly. "I know. I just don't like the idea of having to look for another job in a week or so." He sighed. "I suppose we might as well enjoy our freedom while it lasts."

"We're talking about a job, not being locked up in prison," Ace said with a smile.

"Not that much difference as far as I'm concerned."

As they approached the livery barn, they saw Patterson going into the office with several women. Having no idea what that was about, Ace and Chance walked into the barn and went to the stalls where their mounts were. It didn't take long to get blankets, saddles, and the rest of their gear on Ace's big chestnut and Chance's cream-colored gelding. Holding the reins, they led the animals up the aisle and out of the building.

As they emerged into the street, Ace heard Patterson say. "How about those Jensen boys?"

Chance heard it, too. He looked in the direction of the stableman and his companions, and stood there with his eyes slowly widening as he said under his breath. "Good Lord, Ace. Would you look at that?"

"I see them," Ace replied, trying not to stare. Actually, he had seen the women a few minutes earlier when they were going into the office with Patterson, but he was getting his first good look at them.

It was a sight that no red-blooded young man was going to forget any time soon.

If somebody had set out to assemble a collection of different types of beautiful women, those four might be the result. Two blondes, one exotic-looking brunette, and a mighty cute redhead.

All of them looked to be about the same age as the Jensen brothers except the one with honey-colored hair, who was a few years older but still as lovely as her companions. They wore nice traveling outfits and hats, stylish and well cared for but probably not luxuriously expensive. The women just made the clothes look that way.

Patterson beckoned Ace and Chance. "Come over here, fellas. These ladies have a business proposition for you."

"We didn't agree to that at all," the honey-blonde

said. "Who are these young men? What do you know about them?"

Ace and Chance led their horses closer while the woman was asking her questions.

Stopping, Ace pinched the brim of his hat and nodded politely. "Ma'am. My name is Ace Jensen, and this is my brother Chance."

"Those can't possibly be your given names," the sultry brunette said.

"No, ma'am, but they're all we ever go by."

The honey-blonde said. "Don't call us ma'am. None of us is your mother. My name is Lorena Hutton. *Miss* Lorena Hutton." She introduced the others. "Miss Isabel Sheridan, Miss Jamie Gregory, and Miss Molly Brock."

"Ladies." Chance swept off his hat and held it over his heart as he leaned forward in a little bow. "It's our pleasure and privilege to make your acquaintance, and may I say, being in your presence has brightened immensely a morning that promised to be nothing but dreary."

"Stop running your mouth," Lorena said. "You're not going to impress us, or charm us. But if you're looking for work, you might be able to help us."

"What sort of work?" Ace asked, suddenly wary.

"These ladies and I"—Lorena gestured to indicate her companions—"are heading west to San Angelo. Are you familiar with the town?"

"Heard of it," Ace said. "Haven't actually been there, as I recall."

"But you could find it?"

"Of course," Chance said without hesitation, still smiling broadly. "We've traveled all over. We've very experienced frontiersmen."

Lorena snorted and almost succeeded in making it sound ladylike. "You two aren't old enough to be very experienced at anything."

"You might be surprised, ma'am—I mean, Miss Lorena," Chance said. His smile widened into a grin.

Lorena turned to Ace. "You seem to be the more practical of the two. We need someone to accompany us to San Angelo and act as guides and, well, protectors, I suppose you could call it. Would you and your brother be interested in the job?"

"We're twins, actually, just not identical," Ace said. "How about it, Chance? What do you think?"

"Absolutely!" Chance replied. "We were leaving town and heading west anyway. The opportunity to travel in such lovely, charming company . . . why, *we* ought to pay *you* for that privilege!"

Ace frowned and said, "Yeah, but we, ah, can't afford that—"

Lorena raised a hand to stop him. "Don't worry, we'll pay you. Give me a minute and I can tell you how much."

She turned and went back into the livery stable's office.

While Lorena was gone, Chance tried to engage in conversation with the other three young women, asking each of them where they were from. Jamie Gregory was the only one who really responded, explaining that she was from St. Louis.

"How did the four of you ladies come to be traveling together?" Chance asked.

"Actually, there are five of us. We left Agnes back at the hotel to keep an eye on our bags while we came to see what had happened to Mr. Keegan."

"Agnes?" Chance repeated.

"Yes, Agnes Hampel."

Ace asked. "Who's this Keegan fella?"

"He's the one who was supposed to take us to San Angelo. But I'm afraid he's injured. A horse kicked him and broke his leg."

"All right." Ace still felt a little lost. None of the women seemed to be related, so why were they going to San Angelo together?

Before he could press for more of an explanation, Lorena came out of the office with some money in her hand. "We'll pay you eighty-seven dollars and provide the supplies, since they're already paid for and should be plenty for all of us. That's all the money Keegan had in his pockets."

Patterson exclaimed. "You robbed him?"

Lorena fixed the stableman with a stony glare. "He couldn't stay sober enough to do the job he was paid to do. He doesn't deserve the money. These boys do—if they take the job. And if we offer it." She looked at Ace and Chance again. "I don't know anything about you two. How do we know we can trust you?"

Chance said, "Well, I'd like to believe we have honest faces—"

"If I pay a visit to the local law and ask about you, what am I going to find out?"

The brothers exchanged a worried glance.

Ace said, "If there's a possibility we'll be traveling together, you deserve to know the truth, ladies. Marshal Courtright's probably not that fond of us right now. In fact, we've been involved in some trouble recently, and he told us it would be better if we got out of town."

"In other words, you're criminals," Isabel snapped.

"Not hardly!" Chance said. "There was this rattlesnake in a jar and a bet that I won, and this gunslinger and a crazy Indian—"

"Hold on," Ace said. "Let me tell it."

For the next few minutes, he did exactly that, laying out the events of the previous night. He didn't try to sugarcoat any of it, either. He wanted the ladies to know what the situation was.

When Ace was finished, Jamie Gregory said, "Well, that doesn't sound like any of it was really their fault, Lorena. It was those other men who caused all the trouble, and they're in jail."

"For a little while longer," Ace said. "Marshal Courtright will be letting them out this morning."

"Except the Indian," Lorena said. "He's loose already."

"Yes, but none of them have any real reason to come after us." A note of bitterness came into Ace's voice as he added, "They already have all our money, and I doubt if they would go to the trouble of following us just because of a grudge over a bet."

Lorena considered that for a moment, then said, "You're probably right. From the way you describe them, I've known men like this Shelby and Baylor before. They're more interested in money than anything else. The marshal's right about it being a good idea for you to get out of town, though. Out of sight, out of mind, as the old saying goes." She looked at the other three. "What do you think?"

"We need to get started," Isabel said. "I wish things had worked out differently, but since they have not . . ." She shrugged.

"They look honest to me," Jamie added. "I think we can trust them."

"How about you, Molly?" Lorena asked the redhead, who hesitated before answering.

Finally, she said, "We don't have any other choice, do we? Mr. Patterson said it wouldn't be safe for us to start out on our own, and I believe him. And we really do need to get started."

Lorena nodded and turned back to Ace and Chance. "I guess it's settled, then, if you want the job."

"We'll take it," Chance replied instantly.

After a second, Ace shrugged and nodded in agreement.

"Try not to be so enthusiastic, cowboy," Lorena said dryly. "Come on. I'll show you the wagon."

It was a good-sized wagon with a long bed and a canvas cover over the back. A team of four draft horses went with it. Ace took a glance in the back and saw crates and bags of supplies, as well as bunks built along the walls, two on each side.

Since there were five women going on this trip—although Ace and Chance hadn't seen the fifth one yet—that meant one would have to make a pallet and sleep on the floor of the wagon bed. The brothers had their bedrolls and would sleep outside, of course.

"Looks like a good sturdy vehicle, and the team is fine," Ace told Lorena. "One thing worries me. Unmarried ladies traveling a couple hundred miles with two men . . . well, that may not do your reputations much good."

"Don't worry about our reputations, honey," Lorena told him. "You see, we're already bought and paid for, and I don't think any of the men who made the arrangements will want to back out on the deal."

"Bought and paid for? You mean—"

"That's right. We're mail-order brides."

CHAPTER SEVEN

Actually, that wasn't *exactly* the first thought that went through Ace's mind when Lorena used the phrase *bought and paid for*—but once he considered what she'd said, it made sense.

Chance said. "I've heard of such a thing, but I don't reckon I've met a real, live mail-order bride until now." He frowned. "But I don't understand—"

"Come on. We need to get that team hitched up," Ace said, not letting his brother continue. He had a hunch Chance was about to say something indiscreet about wondering why such beautiful women had to resort to becoming mail-order brides in order to find husbands.

That was a puzzle, all right, but it was also none of his and Chance's business. Everybody had their own story, their own reasons for arriving at the places in life where they found themselves, and other folks didn't have the right to pry uninvited into that.

"Agnes is probably getting a little worried about us," Lorena said. "Jamie, why don't you and Molly go on back to the hotel and let her know what's going on.

Isabel and I will stay here and make sure these two don't steal our wagon."

"Doesn't the wagon actually belong to that Mr. Keegan?" Ace asked. "And if you don't trust us any more than that, are you sure you want to go all the way to San Angelo with us?"

"There are bound to be more suitable guides to be found in Fort Worth," Lorena said coolly, "but it would take time to find one, and I want to get started. And the two of you need to be lighting a shuck, if what you told us is true, so it seems like fate brought us together." She paused, then went on. "I've never trusted fate, not completely. We'll all just have to get used to each other along the way, I guess. As for the wagon, Keegan can pay somebody to go to San Angelo and bring it back, once he sobers up enough. That's his problem, not ours."

"Fair enough," Ace said. "I reckon you're not going to pay us any of that eighty-seven dollars until we get there, are you?"

Lorena smiled. "That's right, cowboy. Payment on delivery, so to speak."

"That's fine. And my name's Ace, not *cowboy*."

"You've punched cattle, though, haven't you? Unlike your soft-handed brother here."

"Hey!" Chance objected. "I've worked cows, too."

"Not nearly as much as your brother, I'm thinking. No, you strike me as the sort who's more at home sitting at a poker table in a smoky saloon. A knight of the green felt."

That put a smile on Chance's face as he repeated musingly, "A knight of the green felt . . . I kind of like that. And to tell the truth, you're probably right about us, Miss Lorena."

"If there's one thing I know," she said, "it's men."

Ace figured it would be best not to ponder too much about that statement. Instead, he and Chance got busy maneuvering the horses into their places and hooking up the harness.

When they were done and the wagon was ready to roll, Chance said to Ace, "Flip a coin to see who handles the team and who rides horseback?"

"No need," Ace said. "You pick, and I'll be satisfied doing the other."

"In that case, I'll handle the team."

That decision came as no surprise to Ace. He knew his brother was looking forward to sitting next to one of the women. Chance would be happy to have either Lorena or Isabel that close to him. Both were lovely.

He was in for a disappointment. Both women climbed into the back of the wagon without even giving the Jensen brothers a chance to help them up.

"We'll ride back here," Lorena said. "I believe Agnes, the fifth member of our group, grew up on a farm. She can probably handle the team once we pick up her and the others. That way you can ride alongside with your brother, Mr. Jensen."

As Chance stepped up to the wagon seat, he said, "You'd better start calling us Ace and Chance. You holler 'Hey, Jensen!', we won't know which one you're talking to."

"I'll keep that in mind," Lorena said from the back of the wagon.

Ace chuckled, which drew a quick glare from his brother, whose gelding he led to the back of the wagon and tied the reins there so the horse would follow. Then he swung up into the saddle on his chestnut and waved Chance out of the livery barn.

Flicking the reins, he got the team moving, and the wagon rolled slowly out into the street.

Ace saw Patterson leaning against the wall next to the office door with a dubious look on his face. He reined closer and said, "We still owe you for a couple nights."

"Send the bill to that Keegan hombre," Chance suggested to Patterson from the wagon seat. "In a sense, we're working for him now."

Ace shook his head. "You don't need to do that." He dug out a couple silver dollars he had gotten in change earlier and leaned down from the saddle to hand them to the stableman. "Thanks for taking good care of our horses, Mr. Patterson."

"Glad to do it," Patterson said. "Come back to see me, the next time you're in Fort Worth."

"Considering the way Fort Worth has treated us," Chance said, "that may be never."

Lorena gave Chance directions to the hotel where she and her companions had been staying.

As he drove, Chance asked over his shoulder. "This fella Keegan—does he run some sort of mail-order-bride business?"

"It's called a matrimonial agency," Lorena said. "He finds brides for men all over Texas and New Mexico Territory."

"He seemed like a respectable gentleman when we arrived," Isabel put in.

"Not to me. I know a drunk when I see one. I just hoped he could keep it under control until he got us to San Angelo." Lorena blew out a disgusted breath. "Turned out he couldn't . . . which comes as no real surprise. I learned a long time ago not to depend too much on any man."

"And yet you're going to marry one of them," Chance pointed out.

"I have a business arrangement with one of them," Lorena corrected. "I believe in business. How far it goes beyond that, we'll just have to wait and see."

The street was busy, so most of Chance's attention was focused on handling the team and the wagon. Ace rode easily alongside with his hat thumbed back on his head. Their visit to Fort Worth hadn't worked out like he had expected, especially the last part of it, but to be fair, things seldom did. Trouble had a way of finding the Jensen brothers.

"There's the hotel, up there on the left," Lorena said as she moved up just behind the seat and bent to look past Chance's shoulder.

"I see it," he said. "There's Miss Jamie and Miss Molly on the porch, too."

"You're being pretty informal."

"We're going to be traveling companions for the next week or so. No need to be stuffy during that time."

Lorena nodded after a second. "I suppose you're right."

"The other lady, that's, ah, Miss Agnes?"

"Yeah. You can see why I said she can probably handle the wagon."

"I don't mind driving—"

"I'd rather have you and your brother on horseback. You can keep an eye out for trouble better that way and be quicker to handle any problems that crop up."

Riding close enough, Ace heard what Lorena said. He leaned toward the wagon and agreed. "You're right, ma'am. I mean, Miss Lorena. But Chance and I can take turns driving the wagon if it turns out to be too much for Miss Agnes."

Chance was hauling back on the reins and bringing the team to a stop as Ace spoke.

The dark-haired young woman heard what he said and asked, "Are you talking about me?"

Jamie said, "I told you Lorena wants you to drive the wagon, Agnes."

Ace took his hat off. "Only if you think you can handle it, ma'am. I mean, Miss Agnes."

She definitely wasn't a beauty like the others, but she had a pleasant look about her. At least, she might have whenever she wasn't standing next to someone like Jamie Gregory, who was pretty enough to throw most women into the shade.

"I used to drive a hay wagon," Agnes said. "This can't be much more difficult than that, I suppose."

"I don't know," Chance said with a smile. "A load of hay can't complain if the ride's too rough."

Agnes looked at him—and her face seemed to light up from the inside.

Ace bit back a groan. He had seen that same expression on the faces of too many women too many times before. Agnes was instantly smitten with Chance, and sooner or later, one way or another, that usually led to trouble.

But maybe not this time, Ace told himself, because Agnes, pleasant or not, certainly wasn't the sort of woman Chance was inclined to pursue. That was a good thing. Like the rest of the women, she was already spoken for.

"Those are our bags on the porch," Lorena said.

Without being asked, Ace dismounted and Chance wrapped the reins around the wagon's brake lever, then jumped lithely to the ground. It didn't take them long to load the bags into the back, next to the supplies.

There was a canvas sling underneath the wagon for extra storage, but it wasn't needed.

Agnes stood next to the front wheel and the driver's box and seemed to be waiting for something. When Chance walked by, she asked him. "Could you give me a hand, please?"

"Uh, sure." He took hold of Agnes's right arm and steadied her as she used the wheel to climb up onto the driver's box. She rested her hand on his shoulder as she made the final effort to climb to the high seat.

At the back of the wagon, Ace helped Jamie and Molly climb onto the lowered tailgate, from which they were able to step into the wagon bed through a narrow aisle in the supplies and baggage. They sat down on the other bunks.

"Are you ladies ready to go?" Ace asked.

"More than ready," Lorena replied. "It's already more than an hour later than we were supposed to leave. Drat that drunken sot Keegan."

Chance untied his horse from the back of the wagon and stepped up into the saddle. Ace mounted as well and brought his horse alongside the driver's box on the right side. Chance moved up on the left. Agnes had settled herself on the seat and grasped the reins in both hands.

"Ready?" Chance asked her.

"Oh, yes. Very ready." She smiled.

Ace said, "You'll have to turn the wagon around and head west." He turned his head to check the traffic in the street. "Looks like you've got room."

Agnes slapped the reins against the backs of the team and called out to the animals. They leaned forward into the harness. She hauled back on the lines to turn the leaders to the right. The wagon lumbered around and started west along Throckmorton Street toward the river.

Crossing the Trinity required a jog in front of the courthouse up to Main Street, where there was a bridge over the stream. That meant they would go past the jail, too, Ace realized. He hoped Lew Shelby, Henry Baylor, Loomis, and Prewitt were still locked up.

At least the men weren't standing out on the street when the wagon rolled by, to witness the Jensen brothers leaving town with the five women. There was no point in asking for trouble.

Especially since it was liable to find them anyway. It always did.

CHAPTER EIGHT

Marshal Jim Courtright slid Lew Shelby's gun across the desk and leaned back in his chair to watch the man in black pick up the fancy revolver. "You've been fortunate so far, Shelby. You haven't done anything in Fort Worth to merit a hanging. But you'd be wise not to push your luck."

Henry Baylor took hold of the lapels of his frock coat and said, "That sounds a bit like a threat, Marshal."

"No threat," Courtright said, "just a warning. I'm getting tired of being summoned to deal with some sort of fracas and finding you fellas there. Why don't you mosey on over to Dallas? It's only thirty miles, and I'm sure you'd like it there."

"We like it here just fine." Shelby thumbed bullets back into his gun, which Courtright had unloaded the previous night, just as he'd unloaded the weapons he collected from the other three men. "Besides, I need to look up a couple gents and have a word with them."

"If you're talking about those Jensen boys, they're gone. I'm told they rode out early this morning."

Actually, Courtright hadn't been told any such thing.

He didn't know if Ace and Chance Jensen were still in Fort Worth, but he hoped they had taken his advice and put the town behind them. If he could convince Shelby and Baylor that was the case, maybe they wouldn't even bother looking.

Shelby pouched his iron, shoving it into the holster with added vehemence. "Which way did they head?"

Courtright's eyes narrowed as he said, "You don't think I'd tell you, even if I knew, do you? But as a matter of fact, I *don't* know. Don't have any idea. Nor do I care, as long as they're not in Fort Worth anymore."

"How do I know you're telling the truth about that, Marshal?"

Courtright tensed and came slowly to his feet behind the desk. He brushed back his coat a little, so his hand wasn't far from the butt of the gun on his hip. "Are you calling me a liar, Shelby?" he asked in a cool, dangerous voice.

Baylor put a hand on Shelby's arm and shook his head. "Lew's not saying anything of the sort, Marshal, and we're certainly not looking for any more trouble. We've had our share for a while."

Courtright had a reputation as a gun-handler, and he could tell by the look in Shelby's dark, deep-set eyes that the man wanted to challenge him . . . felt the need to find out which of them was really faster.

Baylor was too cautious to allow that. He and Shelby had done well for themselves in Fort Worth so far. A gunfight between Shelby and the local law could have only one out of two possible outcomes, and either would damage the gambler's future plans.

Shelby gave a little shake of his whole body, sort of like a wet dog but not as violent. Courtright realized the man was shaking off the killing rage that had gripped him for a moment.

"Anyway, your Kiowa friend broke into the Jensen brothers' hotel room last night, tried to kill them, and wound up stealing their bankroll," Courtright went on, now that the moment of impending violence had passed. "So they've already suffered enough of a loss that evens the score."

Baylor arched an eyebrow. "Is that so, Marshal? We don't know anything about it. How could we? We were locked up last night, remember?"

"I'm sure it won't be long before you find the Indian, or vice versa."

"I'm tired of listening to this," Shelby said. "Let's get out of here."

Still holding Shelby's arm, Baylor steered the gunman toward the door of Courtright's office. Loomis and Prewitt, both as taciturn as ever, picked up their guns from the desk as they left.

Courtright straightened his coat and sat down again, glad to see them all go. As far as he was concerned, they could keep going—right on out of his town.

Outside the jail, Shelby stopped and flexed the fingers of both hands. "I want those damn brothers. And when I'm through with them, sooner or later Courtright and me are gonna settle things between us, too."

"Courtright's high-handed manner will catch up to him sooner or later," Baylor said. "As for the Jensens, I believe the marshal. It seems very likely they've left town."

"We could ask around, find out which way they went. The Kiowa can track them. You know that."

"Go to that much trouble simply so you can shoot them?" Baylor shook his head. "I have no objection to you killing anyone, Lew, you know that—as long as there's a good reason for it. And by good reason I mean—"

"Something that makes money for us," Shelby said with traces of impatience and disgust in his voice. "I know, I know. But you don't understand, Henry, sometimes there are more important things than money. Like a man's pride."

"We'll talk about it later. Right now, we should head for our usual haunts so the Kiowa won't have any trouble locating us." Baylor's voice hardened a little. "I want to discuss that two hundred dollars with him."

"Fifty thousand dollars," the man said as he gazed at the amber liquid in the glass he held.

It was a little early in the morning for whiskey, but some things merited taking a drink no matter what time it was. Brooding about the betrayal that had stabbed a knife in his guts was one of those things.

"Here's to the cold-blooded bitch who stole it from me." He tossed the drink back and thumped the empty on the bar in front of him. He was a big man, heavy through the shoulders but lean-hipped from all the riding he had done, mostly to shake off posses that were chasing him for one reason or another. His black hat was tipped back on rumpled fair hair above a slightly lantern-jawed face.

"You ain't tellin' us anything we don't already know, Earl," said one of the two men who had accompanied him into the saloon in Dallas.

At that hour, they were the only customers except for a drunk who lay facedown over one of the tables, snoring. The only other person in the place was a sleepy-looking bartender wiping idly at the mahogany with a rag.

"Yeah, you talk about her all the time," said the other man who had come in with Earl. As the big man swung a glare toward him, he added hastily, "Not that that's a problem or anything. Whatever you want to say, Earl, me and Cooper are mighty happy to listen. Ain't we, Coop?"

"That's right, Ben," the first man, whose name was Seth Cooper, quickly agreed. Neither he nor his companion, Ben Hawthorne, wanted to make Earl any angrier than he already was.

Earl was usually pretty proddy to begin with. Having his woman take off with fifty grand in loot he and the rest of the gang had stolen from various banks in Texas, Arkansas, and Missouri had made him just about loco.

Cooper and Hawthorne understood that. They were glad their leader had picked them to come with him while he tracked down the thief. That showed Earl trusted them and might result in bigger payoffs later on.

For the time being, the rest of the gang had scattered to the four winds. They were supposed to rendezvous in Fort Smith in two months. Earl, Cooper, and Hawthorne would go there when they had recovered the stolen loot.

They had tracked the woman all the way from Missouri to Dallas, but they didn't know which direction she had gone from there. Cooper and Hawthorne had been all over town, questioning hotel porters, livery hostlers, ticket clerks at the railroad depot and the stagecoach line, anybody they could think of who might have seen her. They'd been making the rounds for two days without any luck.

That lack of success was grating on Earl's nerves. And that meant it was only a matter of time until he exploded. Cooper and Hawthorne didn't want to be around when that happened.

The hinges on the saloon's batwing doors squealed a little as a man pushed through them. He wore a white shirt and dark brown vest, with garters around the shirt's sleeves, and sported a black eyeshade, as well. It didn't take much looking around the room for him to spot the three outlaws at the bar.

The newcomer headed toward them. "Are you fellas looking for a woman?"

The question made Earl look around with a snarl on his face. "What the hell is it to you?"

"I just got back to work at the telegraph office today after taking a few days off," the man replied, unfazed by Earl's bad attitude. "The gent who took my place told me some men were asking around about a woman." He described the object of the owlhoots' search and then added, "About a week ago I handled some telegrams for a woman who looked like that. When I heard somebody was looking for her, I asked around until I was told you might be here getting a drink."

Earl reached out with his left hand, grabbed the man's shirtfront, and jerked him closer. "Who the hell was she sending telegrams to?" he demanded.

The telegraph operator's eyes widened with fear, but he stood his ground and replied in a firm voice, "I figured it might be worth something to you."

Earl's right hand pulled the gun from the holster on his hip, shoved the barrel up under the telegrapher's jaw, and dug the muzzle into the soft flesh there, causing a gasp of pain. "It'll be worth your life if you don't tell me what I want to know."

The drunk still snored away in the corner. The bartender edged toward the far end of the bar, still pretending to wipe the hardwood with the rag but obviously not wanting anything to do with what was going on.

"Earl," Cooper said, "you can't go stickin' a gun in a fella's throat like that. Somebody's liable to come in, see what you're doin', and call the law on us."

"We can't afford that," Hawthorne put in. He took a coin from his pocket. "Ten bucks, mister. That enough to pay for what you know?"

The telegrapher managed to nod, which was no easy feat with Earl's gun pressed against his throat.

Earl growled, lowered the weapon, and stepped back. "Talk," he grated.

"The lady . . . the lady wired a man in Fort Worth." The telegrapher rubbed his sore neck for a second, then went on. "A man named Keegan. He runs a . . . a matrimonial agency, whatever that is. The lady made some sort of deal with him and was going to meet him in Fort Worth. I couldn't really make heads or tails of it beyond that."

"Fort Worth's only thirty miles from here," Cooper said.

"Get the horses," Earl snapped. "We're ridin'."

Hawthorne handed the ten-dollar gold piece to the telegrapher, who said, "I hope you boys won't tell anybody how you found out about this. All telegraphic communications are supposed to be confidential. I'm betraying a sacred trust."

"Sacred trusts come cheap around here, then," Hawthorne said. "We won't say nothin', don't worry about that. All we want to do is find the woman."

"Could I ask—"

"No. You sure as hell can't."

"I told you to get the horses," Earl said with a scowl. "We're gonna find this man Keegan, and he'll tell us what we need to know. Either that, or I'll break every bone in the son of a bitch's body."

Steam billowed around the train sitting alongside the platform in New Orleans. It would be pulling out soon, but not all the passengers were aboard just yet.

In fact, one of the passengers, a slender young man in an expensive suit and hat, watched with a frown of disapproval as porters lifted his trunk and bags from a cart and carried them into a private car.

"These men are lazy," he snapped to his companion. "If their sloth causes me to miss this train, Leon—"

"There's no way you'll miss the train, Mr. Kirkwood," the man called Leon said. "The conductor knows to hold it as long as necessary." A faint twitching at the corners of his mouth might have been a smile . . . or it might not have been. "Trains don't go off and leave passengers who can afford a private car."

"Well, I suppose you're right about that," Kirkwood said.

He was twenty-five years old, with a delicately handsome face adorned by a thin mustache. His companion was twice as old and at least seventy pounds heavier, a bulky man whose thick arms and shoulders strained the fabric of his cheap black suit. A black bowler hat sat on a mostly bald head above very prominent ears and a chin as square and sturdy as a block of stone. Opponents in the prizefight ring had tried pounding that chin for years and never succeeded in doing anything except breaking their knuckles.

One of the porters emerged from the railroad car and said, "That's the last of 'em, Mist' Kirkwood. You's ready to go. I'll go tell the conductor."

Kirkwood jerked his head in a nod of acknowledgment. He didn't thank the porter. Who wasted time and breath thanking a servant for doing his job?

Kirkwood climbed aboard, followed by Leon, who moved with unusual grace for such a big, bulky man. Inside, the car was comfortably, luxuriously appointed.

Kirkwood tossed his hat onto a chair and then sat down on a well-upholstered divan. "I need a drink."

Leon moved to a small bar located near the front end of the private car. He picked up one of the several snifters that sat upside down on a silver tray. His fingers were so thick and strong it seemed like the delicate glass would snap and shatter just from him handling it.

His touch was deft, however, and he had no trouble pouring brandy from a crystal decanter into the snifter. He took it to Kirkwood and handed it to the young man, who swirled the liquid, sniffed it delicately, and took a sip. "Acceptable, I suppose. How long will it take us to reach Fort Worth?"

"We have to go north to St. Louis first," Leon said, "and change trains there. Then on down into Texas. We'll be there tomorrow morning, if there are no delays."

Kirkwood took some papers from an inside coat pocket, unfolded them, and studied them, even though he had already read over the detective's report a score of times. "There had better not be any delays. According to this, she arrived in Fort Worth several days ago. Do you think she'll still be there, Leon?"

"I don't know, sir. But if she isn't, we'll find her." The big man nodded solemnly. "We'll keep looking until you find her, just as you vowed that you would."

"And when we do, she'll see the error of her ways. She'll regret breaking our engagement. She'll promise to come back and remain faithfully at my side from now on." Kirkwood lifted the snifter and drank down all the brandy. He licked his lips. "If she doesn't, you have my permission to twist her pretty little head right off her shoulders, Leon. You'd enjoy that, wouldn't you?"

Leon just grunted.

CHAPTER NINE

Agnes Hampel proved to be quite skilled at handling the team and wagon. She must have learned quite a bit hauling hay on the farm where she was raised, Ace thought. He could tell that having Chance riding along-side distracted her at times, but for the most part she kept her attention on what she was doing.

Ace needed to have a talk with Chance and let him know how Agnes felt. Whenever pretty girls were around, Chance sometimes completely ignored other things that were going on—and there were four beauti-ful ones riding in the back of that wagon.

Once they were across the river, the road split into several trails, with arrow-shaped signs nailed to a single post to identify each route. Ace drew rein and frowned at the signs, which read DENTON, JACKSBORO, and WEATHERFORD.

He looked across the backs of the team and asked Chance, "You know which way we're supposed to go?"

"I haven't been here before. How would I know?"

Lorena leaned out past Agnes. "I have a map I bought when I found out where we were going. I didn't expect to need it, since Cyrus Keegan claimed he knew the way, but I was curious. Now I'm glad I did."

She retreated into the wagon to find the map in her belongings and then climbed out onto the seat and motioned for Ace to come closer. He brought his horse in until his leg was brushing the side of the driver's box.

"Here's Fort Worth," Lorena said as she rested a fingernail on the map. She traced a path with it across the paper. "And here's San Angelo."

Ace leaned closer to study the map in Lorena's hand. As he did, he smelled the scent of lilac water coming from her, along with something else indefinable that stirred his senses. He was conscious that their heads were only a few inches apart. "Looks like we need to go through Weatherford. Then we head on out to Abilene and angle southwest from there to San Angelo."

From the other side of the driver's box, Chance said, "Abilene's in Kansas. You should know. We had some trouble there a while back, remember?"

Ace wasn't likely to forget. "Well, there's an Abilene in Texas, too. There it is, right on the map."

Agnes said to Chance, "You can crowd on in here, if you need to see the map better."

Chance shook his head. "No, I trust Ace to know where he's going. He's always been the level-headed one."

Agnes looked disappointed that Chance didn't want to lean across her to study the map. He didn't appear to notice her reaction.

Ace straightened in his saddle. "All right. We head for Weatherford, then. That was pretty smart of you, Miss Lorena, buying that map."

"I like to be prepared for whatever comes up."

"Yes," Isabel said from inside the wagon, "I imagine you do."

Lorena sent a quick, over-the-shoulder glare at the sultry brunette then folded the map. "I'll ride up here for a while if that's all right with you, Agnes."

"Sure. I won't mind the company." Agnes flicked the reins again and got the team moving onto the trail that led to Weatherford.

It was a nice spring morning, although a low line of dark clouds far to the west promised the possibility of rain later. That time of year, storms were common all up and down the plains that ran through the middle of the country from Canada to the Rio Grande. Good weather for the whole trip would have been welcome, but Ace knew better than to expect it.

The trail ran almost due west through territory covered with small, grassy hills and stretches of woods, especially along the little creeks that trickled through the countryside every few miles. A line of thicker vegetation to the south marked the course of the Trinity River. They passed a number of farms and small ranches and rolled through a small settlement around midday.

Not long after that, Ace spotted some dust rising behind them, and a few minutes later he heard pounding hoofbeats and the rattle of wheels. "Better pull off to the side where there's a good level spot," he told Agnes. "I think we've got a stagecoach coming up behind us, and the driver's liable to be in a hurry to get through."

"We've got as much right to be on this road as any stagecoach does," Chance protested.

"Legally, maybe, but what's the point in arguing? It's easier just to let him by."

Chance snorted to show that he didn't fully agree with his brother on the issue, but he didn't argue as Agnes directed the wagon to the side of the road.

Sure enough, a fast-moving stagecoach came into view less than a minute later. It was several hundred yards behind the wagon, but it covered that ground quickly.

The driver was a white-bearded old-timer with the brim of his hat turned up in front. He hunched forward on the seat, popped his whip around the ears of his team, and yelled at the six-horse hitch. The coach swayed on its wide leather thoroughbraces as the horses thundered past without slowing down.

The four women in the back of the wagon watched the coach race past. "Merciful heavens!" Jamie exclaimed. "I think I'd be positively ill if I was jolted around as much as the poor people in that coach must be."

"That's one more reason I'm glad you ladies have your own wagon and can travel at a more leisurely pace," Chance said as he unleashed a dazzling smile on the innocent-looking blonde. "Someone as beautiful as you should never have to worry about being sick."

"Good looks will ward off some of life's hardships," Lorena said, "but not all of them."

The stagecoach went around a bend in the trail and some trees cut it off from view. Agnes got the wagon moving again. They had been traveling at a decent rate of speed, but nothing like the breakneck pace of the stagecoach.

Molly suddenly said, "You don't suppose that coach

was moving so fast because outlaws were chasing it, do you?"

Ace noticed the expression of concern on her wholesomely pretty face and assured her, "I don't see anybody else, Miss Molly. I reckon that driver was just in a hurry because he's running behind schedule."

"Or else he just likes driving like a bat out of hell," Chance added.

Lorena laughed. "I've known plenty of fellas like that. Never want to slow down for anything."

"Their loss, I imagine," Isabel said.

Ace saw the quick look of veiled hostility that passed between the two women following Isabel's comment. He wasn't sure what was behind it—but maybe it would be better if he didn't know for certain.

As it was, he could guess that Isabel was hinting Lorena had something unsavory in her past. Lorena *did* have a sensuous, worldly air about her. It went along with a pragmatic fatalism, the kind of look and attitude that was common in women who had spent much time in saloons and sporting houses.

In short, it seemed to Ace that she might have been a soiled dove at one time, maybe even recently. The fact that she was on her way to get married didn't rule that out. On the frontier, plenty of ranchers and farmers married women they met in sporting houses. The relative scarcity of females made it easier to overlook what some might consider sordid pasts.

Besides, Ace thought wryly, some of those hombres, especially the ones who sent off for mail-order brides, probably weren't exactly prizes themselves.

A while later, they reached a stone ranch house set in some trees atop one of the rolling hills. Lathered horses stood in the corral near a big barn off to the side and Ace realized they had come from the stage-coach. The driver had switched teams there, which meant the place was probably a regular stop.

That guess was confirmed by a man who came out of the barn and gave the travelers a friendly smile. "Howdy," he called. "Want to water your horses? I don't think old Salty's team drank the well quite dry." He pointed to the well in front of the house.

"We're obliged to you," Ace told him. "I'm sure the horses could use a drink, and some rest, too. We've been traveling all morning."

"You're welcome to stop a while," the man said. "My wife's got coffee and cornbread and beans ready in the house, if you and your, uh . . ." His voice trailed off as he looked at the five women—Agnes on the driver's seat and the other four looking out around her. With a dubious frown, the man went on. "Are you fellas Mormons a long way from Utah, by any chance?"

Ace laughed and shook his head. "No, sir. These ladies are on their way to San Angelo to marry up with men they're supposed to meet there. My brother and I are guiding them and looking out for them."

Since Lorena was the one with the map, it could be said that *she* was the one doing the guiding, but Ace and Chance would handle any trouble that cropped up, so Ace didn't think what he said stretched the truth too much.

The man reached up and tugged on his hat brim. "You ladies light and set a spell, then. My name's John Spencer. This is my ranch."

"We're pleased to meet you, Mr. Spencer," Lorena said without introducing herself or the others. They would likely never be back here, so it wasn't really necessary. "We haven't stopped for dinner yet, so your wife's cornbread and beans sounds just fine. We can pay for our meals, of course."

"Four bits apiece, and worth every penny," Spencer said proudly.

Ace and Chance dismounted and helped the women down from the wagon. Again, Agnes made sure it was Chance who gave her a hand, even though he seemed more interested in clasping Jamie's trim waist as he assisted her from the lowered tailgate to the ground.

Lorena took Ace's hand as she stepped down and seemed to hang on to it for a second or two longer than he thought was really necessary. Earlier, back in Fort Worth, she had been rather tart-tongued, but she smiled mighty nice at him as she said, "Thank you." She must have decided that he was all right after all.

"Glad to help, ma'am."

"I've told you about that ma'am business."

"Yes'm. I mean, Miss Lorena."

"Behave yourself, and maybe by the time we get to San Angelo you can forget about the *miss*, too, and just call me Lorena." She went on into the stone ranch house with maybe just a tad more sway in her hips than she'd displayed before. Clearly, she had relaxed a bit now that they were actually on their way.

Once all the women were inside, Ace and Chance moved to the well.

"It looks to me like Miss Lorena might be a little sweet on you, Ace," Chance said with a grin as they drew up the bucket from the well so the horses could drink.

"I don't think so," Ace said. "She's just being friendly."

Chance lowered an eyelid in an exaggerated wink.

"I've got a hunch she can be *real* friendly, if you know what I mean."

"Blast it, Chance, she's engaged to be married. You need to talk about her like she's a respectable lady."

"So I'm not the only one who thinks that maybe she wasn't always a respectable lady, eh?"

Ace shot a glance toward the house. "Don't you let her hear you saying things like that," he warned. "Whatever Miss Lorena was—or wasn't—is not any of our business."

"Well, I suppose you're right about that."

"Anyway, she's older than us—"

Chance broke in with a laugh. "Yeah, a whole six or seven years older! I don't think that makes a whole heap of difference, Ace, especially to her."

Ace started to say something about how Agnes had been looking at Chance, but he held his tongue. No matter how oblivious Chance could be at times, he would figure it out sooner or later. And then he would have his own problem to deal with.

When the horses had been watered sufficiently, the Jensen brothers left the team to rest and went into the house. The five women were sitting at a long table with Mr. and Mrs. Spencer. Ace and Chance said hello to Mrs. Spencer, a pleasant-faced, middle-aged woman.

When she stood up to get them some coffee and food, Ace waved her back onto the bench next to the table. "We can serve ourselves, ma'am. No need for you to get up."

"You're a very polite young man," she said.

"He is," Lorena agreed, and that was enough to make Chance give his brother another sly grin.

They lingered at the ranch/stagecoach station for an hour. The women were eager to reach San Angelo, but at the same time, allowing the horses to rest meant they could cover more ground overall.

Spencer helped pass the time by spinning yarns about life at the stage station, including antics from the colorful old jehu Salty Stevens, who had been at the reins of the coach that had passed the wagon earlier.

Ace and Chance eventually introduced themselves, and when Spencer heard the brothers' last name, he exclaimed, "Say, you boys aren't related to Smoke Jensen, are you? I met him a couple years ago when he came through here, traveling on a stagecoach with his wife Sally."

"We've met Mr. and Mrs. Jensen," Ace said. "A couple times, in fact. But we're not blood kin as far as we know."

"He seemed like a fine man. I know there are some who still say he's an outlaw, but I don't believe it for a second. A gunfighter, sure, you can tell that about him, but he's on the side of law and order."

Ace nodded. "We've always figured it the same way."

"I hear tell he's got a brother who's a bounty hunter." Spencer frowned. "Never did cotton much to that sort."

"We've met him, too," Chance said. "Luke's not bad . . . for a bounty hunter."

"Of course, a couple drifters like us can't exactly claim to be respectable," Ace added with a smile.

Lorena raised her cup of coffee as if toasting with a drink. "Respectability is sometimes overrated."

Ace didn't know what to say to that other than, "Yes, ma'am. Miss Lorena."

CHAPTER TEN

Ace had been keeping an eye on the clouds in the west all day. They didn't seem to be moving much, just hanging there and looking vaguely threatening, but an hour or so after the wagon left the Spencer place, the wind picked up and the clouds began edging closer and getting darker, shading from blue to gray to black. The sun was still shining brightly where Ace, Chance, and the women were, but it might not stay that way much longer.

They were passing a fairly tall hill when Ace signaled for Agnes to stop the wagon. "I want to take a ride up there and have a look around," he told Chance as he gestured toward the hilltop.

"You're worried about those clouds?"

"A little," Ace admitted. "It might not be a bad idea to find a place where we can hole up for a while, maybe all night."

From the front of the wagon where she looked out past Agnes, Lorena objected, "We haven't come much more than ten miles from Fort Worth! You can't be talking about stopping for the day already, especially when we got a late start."

Ace pointed to the west. "Those clouds may not look like much now, but I've seen some pretty bad storms blow up from clouds that didn't look any worse." He waved his hand to indicate the trail in front of them, which continued through open, gently rolling hills. "If we get caught out there in a storm, there won't be any shelter. I don't mind getting soaked by rain, but we have to worry about lightning and wind, too."

"Mr. Patterson said something about tornadoes," Jamie put in. "I've seen what they can do, and I don't want to be anywhere around one of them."

"You're right about that," Lorena admitted. "All right. We'll wait here. Just don't be gone too long."

Ace and Chance nudged their mounts into motion and rode up the hill that loomed to the north. The slope wasn't too bad, but when they reached the crest about half a mile from where they had left the wagon, both brothers reined in and gazed in surprise at how the land fell away sharply into a thickly wooded valley several miles wide.

"You think the wagon can get down there?" Chance asked.

Ace pointed to a path that zigzagged down the slope. It had probably started as a game trail and been widened by men on horseback.

"I wish that path was a little wider, but I think we're going to have to try it," he said as lightning flickered in the distant clouds. "I'll drive the wagon. I don't reckon Agnes needs to be tackling that chore."

"I won't fight you for the job," Chance said. "Remember that stagecoach line we worked on up in Wyoming? I got my share of hair-raising trails up there!"

They turned their horses and rode back down to the wagon through the freshening wind, which was carrying a hint of coolness. Most times, that would be welcome, but not caught out in the open as they were.

"Climb on in back, Miss Agnes," Ace told her. "I'm taking the reins."

"Is there a problem?" Agnes asked. "You think I haven't been handling the team all right?"

"You've been doing a fine job," Ace said. "But where we're headed, the going will be a mite rougher."

She looked like she wanted to argue with him, but after a moment she shrugged and stood up to climb over the seat and into the wagon bed with the other four women.

Ace handed the chestnut's reins to Chance and then stepped directly from the saddle onto the driver's box. He settled himself on the seat, took up the reins, and swung the team to the north. The horses plodded up the hill.

When they reached the top, Ace brought them to a stop. "I hate to say this, ladies, but I think it would be best now if you got down and walked."

"Why is that?" Lorena asked.

"Because if this wagon turns over and goes tumbling down the hill, it'll be better if you're not in it."

"No one with any sense can argue with that," Isabel said. "Come on, ladies."

Lorena frowned. Ace thought there was a good chance she and Isabel were vying for unofficial leadership of the group. Lorena probably believed that was her right, since she was the oldest. but it appeared Isabel might not agree with that.

At the moment, the rivalry between the two women—

if indeed there was one—didn't matter. Ace was more concerned about the weather.

While Chance helped the ladies out of the wagon, Ace watched the clouds, which were scudding through the sky faster. He saw more lightning in the gathering gloom, and he thought he heard a faint rumble of thunder to go with it.

Agnes heard it, too, and smiled. "Tater wagon's rolling over. That's what my pa always told us kids every time we heard thunder."

"I don't know about the tater wagon," Ace said. "I just hope *this* wagon doesn't roll over."

When the ladies were clear, he lifted the reins and got the horses moving again. The trail, such as it was, angled sharply to the right as it started down the slope, making the wagon lean slightly to the left. Ace shifted on the seat to keep the weight balanced as much as he could.

It was a nerve-wracking few minutes before he reached the point about a third of the way down the hill where the trail turned back on itself. Since the turn wasn't as sharp nor the angle quite as steep, he risked taking his eyes off the ground in front of the horses for a second and glanced back up the trail. Chance had dismounted and was leading the saddle horses down, bringing up the rear behind the five young women. With the exception of Agnes's shoes, none of their footwear was made for walking, so they stepped gingerly along the trail.

As he neared the bottom of the trail, still without incident, Ace saw a limestone ledge thrusting out from the hillside to his left. The outcropping was large and slanted enough at the bottom to create an overhang. The ledge would offer some protection from the rain and wind, and under it there would be less danger from lightning as well.

Thinking there was room for the wagon and the horses, Ace swung the team off the trail and drove over rough, rocky ground, taking it slow so the jolting wouldn't damage the wagon. He glanced back to make sure Chance and the women were following.

The wind picked up and began to moan. They hadn't looked for shelter any too soon, Ace realized. If they had waited much longer it would have been too late.

The limestone outcropping cut off some of the wind's force as he drove in front of it and brought the wagon to a stop. Chance and the women were right behind him. He set the brake, put a hand on the end of the seat, and vaulted to the ground.

"We need to get these horses unhitched and tied up good and secure," Chance said. "That storm will be here in just a few minutes."

"I can help," Agnes offered.

Ace was about to tell her to climb into the wagon with the other women, then he remembered that Agnes had been a good hand with the team so far. He nodded and said. "Thanks."

Maybe she just wanted to impress Chance, but the assistance would be welcome either way.

With the Jensen brothers and Agnes busy tending to the horses, Lorena and the other three women had to climb back into the wagon without any help.

Ace paused in what he was doing to tell them, "Once Agnes is inside, you'll want to close the flaps and cinch in those openings at the front and back of the wagon bed as much as you can. That'll help keep the rain out."

"What about you and Chance?" Lorena asked.

"We can wait it out underneath the wagon."

Chance grimaced at that, but Ace figured it would be too crowded inside the wagon if they climbed in there, too.

Lorena agreed with Chance. She said briskly, "Nonsense. You'll come inside. If it rains, water will run under the wagon and you'll get soaked. There's no need for that."

"We don't want to push our way in—"

"You won't be. We're inviting you. Isn't that right, ladies?"

"It would be better if you joined us," Isabel agreed, and Jamie nodded, too. Molly didn't say anything, but she tended to be quiet. Ace had noticed that about her already.

Ace and Chance tied the horses to several post oaks with thick trunks growing nearby. The trees would shelter the animals, and the ropes were sturdy enough that the horses couldn't break them.

As the brothers were finishing up that chore, the rain began to fall, occasional big heavy drops that landed with loud thumps on their hats. They trotted over to the wagon and climbed in. The ladies had cinched up the opening at the front as much as possible. Chance raised the tailgate and tightened up the cord running around the inside of the canvas.

That didn't close off the wagon bed completely. There were still gaps where the wind whipped in.

With the overcast that had rushed in, it was fairly dark inside now that both openings were cinched up. Rain peppered the canvas over their heads, getting heavier and heavier until it was a dull roar.

Ace and Chance sat on crates of supplies at the back of the wagon.

Lorena asked, "How bad is it going to get?"

"Hard to say—"

That was as far as Ace got in his answer before thunder crashed and drowned out anything else he might have said.

"Oh!" Jamie cried in alarm.

Chance was beside her on the bunk by the time the flash of lightning that accompanied the thunder had faded. "It's all right," he told her as he put his arm around her shoulders in a comforting gesture. "You're safe here inside the wagon."

Ace heard a sniff of disdain and figured it came from Agnes, who sat on one of the bunks with Molly.

Rain began to pelt down even harder. Lightning lit up the inside of the wagon with a near-constant flicker. Thunder rumbled and boomed so loudly Ace felt the vibration coming up from the ground through the wagon wheels.

"This is what they call a real gully-washer," he commented in an attempt to lighten the strained mood.

"Back home we called them toad-stranglers," Lorena said.

"Where's that?" Ace asked.

Earlier in the day, he and Chance had tried to find out where each of the ladies came from, but Lorena, Isabel, and Molly had all brushed aside the question. They weren't rude about it, just didn't really answer.

This time Lorena said, "Mississippi. I was raised down on the coast, the daughter of a fisherman."

As if she didn't want to be outdone by Lorena, Isabel said, "I am from New Orleans. My father was an . . . adventurer, I suppose you would say. A mad Irishman who went to Mexico to fight for one would-be dictator or another. He was never very clear about that. But he met and married my mother, and when they got out of the country, he was one step in front of a firing squad, or so he always claimed." She laughed. "With my father, it was sometimes difficult to tell what was the truth and what was some flight of wild Irish fancy."

That was the most Ace had heard Isabel say at one time.

Lorena evidently thought so, too. "Nobody asked you for your life story, honey."

"What about yours?" Isabel shot back in a challenging tone. "How does a fisherman's daughter from Mississippi wind up being a mail-order bride on her way to marry a man in West Texas?"

"Her father drowns when she's fifteen and her ma dies six months later and she's left to learn how to fend for herself," Lorena snapped. "That's how."

"I am sorry," Isabel murmured. "I did not mean to bring up painful memories."

"Didn't you?"

A particularly hard gust of wind slammed against the wagon's canvas cover at that moment and shook the whole vehicle, distracting everyone inside from the tense exchange between the two women.

When the shaking stopped, Agnes asked, "The wagon's not going to be blown over, is it?"

"Not likely," Ace said. "With the wind like this, though, it's hard to say anything for sure."

The rain was falling so hard it was like a thick gray curtain outside. Through occasional gaps in the downpour, Ace caught glimpses of tree branches waving wildly in the wind.

"Are the horses going to be all right?" Agnes asked.

"They should be. Those draft horses may get spooked, but we tied them securely enough they shouldn't be able to break free. If they do somehow, Chance and I can round them up once the storm's over."

"How do you know your horses won't run away?" Jamie asked.

"Oh, they're used to loud noises," Chance told her. "Although usually it's gunshots, not thunder. Not much difference to a horse, I suppose."

"So your horses are used to gunfire," Lorena said. "Just how much trouble do you boys get into?"

"More than our share," Ace said.

Isabel said. "That means either we should not have chosen you to be our guides and protectors . . . or else we could not have picked more wisely."

Ace grinned. "I reckon we'll have to wait and see which one it turns out to be."

CHAPTER ELEVEN

Storms that violent usually didn't last very long, so Ace wasn't surprised when the rain began to taper off an hour later. The wind stopped blowing quite as hard, too, and the thunder and lightning moved slowly off to the east.

As the sky lightened, he looked outside. "I can see all the horses. None of them broke loose and stampeded. We had a little luck on our side there, I guess."

"It's going to be too late to travel any farther today, isn't it?" Lorena said.

"I'm afraid so." Ace moved the canvas cover a little so he could see better and watched water cascading down the hill in several miniature rivers. "Anyway, it's likely that trail is too muddy right now and won't dry out enough for the wagon to make it up the hill until sometime tomorrow—if it stops raining pretty soon."

Molly said, "You mean we may be stuck here for a day or even longer?" She sounded worried.

Maybe even more than worried, Ace thought. She almost sounded scared.

"We'll get started again as soon as we can," he promised. "If all the storms have blown over by tomorrow, we might be able to find an easier way out of this valley. Today we were hurrying, just trying to get to some shelter before that squall hit."

"It's a good thing we did, too," Chance added. "The way the lightning was popping and crackling all around us, if we'd been out in the open one of those bolts probably would have struck the wagon. And a man on horseback would be a natural target to get hit."

"I guess it's also a good thing we didn't start off by ourselves the way we talked about doing," Lorena said. "I'm not sure any of us would have known what to do when that storm came in."

Jamie said, "You may have saved our lives already, and it hasn't even been twelve hours since we met you!"

"You're our heroes," Agnes said.

Ace didn't care for such effusive praise, but Chance grinned and basked in it. With a certain degree of false modesty, he said, "Just doing our job, ladies."

"Our job is going to be getting out and checking on those horses pretty soon," Ace said. "And I'll bet your slicker is in your saddlebags, like mine is."

"Well, yeah, but we can wait for it to stop raining, can't we? Or at least until it lets up some more." Chance beamed around the inside of the wagon. "Right now I think we should all just sit here and enjoy the company. It's cozy, right?"

"Very cozy," Agnes agreed immediately, but Chance didn't turn away from Jamie to respond to her.

It was still pretty gloomy inside the wagon, but Ace could see well enough to take note of Agnes's expression, which was a mixture of irritation and disappointment. He had never understood why some women fell so hard, so fast, so completely, for his brother, but Chance's appeal to the ladies was undeniable and always had been.

They chatted idly while the storm continued to weaken.

When the rain was just a patter on the canvas, Ace lowered the tailgate and climbed out. "Come on, Chance."

Obviously reluctant to leave the company of the women, especially Jamie, Chance got out of the wagon, too, and the brothers walked across to the horses. The ground was slick with mud, and runoff still gurgled through several nearby channels that had washed out during the storm. They funneled together at the bottom of the hill to form a fast-flowing, temporary stream a foot deep and several feet wide that dropped down over several smaller limestone ledges into a deep gully, forming miniature waterfalls.

The animals appeared to be unharmed. There hadn't been any hail as far as Ace could tell, just wind and rain, thunder and lightning, and none of the horses had pulled against the ropes hard enough to cause injuries.

A break suddenly appeared in the clouds to the west. The low-hanging sun blazed through it like a torch, sending a giant shaft of light slanting along the length of the valley, illuminating it dramatically. The glow made the clouds that had moved off to the east look even blacker than they really were. A rainbow appeared, arching through the sky with its myriad of colors.

The strikingly beautiful scene drew several exclamations of awe from the ladies as they climbed out of the wagon and stood carefully on the muddy ground.

"I see what you mean about not going anywhere

today," Lorena said to Ace. "That trail's like a river, even though the rain has stopped."

"It'll take a while for all the water to run off, but we should be able to get back on the road to San Angelo again tomorrow."

"I suppose we made a good enough start." Lorena smiled. "We're still alive."

The storm moved into Fort Worth in the late afternoon, and the clouds were so dark that in a matter of minutes it looked almost like night. Lights glowed from the saloons and gambling dens and bawdy houses of Hell's Half Acre. Sheets of rain swept through the streets and chased nearly everyone inside. Only a few people ran here and there, most with coats pulled up over their heads in a futile effort to keep from getting soaked.

Few riders—only three in fact—rode on that stretch of Throckmorton Street. They pulled their tired mounts to a halt in front of a saloon.

All three men wore yellow oilcloth slickers, but the rain was so hard that water inevitably seeped in under the garments. They weren't soaked to the skin yet but were getting there in a hurry. Rain trickled in streams off the brims of their pulled-down hats.

They dismounted and tied their horses at a half-empty hitch rail. The animals stood with drooping heads and let the rain pelt them.

The men stepped up onto the boardwalk, under the awning and out of the downpour. Gusts of wind tugged at their slickers.

Earl tipped his head forward to let more of the

water run off his hat. "My God, this is miserable weather!"

Cooper's wet face creased in a grin. "Just a little spring shower."

A bright flash and a deafening clap of thunder followed his words.

The third man, Hawthorne, jumped a little. "Damn. Spring shower, my hind foot."

Earl stepped over to the saloon's entrance. The doors had been closed to keep rain from blowing in. The batwings were swung in and latched back, he saw as he went inside with Cooper and Hawthorne behind him. Hawthorne closed the doors.

Two men sat playing cards at one of the tables. From the looks of the coins in front of them, the stakes in the game were so low as to be almost nonexistent. Four more men stood at the bar nursing beers, and a single bartender was behind the hardwood, polishing glasses.

He nodded to the three newcomers as they stepped up to the brass rail. "Nasty day to be outside. Want a drink to cut the chill a mite?"

"Three whiskies," Earl said. "Leave the bottle, and give us three mugs of beer, too."

"Sure thing, mister."

Water dripped steadily from the slickers and formed little puddles before the sawdust on the floor soaked it up.

Earl picked up the glass the bartender put in front of him and threw back the whiskey in it. He grunted as the welcome burst of fire hit his belly. Next to him, Cooper and Hawthorne put away their slugs, too.

Earl snagged the bottle and refilled the glasses, then alternated sips of whiskey and swallows of beer. The warmth inside him grew and he began to feel better.

They had been in the saddle for most of the day as they rode from Dallas, and the men were almost as tired as the horses that had carried them. Earl had pushed them hard, himself included.

"Don't recall seein' you fellas around here before," the bartender commented. His brown hair was parted in the middle and slicked down. His weak chin and prominent Adam's apple gave him a funny in-and-out look.

"We're new to Fort Worth." Earl fought down the impulse to be curt. He hated small talk—but he needed information. The only way to get it was to talk to people, so he went on. "Came to see an old friend of ours. Fella name of Cyrus Keegan. Maybe you know him?"

"Keegan, Keegan," the bartender repeated in a musing tone. "Knew a Jim Keegan once. Don't think he had any relatives named Cyrus. And this was back in Wichita, so it wouldn't be likely any of old Jim's kin would be down here in Fort Worth. Not impossible, though."

Cooper and Hawthorne exchanged a glance. They saw the look of dark fury stealing over Earl's face and knew that his patience was nearing an end.

Cooper nudged the glass of whiskey closer to Earl's hand and said, "Drink up, boss, and then maybe you'd like to sit down for a spell. It's been a long day."

"Yeah," Earl rasped. "A real long day." He downed the slug and took his beer over to a table in the corner, where he slumped down in one of the chairs and thrust his long legs out in front of him.

"Fellas," the bartender said quietly as he leaned toward Cooper and Hawthorne, "did I say something to make your friend upset? He looked a little mad there."

"He's just tired," Cooper said, "and he really wants

to find his old pard Cyrus. You positive that you don't know any Keegans in these parts?"

"Nope, I sure don't. Sorry." The bartender brightened. "Tomorrow you could go to the courthouse. They ought to have a city directory there, and you could look and see if this fella Keegan lives around here. Handy thing, those city directories."

That actually wasn't a bad idea. Cooper and Hawthorne looked at each other and nodded. That late in the day, in bad weather, there wasn't much they could do, anyway, except wait out the storm. They took their glasses, the bottle, and their beers over to the table and sat down with Earl.

Cooper said, "No luck, boss. But the drink juggler said we could go to the courthouse tomorrow and check the city directory for Keegan. Then we can find him, and he can tell us where your, uh . . . wife . . . went."

"Yeah," Earl said as he picked up the bottle and tipped more busthead into the glass Cooper had set in front of him. "My sweet little wife. I've got a score to settle with her, so I reckon that makes fifty thousand and *one* good reasons to find the lying, stealing, redheaded bitch."

Finding enough dry wood for a fire was impossible, so the Jensen brothers and the five young women made a cold camp that night. They had brought sandwiches—thick slices of roast beef and bread—from the hotel dining room, intending to make a midday meal of them, but the stop at Spencer's meant they had been able to save the food for supper. That was a stroke of luck, since under the circumstances, they couldn't cook anything.

One sandwich had been intended for Cyrus Keegan. Ace and Chance would have been satisfied to split it, but Agnes and Jamie insisted on giving part of their meals to Ace and Chance so the brothers would get enough to eat. That prompted the other three women to tear off part of their sandwiches and pass the pieces over, as well.

"This is mighty kind of you ladies," Ace told them.

"You deserve it after you kept us from getting caught in that storm," Lorena said.

Isabel chewed daintily and swallowed. "The two of you can't sleep out on the ground tonight. It's too muddy."

Ace smiled. "This won't be the first time we've slept on muddy ground, Miss Isabel. We'll be fine."

"Surely we could make room in here," Agnes suggested.

Jamie frowned. "I'm not sure that would be . . . proper."

"It didn't get as wet over under the trees," Chance said. "Don't worry about us. We'll find a good spot."

"Are you sure?" Lorena asked. "I don't really give a damn about propriety."

"This we know," Isabel said.

Lorena narrowed her eyes and leaned forward on the bunk where she was sitting. "If you've got something to say, honey, it might be best for you to go ahead and spit it out."

With a cool smile on her face, Isabel shook her head. "I have nothing to say . . . honey."

Ace figured the women had stayed in separate rooms

at the hotel in Fort Worth. Now that they would be spending all their time together in such close quarters, he wondered if Lorena and Isabel would make it all the way to San Angelo without winding up rolling around on the ground, pulling hair, and trying to claw each other's eyes out.

He hoped that wouldn't happen. He hated having to break up a catfight. Such things tended to be even more dangerous for anybody who tried to interfere.

The stars were beginning to come out and the last shreds of wispy clouds were blowing away as Ace and Chance carried their bedrolls into the trees and searched for a relatively dry spot to spread them. They found a place that wasn't too damp where they still had a good view of the wagon sixty feet away.

"You think we need to take turns standing guard?" Chance asked.

"I'm not sure that's necessary," Ace said. "It's been a long time since any hostile Comanches ventured this far east . . . if there are even any left. Texas has been pretty quiet in the past few years as far as Indian trouble goes."

"Yeah. And that storm probably has any bad men lying low. Besides," Chance added, "our horses will let us know if anybody comes sneaking around."

"That's what I thought," Ace agreed. "It's been a long enough day we can both use the sleep."

They settled down, using their saddles as pillows.

Chance muttered, "Seems hard to believe it's been less than twenty-four hours since we were looking at that damned snake in a jar. I hope Shelby and Baylor and the rest of that bunch don't come after us. Those sweet, innocent young ladies don't need our trouble coming around to bother them."

"Amen to that," Ace agreed. He dozed off a few minutes later.

He wasn't sure how long he had been asleep when something roused him. The horses were quiet. That was the first thing he checked when he pushed himself up on an elbow and peered around in the darkness.

Nothing seemed to be going on. The limestone ledge loomed over the wagon. The vehicle's canvas cover was easy to see in the starlight.

Also easy to see was the dark shape that moved between him and the wagon. He reached out to his shell belt, which he had coiled and placed on the bedroll beside him. His hand closed around the butt of his Colt.

The shape stood upright and was human. Somebody was sneaking around the wagon while the women slept. Ace glanced over at the other bedroll for a second and saw Chance stretched out there, breathing deeply and regularly.

Ace felt a little bad that for an instant he had suspected his brother of trying to pay a nocturnal visit where he had no business being.

That still left the question of who was skulking around the wagon. Ace pushed his blankets aside and rose silently to his feet, gun in hand. He intended to find out who the intruder was.

CHAPTER TWELVE

Ace's bare feet didn't make much noise on the muddy ground as he crept closer to the wagon. He didn't want any shooting—bullets flying around wildly would endanger the women—but he was ready if he needed to use his gun.

He kept thinking about the Kiowa. The Indian could have trailed them from Fort Worth. Ace hadn't considered that a likely possibility, but he couldn't rule it out. And now that he was closer to the mysterious intruder, he could tell that the hombre wasn't very big. Neither was the Kiowa.

He leveled the Colt, looped his thumb over the hammer, and said quietly, "Don't move."

A shocked hiss of sharply indrawn breath came from the person next to the wagon. The shape lunged to the side. Ace made a grab with his left arm, aiming to smack the stranger over the head with the gun if it took that to subdue him.

As Ace encircled the shape and clamped down with his forearm, he felt it pressing against mounds of soft flesh and realized they were breasts.

Warm, firm, female breasts.

He had grabbed one of the mail-order brides—who, by the feel of it, was wearing a thin shift and not much else.

Ace let go of the woman and jumped back. "I'm sorry!" he blurted. "I didn't mean to—I mean, I thought you were somebody else—I mean, somebody sneaking around the wagon—"

Roused from sleep by Ace's exclamation, Chance came up out of his bedroll with his .38 gripped in his hand. "Ace?" he said sharply. "What's going on?"

Ace's face was hot with embarrassment, and it grew even warmer when Lorena stuck her head out the back of the wagon and asked, "What in blazes is all this?"

From the front of the wagon, Isabel added, "Is there some sort of trouble?"

Two of them were accounted for. Ace still didn't know which young woman he had grabbed. If he had to guess, judging by the impression of the body he had gotten during the brief, too-intimate encounter, he would have said Jamie or Molly.

It proved to be the redhead. He recognized her voice as she said, "It's all right, Mr. Jensen—Ace. Don't worry, ladies. Everything is fine."

"I never meant to—" Ace began again.

"I know that," Molly assured him. "You were just making sure we were safe, and I appreciate that."

"But what are you doing out here?"

"Really, there are some questions that a gentleman just doesn't ask a lady."

Ace wouldn't have thought it was possible that he could get any more embarrassed—but he would have been wrong. His face felt like it was on fire. "Of course," he muttered. "My apologies, Miss Molly."

"That's all right." She laughed, but it sounded a little strained. "Now that I've disturbed everyone's sleep, I think we should all go back to bed, don't you?"

"That sounds good to me," Isabel said. "Who knew that riding in a wagon could be so tiring?"

Instinctively, Ace started to step forward and offer to help Molly climb into the wagon, but then he remembered her state of partial undress and thought better of the idea. Under the circumstances, she could manage by herself.

She climbed into the wagon, and Ace and Chance went back to their bedrolls.

As he stretched out, Chance chuckled and said quietly, "You're the one who always accuses me of taking too many liberties with the ladies, Ace. But it was you putting your hands all over Miss Molly, not me."

"I didn't put my hands all over her." Ace scowled in the darkness as he slid the Colt back into its holster. "It was more like my arm that, uh, got up against some things it shouldn't have, just for a second." He heard a muffled noise and went on. "You're trying not to laugh out loud, aren't you?"

"Trying not to," Chance admitted, "but I don't know if I'll succeed!"

The sky—deep blue with not a cloud in sight—was completely clear the next morning. A light wind containing a hint of coolness blew across the valley. The weather wouldn't stay that pleasant for very long. In another month or six weeks, summer would set in with its full force, and Texas would be blisteringly hot and dry.

Ace and Chance and the five women would reach

San Angelo long before that. The ladies would be married to the men who were waiting for them, and in all likelihood, the Jensen brothers would have moved on, heading wherever their fiddle-footed nature took them.

Ace not only had trouble meeting Molly Brock's eyes, he didn't want to look at her at all. He concentrated on checking on the horses then looking for wood that had dried out enough overnight to serve as fuel for a fire.

He had wandered down through some trees toward a gully at the bottom of the hill when he realized that somebody had followed him. He glanced over his shoulder, expecting to see Chance, but it was Lorena Hutton who stood there with a faint smile on her face.

"You're looking for firewood, aren't you?" she asked. "I thought I would give you a hand."

"Well, that's generous of you, but you don't have to. I can manage."

"I'm sure you can, but I want to do my part." Her smile got a little bigger. "If we can get a fire going, I'll be drinking the coffee we brew on it, as well as eating hotcakes and bacon."

That sounded mighty good to Ace. After the day and the night they'd had, a nice hot breakfast would make a heap of difference in how he felt.

"I saw the way you couldn't even look at Molly this morning," Lorena went on. "There's no need to torment yourself about it. I don't think she's the least bit upset."

"That's just because she's being nice," Ace said. "I had no right to grab her like that, especially with her being, well, spoken for by another man."

"It was an accident, and Molly knows it." Lorena moved close enough to reach out and rest the fingertips of her right hand on his left forearm. "Anyway, even though she's spoken for, as you put it, she's not married yet. Some of us figure that until we've said 'I do' and the preacher's done his part, we can still do whatever we want and no one is hurt by it." She didn't withdraw her hand. In fact, she increased the pressure and slid her palm up his arm.

He felt the warmth of her touch through the sleeve of his faded blue shirt. Somehow, she had gotten even closer. If he leaned forward just a few inches, their lips would be together . . .

The sound of voices nearby made Ace pull back. He looked toward the wagon. He could see movement through the trees, although the thick trunks obscured any details. Chance and the women were moving around over there, and it had been his brother Ace heard talking.

"We, uh, we need to find that firewood."

"Sure." Lorena's hand tightened a little on his arm. "But you remember what I said, Ace. It's a long trip to San Angelo, and I don't see any reason why we can't be friends along the way. Good friends."

Ace had a pretty strong hunch what she meant by being good friends. While he was as healthy as any young man his age and responded instantly to the beautiful woman's touch, he also felt like it would be wrong to take advantage of the situation that had brought them together.

Of course, if there was any taking advantage to be done, it might not be him doing it.

He swallowed hard, turned away, and resumed his

search for firewood. Lorena helped him, although her assistance consisted mostly of walking around and being distractingly pretty.

Despite that, in a short time Ace was able to gather up an armload of branches he believed might be dry enough to burn.

Chance frowned a little when he saw Ace and Lorena walking back up to the wagon together, but he didn't say anything.

That would be just what he needed, Ace thought— his rake of a brother lecturing him about women!

He was able to get a fire going. He'd expected to prepare breakfast, since he usually did that when he and Chance were on the trail, but Agnes moved in and said, "I'll take care of this, Ace. You did enough by gathering the wood."

"All right." Ace straightened from the fire. He hoped she was a good cook. He had a hunch that she was, since she had proven competent at every other task she had tackled so far. He backed off and let Agnes get to work.

Chance came up beside him as he was watching her prepare breakfast. Quietly, he said, "She's a mighty hard worker, isn't she?"

"You could say that."

"She'll make some farmer or rancher a fine wife, I reckon."

"Because she works so hard?"

"Well . . . yeah. Why else?"

Ace just gave a little shake of his head and didn't say anything else. It wasn't his job to point out the obvious to his brother. He moved toward the wagon to have a look at it and make sure it hadn't been damaged in the rough ride down the hill the previous afternoon.

However, before he could get there, Molly intercepted him and linked her arm with his, steering him away from the vehicle.

That wasn't like her, Ace thought, although he hadn't really known her long enough to make such a judgment.

"I hope you've gotten over feeling bad about what happened last night. It was purely an accident, Ace. I'm not angry or embarrassed about it, and you shouldn't be, either."

"I always try to oblige a lady. If that's the way you feel about it, Miss Molly, I'm mighty happy to go along with what you say. I wouldn't want bad feelings between us all the way to San Angelo."

"And there won't be any," she promised, smiling. "Do you think the ground is dried up enough for us to get back to the main trail? Why don't we go have a look?"

"Sure," Ace said with a shrug. It seemed like it was his day to receive more feminine attention than usual, he thought as they walked over to have a look at the trail leading back up the hill.

First the worldly Lorena and now shy, quiet Molly. Those two were just about the opposite of each other, but Ace had to admit the interest they were taking in him was gratifying. Not that it really meant anything, of course.

The path was still muddy, but Ace thought the wagon and the team would be able to manage. The women would need to walk to the top of the hill, since the wagon needed to be as light as possible going up the slope.

The coffee, flapjacks, and bacon were all good, and breakfast was a friendly meal, with none of the tension between Lorena and Isabel that had been present the day before. Ace didn't know how long that truce would last, but he planned to enjoy the peace while it did.

When breakfast was over and Agnes had cleaned up, Ace and Chance hitched the team to the wagon.

Ace said, "I'm afraid I'm going to have to ask you ladies to walk for now. That way the horses won't have to pull as much weight up the slope."

"Didn't anybody ever tell you not to use the words *ladies* and *weight* that close together?" Lorena asked with a smile.

"Sorry, I just mean—"

She stopped him with a wave of her hand. "I'm joshing you, honey. We can hoof it, can't we, ladies?"

"I do not care for the idea of walking in the mud," Isabel said with a doubtful frown.

"Stay there at the edge of the trail where there's some grass," Chance told her. "It won't be too bad."

It wasn't. Chance led the saddle horses and went first, while the mail-order brides followed him in a straggling line. Agnes gave the other women a hand now and then when the ground proved slippery.

Ace handled the team. The horses pulled valiantly and stubbornly against the wagon's weight and fought against the mud, as well. They were able to get enough traction to keep going and not let the vehicle get bogged down.

When he reached the crest, Ace brought the wagon to a halt and looked to the east, toward Fort Worth. From that elevation, with the air so clear, he could see a good ten or fifteen miles, all the way to the town on the bluffs above the Trinity. He couldn't see any buildings, of course, but he knew Fort Worth was there.

He hoped that Lew Shelby, Henry Baylor, and the other three were still there, as well, and not somewhere on their back trail. The last thing he wanted was trouble dogging them all the way to San Angelo.

All the women except Agnes were a little winded from the steep walk. Ace climbed down from the wagon, and he and Chance let them catch their breath before they helped them into the vehicle. Agnes took the reins again while Ace swung up into the chestnut's saddle.

"Ready, ladies?" he asked them.

"Ready for anything," Lorena said.

Ace sort of doubted that but hoped they wouldn't have to find out.

CHAPTER THIRTEEN

Still in Fort Worth, Earl, Cooper, and Hawthorne spent the night in rented rooms on the second floor of the saloon after Hawthorne had gone back out into the storm to lead their horses to a nearby livery stable. The task had fallen to him because he had lost while cutting cards with Cooper.

The bad weather had moved on by the next morning, but the three men had to avoid large puddles of water as they walked toward the courthouse. By later in the day, horses' hooves and wagon wheels would have churned the street into a muddy mess, but it wasn't too bad except for the puddles.

They had all guzzled too much who-hit-John the night before. Cooper and Hawthorne were bleary-eyed and stumbling, able to move only because they were fortified with several cups of strong black coffee.

Earl had his hate and anger to fuel him. That was more than enough to keep him striding along purposefully.

Fort Worth didn't have a courthouse square like most county seats in Texas. The courthouse sat at the north end of town on Belknap Street, facing the block between Throckmorton and Houston Streets. The three outlaws went up the steps and into the big stone edifice.

A clerk behind a counter greeted them. "How can I help you . . . gentlemen?" The slight hesitation showed that during his habitual greeting, he realized that these three didn't quite fit the description.

Still, it was a public building and they had as much right to be there as anybody else.

"City directory," Earl snapped.

"This is the, ah, Tarrant *County* Courthouse—"

"Do you have one or don't you?"

"As a matter of fact, I do have one on hand." The clerk reached under the counter and brought up a thin, leather-bound book. He held it out toward Earl, who motioned brusquely for Cooper to take it.

Cooper knew that Earl could read, but it was a laborious process for the boss outlaw. It would be faster and less embarrassing if Cooper checked the directory for Cyrus Keegan.

There were two listings—one for the Keegan Matrimonial Agency on Rusk Street, a few blocks over, the other on Bluff Street that was probably the man's residence. Cooper committed both addresses to memory and slid the directory back across the counter. "Obliged, amigo. Maybe you could give us some directions now."

"I'll try," the man said. It didn't take long for him to tell the three men how to find the places they were looking for.

Earl and the other two outlaws left the courthouse. Cooper and Hawthorne were glad to get out of there.

Courthouses reeked too much of law and order to suit them.

As they walked toward the matrimonial agency, Hawthorne said, "How do folks stand to live in a place like this with the buildings all crowded up against each other?"

"I wouldn't like it, that's for sure," Cooper agreed. "I'm used to bein' out in the open."

Earl grunted. "Running from posses, you mean."

"Well, that's part of it, I reckon. But you can't deny we get plenty of fresh air that way, Earl."

Earl ignored the comment and stopped in front of a door that opened between two businesses. A sign on it read KEEGAN MATRIMONIAL AGENCY—ONE FLIGHT UP. Below that, a hand-printed sign that appeared to have been tacked up recently announced CLOSED TEMPORARILY ON ACC'T OF INJURY.

"What the hell does that mean?" Cooper said. Then, realizing that Earl might not understand completely, he added, "Closed on account of injury."

"Keegan must be hurt," Hawthorne said.

"Then he'll be home," Earl said. "That's where we'll find him. Come on."

It was a long walk to the stretch of Bluff Street—so named because it followed the bluff above the river—where Cyrus Keegan's house was located. If the three outlaws had known how far, they might have gotten their horses from the livery stable and ridden over there.

But they didn't know, this being their first time in Fort Worth. Like cowboys, they made most of their living while on horseback and so wore boots better for riding than walking. Because of that, they were all footsore by the time they reached the neat little whitewashed house, which didn't do a thing to improve Earl's already surly mood.

Cooper knocked on the door. A minute or so later, a heavyset, middle-aged black woman in an apron opened it and looked out at them in surprise. Politely, she said, "Yes, sirs? What can I do for you?"

"We need to see Mr. Keegan," Cooper said. He was the smoothest-spoken of the trio, when he put some effort into being polite.

"Are, uh, you gentlemen in the market for brides? Because I got to tell you, Mr. Keegan is plumb laid up right now and ain't workin' 'cause he's hurt."

Earl's patience ran out in a hurry. "I don't have time to be arguing with some mammy. If Keegan's laid up, that means he's here. Get out of the way." He bulled ahead, forcing the woman to step back even though she tried to hold her ground.

"Mister, you can't do that—"

"Grab her and shut her up," Earl told the other two.

A little wide-eyed, Hawthorne said, "You mean kill her?"

"No, just keep her from yammering in my ear, you idiot!"

The two outlaws took hold of the woman's arms. Hawthorne clapped a hand over her mouth as she started to yell. Earl shoved past. He didn't know exactly where Keegan was, but the house wasn't very big so he didn't think he'd have any trouble finding the man.

Keegan helped with that by calling through an open door down a hallway, "Lantana, who was that at the door?"

Earl stalked down the corridor and stopped in the doorway. The man in the room was in bed with his back propped against several pillows piled behind him. His splinted and bandaged right leg stuck straight out in front of him. He stared in alarm at the rugged-looking stranger in his house. "Who are you?"

"You're Cyrus Keegan?" Earl asked.

"That's right."

Earl took a couple steps into the room. Keegan wasn't a young man. He was fifty years old, maybe more. Hard to say how big he was with him stuck in bed like that, but he seemed medium-sized, at best. A fringe of gray hair ran around his ears and the back of his head. Watery blue eyes peered at Earl through wire-rimmed spectacles.

"I'm looking for Molly Brock. You know where she is."

Keegan shook his head. "You're mistaken, sir. What have you done to my housekeeper? Where's Lantana?"

"Don't worry about her. A couple of my pards are keeping her company." Earl went closer to the bed. "Molly Brock. Where can I find her?"

"I don't know who you're talking about."

Earl loomed over the bed and drew his gun. That caused Keegan to flinch back against the headboard as much as he could with the pillows behind him.

"You traded telegrams with her a few days ago. Is she here in town? By God, you'd better tell me."

"I have nothing to say to you." Keegan couldn't keep his voice from shaking, but he didn't lack for courage—or foolishness. "You get out of my house right now—"

Earl chopped down with the gun in his hand, slamming it against the splinted leg. Keegan's back arched. He screamed in pain, a shriek that was cut off when Earl backhanded him across the mouth with his other hand.

Earl drew back the revolver's hammer and put the barrel against Keegan's head. Keegan whimpered and tried to pull away from the gun, but there was nowhere for him to go.

"Molly Brock," Earl said again.

"Miss . . . Miss Brock is a client! I can't betray her trust—"

"It's *Mrs.* Brock. I'm her husband." A humorless grin tugged at Earl's mouth. "So if you sent her off as a mail-order bride, you broke the law, Keegan. She can't marry anybody else. She's already married to me."

"I . . . I swear I didn't know that! I can only go by what my clients tell me. There's no way to check all their stories and make sure they're telling the truth."

With his free hand, Earl took hold of Keegan's chin and squeezed, forcing the man's mouth into an O of pain and fear. He twisted Keegan's head back and forth. "I don't give a damn about the marrying part. I wouldn't have that bitch back on a bet. But she stole from me, and I'm not gonna put up with that. So tell me, Keegan . . . where is she?"

Keegan made noises, but he couldn't form words with Earl Brock holding his chin in such a brutal grip.

After a moment, Earl let go, and Keegan gasped. "San Angelo! She left here with some other ladies yesterday, bound for San Angelo!"

"Got husbands waiting for them, do they?"

"That . . . that's right."

"Well, at least one of them is gonna be disappointed, then." Earl leaned closer. "You wouldn't be lying to me, now would you, Keegan?"

"It's the truth, I . . . I swear it! They left here in a

wagon yesterday morning. Five women. One of them was your . . . your wife."

Earl frowned a little. "You sent five women across Texas in a wagon by themselves?"

"I was supposed to go with them. But then, this happened"—he nodded toward his broken leg—"and I couldn't go. I was told later that they hired a couple men as guides and to, you know, look after them in case of trouble."

"They're gonna have trouble, all right. Bad trouble." Earl lowered the hammer on the gun and moved it away from Keegan's head.

Then he struck, slamming the barrel against the man's mostly bald dome. Keegan groaned and slumped over on his side, the splinted leg causing him to twist grotesquely. It must have been a painful position, but he wouldn't know because he was out cold.

Earl went back to the front room and found that Cooper and Hawthorne had tied and gagged the black housekeeper. She sat on a chair, glaring murderously at them.

"Find out what you needed to know, Earl?" Cooper asked.

"I did. We'll be riding as soon as we can get the horses."

"What about her?" Hawthorne gestured toward the housekeeper. His voice held a slight tone of dread, as if he still expected Earl to order them to kill the woman.

"By the time she gets loose and can raise a ruckus, we'll be long gone. Just leave her."

Cooper said, "What about the, uh . . ." He pointed with a thumb down the hall toward the room where Earl had been.

"He's out cold." Earl went to the front door, opened it, and walked out.

The other two hurried after him.

Over his shoulder, Earl asked, "Either of you two know where San Angelo is?"

"Yeah, about two hundred and fifty miles west of here, I'd say," Hawthorne replied. "Fort Concho's there. I used to work for a rancher who sold some horses to the army, and we delivered 'em to the fort." Hawthorne grinned. "That wasn't long before I figured out I'd rather *steal* horses."

"You can point us in the right direction, then."

"Molly's gone to San Angelo?" Cooper asked.

"She's pretending to be a mail-order bride, but I know she's just trying to get as far away from me as she can, in the hope that I'll never find her. I will, though. We'll catch up to her before she ever gets there."

Five women—and two men, Earl thought. Whoever those hombres were, they wouldn't be any match for him and his companions. They would catch up, kill the men, get his $50,000 back, and see how good-looking the women were before they decided what to do with them.

It couldn't be any simpler than that.

CHAPTER FOURTEEN

The train pulled into the Texas & Pacific depot at the southern end of downtown Fort Worth a little after ten in the morning.

Ripley Kirkwood's private car had been switched to the train in St. Louis. It would be detached and kept on a siding until Kirkwood needed it again, whenever that might be. The young man's father was an important stockholder in the T&P, so the line did what it could—within reason—to assist him.

Porters removed Kirkwood's bags from the car and loaded them onto a wagon hired by Kirkwood's efficient and brutal assistant. Leon had also made arrangements for rooms in the city's best hotel a few blocks from the depot.

Kirkwood told him, "See to it that the bags are delivered. I need a drink."

"I should stay with you, sir."

"I can take care of myself," Kirkwood snapped.

Deep down, he knew that he probably couldn't. More than once, he had needed his father's money as well as Leon's violent and ruthless methods to get him out of trouble. But he would be all right in broad daylight in the middle of a city, even a half-civilized cow town like Fort Worth.

Leon made a low, rumbling sound in his throat, but he didn't argue. He knew from experience that once his boss's mind was made up, no one could change it.

What Kirkwood didn't know wouldn't hurt him. As the young man strolled off in search of a place where he could get a drink at the relatively early hour, Leon spoke to the wagon driver and slipped the man a five-dollar gold piece to ensure that he would take care of delivering the bags to the hotel.

With that done, Leon followed his employer. For such a big, bulky man, he moved smoothly and swiftly, blending into the background so that even if Kirkwood glanced back, he probably wouldn't notice that he was being trailed.

Kirkwood went into a saloon a couple blocks north of the depot. It wasn't the fine sort of drinking establishment he was accustomed to in New Orleans, but it wasn't *too* squalid, he decided. The front windows were relatively clean, and so was the bar he saw as he stepped up to it.

A couple men sat at one of the tables drinking coffee. They had a bottle of whiskey on the table, as well, and from time to time they picked it up and splashed a little liquor into their cups. If they had been at it for very long, the mixture was probably more whiskey than coffee by now.

Two more men stood at the far end of the bar with mugs of beer in front of them. A fifth customer sat at a table in the rear corner, leaning back in his chair with his legs stretched out in front of him and his hat tipped down over his eyes. As far as Kirkwood could tell, the man might be asleep.

It was quiet enough in there to sleep, no doubt about that. The men at the table conversed in voices too low to make out their words. The pair at the bar didn't appear to be interested in talking. Sunlight slanting in through the front windows struck sparkling reflections on dust motes floating in the air.

The place felt almost like a church—the Church of the Early Morning Drunk.

The bartender wore a white shirt. No apron or vest. Or tie, for that matter. He had a weathered, rawboned look as if he might have been a cowboy at one time. The heavy limp in his step as he came along the bar toward Kirkwood explained why he no longer rode the range. Some sort of accident had crippled him, more than likely.

"What can I get you, mister?"

"Brandy," Kirkwood said.

The bartender smiled. "Hope you didn't have a particular brand in mind, because we've only got the one bottle. Not much call for it in these parts. It'll have to be in a regular glass, too. Don't have any of those— what do you call them? Snifters."

"That's fine," Kirkwood said, trying not to let his impatience show. He was there for a drink, not conversation.

The bartender got the bottle from a shelf, set a glass on the bar, and poured it half-full. He looked at the ten-dollar gold piece Kirkwood pushed across the hardwood and said, "Not even brandy costs that much around here, mister."

"You don't know how badly I need it." Kirkwood fought the temptation to gulp down the whole drink.

He sipped the brandy and went on. "The rest is for information. I'm looking for a woman."

"This ain't that kind of a place, mister," the bartender replied with a shake of his head.

"Not that sort of woman," Kirkwood said. "And not just *any* woman."

It was a long shot that Isabel would have ever been there, but one had to start somewhere. He couldn't rely on Leon for everything.

"Her name is Isabel Sheridan. She has dark hair and eyes, and if you ever saw her, you wouldn't forget her. She's one of the most beautiful women I've ever known."

"Well, we have some good lookers around here, I'll give you that. But I don't recall any by that name. You have a reason to think she may have come in here?"

"Not really. I just know she arrived in Fort Worth a few days ago. I'll ask about her in every saloon, every restaurant, and every hotel, if I have to."

Well . . . Leon would ask about Isabel in those places, but practically speaking, it was the same thing.

"You must really want to find her."

"We were supposed to be married." Kirkwood wasn't sure why he was spilling his guts to this bartender. Maybe he had held in all the hurt and rage for too long. "I have to find her. She has to tell me what went wrong."

"Ran away, did she?" The bartender shook his head ruefully. "Gals are like that. Changeable, you know? You never know what sort of notions they'll take into their heads. Young fella like you—handsome, I mean, and you look like you got money—I'm sure you won't have any trouble findin' some other gal who'd be plumb happy to marry you."

"You don't understand. *She was mine—and she ran away from me.* I can't abide that. I remember I used to have a dog that kept running away from me." Kirkwood stopped short, deciding it might be better not to finish that story.

The bartender frowned anyway, evidently not liking what he heard in Kirkwood's voice. "You want another drink?"

"I haven't finished this one."

"Well, it might be best if you go ahead and finish it, then take your business somewhere else, friend. I'm not sure this is the right place for you."

Kirkwood's fingers tightened on the glass. "Are you telling me to get out?"

"Just call it a suggestion."

Kirkwood wanted to reach across the bar and slam the glass against the man's head. He could see it shattering, the jagged edges slicing into flesh, blood spurting. How dare someone even think of throwing him out of a cheap place like this! Didn't the bartender know he was Ripley Kirkwood? Didn't he know who his father was?

No, of course he didn't, but that didn't matter. The bartender should have been able to tell just by looking at him that he was a man of quality.

The bartender must have been able to tell *something* by looking at him, all right, because he put his hands on the bar and said. "Now listen, mister, don't even start thinking about causin' any trouble in here."

"I just asked you a question," Kirkwood said, spacing the words out through clenched teeth.

"Yeah, and I gave you an honest answer, and now I think it's time you went on your way."

The two men at the bar finally noticed what was going on. One of them said, "This fancy-pants fella givin' you trouble, Gene?"

The bartender raised a hand. "No trouble. He's gonna finish his drink and leave, aren't you, mister?"

"I'll leave when I'm damned well ready." Kirkwood knew he wasn't going to find what he was looking for, but he couldn't tolerate it when inferiors defied his will.

And Ripley Kirkwood considered just about everyone he encountered to be his inferior.

The two cowboys started toward him. "He don't need to finish his fancy drink," one said. "But I'll pour the rest of it over his head if he wants me to."

"Damn it, Ross," the bartender began. "I don't want the place busted up."

A sneer twisted Kirkwood's mouth as he said, "I'll finish the drink my way." With a casual flick of his wrist, he dashed the rest of the brandy into the first cowboy's face.

The man howled a curse and staggered back, pawing at his burning eyes. The second man spewed an obscenity and lunged at Kirkwood, who twisted at the hips and met him with a straight right to the jaw. Anyone who thought he was weak and defenseless just because he was rich was making a bad mistake.

The punch landed solidly and rocked the cowboy's head back. Kirkwood hooked a left into the man's midsection that doubled him over. He clasped his hands together and raised them, poised to bring them down in a clubbed blow to the back of the cowboy's neck that would drive him senseless to the floor and maybe even kill him.

Before that blow could fall, the bartender reached over the hardwood and grabbed Kirkwood from behind. His arms went around Kirkwood's chest and jerked him back against the bar. The edge dug painfully into Kirkwood's back.

"I got him!" the bartender yelled.

His face dripping brandy, the cowboy had recovered enough to clench his fists and move in. He blinked rapidly. His vision still wasn't completely clear, but he could see well enough to slug punches into Kirkwood's body.

The impacts made Kirkwood grunt. He jerked up his right leg, planted that foot in the middle of the attacker's chest, and shoved. The cowboy flew backwards, arms flailing, and landed on the table where the two men were drinking spiked coffee. It collapsed with a crash. Cups and whiskey bottle went flying. The men fell over backwards in their chairs.

"That's it, damn it!" the bartender cried. "Teach this bastard a lesson, boys! I'll hang on to him!"

Kirkwood twisted back and forth but couldn't break the bartender's grip. His hat fell off. He panted from anger and exertion.

The fifth man, the one sitting alone, hadn't budged or even lifted his head, but the other four closed in on Kirkwood, fists poised to hammer him insensible. If they got him on the floor, they might stomp him to death. He knew that, but in his wild rage, he didn't care. He just wanted a chance to strike out at them.

He didn't get that chance. Massive hands reached from behind and caught hold of two men by the neck. The newcomer smashed their skulls together with near-fatal force. then let go of them. They dropped like puppets with their strings cut.

Leon's stony face never changed expression as he stepped over the men he had knocked out and back-handed another one in the face. Blood spurted and cartilage crunched as the man's nose flattened. He reeled back, gasping and moaning, and collapsed with both hands pressed to his ruined nose.

The fourth man was the only one who actually swung a punch at Leon. The big man swayed aside from the blow, caught hold of the man's arm at the wrist and elbow, and smashed it down on his rising knee.

The man's forearm snapped like a breaking branch. He screamed, dropped to his knees, and then huddled against the front of the bar, cradling the broken limb.

The bartender shoved Kirkwood at Leon and reached hastily under the bar. He came up with a sawed-off shotgun. Leon caught hold of Kirkwood with his left hand and moved him aside. His right moved too fast to follow as he plucked a short-barreled revolver from a shoulder holster under his left arm.

The gun popped before the bartender could get the scattergun's hammers pulled back. The small-caliber slug tore through his right shoulder and did enough damage to make him drop the shotgun onto the bar. He grabbed the wound, slumped against the back bar, and groaned.

Leon darted a glance at the motionless man in the rear corner, decided that he wasn't a threat, and hol-stered the gun. Leon straightened Kirkwood's coat and picked up his hat. Kirkwood took it, brushed sawdust from it, and put it on.

"Let's get you out of here, sir," Leon said.

"I should reprimand you for not following my orders . . . but I'll admit I was glad to see you," Kirkwood said.

They left the saloon, Kirkwood striding out as if he owned the place, Leon backing to the door just in case anyone else wanted to make a try despite the punishment he had handed out.

No one did. The only sounds in the saloon were moans and whimpers.

"They didn't know anything about Isabel in there," Kirkwood said as Leon came alongside him. "Of course, I didn't really expect them to, but since I was in there, I thought I'd ask. We'll probably be better off checking with all the hotels in town."

The bodyguard grunted. "I'll get started on that, sir, as soon as you're settled in where we're staying."

"I can help with that—"

"No need, sir. I'll find Miss Sheridan, and then you can deal with her as you see fit."

Kirkwood smiled. He liked the sound of that. He really did.

CHAPTER FIFTEEN

Weatherford was a farming community and the seat of the next county over from Tarrant. The wagon reached the settlement around the middle of the afternoon. The courthouse and the town square were visible up ahead, at the top of a long, gentle slope. The horses had rested when the group stopped for the midday meal, but they could use another short break.

Ace told Agnes, "We'll stop up there at the square. You and the other ladies can walk around for a while if you'd like."

On Saturdays, the square would be packed with people, horses, mules, and wagons as all the farmers and their families from the surrounding area would be in town to buy supplies and visit with their friends and neighbors. The farmers' market a couple blocks east of the square would do a booming business, as well.

Even though it wasn't Saturday, the settlement was crowded. Plenty of immigrants passed through on their way farther west.

Navigating with skill through the traffic in the street, Agnes brought the wagon to a stop in front of a large building facing the square. A sign across its front read JEFFREYS' EMPORIUM AND HARDWARE.

"We don't really need any more supplies yet," she said to Ace and Chance, "but I suppose it wouldn't hurt to stock up on a few things."

"It's handy to the public well," Chance said, pointing. "We can water the horses while you ladies look around inside."

"I can give you a hand with the watering," Agnes offered without hesitation.

"No, that's all right." Chance grinned. "Ace and I need to do something to earn our pay."

Ace could tell that Agnes would have preferred helping Chance, but she climbed down and went into the store with the other four women. After what he had said, she didn't have much choice.

No one was drawing water from the well at the moment, so Ace lowered the bucket attached to a rope and let it fill, then pulled it back up. Chance brought a bucket from the wagon, Ace emptied the water into it, and Chance carried that bucket over to the horses to let them drink.

Ace followed alongside. "She's sure sweet on you, you know."

"Who, this horse?" Grinning, Chance scratched the drinking horse between the ears.

"You know good and well I'm talking about Agnes."

"And *you* know good and well that she's not the sort of gal who catches my fancy, Ace."

"Because she's not pretty enough?"

Chance shook his head. "Pretty's got nothing to do with it. Well, maybe not nothing, but there are more important things than looks, you know."

"I'm glad to hear you say that. Of course, I've never

seen any evidence that you really feel that way. You perked right up as soon as you saw Miss Jamie, for example."

"What man wouldn't perk up if she was around?" Chance carried the bucket over to one of the other horses. "Anyway, you're a fine one to talk, Ace Jensen, after you went off *gathering wood* with Miss Lorena this morning."

Ace felt his face warming. "She followed me. I didn't ask her to come along."

"Either way, you were alone in the woods together, and I've seen the way her hand lingers any time she finds an excuse to touch you."

"We weren't really alone in the woods," Ace pointed out. "We were twenty yards away from the camp."

"Yeah, but I couldn't see you very well. The two of you could've been doing who knows what out there."

"We weren't doing anything," Ace insisted, "except trying to find some firewood."

"You tell the story any way you want," Chance said. "It doesn't really matter to me."

When the horses all had a good drink, Chance put away the empty bucket in the back of the wagon. As he rejoined Ace at the front of the vehicle, a large group of men walked up onto the high porch in front of the store that also served as a loading dock.

The Jensen brothers couldn't help but look at those men. They were the sort of hombres who would draw a lot of attention wherever they went.

All of them wore a mixture of buckskin and home-spun garments and looked like they would be more at home in the mountains. And they were big, all towering over six feet. Beards covered their faces, most of them dark but a few blond and one, hanging from the chin of the man in the lead, was long and white as snow.

Ace counted eight men in all, and although it was difficult to be sure because of the beards, he thought they all shared a family resemblance.

As the men disappeared into the store, Chance said quietly, "That's a pretty woolly-looking bunch."

"They remind me of men Preacher would know," Ace commented, referring to the legendary mountain man who was Smoke Jensen's mentor and oldest friend. The brothers had met Preacher on Smoke's Sugarloaf Ranch in Colorado the previous Christmas.

"We'd better go see how the ladies are doing," Chance said.

They climbed the steps at the end of the porch and went through the open double front doors.

A man somewhere in the rear of the store was saying, "I've explained this to you before, Mr. Fairweather. You have to pay what you already owe before I can extend you any more credit."

"Well, that just don't make sense," a booming voice replied. "I don't follow your reasonin', son."

"You have to pay for the supplies you already took before you can get any more."

"Do you know how much food it takes to feed a family of seven growin' boys?" The white-bearded patriarch of the clan was the one arguing with a clerk who stood behind a counter. The old-timer rested his big, knobby-knuckled hands on the counter and leaned forward in a menacing stance.

A couple of his sons stood behind him, while the others had spread out through the emporium to look at the goods on the shelves. Ace wasn't sure he would refer to any of them as *growing boys*. They all looked full-grown to him.

One of the blond-bearded sons nudged a dark-bearded brother with an elbow and nodded toward the five mail-order brides gathered around a long table where bolts of cloth were on display. The two Fairweathers grinned and chuckled, obviously impressed by the beautiful young women.

Aware of the scrutiny from the big, rugged strangers, the ladies clustered together defensively and kept shooting wary glances toward the Fairweathers.

Most Western men treated respectable women with the utmost politeness, but that might not have been the case in whatever mountains the Fairweathers came from. Ace could tell their behavior was making the ladies uncomfortable.

Chance saw what was going on, too, and bristled at it. "Look at the way those hillbillies are leering at the ladies," he said to Ace. "I'm going over there and tell them to act like gentlemen."

For once Ace wasn't going to try to keep his brother's impulsive nature in check. He agreed with Chance. Those two needed to leave the ladies alone, and that included ogling them.

The Jensens started forward, but before they could reach the mountaineers, the white-bearded man turned away from the counter and bellowed, "Barnaby! Fergus! Get over here!"

The blond-bearded one said. "Aw, Pa, we was just—"

"I know what you was just. Fergus, you got the most book-learnin'. I want you to explain to this feller what *credit* means."

Testily, the clerk said, "I know how credit works,

Mr. Fairweather. You're the one who seems to be having trouble grasping the concept."

With obvious reluctance, the two men turned away from their intense scrutiny of the mail-order brides and joined their father at the rear counter.

The blond one, whose name evidently was Fergus, said to the clerk, "Now, mister, this is the way it's gonna be. We need more supplies before we head on west. You're gonna give 'em to us, and we'll pay you later. That's credit."

"You and your family already owe seventeen dollars and fifty cents," the clerk said. "That's as much credit as the owner is willing to extend. And even if you were to pay that off, you just admitted that you're moving on west. When did you intend to pay for what you wanted today? You're not even going to be here!"

"Well . . . we'll settle up with you later. That's credit," Fergus insisted.

"So you intend to run out on your previous bill, as well as the one you were going to run up today." The clerk folded his arms across his chest. "I'm going to advise Mr. Jeffreys that he needs to ask the marshal to keep you from leaving town until you've settled your debt."

The dark-bearded son, Barnaby, balled his hands into fists and scowled at the clerk. "Now that ain't bein' friendly at all. How do you figure on stayin' in business when you talk to your customers like that?"

Ace and Chance were watching the confrontation at the counter, but a short scream jerked their attention back to the ladies. Unknown to any of them, three more of the Fairweather sons had slipped up behind them.

One of them had hold of Jamie, sliding his arms around her trim waist. "Pa! When you get things squared away over there, we found somethin' else we want to buy!"

The other two grabbed Isabel and Molly, both of whom cried out and tried to twist free.

The one who had hold of Isabel said, "These gals is just what we need, Pa!"

"We'll have wives when we get to our new home!" the third Fairweather brother chimed in.

Most of the other customers had drifted out of the store, spooked perhaps by the Fairweathers. Ace and Chance acted instinctively, drawing their revolvers and leveling them at the three men.

"Get your hands off those women!" Chance ordered. "Now!"

"You heard him," Ace added. "Step away from them!"

The threat was a hollow one. The way the men were holding on to the ladies, Ace and Chance couldn't risk any shots.

Agnes took action. Grabbing a bolt of cloth, she swung it hard and smacked one of the Fairweathers across the face with it. As the bearded man grunted in surprise and loosened his grip on Isabel, she kicked backwards and drove the heel of her shoe against his shin. He yelped and let go of her.

Still holding the bolt of cloth, Agnes began whaling away at another Fairweather with it. She wasn't going to do any real damage wielding such a "weapon," but it served as a good distraction. Ace and Chance holstered their guns and lunged forward, ready to tackle the hillbillies.

The Jensens were immediately hit from the side by two more of the bearded brothers, tackled, and driven off their feet. They sprawled in an aisle between shelves, hulking Fairweathers on top of them raining down punches.

Ace saw a fist coming at his face and jerked his head aside just in time. His attacker's fist slammed into the plank floor with enough force to make the man bawl in pain. Ace cupped his hands and clapped them against the man's ears, producing more agonized yelling.

A few feet away, Chance ducked his head to shield it as much as possible and grabbed his opponent by the ears. He rose up as he pulled the man down. The top of Chance's head smacked hard into the middle of his opponent's face. Chance caught hold of him by the neck and heaved to the side. He rolled on top as the Fairweather went over. Chance's right knee sunk into the man's belly. Still holding him by the neck, Chance banged the back of the Fairweather's head on the floor a couple times.

That should have ended the fight, as the man's eyes turned glassy. He was out cold. But before Chance could feel any satisfaction from that triumph, someone else grabbed him from behind, looping an arm around his neck to jerk him up and back.

"I got him!" a voice brayed in Chance's ear. "Whup the son of a bitch!"

Ace wasn't out of the woods, either. He bucked up from the floor and threw his attacker off, but before he could follow up on that advantage, a foot crashed into his ribs. The vicious kick sent him rolling.

"Stomp him!" somebody yelled. "Stomp him into little pieces!"

A boot heel came at Ace's face. He got his hands up and grabbed it barely in time to save himself from being badly injured, if not worse. He yanked and heard a startled yelp, followed by a loud noise as the man who'd just tried to bust his head open came crashing down instead.

Heavy footsteps pounded nearby. One of the blond-bearded mountaineers was charging him. Ace couldn't tell if it was the one called Fergus or the other blond brother . . . not that it mattered. He rolled, stuck out a leg, and swept the man's feet out from under him. As the man fell, he tried to hold himself up by grabbing a set of shelves, but all he managed to do was pull it down on top of him. The shelves were loaded with pots and pans, and they set up a tremendous clangor as they fell around him.

Ace made it to hands and knees and spotted Chance a few feet away. One of the Fairweathers had an arm around Chance's neck, strangling him, while another of the brothers hammered punches to Chance's body.

Ace surged to his feet, snatched up one of the fallen pots, and banged it off the skull of the man assaulting Chance. The man's knees buckled and he dropped to the floor, senseless from the blow.

"Look out!" someone shouted.

Ace darted a glance over his shoulder and saw the white-bearded patriarch coming at him. The seamed and weathered face above the beard was twisted in lines of rage. Fairweather held a shotgun, and from Ace's perspective, the twin barrels loomed as large as a pair of cannon.

"Move, Grover!" one of the other men yelled. "Pa's on a rampage!"

Ace saw the killing frenzy in Fairweather's eyes. He wasn't the only one aware of it. The man holding

Chance let go of him and dived to the side, out of the line of fire.

Ace whirled and left his feet, throwing himself toward a half-stunned Chance. A heartbeat later, both of the shotgun's barrels exploded with a thunderous roar as smoke and flame spurted from them.

CHAPTER SIXTEEN

Ace wrapped his arms around Chance and carried them both to the floor just as the deafening shotgun blast filled the store and pounded his ears like giant fists. Ace couldn't hear anything, his head was ringing so badly. He didn't feel any pain when he landed, other than from the fight, and didn't think any of the buckshot had hit him.

He rolled onto his belly and pushed up on hands and knees, lifting his head to look around. He might not be able to hear anything, but his eyes still worked just fine. He saw Fairweather standing there with the shotgun broken open, fumbling to replace the shells he had just fired.

Before the old-timer managed to reload, a shapely, well-dressed, honey-haired figure stepped up beside him. Lorena put the barrel of a small pistol to his head and said something. Ace saw her lips move even though he couldn't make out the words.

Fairweather's gnarled fingers opened and let the empty shotgun fall to the floor.

His sons—the ones who were still conscious after

the battle with the Jensen brothers—gathered their wits and converged on their father and Lorena. Ace and Chance came to their feet at the same time and drew their guns again.

"That's far enough," Chance said.

Ace understood the words and knew his hearing was coming back. He covered the Fairweathers along with Chance, but from the corner of his eye he searched for the other four women. He spotted them over to the side, huddled in front of a wall where tools and farm implements hung on hooks. Agnes stood a little in front of Isabel, Jamie, and Molly as if she intended to protect them if need be. The look on her face was fierce.

"You fellas better stay back," Lorena warned the rest of the Fairweathers. "Come any closer and I'll put a bullet in your pa's head."

"They'll hang you for it if you do, you hussy!" one of the bearded brothers yelled.

A new voice said, "I don't think so."

Ace glanced toward the sound and saw a medium-sized man with a close-cropped salt-and-pepper beard. He wore a black hat and suit and carried a Winchester repeater. A star was pinned to his vest.

The lawman gave Ace and Chance a look and went on. "You boys pouch those irons. If there's any more shooting to be done here, I'll do it."

Ace and Chance exchanged a glance. Chance shrugged. Ace nodded and slid his Colt into leather. Chance followed suit with the Smith & Wesson. At least the sheriff or marshal or whatever he was hadn't demanded that they give up their guns. The Jensen brothers would have been less likely to do that willingly.

"All right. Ma'am, I'd appreciate it if you'd step back and put your gun away."

"I don't know if I ought to do that," Lorena said. "This old man is crazy. He could have killed some of his own kin, firing off a shotgun inside the building like that."

"Yes, ma'am. I know," the lawman replied. "This isn't the first run-in I've had with these Fairweathers." His voice hardened. "It's going to be the last, though. I'm locking them up overnight, and in the morning they're getting out of my town!"

"You can't do that!" one of the Fairweathers objected. "We ain't done nothin' wrong! We was just defendin' ourselves from these fellas and their whores!"

The old-timer said, "Angus, boy, don't go callin' a woman a whore when she's holdin' a gun to your poor ol' daddy's head. I know you ain't very bright, but use what little sense the Good Lord gave you!"

Lorena pulled the little pistol back, then banged it sharply against Fairweather's head. "That's for what your boy just called us."

Fairweather gingerly touched his scalp and glared at the brother called Angus. "See? What'd I tell you?"

Lorena stepped back and slipped the gun into a pocket on her dress that Ace wouldn't have been able to tell was there if he didn't see her do it. She joined the other four women over by the wall.

"Now," the star packer said, "somebody needs to tell me what in blazes went on here."

From behind the counter, the clerk said, "These . . . these Fairweathers came in and demanded more credit, Marshal. They haven't paid what they already owe Mr. Jeffreys. And they admitted that they're going to leave town. They're planning to run out on their debt, and still they want to add to it!"

"We just want credit," said the white-bearded old-timer. "Get the goods now, pay for 'em later. The store gives credit to other folks. 'Tain't fair they won't give us none!"

"Even when you buy something on credit, you have to pay for it sooner or later," the marshal said.

"We'll pay what we owe," Fairweather insisted. "One o' these days."

The clerk's disgusted snort testified to how unlikely he found that idea.

"Squabbling over what you owe aside," the marshal said, "you can't go around shooting off guns inside stores, especially shotguns. And from the looks of it, there was a brawl, as well."

One of the blond Fairweathers pointed at Ace and Chance and said, "Arrest 'em, Marshal. They done started it!"

"That's a lie," Lorena said coldly. "Ace and Chance weren't doing anything except defending us from these louts."

"Who are you, ma'am?"

"Miss Lorena Hutton," she answered. "These other ladies are Miss Sheridan, Miss Gregory, Miss Brock, and Miss Hampel. We're on our way to San Angelo to meet our future husbands. Ace and Chance Jensen are working as our guides and protectors."

"Mail-order brides, eh?" the marshal said. "I've heard about that, but I reckon you ladies are the first I've met. Are any of you injured?"

"Only our dignity," Lorena said.

A faint smile tugged at the lawman's mouth. "I suppose offending a lady's dignity could fall under the charge of disturbing the peace, too." He grew more stern as he faced the Fairweathers. "You're going to jail. I can hold you tonight, and what happens in the morning is up to you. You can leave town or I can convince the judge to find you all guilty and sentence you to thirty days, plus a hefty fine."

The old man sputtered. "That . . . that ain't right!"

"And," the marshal went on, "you're going to pay what you owe the store right now or we'll add theft to the charges and get you another thirty days. Maybe sixty." He looked at the clerk. "How much is their bill?"

"Seventeen dollars and fifty cents, Marshal."

The lawman gestured with the Winchester's barrel. "Let's have it."

Glaring murderously, Fairweather dug around inside his homespun shirt and finally came up with a small buckskin poke closed with a strip of rawhide. He unlaced it, delved inside, and brought out several coins. He slapped them down on the counter so hard the clerk flinched a little.

"I'll get you your change," the clerk said.

"Damn well better," Fairweather snapped.

"This is a mighty sorry state of affairs," one of his sons lamented. "We have to pay to go to jail."

The clerk slid some coins across the counter to Fairweather, who scooped them up and growled. Then the lawman gestured with the rifle to start his prisoners toward the front of the store, with some of the brothers helping their groggy siblings who were just now regaining consciousness.

As they went, one of the bearded men said, "I still say you ought to arrest them two varmints. They was fightin' just like we was."

"I intend to talk to them." The marshal glanced

back at Ace, Chance, and the ladies. "You mind waiting here until I get these fellas locked up?"

"Just put them behind bars where they belong, Marshal," Lorena said. "I suppose we can wait for a while."

Ace and Chance nodded in agreement.

Once the marshal and the Fairweathers were gone, customers began filtering back into the store. The clerk came out from behind the counter to try to clean up the mess that had been made when the shelves fell over.

"We can give you a hand with that," Ace offered.

He and Chance set the shelves upright. The clerk and Agnes picked up the scattered pots and pans.

"How in the world did you avoid getting shot?" Agnes asked Chance. "That madman was almost right on top of you with that shotgun."

"I reckon I owe my life to Ace," Chance replied. "He knocked me down just as the scattergun went off. It was probably good that Fairweather was that close to us. The charge didn't spread out much."

"Look what it did to that big sack of flour," Ace said as he nodded toward a burlap sack with a big, shredded hole in it. A considerable amount of flour had spilled out of it. "That could have been one of us."

"And that flour could've been our blood and guts," Chance added with a grin.

"I kept back some to pay for that when I gave Linus Fairweather his change," the clerk put in. "Seemed only fair."

"That's his name?" Ace asked.

"Yeah. Highfalutin name for a dirty hillbilly, isn't it?"

"Where a fella's from isn't as important as how he acts."

"Yeah, that's true, but that bunch will give a bad

name to mountain folks everywhere. Marshal Newsom's had nothing but trouble with them ever since they hit town a week or so ago. I don't blame him for getting fed up and running them out."

Lorena said to Agnes, "What were you thinking, hitting that man with that bolt of cloth? You could've gotten hurt."

"So could any of you," Agnes said. "I was just trying to show them that they couldn't run roughshod over us."

"You made that point quite well," Isabel said. She regarded Lorena coolly. "I didn't know you carry a gun."

"You never asked me," Lorena replied. "And if you had, I probably would have told you it's none of your business."

"I was thinking about using this if that man hadn't let go of me," Isabel said as she produced a short, slim dagger.

Ace couldn't see where she got it from, nor where it disappeared to when she put it away.

Agnes asked Jamie and Molly, "Are you two armed as well?"

"Goodness, I wouldn't know how to use a gun or a knife," Jamie replied.

"That's right, you have other weapons, don't you, honey?" Lorena said.

"Guns scare me," Molly said. "I don't like being around them unless they're necessary."

Ace said, "Out here on the frontier, that can be pretty much everywhere, Miss Molly. Except maybe in church."

"And I wouldn't count on that," Chance added.

A few minutes later, the marshal came back into the store. "Matt Newsom," he introduced himself. He had the Winchester tucked under his arm and didn't offer to shake hands.

"Are you going to do like the Fairweathers wanted and arrest us, too?" Chance asked.

"No, I just wanted to warn you that you've made some bad enemies here today. Those Fairweathers are trouble, pure and simple."

"Are there any more of them?" Ace asked.

"As a matter of fact, yes. The two oldest boys, Angus and Barnaby, are married, and their wives have kids. It takes five wagons to haul all of them and their gear. The others—Claude, Dennis, Elmer, Fergus, and Grover are their names—they're in the market for brides."

"Not us," Lorena snapped.

"They're like little kids," Newsom said. "They see something shiny, they want it. And you ladies, begging your pardon, are definitely shiny."

Jamie smiled. "I like that."

Ace said, "So what you're getting at, Marshal, is that we ought to be moving on, too, so we can get ahead of the Fairweathers and maybe they won't be able to follow us."

Chance said, "This is just like back in Fort Worth. I still don't like it. It's too much like running away."

"What happened in Fort Worth?" Newsom asked.

Ace waved the question away. "Nothing worth worrying about. Just a run-in with some fellas."

"Lew Shelby and Henry Baylor," Chance said. "Heard of them?"

Newsom frowned. "I don't know Baylor's name, but I've heard of Shelby. He's a gunslinger. A dangerous one. He's not on your trail, is he?"

"Not that we know of," Ace said.

"We've been keeping a sharp eye out behind us," Chance said.

"Good. You'd better keep on doing that. I'm sure the Fairweathers will agree to leave town in the morning instead of going to jail. That sort can't stand to be locked up. You're heading west, they're heading west . . ." Newsom's voice became grim. "So they're going to be somewhere behind you, and, trust me, you don't want that wild bunch to catch up."

CHAPTER SEVENTEEN

Normally, in a settlement that late in the day, Ace would have suggested that they just go ahead and spend the night there, but under the circumstances he thought it best they follow the marshal's advice and put Weatherford behind them.

Chance agreed with him. They could cover probably half the distance to the Brazos River in the daylight they had left, then ford the river in the middle of the day tomorrow.

The terrain became more hilly west of town, but Agnes continued to do a good job handling the team. They pushed on as the sun lowered in the sky ahead of them and didn't stop until it had dipped below the horizon, leaving the thin white clouds awash in orange and gold like streaks of flame in the heavens.

They made camp in a meadow beside a creek. Plenty of water and grass for the horses. Ace could tell that a pleasant night was in the offing. He and Chance would have no trouble sleeping outside.

As far as he could tell, it hadn't rained as much there the day before. Finding wood dry enough for a campfire was a lot easier. Agnes heated beans, fried some salt pork, and baked biscuits in a Dutch oven. Ace brewed the coffee. It was a good meal.

After everyone had eaten and the dishes were cleaned up, Isabel and Jamie retreated into the wagon. Molly and Agnes sat on a log with the light from the campfire playing over their faces as they talked quietly. Chance took a comb and began currying the horses.

"I was wondering if I could have another look at that map of yours," Ace said to Lorena. "I want to make sure we're following the best route."

"Of course," she said. "I'll get it and fetch a lantern, too, so we can see better."

She got the lantern and the map from inside the wagon and placed them on the lowered tailgate. Ace fished a lucifer from his shirt pocket and snapped it to life with his thumbnail, then held the flame to the lantern's wick. It caught and cast a yellow glow over the map as Lorena unfolded it.

"Here's Weatherford," Ace said as he rested the tip of his index finger on the map and then moved it along to trace their route, "and here's the Brazos River. We'll be beyond it tomorrow, unless we run into problems. I was thinking we'd keep on heading west until we got to Abilene, then cut south for San Angelo, but now that I look closer, it appears there's another trail running southwest that would get us there maybe a day sooner."

Lorena smiled. "Are you in that much of a hurry to rid yourself of our company, Ace?"

"Oh, no, ma'am . . . I mean Miss Lorena. That's not it at all."

"Just Lorena. Please."

Ace nodded. She had said it might take until they reached San Angelo for him to drop the *miss*, but evidently she had changed her mind.

"All right. Lorena. That's a mighty pretty name. It suits you."

"Thank you." She put her hand on his upper right arm as she stood close beside him. "Ace suits you. The top card in the deck."

"I don't know about that. Chance and me, we're just drifters. I sort of hate to say it, but we really don't amount to much."

"Now that's just not true at all. You've already helped us a great deal, and I'd be willing to bet you've helped plenty of other folks as well. That's what you do, isn't it? Ride around giving people a hand who need one? Like noble knights in some old book."

"I don't know," Ace said. "Comparing us to knights seems pretty far-fetched to me."

"You've probably won the hearts of a lot of fair maidens, too."

She'd stepped closer to him. She had a way of doing that without him even noticing what she was up to until it was too late and she was pressed against him.

"I'm afraid our armor's pretty tarnished," he said.

"Well . . . I'm not exactly a maiden, either."

Her hand came up, cupped the back of his neck, and held his head in place while she lifted herself on her toes and kissed him.

Ace's instincts took over. He lowered his head a little so their lips could come together with urgency and passion. His arms reached around her waist and hugged her tightly to him. She tasted and felt mighty good.

That reaction lasted only a moment, though, before he remembered that there were people all around them, including his own brother. True, the canvas flap at the back of the wagon was closed, and Chance, Agnes, and Molly were around on the other side of the vehicle. None of the others had a really good view of them. That could change at any second, though.

Ace moved his hands to Lorena's shoulders and held her in place as he broke the kiss and moved back. "We shouldn't be doing this. You're engaged to be married to somebody else."

"I told you, until I say my vows, I'm not worried about that."

"Well, maybe you should be. You gave the fella your word, after all."

Anger flashed in Lorena's eyes. "I've never even met the man. He's just a name on a piece of paper to me. How can I feel any sort of loyalty to him until the deal is actually done?"

"That's what marriage is to you? A deal?"

"Don't you go judging me, Ace Jensen. All I'm saying is there's no reason we can't make this trip enjoyable for both of us. It doesn't have to mean anything other than that."

"Maybe not to you," Ace said.

"Why, you pompous, stiff-necked—" Lorena stopped short, glared at him, and then started folding up the map. "I guess you've decided where you want to go—so I don't have to tell you."

"Yeah, I got a good enough look at the map," Ace said, knowing full well that wasn't all she meant.

"Then I'll take it and turn in." She leaned over and blew out the lantern, causing darkness to fall around him. She started to turn away with it and the map, but then she paused and couldn't resist adding, "If you change your mind, it shouldn't be any trouble for you to find me. I won't be very far away, now will I?"

That was true, Ace thought as Lorena went back around to the front of the wagon, and it certainly didn't make things any easier being around her all the time and knowing the way she felt about him.

"What's her problem?" Chance asked as he stepped out of the shadows nearby. Ace wondered how much his brother had seen and heard.

"Nothing," he said. "Lorena and I just see things a little differently, that's all."

"So it's Lorena now, instead of Miss Lorena. That's interesting."

"No, it's not," Ace snapped.

But it could get interesting before they got to San Angelo, he thought. He gazed off into the darkness toward the east, wondering how much trouble lurked behind them.

And ahead.

In his hotel room in Fort Worth, Ripley Kirkwood was pacing. The knock at the hotel room door made him stop and swing toward it. "Yes?"

The door opened and Leon came in wearing his black bowler hat. He took it off and held it in one big hand as he said, "I've located her, sir." He held up his other hand to forestall the eager expression that appeared suddenly on Kirkwood's face. "I should say, I've found out where she was. She left Fort Worth yesterday morning."

"Do you know where she went?"

"Not exactly. But I have a lead on it."

Kirkwood struggled to control his impatience. He had been taking his ease in the hotel room all day, and although it was comfortably furnished, it was nothing compared to his father's mansion in New Orleans.

He'd had supper sent up; the tray with the empty dishes sat on a side table. Kirkwood wore silk pajamas and a dressing gown. He had a glass of whiskey in his hand, so he downed what was left of the fiery liquor. "All right. Tell me about it."

"She's been staying at a hotel seven or eight blocks from here, at the other end of town." Leon had set out to question desk clerks at every hotel in Fort Worth, if he needed to. "Some other women joined her while she was there. They weren't staying together, exactly, but they all seemed to know each other."

Kirkwood frowned. "Other women? I can't be certain, of course, but I would have sworn Isabel didn't know anyone here in Fort Worth."

"They could have come from other places and met here," Leon suggested. "Since they were all staying in a hotel, that's a more likely explanation."

Kirkwood's frown deepened as he considered that. He supposed Leon's theory was possible, but it still didn't explain anything. "You said Isabel left town. Did the other women go, too?"

Leon nodded solemnly. "They did. Wherever they went, they were all together, riding in a covered wagon."

"A covered wagon!" Kirkwood laughed. "That doesn't sound like Isabel at all. I can't imagine that spoiled little beauty in a covered wagon."

Leon tipped his head a little to the side but didn't say anything. His expression made it clear that he was just telling his employer what he had found out, whether Kirkwood wanted to believe it or not.

Kirkwood picked up the whiskey bottle and splashed more amber liquid into the empty glass. "Go on. Did you find out anything about the other women?"

Leon shook his head. "The clerk didn't want to tell me their names, and I didn't push it. I know you don't want too much disturbance or notoriety."

"I want Isabel," Kirkwood snapped. "And if it takes some disturbance and notoriety to get her, then so be it. What, exactly, *did* you find out, Leon? She was here. Hell, man, we knew that already!"

"We know she left in a wagon with four other women. They had to get the wagon from somewhere. First thing in the morning, I'll check with the places where they might have bought or rented it, and I'll start with the ones closest to the hotel where she was staying."

"I suppose that makes sense," Kirkwood admitted grudgingly. "All right. Good work."

He seldom praised or thanked anyone who worked for him, but Leon was different. He knew how much he depended on Leon.

"There's one other thing," the big man said. "Miss Sheridan and the other young ladies weren't alone when they left town."

"What do you mean, they weren't alone?"

"They had two men with them. I wasn't able to find out anything about them, but it's safe to assume that they're either connected with the other women, or else they were hired to go along."

"That doesn't really matter, does it? If they try to interfere with us, you can just kill them."

Leon inclined his head again, this time in agreement.

"We'll start after them as soon as you find out which

way they went," Kirkwood went on. "I suppose it's too much to hope that there'll be a train where we're going?"

"We don't really know where that is yet, but since the women are traveling in a wagon, it's a safe bet there's no train."

"Well, then, we'll go on horseback. I'm an excellent rider, you know."

"Yes, sir. Until then, I thought you might need something to pass the time."

Kirkwood perked up at that. A distraction *would* be welcome. Something to get his mind off Isabel's betrayal for a while. A sly smile tugged at his mouth as he asked, "What have you done, Leon?"

"Made arrangements, sir." The big man went to the door, opened it, and beckoned to someone in the hall. He moved back to let a woman walk into the room.

She was Spanish, Kirkwood saw, catching his breath. A bit more dusky-skinned than Isabel, who had gotten some of her heritage from her Irish father even though she had taken more after her Mexican mother. Shorter than Isabel, too, but this girl had the same brown eyes and midnight dark hair and intriguing smile. She wore a long brown skirt and a short-sleeved, dark blue blouse that dipped dramatically in the front to bare her shoulders and reveal the inviting cleft between her breasts.

"Hello, *señor*," she said in a husky voice.

The huskiness might have been real, maybe a pretense, but it was exciting either way.

"Your friend here tells me that you are in need of company for the evening."

"Oh, my, yes," Kirkwood said as he stepped toward her. He rested his left hand on her right shoulder, sliding it over the smooth, warm skin. His right hand went behind her head and his fingers tangled in the thick waves of black hair. He pulled her against him and brought his mouth down on hers.

She twined her arms around his neck and returned the kiss eagerly. Then his grip on her got a little too forceful, and she tried to pull away. He tightened his hands on her, not allowing that. She panted against his mouth and managed to draw her head back slightly. He saw in her eyes . . . not fear, exactly, but perhaps the thought that she shouldn't have accepted whatever offer Leon had made to her.

Kirkwood held on to the girl as she started to struggle. He looked over her shoulder at the big man and grinned. "Leon, what in the world would I do without you?"

CHAPTER EIGHTEEN

Ace could tell that Lorena was still angry with him the next morning. Her eyes flashed when she looked at him, and her tone was cool and reserved whenever she spoke to him. He regretted that a little but was certain he had done the right thing when he told her she ought to honor the promise she had made to the man she was going to marry.

They got a good early start and followed the trail westward over rolling, often wooded hills. It was good country for both farming and ranching. They saw plenty of cattle, as well as some cultivated fields here and there, along with farmhouses where smoke rose from stone chimneys.

The weather was so pleasant that the women had rolled up the canvas on the sides of the wagon. Every so often a wagon loaded with produce rattled past, headed the other way toward Weatherford. The farmers tried not to gawk at the lovelies inside the vehicle, but most of them didn't succeed very well.

More clouds were in the sky today, but they were the big, white, fluffy kind, not dark storm clouds like a couple days earlier. Ace and Chance rode on either side of the wagon part of the time, but Ace also scouted ahead now and then and Chance dropped back to check the trail behind them.

Late in the morning, they came in sight of the Brazos River, its course marked by an even thicker line of dark green vegetation. Hills rose north and south of the trail, but the route dropped down into a saddle where a ford was located, at least according to the map.

As the wagon and the riders approached, Ace studied the river and frowned. The Brazos was higher than he had hoped it would be, filling the broad riverbed from bank to bank. It was flowing fairly fast, too, and had a slightly muddy cast to it.

"The river's up because of all the rain the other day, I suppose," he said to Chance as they rode about twenty feet in front of the wagon.

"You reckon we can still ford it?" Chance asked.

"I don't know." Ace pointed to a large frame building that sat just south of the trail. Five wagons were tied up in front of it. "That doesn't look too promising. Those wagons probably belong to pilgrims who weren't able to get across the river."

From the driver's seat of the wagon, Agnes called, "Are we going to have to stop up here?"

Ace hipped around in the saddle. "Yes, at least until we find out what the situation is. The river may be too high to cross right now."

"That'll put us even further behind schedule," she said with a frown.

"Yes, but there may not be anything we can do about it."

Ace didn't like it, either. He hadn't forgotten that Linus Fairweather and his seven hulking sons were

back there somewhere behind them. They seemed the
sort who would hold a grudge. The night they had
spent in Marshal Newsom's jail would just make them
angrier. Ace wanted to put the river behind them and
keep going.

Instead, Agnes had to bring the wagon to a halt in
front of the sprawling building. A crudely painted sign
nailed to the awning that overhung the porch pro-
claimed that it was Blanchard's Traydin Post.

A scrawny man with a brush of gray beard stepped
out onto the porch. He wore a black vest over a dirty
white shirt and had a black plug hat on his head.
"More pilgrims! Welcome, folks! I'm Dingus Blanchard, the owner o' this here fine ee-stablishment.
Light down and come on in. Got plenty o' drink and
food and anything else you might need."

Ace didn't dismount just yet. He rested both hands
on his saddle horn and leaned forward as he asked, "Is
the river too high to cross here?"

"Here and ever'where else this side o' the Gulf of
Mexico, I expect," Blanchard said. He hooked his
thumbs in his vest pockets. "Big cloudburst upstream a
couple days ago."

Chance said, "We got caught in it between Weatherford and Fort Worth, when it blew through there."

"Then you know how bad it was. All that water's
got to run off 'fore the river goes down. Might be low
enough tomorrow. Might not. But lucky for you folks,
you got a place to stay until it does. I rent rooms
here, too."

Ace figured the price would be pretty steep. Probably for the food and drink Blanchard had mentioned,
as well. The man struck him as the type who wouldn't
pass up any opportunity to make a nickel.

Blanchard waved to the women. "Come on in, ladies, and make yourselves to home. My, my, I ain't seen such a collection of purty gals in these parts in all my borned days."

Chance lifted a hand and motioned for the women to remain where they were as he said, "You ladies stay right there in the wagon for now. Ace and I will ride down and have a closer look at the river."

"Won't do you no good," Blanchard insisted. "I been livin' alongside the Brazos longer 'n anybody around here 'cept the Comanches, and they've all done moved farther west. I know the Brazos, seen all of its moods and tricks. You ain't gettin' across it today."

"We just want to see it better ourselves." Ace wasn't sure about leaving the women alone, but the river was only a few hundred yards away and they wouldn't be out of sight.

Blanchard shrugged skinny shoulders. "Suit your own selves."

Ace and Chance nudged their horses into motion again. They trotted down to the Brazos and reined in on the grassy bank. Ace looked north along the river, which flowed between tall wooded bluffs in that direction. The terrain wasn't quite as rugged to the south.

But the river was just as high in both directions, and now that they were closer, Ace and Chance were convinced the wagon wouldn't be able to cross it.

"You might could swim a horse to the other side," Chance said, "but that wagon would wash away for sure."

Ace nodded. "Yeah. We don't have any choice but to wait here until it goes down."

"That'll give the Fairweathers time to catch up to us."

"I know," Ace said, his face and voice grim. "So we'll have to be ready for trouble."

Chance laughed humorlessly. "Same as we always are."

Ace couldn't disagree with that. He turned the chestnut's head and rode back toward the trading post and the five women waiting in the wagon. Chance's cream-colored gelding loped alongside.

Some of the other travelers who had been stopped at the trading post by the high water had emerged from the building and were gathered around the wagon. Ace saw women and children among them, so he figured they weren't out to cause any trouble. They were just farm families on their way to new homesteads, visiting with the newcomers.

As Ace and Chance rode up, the ladies looked curiously at them.

Ace nodded and told them. "We'll have to spend the night here, all right, and hope the river goes down by tomorrow."

"If there is nothing else we can do, we must make the best of it," Isabel said.

"There aren't any other fords around here?" Lorena asked.

From the porch, Blanchard answered the question. "Closest one is fifteen miles downstream, and the water'll be too high to cross there, too. This time o' year, what with all the storms, you got to expect a few delays on account of high water."

"What about our horses?" Agnes said. "Those other teams are still hitched up. They shouldn't be left that way overnight, and neither should our animals."

Blanchard jerked a thumb over his shoulder. "I got a corral out back and a shed with some hay in it. It's liable to get a mite crowded with this many critters in it, but I reckon they'll be all right."

Chance said, "I suppose you charge for the feed and the use of the corral."

"This ain't a charitable institution, sonny. My prices is fair, don't you worry about that."

Fair or not, they would have to pay what he asked, Ace thought. He said, "Why don't you ladies go on inside? Agnes, you can drive on around to the back and we'll get the horses in the corral. No need in waiting, since it's clear we're going to be here for a while."

Lorena, Isabel, Jamie, and Molly climbed down from the wagon and went into the trading post, surrounded by the immigrants who had come out to greet them. Ace, Chance, and Agnes tended to the team. Some of the farmers who had stopped earlier brought their horses and mules around to the roughly built pole corral, as well. They introduced themselves, shook hands with the Jensen brothers, and tipped their hats to Agnes, who seemed pleased by the politeness.

The inside of the trading post was even more crowded with goods than the emporium back in Weatherford had been. The aisles between shelves were narrow and stacked with crates, piles of burlap sacks, barrels, and kegs.

One section of the place had half a dozen rough-hewn tables crammed into it. The other four ladies sat at one of them with cups of coffee in front of them. Jamie motioned Ace, Chance, and Agnes over to join them.

They had to scoot their chairs together closely for there to be enough room. Agnes made sure she was next to Chance, Ace noted. Chance smiled at her, but there was nothing special about the expression.

Ace had to give his brother a little credit. He wasn't trying to take advantage of Agnes's infatuation with him. He certainly hadn't led her on or tried to make her believe he was more interested than he really was.

Blanchard brought over a coffeepot and three more cups. "Got a big pot o' stew simmerin' on the stove in the back. I'll have my Injun woman bring some to y'all when it's ready."

"Do we need to go ahead and pay you for everything?" Lorena asked.

"Oh, no, ma'am. You can settle up in the mornin' or whenever you go to leave. I'm a trustin' sort." Blanchard paused. "And I got some Injun boys around the place to make sure nobody tries to cheat me."

"Don't worry about us," Chance snapped. "We're not going to cheat anybody."

"Didn't say you would, sonny, didn't say you would. I just like to be careful, is all. That's the way I've stayed in business as long as I have. And kept my hair, too, which weren't easy back in the days when the Comanch' were roamin' all over these hills and it was worth your life to cross the Brazos. Some of us old-timers took to callin' it the Black River, because that was what you had waitin' for you if you dared to go beyond it—the eternal darkness o' death."

After Blanchard had retreated through a door in the back of the room, Jamie shuddered. "I'm starting to wish I'd never agreed to any of this. I don't think it's really safe out here."

"No matter where you are," Lorena said, "a place is only as safe as you make it. That's why I carry a gun and why Ace and Chance are packing irons as well. You never know when trouble will walk in."

Ace glanced at the door and stiffened on his chair. "Actually, it just did."

The tall, erect figure of Linus Fairweather stood in the doorway, his hawkish eyes under bushy white brows searching around the room.

CHAPTER NINETEEN

Molly let out an audible gasp, and Ace knew she had spotted Fairweather, too. So had Chance, who leaned forward and moved his hand toward the Smith & Wesson under his coat.

"Take it easy," Ace said quietly to his brother. "There are too many innocent folks in here. We don't want to start throwing lead around."

"Tell it to that loco old man," Chance snapped. "He wasn't worried about innocent bystanders when he fired off that double load of buckshot back in Weatherford."

All the women were aware of Fairweather's arrival. Jamie cast an apprehensive glance over her shoulder toward the door and asked in a nervous half-whisper, "Do you think he's looking for us?"

"He and the rest of his family were heading west, remember? Could be he's just looking around, since the river's too high to cross." Even though Ace knew logically that was true, he didn't really believe it. He was even more convinced of that when Fairweather's gaze landed on the table where the Jensen brothers and the five women sat. A look of savage triumph flashed through the eyes of the white-bearded patriarch.

Dingus Blanchard had spotted the newcomer and strode toward Fairweather. "Welcome, friend, welcome. Come on in and sit yourself right down. We got stew and coffee and somethin' stronger to drink if you're of a mind to—"

Fairweather brushed past Blanchard and stalked toward Ace, Chance, and the ladies. The immigrants in his way saw him coming and nervously stepped aside.

Ace and Chance stood up and moved around the table to block Fairweather's path. Both of them looked determined that he wasn't going to get anywhere near the five women.

Fairweather's mouth twisted in a wolfish grin under the white whiskers. "I figured I'd see you two boys again. We're all headin' the same direction, after all. You could almost say we're travelin' together."

"No, you couldn't," Ace said. "We're not looking for trouble, Mr. Fairweather, but we don't want anything to do with you and your boys."

"There was no need for that ruckus back in Weatherford. If you two hadn't horned in—"

"Your sons were molesting these ladies, and it's our job to look out for them," Chance said. "Anyway, we're not in the habit of standing by and doing nothing while a bunch of unwashed mountaineers paw respectable women."

"Respectable women don't go traipsin' across Texas with two fellers who ain't related to 'em," Fairweather barked back.

Lorena stood up and looked past Ace and Chance. "We're all engaged to be married, you evil-minded old coot."

Blanchard came up behind Fairweather. "Say, now, if there's gonna be any trouble, I sure wish you fellas would take it outside—"

"No trouble," Fairweather said. "I just saw these folks and wanted to say howdy to 'em. And let 'em know I'll be seein' 'em again, once my boys get here. I'm ridin' scout ahead of the rest, you see."

"Two of your sons have wives and children with them, don't they?" Ace said.

Fairweather looked surprised by the question and frowned. "What if they do?"

"For the sake of those families, you shouldn't be looking for trouble. Just move on wherever it is you're going and leave us alone. Everybody go their separate ways."

Fairweather's deep-set eyes narrowed. "Five of my boys don't have wives, and they's five unmarried women right here."

"You practically accused us of being whores." Lorena flung the words angrily at him.

Isabel added. "You came right out and called us by that name back in Weatherford. And yet now you say you want us to marry your sons?"

"A man needs a wife," Fairweather said. "God gave Eve to Adam, back there in them Bible days, and that's the way it's been ever since. We're goin' west to prove up on some land and start farms. There'll be plenty of hard work from before dawn to after dark. You won't have time for your whorish ways."

"In other words, you don't need wives for your sons so much as you need farm hands," Lorena said. "I'm starting to understand now."

"You don't understand nothin', woman," Fairweather

said. "You best keep a respectful tongue in your mouth, or I'll—"

"You won't do a damned thing," Chance interrupted him. "Go on and get out of here."

The whole trading post was quiet and tense as everyone watched the confrontation.

Blanchard broke that hush by saying, "Hold on, hold on. Sonny, you ain't got the right to chase away my customers. Ever'body is welcome at this here tradin' post—Injuns, black folks, Messicans . . . Hell, I wouldn't even turn away a Chinaman, even though I don't reckon I've ever seen one come in here."

"Stay out of this, Mr. Blanchard," Ace said quietly. "This is between us and Mr. Fairweather."

"I seem to be outnumbered. And outgunned." Fairweather reached up with his left hand to stroke the long white beard. "Reckon that won't always be the case. I'll see you boys when it ain't." He turned and walked out of the trading post without looking back.

A few seconds of silence lingered after Fairweather was gone, then a low hubbub of conversation began as the other people in the building began talking about what had just happened. Ace and Chance turned back to the table.

Lorena sat down and sighed. "I thought for a moment there that he was going to start shooting."

Chance shook his head. "No, that sort likes to have all the odds on his side. If he'd had his sons backing his play . . ." His voice trailed off as he shrugged.

"There's no telling what might have happened," Ace concluded. "I sure wish there was some way to get across that river."

Agnes spoke up. "I'm willing to risk it. The wagon

will float, and if the horses are strong enough swimmers, I believe we could make it."

"The river's too high and the current is too fast," Ace said with a note of finality in his voice. "And we don't know how the team would handle it. We can't risk it."

"Then we'll stay here and be sitting ducks," Isabel said. "You heard the old man. He was scouting ahead of the others. But they're probably not very far behind him."

"They won't try anything too bad," Ace said, "not with so many witnesses here." He nodded toward the other people crowded into the trading post.

"I'd say that depends on just how loco that bunch really is," Chance countered. "They might decide to wipe out everybody here and burn the place to the ground."

Ace couldn't argue with his brother about that. It was impossible to predict just how far a madman would go to get what he wanted.

"This is the place?" Ripley Kirkwood stood in front of a house in Fort Worth.

Leon nodded. "According to the man at the livery stable, this is where we'll find Cyrus Keegan."

"Perhaps he'll cooperate with us. I'll handle the conversation starting out. Then, if Keegan proves reluctant to tell us what we need to know, we can employ your special skills, Leon."

The big man didn't say anything and was as impassive as ever.

Wearing a cream-colored suit and a planter's hat, Kirkwood looked every bit the wealthy young man

about town as he went to the porch of the small, neatly
kept frame house and knocked on the door. A middle-
aged black woman answered the summons, jerking the
door open more abruptly than he expected.

One of Kirkwood's eyebrows rose in surprise when
he saw that she clutched a heavy butcher knife in her
right hand while she used her left to open the door.
The look on her round face was none too friendly,
either.

"What you want?" she demanded in an equally hostile tone.

Inside, Kirkwood bristled at being spoken to in that
manner by a black servant. He was old enough to remember the war and even had a few memories from
earlier than that, from his life as a small child. He had
grown up listening to his father's bitter comparisons of
the way things had been to the way they were now.

Kirkwood didn't think of himself as being particularly prejudiced. He looked down on all servants,
not just the black ones. A man couldn't be more fair
than that.

He kept his emotions under tight control and put a
smile on his face. He even took his hat off as a show of
respect he didn't feel. "Good morning. My friend and
I are looking for Mr. Cyrus Keegan. We were told that
he lives here."

His charm had little effect on the woman, but her
scowl eased slightly. The glance she directed at Leon
was still suspicious. Most people felt that way about him.

She turned her attention back to Kirkwood. "This is
Mr. Keegan's house, all right, but he's laid up right now.
Ain't doin' no business."

"A broken leg, yes, so we were told," Kirkwood said,

nodding. "And I hate to bother him, but it really is imperative that I speak with him. It concerns . . . a matter of the heart."

The woman grunted in surprise. "You? You're lookin' for a mail-order bride? Handsome, well-to-do fella like yourself, you'd think the gals 'd be linin' up for a chance to get hitched to you."

A friendly laugh came from Kirkwood. "Not everything is always as it appears to be, madam. I assure you, it's vital that I speak with Mr. Keegan."

"Well . . . come on in. I reckon your . . . friend . . . can wait in the parlor. I'll take you back to see Mr. Keegan." She stepped back to let Kirkwood and Leon in. She had lowered the butcher knife to her side, but she still gripped the wooden handle tightly.

"Do you always answer the door prepared for trouble?" Kirkwood asked as he stepped inside.

"Since yesterday I do."

That set off an alarm bell in Kirkwood's mind. "What happened yesterday?"

The woman hesitated, obviously trying to decide whether she wanted to answer the question. Finally she said, "Some other fellas showed up outta the blue wantin' to talk to Mr. Keegan, sort of like you just done. They got rough with the both of us. Tied me up and stuck a gag in my mouth! That was bad enough, but they hurt Mr. Keegan. One o' them varmints walloped him with a gun . . . right on his busted leg."

"Good Lord," Kirkwood said. The surprised exclamation wasn't feigned. "Why in the world would they do such a thing? Were they thieves?"

"No, they didn't steal nothin'. They just wanted Mr. Keegan to tell 'em where some o' them mail-order brides o' his went."

Kirkwood stiffened. It had been enough of a surprise when he and Leon had found out from the liveryman that Isabel and four other women had left Fort Worth in a wagon belonging to a man who ran a matrimonial agency. When he had stopped to think about it, though, the idea made a certain amount of sense. Isabel had fled from New Orleans and evidently wanted to get as far away from him as she could. She wasn't rich and had few relatives who could help her. The money she had taken had gotten her to Fort Worth, but she would have needed help in continuing her flight.

He didn't believe for a second that she really intended to marry whatever unfortunate fellow had paid for her journey farther west. She would betray him, break his heart just as she had with her fiancée in New Orleans. Isabel's hurtful ways had to be stopped, whatever it took.

According to what the black woman had just said, it appeared that someone else was on the trail of the women who had left Fort Worth. Kirkwood had no idea who they might have been, but from the sound of the woman's story, they weren't to be trifled with.

"How many of these men were there?" he asked.

"Three. All of 'em mean and ugly. Wouldn't surprise me a bit if they was outlaws."

That *was* worrisome. Kirkwood didn't want anything to happen to Isabel before he caught up to her. Whatever befell after that would be on her own head, but he didn't want to be cheated out of his satisfaction.

"And they wanted to know about a group of mail-order brides? That's what I need to ask Mr. Keegan about as well. Unless you happen to know where they went?"

"I don't know nothin' about the mister's business.

Lemme go see if he's awake." She went down a hall, knocked softly on a door, and then opened it. A bit of quiet conversation occurred and then the woman motioned for Kirkwood to come.

Cyrus Keegan was propped up in bed, his splinted and bandaged broken leg in front of him. He held a pistol in his lap. "What do you want?" His tone didn't hold an ounce of friendliness.

Kirkwood smiled again. "You won't need that gun, sir. My name is Ripley Kirkwood, of the New Orleans Kirkwoods. I'm here on a matter of business." He knew instinctively how to deal with the pale, middle-aged fellow.

"I run a matrimonial agency," Keegan snapped. "You don't strike me as the sort who would need to send away for a wife."

"I done told him the same thing," the woman said.

"I *am* looking for a woman," Kirkwood admitted.

"Not Molly Brock, I hope."

Kirkwood shook his head. "That name means absolutely nothing to me, sir. The lady I referred to is Miss Isabel Sheridan." He could tell by the look in Keegan's eyes that the name had struck a chord.

Keegan said, "You're not already married to her, are you?"

"No . . . but I *am* betrothed to her. Isabel is to become my wife next month."

"Oh, hell." Keegan sighed. "This has never happened to me before, and now twice in the same bunch!" He lifted the pistol. "I'm not going to tell you where they went. Those bastards may have beaten it out of me yesterday, but I won't allow that to happen again."

Kirkwood saw that there was a little steel under

Keegan's meek-looking exterior. He made a placating gesture. "Please, sir, don't even think that I would do such a thing. I would never resort to violence. I am, however, prepared to make it worth your while to cooperate . . ." His hand strayed toward the inside of his coat, making it clear that he was reaching for a wallet.

"You can't bribe me, either," Keegan snapped. "I have a contract to uphold."

"But sir, I've told you that one of the ladies you made an arrangement with is already engaged to be married. To me." Kirkwood cocked his head a little to the side. "I have no wish to involve the law in this matter, but I have a feeling the courts would not look kindly on anyone who assisted in the destruction of an impending marriage. There is such a legal concept as alienation of affection, after all."

"Are you saying you'd file a lawsuit against me?"

Kirkwood had sensed that this man would fear something that might cost him money more than anything else. He smiled sadly and said, "Only if I were forced to such an extreme measure."

"Damn it. All right." Keegan set the gun aside. "If Miss Sheridan is really your fiancée, I suppose you have a right to know. She left here with the others bound for San Angelo."

Kirkwood remembered something else. "And the men who accompanied the group?"

"I don't know. A couple young drifters, I believe. The marshal was here yesterday after those other men assaulted me and Lantana, and he said their name is Jensen. Brothers, I think. They were in some sort of trouble with the law a few days ago, before any of this other happened. I'm not happy about them going with the ladies, but like this"—he nodded toward his broken leg—"there's nothing I can do about it."

"Of course not. It's out of your hands now."

"Are you going after them?"

"My honor—and my heart—demand it."

"Well then, watch out for those Jensen boys. They might be gunfighters or even outlaws, for all I know."

"I'll take care, I assure you. I'm in your debt, Mr. Keegan."

The man shook his head. "Just go on before the next bunch comes along wanting to know where those ladies went. I swear, I've never had such popular clients before—and I hope I never do again!"

Outside the house, Kirkwood said to Leon, "Find out as much as you can about those two men who went with Isabel and the other women. Keegan said their name is Jensen. Evidently there was some sort of trouble involving them a few days ago, so you should be able to ask around and find someone to tell you."

"Why are you worried about that, sir?" It was highly unusual for Leon to question any of Kirkwood's orders, but in this case likely his pride was hurt. "I can take care of any problems—"

"I have the utmost confidence in you, Leon, you know that. But Keegan seemed to think that these Jensens might be gunfighters. It might be better if we recruited a few guns ourselves."

A low rumble came from Leon's throat. He wouldn't go against what Kirkwood told him to do, but he didn't always have to like it.

Kirkwood didn't care whether Leon approved or not, as long as he carried out his orders. The only thing that mattered was finding Isabel and dealing with her.

If that required hiring a few gunmen, then so be it. And if it required killing those two men named Jensen . . . well, that was just too bad for them.

CHAPTER TWENTY

At least the stew that Dingus Blanchard's Indian wife prepared was very good. In fact, the meal was the high point of the afternoon as they sat with the ladies and waited for the river to go down.

And waited, as well, for Linus Fairweather and his sons to show up and start another ruckus.

The Fairweathers didn't put in an appearance at the trading post, however, and gradually the ladies relaxed.

Not so Ace and Chance, whose natural caution kept their gazes riveted to the door and the windows. If anybody tried to take potshots at them, they would be ready.

Meanwhile, Ace listened with half an ear to the conversation going on at the table. The five women were more comfortable with each other than they had been starting out. Lorena and Isabel might not ever warm up to each other, but at least they weren't making thinly veiled hostile comments.

Jamie talked about being raised in a family with numerous brothers and sisters back in St. Louis where her father had owned a successful furniture store. He'd been well-to-do without actually being rich. "I just had to get away from that crowd. There's hardly ever a moment's privacy in my family's house—and it's a big house!"

"So you wound up stuck in a wagon with four other women," Lorena said.

"Yes, but that's just temporary. My husband—I mean, my husband-to-be—has a ranch, according to the letter I received from him, so there should be lots and lots of wide open spaces. I'm looking forward to it, I really am."

Ace wasn't sure, but he thought Jamie sounded a bit like she was trying to convince herself of that. It took a big leap of faith to set out across the country and marry a man she had never met and had barely even corresponded with. He wouldn't blame her, or any of them, if they were having a few second thoughts about what they were doing.

"How about you, Molly?" Isabel asked. "You haven't said much about your family or where you're from."

"Not that you have to," Lorena said. "We won't pry if you don't want us to."

Molly smiled. "No, that's all right. I know I've been a little standoffish. I've never really been that comfortable around people. It takes me a while to get to know folks. And really, there's almost nothing to say about me. I have a sister and two brothers back in Missouri. My pa, he's the local lawman. My ma passed away a few years ago."

"What made you decide to become a mail-order bride?" Ace asked.

"Well, maybe it was because of my pa's job, but it seemed like the only men I ever met around home were pretty sorry specimens. You know, criminals and the like. So I figured if I was ever going to find myself a decent man, it might be a good idea to get far away from there. Texas sounded like a good place to go."

Agnes said, "My pa thought I was crazy for coming to Texas. He's seen too many drovers push too many herds across our farm and ruin our crops. He said if I ever brought a Texan husband back home with me, he'd pepper his britches with buckshot! I believe he might do it, too." She laughed. "Of course, that just made me even more stubborn. I've never liked being told what to do—or not do."

Isabel laughed. "I can imagine. You're a strong-willed woman, Agnes. That's what I like about you." She looked around the table. "I think we are all strong-willed women. We know what we want—and what we don't want—and will do whatever is required to achieve it."

"Damn right," Lorena said. "Pardon my French."

Isabel looked like she was about to make some cutting response to that comment, but she controlled the impulse in time. Ace was glad to see that. They were all getting along right now, and it would be fine with him if things stayed that way. They had enough potential trouble facing them without fighting among themselves.

As that thought went through his head, he glanced again at the doorway. Still no sign of the Fairweathers. Maybe something had happened to delay them. Maybe the river would go down and he and Chance and the ladies could get across before the Fairweathers arrived.

But on this side of the Brazos or the other, Ace still had a feeling that a reckoning was coming sooner or later.

* * *

As night approached, the immigrant families retreated to their wagons. The charges for taking care of their livestock were high enough; they couldn't afford to pay Blanchard for lodging as well.

Ace thought it would be a good idea if the ladies stayed inside the trading post, though, and Chance agreed.

"We can do a better job of protecting you in here," he told them.

"We'll have to spend plenty of nights on the trail after we leave here," Lorena argued. "And we don't have a lot of extra money to pay what that avaricious old buzzard is going to charge."

"You should be able to afford one night," Ace said. "If you can't, Chance and I can kick in part of the money you've set aside to pay us when we get to San Angelo."

"Now, hold on a minute, brother—" Chance began, then stopped and sighed. "I reckon you're right. It's too risky to stay outside while those Fairweathers are skulking around, if you've got another option."

The ladies agreed, although not without more reluctance.

Ace went and made the arrangements with Blanchard, who pushed aside a curtain that covered a doorway leading to a hall with five doors on each side. "The rooms ain't fancy, but the beds ain't got no varmints in 'em . . . I don't think."

There was no door at the far end of the hall, so no one could get in that way.

Ace asked, "Is anyone else staying here tonight?"

"Nope, them ladies are the only ones."

"Then let's put them all on the right side. We'll put a chair here in the hall and my brother and I will take turns sitting up, just to make sure nothing happens. Whichever one of us isn't on guard duty can get some sleep in one of the other rooms."

"A chair, eh?" Blanchard rubbed his jaw. "I might have to charge you for the use of it—" He stopped when he saw the frown on Ace's face, then waved a hand casually. "Oh, I reckon we can throw that in."

"Thanks," Ace said dryly.

"That fella who was here earlier . . . What sort of grudge is he holdin' against y'all, anyway?"

"We had trouble with him and his sons back in Weatherford, and they wound up spending a night in jail because of it. The main thing, though, is they've made up their minds that the unmarried boys ought to have those ladies as their wives."

"Well, they're mail-order brides, I heard tell." Blanchard spread his hands. "What difference does it make who they get hitched up with?"

"It makes a difference," Ace snapped.

Supper was more of the savory stew. When it was over, the ladies went out to the wagon to fetch a few things they would need. The Jensen brothers went with them. Night was falling, and danger could be lurking out there in the gathering darkness.

At the moment, however, there was a bit of a festive feeling in the air. The immigrant families had built campfires and cooked their own food rather than pay Blanchard's prices. Kids were running around, getting in some last playing before turning in. Men sat on lowered tailgates and smoked pipes. Women finished cleaning up. It was a homey scene, even though they had no permanent home at the moment. They had the wagons and their families, and with the resilience of pioneers everywhere, they were making the best of the situation.

The ladies went back inside and settled into their rooms, which, as Blanchard had said, were not fancy. They were small, with no room for any furniture other than a narrow bed with a straw tick mattress and a tiny table with a candle on it.

"Not that much worse than what I'm used to," Agnes commented, although the other four women looked a little disappointed by the accommodations.

Ace got one of the chairs from the trading post's main room and placed it in the hall, which was lit by a single candle on a shelf.

"Flip a coin for the first shift?" Chance suggested. As always, if there was a way to gamble on something, he would find it.

Ace was about to say that Chance could just go ahead and do whichever he would prefer then sensed that his brother would be disappointed by that. "Sure."

"Call it," Chance said as he took a coin from his pocket and flipped it in the air.

"Tails," Ace said.

Chance caught the coin, slapped it down on the back of his other hand, and then revealed that it was heads. With a grin, he said, "I'll take the first shift. Maybe Miss Jamie will have a bad dream and need some comforting."

"I think somebody else may be the one who's dreaming." Ace took off his hat, gunbelt, and boots but was otherwise fully dressed as he stretched out on the narrow bed. It was more comfortable than a blanket spread out on rocky ground, but that was about all he could say for it. He dozed off pretty quickly anyway.

He had no idea how long he had been asleep when what sounded like a clap of thunder jolted him awake. He lay there for a second before he realized the noise hadn't been thunder at all.

It was a shotgun going off.

Leaping out of bed, he crammed his feet in his boots and snatched the Colt from its holster without taking the time to buckle on the gunbelt or grab his hat. He lunged into the dimly lit hallway and spotted Chance standing tensely by the chair near the entrance to the trading post's main room. He had the Smith & Wesson in his hand.

"The ladies?" Ace asked sharply.

"All right, I guess," Chance replied. "That shot came from somewhere outside."

Both brothers stiffened as they heard someone scream. Then a harsh voice shouted, "Jensen! Ho, you Jensens! You better get on out here right now!"

"That's Fairweather," Chance said.

Ace nodded but said, "We need to check on the ladies before we do anything else."

They didn't have to. All five doors opened, and the young women poked their heads out into the hallway. Jamie and Molly looked frightened but all right. Lorena, Isabel, and Agnes were apprehensive, but their eyes flashed with defiance and a readiness to fight if need be.

"What the hell is all the commotion?" Lorena asked.

"Fairweather's outside," Ace said. "He fired a shotgun, and then somebody screamed. Now he's yelling for me and Chance to come out there."

"You're not going, are you?" Isabel said.

"All those pilgrims are out there," Ace replied grimly. "We can't let Fairweather and his sons harm innocent folks."

"You've been hired to keep *us* safe."

"And we will," Ace said. "Chance, you stay here while I go see what Fairweather wants."

"We know what he wants, more than likely," Chance said. "The trick will be keeping him from getting it."

Ace went out into the main room, which was dark. He thought he would have to make his way through the labyrinth of shelves and goods by feel, but another door opened and Dingus Blanchard stepped into the room, holding a lighted lantern up with one hand and carrying an old Sharps buffalo gun in the other. A nightshirt flapped around his bony knees, but he was still wearing the black plug hat.

"What in blazes?" he demanded.

"Fairweather's back."

"I warned you boys I didn't want no trouble!"

"Then you shouldn't have let us stay here," Ace said. "It seems to follow us around."

"I ain't in the habit of turnin' away customers, no matter who they are. I just don't like it when they drag their problems into my tradin' post!"

Linus Fairweather shouted again from outside, "Jensen! You Jensen boys! You better get out here now!"

The demand was followed by another shrill scream, this one cut off with ominous abruptness.

Ace started toward the front door. Behind him, Blanchard cursed and followed him.

Ace said over his shoulder, "When we get up there, blow out that lantern! We don't want to make ourselves better targets."

"I know that. This ain't the first time I've had trouble come callin', sonny. I've fought Injuns, remember?"

Ace was too busy thinking about what might be going on outside to discuss Blanchard's history. Those screams had come from a woman, and the only women out there were the ones from those immigrant wagons. Ace knew the Fairweathers had a grudge against him and Chance and wanted the ladies traveling with them, but he had hoped that the troublemaking clan wouldn't bother anybody else.

When he reached the door, he held the Colt pointing up beside his head. He looped his thumb over the hammer and glanced back to nod at Blanchard. The man leaned closer to the lantern and blew out its flame. Darkness closed in around them.

Ace found the door latch, twisted it quietly, and eased the door toward himself. Through that narrow gap came the flickering glare of firelight. He moved where he could look out better and spotted a man standing beside one of the parked wagons, a blazing torch in his hand. Judging by the amount of light outside, there had to be more torches—and more vengeful men holding them.

"I saw that door move, Jensen!" Linus Fairweather yelled. "Open it on up! Boys, hold your fire. We'll try talkin' first, before we go to shootin' and burnin' and killin'."

Ace didn't trust Fairweather for a second. Ordering his sons to hold their fire might mean exactly the opposite. They might start shooting as soon as the door opened wider, but Ace had to run that risk. Otherwise he couldn't find out exactly what was going on—and how bad the threat really was.

"You'd best back off some, Mr. Blanchard," he said quietly. "I can't guarantee what's going to come through this door when I open it."

"Well, if any bullets come in, I can guaran-damn-tee you what's goin' back out." The sound of the big Sharps being cocked came to Ace's ears. "A .50 caliber buffalo slug, that's what!"

With no time to argue with Blanchard, Ace held the Colt ready, stood a little to one side, and pulled the door back so he could see what was in front of the trading post.

What he saw made his heart sink and his pulse hammer in his head. Linus Fairweather stood near one of the immigrant wagons with the light from several torches playing over him. He had his right arm around the neck of a middle-aged women as he held her close beside him. Ace recognized her as the mother of several little tow-headed boys from one of the immigrant families.

In Fairweather's left hand was a shotgun with sawed-off twin barrels. He held the muzzles close to the woman's left ear. At that range, if he fired the weapon he would blow the woman's head clean off her shoulders.

"I see you, young Jensen," Fairweather called. "But I only see one of you. Get your brother and both of you come out here where we can talk."

"I can talk just fine from right here," Ace said, "and I speak for both of us. What do you want, Fairweather?"

"That's *Mister* Fairweather to you! Respect your elders, boy. And you know good and well what we want. I got a man standin' next to each of these wagons with a torch and a gun, holdin' the folks inside 'em. You turn over those women to us, or I'll give the order and my boys will burn ever' one o' them wagons and ever'body inside 'em!"

CHAPTER TWENTY-ONE

The horror of what he had just heard struck Ace dumb for a moment. Fairweather was threatening mass murder if he didn't get his way. That possibility had crossed Ace's mind before, but he hadn't really believed anyone could be that depraved.

That was his mistake, he told himself grimly as his brain began to function again. There was no limit to the depravity of some human beings.

"Good Lord!" Blanchard exclaimed, sounding equally shocked. Then he said fearfully. "My boys!"

"The Indian boys you mentioned earlier?" Ace asked.

"Yeah. My wife's boys, really. Three of 'em. Pureblood Lipan. But I helped raise 'em, and they feel like mine, damn it. They sleep out in the shed, next to the corral."

"Fairweather may not know they're there," Ace said. "There's a good chance he hasn't hurt them."

"If he has, I'll kill the bastard," Blanchard vowed. "He'll have to kill me to stop me."

Ace hoped it wouldn't come to that, but he had his

doubts. By threatening to massacre all the immigrants, Fairweather had gone too far. He had to get what he wanted—the five women—if he meant to retain the power in his family. And even if he succeeded, he might decide to wipe out everyone else at the trading post anyway, just to make sure no one was left to spread the story of what he'd done.

"Can you get to the shed without going out this door?" Ace asked Blanchard.

"Yeah, I can go out the back window."

"Fairweather is liable to have somebody watching it."

"I can skulk around damn near as good as an Injun, if I do say so myself. I can get out without bein' spotted." The man sounded confident.

Ace hoped he was right. "Get out there and check on your boys, then. Are they armed?"

"There's a couple rifles and a shotgun in the shed."

"Good. You may need them. If hell breaks loose and you have to shoot, remember that the Fairweathers are the ones with the torches."

"We'll be careful," Blanchard said. "What are you gonna do?"

Ace sighed. "Try to talk some sense into that loco fool."

"Good luck with that," Blanchard said, sounding like he didn't believe such a thing was even remotely possible. He faded back into the darkness while Ace turned his attention again to the partially open door.

Outside, Linus Fairweather called, "I'm losin' my patience here, boy! Send them females out right now, and we might let you little bastards live!"

Something about the way he said that convinced

Ace his hunch was right. Fairweather didn't intend to leave anyone alive when he and his sons left.

Easing closer to the door, Ace said. "Fairweather!"

"Damn it, boy, I've told you about respectin' your elders!"

A split second later, a rifle cracked and a slug chewed into the doorjamb, throwing splinters in the air.

"Hold your fire!" Ace yelled. "Mr. Fairweather! Is that better?"

"Keep talkin' and we'll see."

"Your two oldest boys are married, right?"

"What's that got to do with anything?" Fairweather asked. "We ain't lookin' for wives for them."

"But they *have* wives, and children, too, I'm told."

"So? What the hell does that have to do with anything?"

"Do you really want to turn family men into killers? You want their kids having to grow up knowing that their fathers are murderers?"

"They're Fairweathers, by God! Their loyalty to me and their brothers comes first!"

"What kind of father would ask his sons to do such a thing?" Ace asked. "And what about their families? They're not out there watching this, are they?"

"That's none o' your damn business . . . but we left our wagons a ways back, camped for the night."

"Because you know those women and children don't need to see such horror. And yet you're willing to inflict it on all those innocent folks you're holding prisoner."

"Damn you, boy, hush your argufyin'! Nobody's got to die here. Just give us those women."

There was no reasoning with the man, Ace realized, and no trusting him, either. He was going to have to lunge onto the porch and take a shot at Fairweather, in the faint hope that he could kill the old man before Fairweather could pull the sawed-off's triggers.

That would leave Ace in the open to be riddled by the other Fairweathers, but if Blanchard and his Lipan stepsons were in position to hit them with a surprise attack, everyone else might have a chance to survive.

He wished he'd been able to say so long to Chance before it came to that.

Ace's taut muscles were about to propel him into action when the whiplash of a rifle shot sounded, followed instantly by another and then the boom of a shotgun. Blanchard and his boys were going into action.

Ace kicked the door all the way open and saw that Linus Fairweather had twisted his head away from his prisoner and toward the sound of gunfire. That was enough to make the sawed-off's barrels waver away from the immigrant woman's head.

The Colt boomed and bucked in Ace's hand. He saw Fairweather jerk as the bullet hit him somewhere. The impact was enough to loosen his grip, and the woman tore free from him. She ran screaming toward the wagons.

Fairweather caught his balance and swung the scatter-gun toward Ace. Flame belched from both barrels.

Ace was already diving off the porch. He landed on his shoulder and rolled, then came up on one knee with the Colt roaring again. Two swift shots blasted from it.

Fairweather staggered back and bent forward, then swayed from side to side. Ace could tell from the old man's reaction that at least one of his bullets had punched into Fairweather's midsection. Fairweather fell to his knees but otherwise remained upright, hunched over the wound.

A strident yell came from Ace's left. "Pa!"

Ace turned in that direction and saw one of the blond Fairweather sons charging toward him. The man held a torch that he whipped through the air at Ace. The blazing brand turned over and over, casting flickering light across the ground as the man opened fire with his rifle. The torch sailed over Ace's head and fell to the ground behind him.

He felt as much as heard bullets ripping through the air next to his ears. Steadying the Colt, he triggered a shot that slammed into the charging man's chest and stopped him as suddenly as if he'd run into a stone wall. He dropped his rifle, pressed both hands to his body, and seemed almost to melt down to the ground.

Screams made Ace turn in the other direction. Two of the immigrant wagons were on fire, but the wagons' occupants had scrambled out and escaped the flames because the Fairweathers had their hands full with the attack by Blanchard and his stepsons. Ace saw them darting here and there, firing at the Fairweathers, who returned the shots in a roll of gun-thunder.

Ace snapped a shot at one of the dark-bearded Fairweathers as the man tried to reach cover. He stumbled but kept moving, disappearing behind one of the wagons.

A shot from the trading post's porch made Ace glance in that direction. Chance was there, the .38 in his hand spitting fire. Ace surged to his feet and ran to the porch, bounding onto it to join his brother. As he thumbed fresh rounds into his Colt, he said, "You shouldn't have left the ladies!"

"Lorena and Isabel got a couple shotguns from

Blanchard's stock. Anybody who tries to bother them will get a gut full of buckshot!"

Ace didn't doubt that.

"They chased me out of there and told me to help out here," Chance added.

Ace believed that, too. He hadn't been acquainted with Lorena Hutton and Isabel Sheridan for very long, but he already knew how strong-willed they were.

Gunfire still crashed back and forth across the clearing in front of the trading post. The burning wagons threw a nightmarish glare over the scene. A couple torches, obviously dropped by the Fairweathers when the fighting started, still burned where they lay on the hard-packed dirt, but they were about to gutter out, as was the torch that one of the men had thrown at Ace.

The shots began to dwindle. Between blasts, Ace heard the swift rataplan of hoofbeats. Somebody was lighting a shuck, and he had a pretty good idea who it was.

"Hold your fire!" Ace shouted. "Mr. Blanchard! Hold your fire!"

One by one, the guns around the trading post fell silent. No more shots came from the darkness. The surviving Fairweathers were gone. They had fled back to their camp, wherever that was.

Dingus Blanchard stepped into the light from the burning wagons. He still held his old buffalo gun. The left sleeve of his nightshirt was stained with blood, but he didn't appear to be badly hurt. He waved three more figures into the light—stocky, dark-haired young men—his Lipan stepsons. A couple sported bloodstains from minor wounds, as well.

"Check on those immigrants," Ace said as he came down from the porch. "See if anybody is wounded."

Ace had natural leadership ability that came to the fore in times of trouble. "We'll see about the Fairweathers."

Blanchard nodded.

With Chance beside him, both holding their guns ready, Ace approached Linus Fairweather first. The man lay facedown in the open area between the parked wagons and the building. Chance kept the clan's patriarch covered closely while Ace hooked a boot toe under Fairweather's shoulder and rolled him onto his back.

Fairweather was still alive, but the huge dark stain across his middle was an indication that he wouldn't be for very much longer. He glared up at Ace and Chance and gasped for enough air to curse them. "You damn . . . Jensen boys. You'll be . . . damned sorry . . . you ever crossed the path . . . of the Fairweathers!"

"I reckon we already are," Chance said coldly. "So are plenty of other people, including some of your sons."

Fairweather groaned, whether in pain or grief or both, Ace didn't know. He supposed it didn't really matter.

"I curse you," Fairweather said. "You'll never . . . know peace . . . Blood and death . . . will follow you . . . all your borned days!"

"We're used to it," Chance said.

It bothered Ace a little more to hear such a dire prediction, but Chance had a point. They already seemed to run into more than their fair share of trouble.

"Not fair," the old man muttered. "We was supposed to get . . . what we wanted . . . We're Fairweathers . . . by God . . ." His chest rose as he drew in a sharp breath. Then the air came out of him with an ugly rattling sound, and he was gone.

The Jensens walked over to the blond Fairweather Ace had shot.

He thought it was Fergus but couldn't be sure. That man was dead, too, drilled cleanly through the heart.

Two more Fairweather sons, both sporting dark beards, were dead, as well, crumpled near the wagons where the unexpected volley from Blanchard and his stepsons had dropped them.

Four of them had gotten away. Ace hoped the two men with families had been among them. As loco a bunch as they had been, he hoped no women and children had lost husbands and fathers tonight. Even more so, he hoped that was the case among the immigrants.

He was relieved when Blanchard reported there were no fatalities among the pilgrims who had stopped to wait for the river to go down.

"Couple families lost everything except their livestock, though," Blanchard said with a frown as he looked at what was left of the burned-out wagons. Flames still danced here and there on the blackened husks.

"The Fairweathers ought to have to pay for that," Chance said.

"I'm gonna sic the law on 'em, you can count on that," Blanchard said. "I'll send one of the boys ridin' to Weatherford first thing in the mornin' with word of what happened here. But from what you told me about how they was tryin' to cheat that storekeeper in town, they probably don't have any money. Not enough to make it right for these poor folks, anyway."

Blanchard frowned and rubbed his grizzled jaw. After a moment, he went on. "I got plenty o' goods and supplies here. I can help 'em out, make sure they got enough to head on their way again once they get some new wagons. I can give 'em a hand with that, too."

Ace and Chance stared at him in surprise.

Chance said, "No offense, Mr. Blanchard, but we thought—"

"That I was a penny-pinchin', money-grubbin' son of a bitch?" Blanchard laughed. "Well, I sure as hell am, boys, but ever' now and then you got to put that aside and at least pretend to be a decent human bein'. I can do that . . . as long as those times don't come around too often." He went to talk to the immigrants and start making arrangements to salvage their westward journeys, while Ace and Chance returned to the building.

The five women, all wearing robes over their nightclothes, stood waiting on the porch. Lorena and Isabel still held the shotguns they had commandeered from Blanchard's stock.

"Is it all over?" Lorena asked.

"I hope so," Ace said.

Then he thought about Linus Fairweather's curse and the fact that four of the Fairweather sons were still alive, and he wasn't the least bit sure.

CHAPTER TWENTY-TWO

By the next morning, the flames in the two burned wagons were all out. The families who had lost everything had spent the night inside the trading post. At least two men had stood guard all the time, with Ace and Chance splitting up the duty along with Blanchard's stepsons.

With the coming of a cloudy dawn, Ace walked to the river to see how it looked. The Brazos was down considerably from the day before, and the current was slower. Sandbars poked through the muddy water here and there.

A footstep behind him made him half-turn as his hand moved to the Colt on his hip. Dingus Blanchard raised a hand to forestall Ace's draw. "No need for that hogleg, son. I see we done had the same idea."

"What do you think?" Ace asked. "Will we be able to ford the river today?"

"I reckon so. As long as you know the way to avoid all the snags and sinkholes and quicksand . . . which I happen to know, o' course, since I've lived on this here river for so long. I'll ride on the wagon with you and guide you. One o' my Injun boys can come along behind on his mule, and then he can carry me back across once you folks are on the other side."

"We'll be obliged to you for your help. How much will all that cost?"

Blanchard waved a hand. "Shoot, won't be no charge for that. Nor for anything 'cept the grub y'all and your horses et. I'm feelin' . . . what's the word? . . . *generous* . . . today." He cackled. "First time I been able to say that in a spell. And all it took was gettin' shot at by a bunch o' loco hillbillies."

Ace wasn't going to argue with the man's generosity. The ladies didn't have enough extra cash to spend when it wasn't necessary.

They returned to the trading post where everyone was enjoying a simple but filling breakfast prepared by Blanchard's Indian wife. Ace and Chance washed down the food with cups of steaming black coffee, then went around the building to fetch the team and hitch the horses to the wagon.

Not surprisingly, Agnes tagged along. "I don't mind driving the wagon across the ford."

"I figured I'd do that," Ace said. "No offense."

"None taken, but if you do that and I ride in the back with the others, there'll be that much more weight in the wagon. Wouldn't that increase the chances of it bogging down?"

"Mr. Blanchard says he knows where it's safe to cross. He's riding with us to make sure everything goes all right."

"He can tell me the same as he can tell you," Agnes insisted.

Chance said, "Agnes has a point, Ace. It's not like you're all that fat—"

"Thanks a lot," Ace said dryly.

"But extra weight is extra weight," Chance went on. "Why not let her give it a try?"

Agnes smiled brightly at him. "Thank you for standing up for me."

"Just trying to be reasonable," Chance said, but he returned the smile, and that made Agnes beam even more.

The families that hadn't lost their wagons were getting ready to move on. They had decided to band together and form a little wagon train, since the delay at the Brazos had caused them to bunch up. Ace and Chance didn't intend to wait for the others. They would push on with their charges as soon as they were on the other side of the river.

The sun had been up for about an hour when the ladies climbed into the wagon and Ace and Chance swung into their saddles. Dingus Blanchard pulled himself up onto the seat next to Agnes as she took up the reins. Jamie waved from the back of the wagon to everyone who was still at the trading post as Agnes got the vehicle rolling toward the river.

Blanchard directed Agnes down a grassy slope to the water's edge and told Ace and Chance. "You boys ride on ahead so the lady can use your horses to judge how deep the water is."

The Jensen brothers walked their mounts into the river. The horses seemed to have fairly solid footing. Agnes followed them. Gravel crunched under the wagon's wheels as water rose to the hubs.

It didn't get any deeper than that, though, and in some places it wasn't even that deep. The riverbed was a mix of gravel and sand. As long as Agnes kept the wagon moving, it wasn't likely to bog down.

In a loud voice, Blanchard called out directions to

Ace and Chance, and Agnes followed them unerringly. One of Blanchard's stepsons followed the vehicle on a mule, as the trading post owner had told Ace.

There were no mishaps along the way, so it took only a few minutes for the wagon to ford the river. The horses pulled it out on the western bank, and Agnes brought it to a stop.

Blanchard climbed down and waved Ace and Chance over. He shook hands with the two young men as they leaned down from their saddles. "Good luck to you boys. I'm hopin' you've seen the last o' them blasted Fairweathers."

"I hope we've all seen the last of them," Ace said. "I'm sorry our trouble came down on the heads of you and those immigrant families."

"Nobody can avoid trouble all the time," Blanchard said. "The world won't let that happen. I'm old enough to have figured that out. Take the good times as you find 'em, and deal with the bad ones when they come along and slap you across the mush. That's about all we can do." He waved farewell as the wagon rolled away.

It headed west once again and soon disappeared among the wooded hills.

From the top of a hill a short time later, Ace turned in his saddle and looked northward across a sweeping landscape that fell away into the valley where the Brazos made its way. The distant water sparkled gold in the early morning sunlight, creating a beautiful vista.

"If a fella wanted to settle down, he could find worse places to do it than this," Ace mused.

"Yeah, but that would mean settling down, and we don't want to do that," Chance said.

"I didn't say us. I was just talking about folks in general."

"Well, stop it. I don't like the sound of it. There are way too many hills I haven't seen the other side of to even be thinking about anything like that."

Ace grinned, clucked to his horse, and got the animal moving again.

Earl Brock, Seth Cooper, and Ben Hawthorne were riding west along the trail leading from Weatherford to Abilene and points farther west when Brock abruptly reined in.

"Somebody coming," the outlaw said, "and he looks like he's in a hurry."

Cooper squinted at the man trotting toward them on horseback. "Looks like an Indian, too. A tame Indian, mind you. Those are white man's clothes he's wearin'."

"I don't reckon he's got anything to do with us, Earl," Hawthorne said. "Let's just let him go on about his business."

"I'm not gonna stop him from going about his business," Brock snapped, "but I'm curious what errand he's on."

Behind him, the other two glanced at each other. Cooper shrugged. If Brock wanted to talk to the Indian, it wouldn't hurt anything as far as he could see. He hoped the redskin wouldn't give Earl any lip. Brock had been known to shoot people for that, even white people. He wouldn't hesitate to drill an Indian if he lost his temper.

Brock held up his left hand in a signal for the rider to stop. His right hand rested on the butt of his holstered revolver. If the Indian didn't stop, Brock would pull the gun and make him wish he had.

However, the Indian reined in. He was young, not much more than twenty, and as Cooper had said, he was dressed in a work shirt and a pair of denim trousers like a white man would have been. His reddish-hued face was broad and flat, his black hair cropped off square just above his shoulders.

Brock could identify the Cherokee, Seminole, and the other tribes up in Indian Territory, but he had no idea which tribe the youngster belonged to. "You speak English, buck?" he demanded.

"I speak good," the young man replied. "What you want?"

"Where are you headed in such a hurry?" Brock's eyes narrowed suspiciously. "Did you steal something? Trying to get away?"

"I am not a thief! I go to Weatherford to see the sheriff."

Cooper said. "What in blazes does a redskin need with the sheriff? You don't expect a white lawman to believe any story you tell him, do you?"

The Indian scowled. "Tell truth. Crazy men come to trading post. Try to steal women."

"Women!" The exclamation came from Brock. "What women?"

"White women," the young man said, as if that should have been obvious. He gestured vaguely. "They go west, find husbands."

"Damn it," Hawthorne said. "He's talkin' about those mail-order brides!"

Brock scowled and leaned forward in his saddle. "What did these white women look like? Did one of them have red hair?"

The young man tried to move his mount around them, but the outlaws' horses blocked the trail.

"No talk," he said in a surly voice. "Must find sheriff."

"No, damn your red hide. You're gonna tell me what I want to know." Brock's gun came out of its holster, rose in his hand, and the hammer clicked back under his thumb. "The women," he went on impatiently. "Tell me about them, or I swear, I'll blow you out of the saddle."

"But the sheriff must know about the crazy men—"

"I'm worse than any loco hombre you ever ran into," Brock said, his voice flat and hard and dangerous.

The young Indian quickly realized that was true. Words tumbled out of his mouth in a rather disjointed fashion.

Despite that, Brock and his two companions didn't have any trouble following the story. The young Indian didn't know all the details of what had caused the problems between the Jensen brothers and the mail-order brides on one side and the bunch of bearded men on the other, but the description of the women was what mattered most to Brock.

One of them had to be Molly, all right. The young man's description sounded just like her, which came as no surprise. There couldn't be *two* bunches of mail-order brides traveling across that part of Texas.

Brock interrupted the Indian. "The woman with red hair, she wasn't hurt in all the shooting?"

The young man shook his head. "No women hurt. Four men with beards killed. My father and brothers wounded a little, not bad."

"I don't care about anybody else, just the redheaded woman. Is she still at the trading post?"

The young man's shoulders rose and fell. "Still there

when I rode away. Probably gone now, if river was down enough."

"Whereabouts is this tradin' post?" Cooper asked.

"Five miles." The Indian turned in the saddle and pointed west. "That way."

"It won't take us long to catch up," Brock said. "The bitch is close now, boys. Close enough I can almost smell her! Come on."

The three outlaws spurred their horses into motion and thundered away, following the trail toward the Brazos. The young Lipan just watched them go for a moment, then shook his head and resumed his journey to Weatherford, clearly more puzzled than ever by the behavior of white men but knowing he would never figure them out.

CHAPTER TWENTY-THREE

"That's them," Leon said as he nodded toward the five men who sat around a table toward the back of the big barroom.

"Disreputable-looking bunch, aren't they?" Ripley Kirkwood said with a faint smirk on his handsome face. "Except for the one in the frock coat. He looks as if he might have had some quality in his life at some point in the past."

"The one in black is a killer."

"Well . . . the same thing could be said about you, couldn't it? Ever since that bare-knuckles bout in Omaha, and a number of times since then."

Leon grunted.

"So we have a tinhorn gambler and a notorious gunslinger," Kirkwood went on. "What do we know about the other three?"

"The Indian's a Kiowa. That's all they ever call him. He's supposed to be a good tracker and a pretty dangerous man in his own right. The other two . . ." Leon shrugged. "Blank pages. Prewitt and Loomis, they're called, but nobody seems to know anything else about them."

"It doesn't matter. The gunslinger . . . Shelby, is that right? He's the one we'll need to make the most use of. If he has a grudge against those Jensen brothers already, we might as well take advantage of that."

A low rumble came from Leon's throat. Kirkwood knew he was opposed to the idea of hiring outside help, but that didn't matter. Kirkwood didn't give a damn about a servant's opinion, and no matter how much he relied on Leon, the former prizefighter was still a servant.

Leon was good at finding things out. He had nosed around and discovered that these five men had clashed with the Jensen brothers. Kirkwood still wasn't clear exactly why the Jensens had gone with Isabel and the other women, but the reason didn't really matter. They were a potential obstacle to what Kirkwood wanted, so they had to be eliminated.

If that could be accomplished with minimal risk to himself and Leon, so much the better. These five men were . . . expendable.

Kirkwood walked across the saloon toward the table where the men sat. In his expensive clothing, he was out of place there, but not so much that he drew an excessive amount of attention. Sometimes rich men liked to go out and haunt places that were beneath them. Kirkwood had done that himself on a number of occasions, and he was sure it happened in Fort Worth, too.

A couple gaudily painted and garbed young women took note of Kirkwood and started toward him, knowing a wealthy potential mark when they saw one, only to retreat nervously when Leon glared at them. Kirkwood was there for business, not pleasure.

The gambler—Henry Baylor, according to the gossip Leon had heard—was idly dealing poker hands and then picking them up again. The other four men nursed drinks. A mostly empty bottle of whiskey sat in the middle of the table.

The Indian was the first one to notice Kirkwood and Leon. He was sitting between Shelby and a mostly bald man with a potbelly. He nudged the gunman and said something to him. Shelby looked around and sat up straighter.

The reaction spread around the table to the other men, so that by the time Kirkwood and Leon got there, all five of them were sitting up and tensely alert as if the two strangers might mean trouble.

Kirkwood came to a stop with Leon behind him. He hooked his thumbs in his vest pockets, and smiled. "Good day to you, gentlemen. My name is Ripley Kirkwood."

Baylor said, "Is that supposed to mean something to us, Mr. Kirkwood?" He was probably the smoothest and best-educated of the five and would serve as their spokesman.

"Not unless you've spent much time in New Orleans. The name is well known there, since my father is a very wealthy man."

"Do you just enjoy coming up to strangers and bragging about your father, or is there a point to this?"

"Oh, there's a point, to be sure," Kirkwood said. "I've been told that several days ago you had some trouble with a couple brothers named Jensen."

Baylor set aside the deck of cards at the mention of the name.

Lew Shelby reacted, as well. His lips drew back from his teeth in a grimace, and his hand made what appeared to be an instinctive movement toward the gun on his hip. "Are those bastards friends of yours?" he asked in a growling tone. "Because if they are—"

Kirkwood lifted a slender hand to silence Shelby's blustering threat. "I've never met the two gentlemen."

"They're hardly gentlemen," Baylor said. "They're just a pair of drifters. Saddle tramps. One of them tries to dress well, but you can still tell what sort he really is."

"Well, I have some business with the Jensen brothers."

"Won't do you no good," Shelby said. "They lit a shuck. Ran out because they're afraid of us."

"No doubt." Kirkwood managed not to sound too condescending about it. "But I know where they're going, and I intend to catch up to them." His voice hardened. "They have something of mine, and I'm going to retrieve it."

Baylor asked, "What does that have to do with us?"

"Since you have a score to settle with the Jensens, I thought you might like to come with us. To join forces, if you will."

As if the activity helped him think, Baylor picked up the deck and leaned back in his chair, riffling the cards automatically as he looked intently at Kirkwood. "What you mean," he said after a moment. "is that you're afraid of the Jensens and want our help dealing with them."

Leon stepped around Kirkwood. His face was as impassive as ever, but his eyes seethed with anger. "We don't need your help—"

"Leon," Kirkwood said.

Leon fell silent.

Kirkwood went on. "My assistant is quite capable, thank you. But these Jensens are an unknown quantity. For all I know, they have friends where they're going.

The five of you, or as many of you as care to go along, simply ensure that Leon and I won't find ourselves badly outnumbered."

"I told you we should have gone after them," Shelby snapped. "I wanted to kill those little sons of bitches right from the start."

"Throw in with me, and there's a good chance you'll get your wish," Kirkwood said with a smile. "How about it?"

Shelby and Baylor looked at each other. It seemed obvious that the two of them would make the decision. The other three men hadn't spoken or done anything to indicate that they wouldn't go along with whatever the gunfighter and the gambler wanted.

Shelby was eager to agree, Kirkwood could tell, but Baylor remained cautious.

"What is it that you're really after?" Baylor asked.

"That doesn't matter—"

"It might, if we're going to be risking our lives."

Kirkwood considered for a second, then shrugged. "Very well. The Jensen brothers are traveling with a group of women—"

"Now you're talkin'." The bald, potbellied man spoke up for the first time.

"Be quiet, Jack," Baylor said. "What sort of women?"

"Mail-order brides," Kirkwood said. "One of them is an imposter. She's really my fiancée, and she's running away from me."

"She got cold feet, eh?"

Kirkwood made a curt gesture. "The reason doesn't matter. All you need to know is that I intend to get her back, and if the Jensens get in my way, they'll be disposed of, whatever that takes."

"And the other women?" Shelby rasped.

"I don't have the least bit of interest in them," Kirkwood said. "Does that make a difference?"

"It might. We're in," Shelby declared.

"I concur," Baylor said. "With the understanding that you'll be covering all the expenses *and* a fee for our time and trouble, Mr. Kirkwood."

"I told you that my father is rich," Kirkwood replied with a chuckle. "The cost is no object. How soon can you be ready to leave?"

"There's still plenty of day left," Shelby said. "We can be ready to ride in half an hour. Need to pick up some supplies and ammunition. Jack, you and Prewitt handle that."

Kirkwood said. "Leon, go with them, pay for the supplies, and arrange for good saddle horses for the two of us."

"Better get some extra mounts," Jack Loomis suggested. "Those Jensens are a couple days ahead of us. We'll need to do some hard riding to catch up to them."

"See to it," Kirkwood told Leon.

Loomis apparently surprised the others by continuing. "Give us a few minutes to talk over some things. Personal business, nothing to do with this. Your man can wait over at the bar."

Kirkwood shrugged. "Fine. Leon, you heard the man. I'll be at the hotel. Fetch me when we're ready to depart."

Leon jerked his head in a nod and went to the bar while Kirkwood walked out of the saloon.

Lew Shelby said, "Jack, when the hell did you start giving orders in this bunch?"

Loomis leaned forward and lowered his voice. "Don't look at that Leon fella, so he won't know I'm talkin' about him. Remember I told you about being in a saloon at the other end of town yesterday morning when a couple gents came in and raised a ruckus? Well, that was them."

Shelby's eyebrows rose in surprise. "The fancy pants and his trained ape?"

"That ape busted up five men without any help and without even breakin' a sweat," Loomis said. "I reckon he would have killed all five of them without blinking an eye if he needed to." He looked around at the others. "I know you boys. You're thinkin' about double-crossing Kirkwood or whatever his name is, maybe seeing what he's worth to that rich father of his, once we kill the Jensens and grab those women."

Shelby inclined his head to indicate that Loomis was right. "What if we are thinking about that?"

"I'll be right there with you," Loomis promised. "I'm just sayin', when we make our move . . . kill the ape first. Because if you don't, he'll sure as hell kill us."

CHAPTER TWENTY-FOUR

It was an overcast day on the trail, but the thick gray clouds didn't promise rain. They just made the air more sultry and had all the ladies inside the wagon fanning themselves because of the sticky heat.

Ace and Chance rode with their hats tipped back on their heads and their sleeves rolled up. Ace took the point, as usual, while Chance divided his time between riding in front of the wagon with his brother and dropping back to make sure no pursuit was coming up behind them.

It was their hope that the Fairweathers had suffered enough losses to make them give up the crazy idea of claiming the women for themselves. Linus Fairweather had seemed more than a little loco, and without him to drive them on, the surviving sons might not be so eager for more trouble.

By midafternoon, the terrain had gotten even more rugged, with steep hills and bluffs and valleys choked with thick vegetation. The road twisted around like a snake, following the easiest route. The sandy soil closer to the river had given way to hard red clay. It looked more like mining country to Ace, but there were ranches in the area, too. They saw numerous cattle grazing among the hills and thickets.

Late in the afternoon, they came to a tall ridge rising in front of them. It ran north and south as far as they could see.

Chance reined in. "How in the world are we going to get up there with a wagon?"

Ace brought his horse to a halt and frowned at the steep escarpment. "There's got to be a trail. That map Lorena has shows the road going on west. We just can't see it from here."

Creaking and swaying, the wagon rolled up behind them. Agnes hauled back on the reins and stopped the team. "Are we going the right way?" she called from the driver's seat.

Ace hipped around in his saddle and said, "We were just talking about that. Chance, you stay here while I scout ahead and see if I can find a way to the top."

Chance opened his mouth and looked like he was going to argue, but then he nodded. "You're right, we don't need to leave the ladies alone. Not after what happened back at the river with the Fairweathers."

Ace lifted a hand in farewell and heeled his chestnut into motion again. A mile-wide flat lay in front of the ridge, so it didn't take long for Ace to cross it and reach the base of the escarpment.

When he was closer, he could see the way a number of smaller ridges jutted out like gnarled fingers. The road followed the slope between two of those smaller promontories. It was steep but passable. The horses would have a hard pull getting the wagon to the top. The women would need to get out and walk again. They weren't going to like that.

It would be best to wait until morning to make the climb. The team would be much fresher after a night's rest. With that decided, he swung his horse around and loped back toward the wagon.

The ladies had climbed down and gotten out to stretch their legs. Chance had dismounted and was trying to talk to Jamie, but she didn't appear to be paying much attention to him. As Ace rode up, all of them turned toward him to find out what he had discovered.

"We can make it to the top," he reported. "It won't be easy, but the road goes up there and we can follow it." He swung down from the saddle, holding the chestnut's reins. "I'm afraid you ladies are going to have to walk, though, the way you did a few days ago . . . between Fort Worth and Weatherford. Only it'll be a lot longer hike this time. The way the trail runs, it's probably at least a mile from the base of the ridge to the top."

"A mile on foot, uphill?" Isabel said with a note of alarm in her voice. "In these shoes?"

"There's no need for that," Chance said. "Our horses can carry double, even up a hill like that. We'll take you up two at a time."

Ace frowned. That idea hadn't occurred to him. They would need to give the horses plenty of time to rest once everyone was on top of the ridge, but he had to admit, Chance's plan would work.

"Do you mind driving the wagon?" Ace asked Agnes.

"Not at all. I'm glad to do anything I can to help. You know that."

Jamie put a hand on Chance's forearm and smiled at him. "I'm so glad you thought of that, Chance. I really wasn't looking forward to that long walk."

"You can ride with me," he told her. "I'll take you up first."

"In the morning," Ace said. "We'll make camp here and let all the animals rest overnight. I don't want to tackle that hill until tomorrow morning."

No one argued with that decision. Agnes found a good place for the wagon, near some trees that would provide wood for a fire. There didn't seem to be a creek in the vicinity, but they still had plenty of water in the barrels lashed to the side of the wagon.

They had seen a few riders in the distance during the day, probably cowboys who worked for some of the spreads in the area. They hadn't encountered anyone on the road, however, and hadn't spotted anyone coming up behind them. As night fell, Ace figured it wasn't too much of a stretch to hope that it was a peaceful one.

The clouds meant a starless night, and with the ridge looming above them the darkness seemed even thicker. Their campfire was a lone spot of illumination in a vast sweep of black. Ace didn't take much comfort in that. The fire announced to the world where they were. He and Chance would remain watchful.

As if reading Ace's mind, after supper Lorena said, "You know, we wouldn't mind helping you stand guard at night. Would we, girls?"

"I certainly don't," Agnes said. She was always the first to volunteer for any chore that needed done.

"I'm not sure I'd be any good at it," Jamie said with a frown. "I don't do very well if I don't get a full night's sleep. I might not be able to stay awake."

Molly said, "I'd be willing to help, but I'm not any good with a gun."

"Nor am I," Isabel put in. "But I can remain alert and sound the alarm in case of trouble."

Ace shook his head. "That's what you're paying us for, ladies—to protect you. Chance and I can handle that job."

"Well . . . sometimes it might be easier to stay awake if we had a little company," Chance said.

"It's settled, then," Agnes said immediately. "We can take shifts. The ones of us who are willing to, that is."

Reluctantly, but clearly not wanting to be the only one who didn't volunteer, Jamie said, "All right, I suppose I can give it a try."

Ace smiled a little to himself and shook his head. He knew that Chance would try to arrange things so he was paired with Jamie. At the same time, Agnes would be angling for a shift with Chance.

And as for Lorena . . . she had been a little cool toward Ace, so he hoped she wouldn't figure it was an opportunity to try to seduce him again. But he wasn't sure, since she was the one who had suggested the idea in the first place.

The women drew lots to see which of them would stand guard. That was the only fair way to do it.

Chance was paired with Lorena, which was a relief to Ace on two levels. He didn't have to worry about the honey-blonde trying to take advantage of the situation, and if Agnes was disappointed in not being teamed with Chance, at least Jamie wasn't going to be staying up with him, either.

Molly won—if that was the right term—the draw to be Ace's partner for the night. That development didn't please Ace as much. He still felt a touch of embarrassment whenever he thought about that nocturnal encounter with a scantily dressed Molly several nights earlier.

She smiled across the fire at him, though, and

seemed to be saying that it was all right, so he told himself not to worry too much about it.

Chance and Lorena had the first shift, so Ace crawled under the wagon with his bedroll and got some sleep. As usual, it seemed like he had barely closed his eyes when Chance tapped his foot with a rifle barrel to wake him.

"Anything going on?" Ace asked as he pulled on his boots.

"Not a thing. Lorena dozed off a couple of times. I let her sleep." Chance laughed softly. "I think she was a little annoyed with me for doing that, but shoot, I'm not going to wake a woman who's sleeping. Doc raised us to be gentlemen."

"She's gone to bed?"

"Yep. But she said she'd wake Molly first."

Sure enough, Molly poked her head out of the wagon a minute or so later. When she climbed out, Ace saw by the light of the fire's embers that she was fully dressed.

"Do you want a rifle?" Ace asked her.

"I wouldn't be of any use with one if I had it," she said. "I hope that's all right."

"Sure."

Chance said. "Good night, you two," and disappeared underneath the wagon to seek his bedroll and a few hours of sleep.

"You can sit on the tailgate there if you'd like," Ace told Molly.

"What about you?"

"I'll sit some, but I'll be up roaming around, too. You just keep your eyes and ears open."

"I can do that."

He tucked his Winchester under his arm and sat on

the tailgate beside her for the moment. After a while he asked. "Who's the fella you're supposed to marry in San Angelo?"

"His name is Jonas Blosser. He's a blacksmith. From what I can tell, he's a good, honest man, well respected in the community."

"Sounds like a hard worker," Ace said. "I hope you'll be very happy."

"I'm sure I will be. At least I won't have to be around outlaws all the time."

Ace frowned and was about to ask her what she meant by that, then he remembered. "Oh, yeah, your father's a lawman, right?"

"That's right. He's the marshal in the town where we live. I used to bring meals from the café to the jail for his prisoners. I started doing that when I was twelve years old."

"That doesn't sound like a job for a twelve-year-old," Ace said.

"Oh, I didn't mind. I was glad to help out. A lot of the men who wound up in jail really weren't that bad. They just had bad luck or made bad decisions."

"I suppose." Ace didn't say anything about how he and Chance had run afoul of small-town lawmen in the past and wound up behind bars, usually because of some misunderstanding.

"Those prisoners weren't very good husband material, though," Molly went on. "That's why I decided to leave. I'm sure Jonas will be much better."

"I hope so," Ace told her.

She sighed. "It would be hard for him to be worse than some of the men I met up there in Missouri."

Ace thought she was going to continue, but she fell silent.

After a few minutes she went on. "How about you and Chance? Where are you from?"

"From all over, really." Ace told her about how he and his brother had been raised by Doc Monday. She was easy to talk to, and he kind of regretted it when he realized he needed to get up and walk around the camp to make sure no one was sneaking up on them.

"Do you want me to stay here?" Molly asked.

"That'd be best," Ace said. "I can leave my Colt with you . . ."

She shook her head. "I don't want a gun. I'd be afraid I'd shoot somebody I wasn't supposed to."

"All right. Just keep your eyes and ears open."

He slid down from the tailgate and walked out about twenty yards from the wagon, then began making a circle around the camp. A glance at the sky told him the overcast was beginning to break up. He saw a star peeking through here and there.

The night seemed quiet and peaceful. He was about three-quarters of the way around the camp when a sudden flurry of hoofbeats somewhere nearby shattered the stillness. He stiffened for a second and then broke into a run toward the camp, carrying the Winchester at a slant in front of him.

His first thought was that the surviving Fairweathers were attacking out of the darkness. As he pounded up to the wagon, he realized the hoofbeats were going *away* from the camp, rather than toward it. Somebody was lighting a shuck out of there.

The noise had roused Chance from sleep. He rolled

out from under the wagon and came up on a knee with the .38 in his hand.

"Ace! What the hell?"

"I don't know," Ace said. He hurried to the back of the wagon where he had left Molly.

She was gone.

CHAPTER TWENTY-FIVE

The women had been awakened by Chance's shout. Lorena pushed aside the canvas at the back of the wagon and peered out at the Jensen brothers. The other three tried to look over her shoulders.

"What is it?" Lorena said. "What's wrong, Ace?"

"Molly's gone," Ace replied.

"Gone! What do you mean, gone?"

Ace didn't bother answering that question since it seemed pretty obvious to him.

The question that mattered was—had Molly run away on her own . . . or had someone taken her?

Ace rushed over to the horses and saw that his chestnut and Chance's cream-colored gelding were still there, tossing their heads a little because of the commotion. So were the four big draft horses. If Molly had left on her own, she would have taken one of the saddle mounts.

That meant someone had slipped into the camp and grabbed her, then gotten her away from the wagon without making a sound. Ace's first thought was that one of the Fairweathers had kidnapped the young woman.

The other four ladies chattered in excitement and worry as Ace swung back to his brother. "Stay here. I'll go after them."

"Them?"

"It sounded like more than one horse to me," Ace said grimly.

"That damned Fairweather bunch!"

"More than likely." Ace couldn't think of who else it might have been.

"I'm coming with you," Chance said.

"No, that could be just what they want. They might have grabbed Molly in order to lure us both away from the wagon, so they could swoop in and grab the rest of the ladies."

"Let them try!" Lorena said from the wagon, her eyes flashing with anger and defiance in the dim light. "We'll meet them with hot lead if they do."

"We can't risk it," Ace said. "And we're wasting time arguing."

"You're right," Chance admitted grudgingly. "Go on. I'll see to it that nothing happens to the others, and we'll all wait right here for you to get back with Molly."

"I appreciate the vote of confidence," Ace said as he leaned his rifle against the wagon. He began saddling the chestnut.

Already the hoofbeats that had fled away from the camp had faded away, but Ace knew which way they had been headed—north along the base of the ridge. He would start in that direction and hope for the best.

The alternative was to wait until morning and try to track the kidnappers then, and he wasn't going to do that. He slid his rifle into its scabbard, then swung up into the saddle and turned the chestnut north.

Behind him, Lorena called, "Good luck! Be careful!"

Ace intended to use caution—but rescuing Molly was more important. He would run whatever risks he needed to.

More stars had emerged, which gave him enough light to see where he was going. He had to maintain a fairly slow pace because of the rough terrain. It wouldn't do Molly any good if the horse stumbled and broke a leg or even just lamed itself.

Ace followed the ragged edge of the escarpment. It wasn't likely the kidnappers would try to climb it in the dark. And if the Fairweathers were responsible for grabbing Molly, their camp was probably back to the east somewhere. Finding tracks at night was very difficult, and Ace wished the moon would come out so he could at least make the attempt.

As if the moon had read his mind, it sailed out from behind the thinning clouds and cast a silvery glow over the landscape. Ace reined in and intently studied the ground ahead of him. After a while he dismounted, hunkered on his heels, and snapped a match to life with his thumbnail.

His instincts had guided him well. He was looking at the tracks left by three horses. That matched up with what he had heard back at the camp. They were definitely headed north, not swinging back to the east.

Ace followed on foot, leading the chestnut. Now that he had found the sign, he didn't want to lose it.

That made for slow going. The delay chafed at Ace, but staying on the right path was more important than hurrying.

He covered several miles in that fashion. A few times

he believed he had lost the trail, but diligent searching and some carefully shielded match light turned it up again.

The ragged edge of the escarpment still loomed on his left. It struck him as odd that the Fairweathers would continue in that direction, but there was no telling what those loco hombres might do.

The eastern sky held the faintest tinge of gray, heralding that dawn was a couple hours away, when Ace suddenly stopped and sniffed the air. He thought he had just caught a whiff of wood smoke, and sniffed again. Somebody not too far away had a fire going.

Could be an isolated farm, he told himself. Or a line shack on some ranch. Or it might be that the men who had kidnapped Molly had gone to ground with their prisoner, thinking they were safe from pursuit until the morning.

The smoke was easier to follow than the hoofprints had been. Ace just let his nose guide him. When the smell was strong enough to convince him the fire was close, he tied his horse to a sapling and catfooted ahead.

A faint, flickering glow appeared to his left about a hundred yards away. His quarry had made camp in a narrow canyon formed by two smaller ridges that protruded from the main escarpment. Ace crept closer until he could peer through a gap in the brush and see the fire itself.

The wooded slopes pressed in close on both sides of the camp, but there was room for the fire, three horses, the three men who had ridden them—and Molly Brock.

Ace's eyes narrowed in surprise as he saw that all three men were clean-shaven except for some stubble.

They weren't any of the Fairweather brothers. He had never seen them before.

Molly sat on a slab of rock with her head down and her hands clasped around her knees. Her shoulders were hunched over as if she expected a blow.

The man looming over her looked mad enough— and mean enough—to hit her. He was a big man, tall and broad through the shoulders, with a black hat pushed back on a thatch of curly blond hair. His lantern-jawed face wasn't exactly ugly, but he was far from handsome.

The other two men, in well-worn range clothes, resembled dozens of hardcases and outlaws the Jensen brothers had encountered over the past few years as they drifted through the West. All three were armed and looked like they knew how to use the guns.

As Ace watched from the brush, the big man said to Molly. "I'm tired of talking to you. You'd better give me what I want, or you'll be damned sorry."

That son of a bitch, the normally mild-mannered Ace thought. Even most owlhoots wouldn't talk like that to a woman, and they sure wouldn't threaten her. If the man made a move toward her, Ace would have to shoot him.

But he didn't want to do that. Not out of any compassion for the brutal kidnapper or fear for himself, but if he downed the man threatening Molly, the other two would grab their guns and open fire. The way they were positioned, Molly would be right in the way of those bullets. The likelihood of her catching a stray slug would be high.

He had to do something else. Had to think of some sort of distraction that would allow him to get Molly away from her captors before any shooting started. . . . An idea popped into his head. It seemed like a long shot, but it might be the only chance he had to rescue her without putting her too much at risk. Carefully, silently, he backed away toward the spot where he had left his horse.

When he had put enough distance between himself and the camp, he circled to the north, then onto the ridge that stuck out from the higher escarpment. The slope was steep, but he managed to move along it without falling. He couldn't get in a hurry without making the brush crackle, so he had to be patient.

Ace heard the sound of voices from the camp below him, but he couldn't make out the words. He could tell by the rising tone of the big man's words that time was running out. The man was about to lose his patience, and that didn't bode well for Molly.

Ace went farther up the little canyon, then stopped. He took a couple deep breaths then threw back his head and howled.

It wasn't a dog-like howl. More the shrill, snarling cry of a mountain lion. As kids, Ace and Chance had practiced making animal sounds until they were experts. They could imitate any birdcall that was out there, as well as the chuffing snorts of a bear, the bellow of a moose, even the chittering of squirrels.

The uncanny shriek echoed between the slopes and seemed to grow louder. As Ace fell silent, he heard shouts of alarm coming from the men and frightened whinnies from the horses.

Somebody yelled, "Grab those horses before they pull loose and bolt!"

Another man said, "Get your rifles and go find that

panther! Those big cats love horse meat. We can't afford to lose any of our mounts."

"Damn it, Earl—" That was the voice of the third man.

Ace realized the name belonged to the big man. Clearly he was the boss of the trio.

"Kill it if you can find it, but even if you don't, fire some shots in the air and run it off. We can't have it hangin' around here. The horses are already spooked."

The horses would settle down soon enough, once they realized they had only heard a mountain lion and couldn't smell one. But the three men who had kidnapped Molly didn't know that.

A racket came from the brush below him as the two men tramped through it in search of the "panther" they had heard. Ace heard some grumbling from them as well. Despite their displeasure, they weren't going to defy the big man's orders.

Ace waited until they were past, then began easing back along the slope toward the camp. The light from the fire was brighter. Somebody had thrown more wood on it to make the flames blaze up, probably in hopes that it would keep the big cat away.

Faintly, he could still hear the two men crashing around up the canyon. If there really had been a mountain lion in the vicinity, it probably would have run off already . . . or eaten the two hardcases.

All Ace cared about was that they were out of the way. Crouching low so the brush would conceal him, he crept closer until he could see the camp again.

Holding a rifle in his hands, the big man stood looking up the canyon. His back was to the fire, so Ace couldn't make out his expression, but his attitude was one of tense anticipation. If a mountain lion came bounding out of the shadows, he was ready.

But he wasn't prepared for a human antagonist.

Ace slipped his Colt from its holster and stepped out of the brush. "Drop that rifle, mister, and get your hands in the air!"

Behind the man, Ace had the drop on him, but that wasn't enough to make him surrender.

The man whirled. Bent low, he brought the rifle around. Ace caught a glimpse of a snarling face above the swinging barrel.

He had given the man a chance to cooperate. He wasn't going to wait until the kidnapper opened fire on him. Anybody who would grab a woman and threaten her didn't deserve a whole heap of consideration, anyway.

Ace's gun boomed.

The man flew backwards, the rifle sailing out of his hands as he fell. He clawed at his upper right arm where Ace's slug had ripped a deep crease.

"Molly, run!" Ace shouted at her.

It was good that they hadn't tied her up. She lunged to her feet and dashed away from the camp. Ace knew that path would take her toward his horse. He intended to be close behind her.

The big man landed hard on the ground but rolled over and came up clawing at his holstered revolver with his left arm. His right hung useless for the moment, dripping blood from the bullet wound. He gave up trying to draw his own gun and threw himself to the side as Ace fired again. He saw the man's shirt jerk where the bullet tugged at it.

The man's headlong dive carried him into the bushes at the edge of the camp. Ace snapped another shot in that direction then ran after Molly. The muscles in his back were tense as he halfway expected to feel a bullet smash into him.

Shadows closed in around him. No more shots roared. A couple hundred yards up the canyon, the other two men shouted. They would be on their way back in a hurry to see what all the shooting was about.

"Ace!"

The low-voiced cry made Ace veer toward it. A dark shape loomed up in front of him. It was his horse, he realized. Molly had hold of the reins and was leading the animal.

"Thank God he didn't kill you!" she exclaimed.

Ace took the reins from her, grabbed the saddle horn, stuck his foot in the stirrup, and swung up. The chestnut danced back and forth a little, but Ace tightened the reins and calmed the horse. He reached down with his other hand. Molly grasped his wrist with both hands. He pulled her up behind him. She put her arms around his waist and held on tight.

He heeled the horse into a run and galloped out of the canyon, onto the flats again. They turned south toward the camp where he had left Chance and the other ladies.

Ace didn't hear any more guns go off behind them, but he knew better than to believe they were in the clear just yet.

CHAPTER TWENTY-SIX

Earl Brock clambered to his feet and stumbled out of the brush as Cooper and Hawthorne ran up. Both men looked spooked, but their rifles were ready if they needed to fire.

"Earl, what happened?" Hawthorne asked.

"That was no damn mountain lion doin' that shootin'!" Cooper said. "I never saw one yet that could use a gun."

"You're hit," Hawthorne added as he looked wide-eyed at Brock's bloody sleeve.

"Shut up and let me get a word out, you damn fools," Brock said, tight-lipped with rage. "I know I'm hit. He shot me and took off with Molly."

"Who?"

"One of those blasted hombres traveling with the women."

Brock would have preferred to kill the two young men, but after following the group all day and riding hard to catch up, when the opportunity to grab Molly and make off with her had presented itself unexpectedly, he had seized it. He hadn't figured anybody would come after them until morning.

By then, he intended to force her into revealing what she had done with the money she'd stolen from him. She had either cached it somewhere, maybe even put it in a bank—that would be ironic, since most of it had been stolen from banks—or else she still had it with her.

In which case they would have to go back to the wagon to recover the loot, and they could kill the two men *then*.

But . . . one of the bastards had not only come after them, he had been able to find them. Then he had taken them by surprise.

It infuriated Brock that they had fallen for the trick. "You didn't see a mountain lion, did you?"

Cooper shook his head. "Nope, we didn't see hide nor hair of a big cat, nor hear one again, either. You think—"

"Yeah, it was him," Brock said bitterly. "Of course it was. Get the horses saddled. We're going after—" He stopped short as his head suddenly spun crazily and everything went blurry. The whole world seemed to be whirling around him. He felt himself swaying, then he fell, unable to catch himself as he crashed to the ground.

He didn't pass out completely. He heard the startled exclamations from the other two men, felt hands gripping him and rolling him onto his back. Pain shot out from his wounded arm and filled his entire body. He gasped but couldn't form the curses that wanted to spring from his lips.

"Earl! Boss!" That was Hawthorne, sounding frantic. "Is he dead, Coop?"

"No, he's still breathin'. Reckon he just passed out 'cause of losin' so much blood from that wounded arm. We gotta get him patched up."

Brock forced his mouth to work as his eyes began to focus again. "No! We need to . . . go after Molly . . ." He tried to get up, but Cooper held him down.

"Can't do that, Earl. You're gonna bleed to death if we don't tend to you. Goin' after Molly won't do any good if you die along the way."

Brock hated it whenever anybody argued with him, but somewhere inside his muddled brain, he knew Cooper was right. He sighed and let himself slump back on the ground. "All right," he whispered. "Do what you got to do. But make it fast, and when you've got me fixed up, we're going after that bitch and her protectors again."

"Don't you worry about that, Earl," Cooper said as he started to rip away Brock's bloody sleeve. "We're gonna get that money back, all right, and when it's all over, we'll send those two fellas straight to hell!"

Ace didn't slow the chestnut until they had covered half a mile from the canyon where the kidnappers had been camped. Then he pulled the horse back to a walk and maintained that pace for a couple minutes, listening intently for any sounds of pursuit. When Molly started to say something, he shushed her.

If she took offense at that, she didn't show it.

Finally, when Ace was satisfied that he didn't hear

any hoofbeats in the distance behind them, he said, "I'm sorry, Molly. I didn't mean to be rude just now."

"Rude?" she repeated. "You saved my life, Ace! You can say anything you want to me, and as far as that incident a few nights ago is concerned, I don't want you ever feeling embarrassed about that again."

The fact of the matter was that Ace felt a little embarrassed at that very moment. The way Molly was riding behind him and clinging to him, the soft mounds of her breasts pressed against his back. Every time he swayed in the saddle, he felt their intriguing movement.

It was the second time he had experienced such intimate knowledge of her body, and while it was certainly pleasurable, it also made him uncomfortable.

The horse's sides had stopped heaving from the hard run. Ace allowed it to proceed at the slow pace for a few more minutes, then nudged the animal into a ground-eating lope.

"Did Chance come with you?" Molly asked as she leaned her head forward over Ace's left shoulder.

"No, he stayed with the others. We thought it was probably the Fairweathers who took you, and that it might be a trick to draw both of us away, then swoop in and grab everybody else."

"That was good thinking, even if it didn't turn out that way. And very brave of you to come after me alone."

"Who in blazes *were* those jaspers?" Ace asked. "I don't think I ever saw any of them before. They sure weren't any of the Fairweather brothers."

"No, they weren't." Molly hesitated for a second before going on. "I don't know them, either. They didn't use any names when they were talking to each other. I think maybe . . . maybe they just saw us . . . the ladies, I mean . . . and decided to take one of us for their . . . their pleasure, you know? I was the unlucky one they were able to grab."

"I don't reckon they gave you any warning before they kidnapped you?"

"No. I guess I wasn't as alert as I thought I was. I never heard them sneaking around until one of them grabbed me from behind and clapped his hand over my mouth. I tried to fight him, at least enough to raise a ruckus and let you know something was wrong, but he was just too strong."

"The big one, you're talking about?"

Ace felt a shudder go through her, then she said, "That's right. The big ugly one."

"I thought I heard one of the others call him Earl."

"Did you? That's entirely possible." She gave a shaky little laugh. "I was so scared, I didn't even know what was going on half the time. I was just hoping that somehow, by some miracle, one of you would show up in time to save me. And you did."

Such praise deepened Ace's uneasiness. He didn't want Molly to develop some sort of crush on him out of gratitude. Lorena's on-again, off-again efforts to flirt with him had already been enough of a distraction.

After a while he ran the chestnut hard for another mile, then let the horse walk again. Alternating gaits like that allowed a horse to cover a lot of ground while preserving its strength and not having a bad effect on its wind.

The sky had lightened and gradually turned orange and gold with the approach of dawn, and while they were walking, the sun appeared on the horizon and steadily grew brighter as it rose.

It wasn't long after sunup when they came in sight of the wagon.

Chance had been watching and rode out to meet them, holding his rifle ready in one hand. Ace didn't have the chestnut at a gallop, so that told Chance there was no immediate pursuit. Ace knew his brother would be cautious anyway.

"Thank God!" Chance exclaimed when he drew rein beside them. "You found her. Molly, are you all right?"

"I'm fine, thanks to Ace. He rescued me from those men."

"I hope you killed all those blasted Fairweathers this time," Chance said with savage intensity.

Ace shook his head. "It wasn't the Fairweathers. It was three strangers who stole Molly away. We don't have any idea who they are, except one of them is called Earl."

"Strangers?" A puzzled frown creased Chance's forehead. "Why in the world . . . you mean they intended to . . . ?"

"That's right."

"Well . . . Blast it! I'm sorry, Molly. I'm just glad Ace got to you in time. He *did* get to you in—"

"He did," Molly said. "And I'll always be grateful for that."

They had continued riding toward the wagon while they were talking. The other four women stood beside the vehicle, watching anxiously, and when the riders were close enough for them to see that Molly was with Ace and appeared to be all right, they ran forward to greet her.

Ace reined in, and with his help Molly slid to the ground. The others swarmed around her, hugging her and talking quickly and excitedly. They got the story out of her while the Jensen brothers dismounted. The other four women turned their attention to Ace, gathering around him. Each one in turn hugged him to thank him for rescuing Molly.

Lorena went last, and her hug lasted so long and was so intense that Ace began to wonder if he was going to have to pry her arms from around his neck. Finally the honey-blonde stepped back and gave him a dazzling smile.

"Dadgum it," Chance said. "If you're going to get a reception like that, next time I get to go after the varmints and rescue the girl."

"It'll be just fine with me if there isn't a next time," Ace said.

"Well, sure. You've already had five beautiful women fussing over you. You don't care if I get that sort of treatment."

Ace was glad his brother had included Agnes with the others in that description. Judging by her smile, she liked it, too.

Jamie stepped over to Chance. "Oh, hush. Stop your pouting, Chance Jensen."

She came up on her toes and brushed her lips across his cheek. A grin spread over Chance's face, which caused the expression on Agnes's face to fall a little before she covered it up with a smile. Ace saw it though.

Everyone grew more solemn as Isabel asked a practical question. "Are those men going to come after us?"

"I don't know," Ace said. "They might. I reckon it

depends on how determined they are, and how bad the one I shot is wounded. The other two might decide it's better just to take care of him and leave us alone from here on out. That's what I'm hoping they'll do."

"You and me, both," Lorena said. "We've already had enough trouble on this trip to last us the whole way to San Angelo!"

Ace couldn't agree more with that sentiment. "Let's get some breakfast and then see if we can get up that hill!"

CHAPTER TWENTY-SEVEN

The chestnut was worn out from the hard ride carrying double, so Ace didn't want to ask any more of the animal. To tell the truth, he was pretty tired himself, but there was still work to do.

Because of the possibly increased danger, he and Chance modified their original plan. Ace drove the wagon up the hill while Agnes and Isabel rode alongside him on Chance's cream-colored gelding. Ace's horse was tied behind the wagon and plodded along, bringing up the rear.

Chance remained at the bottom of the hill with Lorena, Jamie, and Molly.

Once they were at the top, Isabel dismounted and Agnes headed back down on horseback to fetch another of the women. She was the best rider in the bunch and had no trouble handling Chance's well-trained mount.

Doing it that way, none of the women were ever alone, except for Agnes during the time she was riding back down the hill to pick up another of the mail-order brides. She traveled with Chance's Winchester across the saddle in front of her. She had assured the Jensen brothers she knew how to use the rifle, and they believed her.

The ascent up the escarpment by the entire group took longer, but it was the easiest for the horses. Out on the frontier, taking good care of their horses was sometimes the difference between life and death.

It was safer for the women, too. They were protected by at least one gun all the time.

While Ace and Isabel were waiting for Agnes to return, Isabel said, "You must be tired. Why don't you go in the back of the wagon, stretch out on one of the bunks, and try to get some rest? I can stand watch, I assure you."

It wasn't a good time for Ace to yawn, but he couldn't help it. He stifled the yawn and said, "I'm fine. Between the Fairweathers and Earl and his two partners, there are too many hombres roaming around these parts who'd like to cause trouble for us. It's better if I stay awake."

"If you insist. But if you change your mind, I will be very watchful."

Ace didn't doubt that. He remembered the way she had produced that dagger from some hidden sheath, when he'd had no idea she was even armed.

To keep himself from dwelling on his weariness, he said, "So you're from New Orleans."

"That's right."

"You still have family there?"

A look of pain briefly crossed her face, causing Ace to wish he hadn't asked the question.

Then she smiled. "No, not anymore. My mother

passed away a number of years ago. My father has been gone for two years now. Perhaps he had relatives somewhere, but he never spoke of them. He was definitely the black sheep of the family, as people say."

"Black sheep are just about all there is in my family, I reckon," Ace said as he returned the smile.

"My mother's family is all back in Mexico," Isabel went on. "She tried to keep in touch with her brothers and sisters when I was young, but it was difficult. So much turmoil below the border all the time, first this *presidenté* in power and then this other emperor, and people do not know from one week to another whether they will live in a palace or be stood in front of a wall for the firing squad."

"It can't be *that* bad," Ace said.

Isabel laughed. "Perhaps I exaggerate. But only slightly." She shrugged. "At any rate, I do not really know any of my relatives in Mexico. They might as well be no kin at all."

"Shame to go through life alone like that."

"Yes . . . but sometimes being with the wrong person is worse than being alone." She waved a slender hand as if to dismiss that thought. "But soon I will be married, and all will be well."

"Who's your new husband going to be?"

"His name is Gilpin. Abner Gilpin. He edits and publishes a newspaper."

Ace had a little trouble imagining someone as glamorous as Isabel being married to a man named Abner Gilpin, but he supposed that wasn't fair. People didn't have much control over what they were named.

"Well, I hope the two of you are happy together."

"From the letters we have exchanged—admittedly,

not that many—he seems like a good man. All of life is a gamble, is it not?"

"Chance and I were raised by a man who made his living with a deck of cards, so I reckon we know that better than most folks."

Not long after that, Agnes appeared at the head of the trail, riding Chance's horse with Jamie perched behind her.

"Any problems?" Ace asked as Agnes reined in beside the wagon.

"No. We didn't run into anybody on the trail, and everything's peaceful down below." Agnes gave Jamie a hand getting off the horse. "I'll fetch Molly and Lorena."

That meant the last two riders up the hill would be Chance and Agnes. If he and Chance hadn't come up with the plan themselves, Ace thought Agnes might have arranged things that way.

He might ask his brother about that ride later, or he might not, Ace decided. Navigating all these would-be romantic entanglements was getting damned tiresome.

By the time all the ladies were atop the escarpment, it was late in the morning. Ace believed the horses hitched to the wagon had recovered enough from the steep pull to continue the journey. He left the chestnut tied to the back and rode on the seat with Agnes.

She took the reins back from him, and he didn't argue with her. She had proven to be quite a capable teamster.

For the most part, the terrain up there was as flat as it was farther east. Hills cropped up here and there, but they were gentle and rolling. Clumps of post oaks dotted the landscape, with broad stretches of sand roughs between them. They were leaving the farmlands behind. It was ranching country, almost exclusively.

"Have we reached the halfway point of the trip?" Agnes asked as she kept the wagon rolling along.

"I don't know," Ace said. "I'd have to study that map of Lorena's again before I could say."

In a quiet voice that wouldn't carry to the women inside the wagon, who were talking among themselves, Agnes commented, "She'd like that."

Ace tried not to wince. He cast a wary glance over his shoulder. "I know. She's got some funny ideas about marriage and fidelity."

"I suppose everybody has a right to their own opinion, even about something as fundamental as that."

"Yeah, I reckon."

Agnes cocked her head a little to the side. "She's a very attractive woman."

"I'm not going to deny that," Ace said.

"Some people like to look down their noses at other folks. I believe in live and let live. If growing up on a farm taught me anything, it's that nature nearly always finds a way to get what it wants."

"Humans are better than animals."

"Sometimes," Agnes said. "But when you think about some of the humans we've run into on this trip . . . I'd have to say not always."

Ace couldn't deny that, either.

Starting out, Ripley Kirkwood had felt complete confidence in his riding abilities.

Riding in a park, or around a training ring at the stables, turned out to be completely different from starting across frontier Texas in a saddle strapped to a four-legged torture machine.

Leon seemed to be suffering as well, although it was hard to tell. Most of the time his face appeared hewn out of granite. Whenever the group stopped, he dismounted and mounted again very carefully and gingerly. That was the only evidence of his discomfort.

Thanks to the extra horses Jack Loomis had suggested, they had been able to maintain a fast pace since leaving Fort Worth, All five of the hardcases had spent a great deal of time in the saddle and had no trouble with the long hours of riding.

Kirkwood's pride wouldn't allow him to reveal how much agony he was in. The burning pain in his thigh muscles alone was almost enough to make him scream. He didn't believe he would ever be able to sit down again without hurting, no matter how soft and comfortable the chair was.

Lew Shelby estimated that they had made up half the ground on the Jensen brothers and the mail-order brides. Another couple days, maybe a day and a half, and they would catch up with their quarry.

Whenever Kirkwood started thinking that he hurt too badly to go on, he conjured up in his mind an image of Isabel's lovely face. Either she would come to her senses and those delicious red lips of hers would promise to worship and adore him and stay with him forever . . . or else she wouldn't be so lovely anymore. Leon would see to that.

The thought kept Kirkwood going.

The taciturn Prewitt, a man so bland and colorless he seemed to fade into the background unless you were looking right at him, turned out to be an excellent trail cook. Nothing approaching the same level as the fine restaurants back in New Orleans to which Kirkwood was accustomed, of course, but Prewitt was able to put together a decent meal out of the supplies Leon had bought before the group left Fort Worth.

Around the campfire that night, while the men were enjoying the stew Prewitt had prepared, Shelby said, "This woman you're looking for, Kirkwood, is she pretty?"

Kirkwood frowned. He didn't like being addressed so familiarly and disrespectfully by a common gunman, but he didn't want a falling-out, so he allowed the insult to pass. "Isabel is very beautiful. One of the loveliest women I've ever seen. And I've been with *many* beautiful women."

"I wonder about the other gals traveling with her."

Loomis said, "They're probably as ugly as the north end of a southbound horse. Who else would become a mail-order bride and get hitched up with a fella she doesn't even know?"

"It's hard to say," Henry Baylor mused. "Perhaps the other women have extenuating circumstances in their background, like our friend Ripley's beautiful Isabel."

Kirkwood wasn't sure which he disliked most, being called *Kirkwood* by Shelby or *Ripley* by the gambler.

"I reckon you can ask 'em," Loomis said as he poured himself another cup of coffee. "After all, we can't be sportin' with 'em all the time. We'll probably have to talk to them a little, here and there, in between bouts in the blankets."

He shook his head as if such a prospect as actually talking to women wasn't appealing at all.

"Yeah, but what if they *are* ugly?" Shelby asked.

Loomis pointed with his thumb. "Give 'em to the Kiowa."

The Indian looked up from his bowl of stew and glared. "Don't want white women. They complain too much. Like crows, always cawing and flapping."

That drew a round of laughter from the other men. Leon even smiled faintly, Kirkwood noted.

"Then why are you here?" Loomis asked the Kiowa.

"Money. Don't want white man's women, but like his money just fine."

"Yeah," Shelby said. "Maybe the hombres who are supposed to marry those women will pay to get 'em back safe and sound. Well . . . safe, maybe. Probably not as sound as they were before they ran into us."

Kirkwood dashed the dregs of his coffee into the fire. He had listened to these crude, tiresome discussions more than once. He might need the help of these men to get what he wanted, but that didn't mean he had to enjoy their company.

With a nod to Leon, he retired to his bedroll to dream about Isabel. Those dreams might be blissful— or they might be bloody.

Either way was all right with Ripley Kirkwood.

CHAPTER TWENTY-EIGHT

By the end of the day, Ace, Chance, and the five ladies had reached a crossroads where a couple arrows with names burned into them were nailed to a signpost. The one that pointed onward in the direction they had been going, almost due west, sported the legend ABILENE.

The other arrow, angled south by southwest, had the name CROSS PLAINS burned into it.

"That sounds familiar," Ace said as he reined in. He was riding the chestnut again, the horse having rested enough to bear a rider once more. "I need to take a look at the map."

"It's plenty late enough for us to stop and make camp," Chance said. "Let's do that, and then you and Lorena can put your heads together over the map."

That sounded like a good idea to Ace. They were on flat ground, but nearby the smaller trail leading to Cross Plains went down a slope into a valley broad enough that Ace couldn't see the other side in the fading light.

They gathered wood for a fire. In an area with sparser

vegetation, they would have been collecting firewood everywhere they found it, taking it along with them in case they had to make camp in an area with no trees. So far, that hadn't been a problem. Post oaks, live oaks, cottonwood, pecan trees, all had been common along their route. It was good country. Ace could understand why settlers had been eager to expand into it, and why the Comanche had fought so hard to keep them out.

Once the team was unhitched and the other horses unsaddled, the fire built, and supper underway with Agnes preparing it, Lorena got her map from inside the wagon and spread it on the tailgate, the best place to open it out so that she and Ace could study it.

Ace pointed. "I thought I remembered a place called Cross Plains. That's where we need to go, all right. From there on southwest to Coleman, then west to Hutchins City and right on to San Angelo." His fingertip followed the route as he spoke. "Another four days ought to do it."

"And not a day too soon," Lorena murmured.

"We've done pretty well so far."

"Considering we've had to deal with lunatics and kidnappers, I suppose you're right. We're all still alive and relatively healthy." Lorena began rolling up the map.

"I'm sorry not everything has worked out the way you wanted it to," Ace said.

"You mean because I've had to deal with some stiff-necked *boy*?"

Ace felt his face warm, but whether it was from embarrassment or anger, he didn't know. "You can think whatever you want about me, but I still have to live with myself. I have to look at myself in the mirror . . . and sleep at night."

She smiled at him and caressed his cheek with the hand that wasn't holding the map. "Oh, honey, people can look themselves in the mirror after doing *lots* worse things than anything you and I might have done. Otherwise most of us would go mad. Trust me on that. I speak from experience."

She tapped the rolled-up map against his head and climbed into the wagon, chuckling to herself. Ace was left standing there, feeling vaguely foolish.

Chance moved from the shadows on the far side of the wagon and said quietly, "I reckon she told you."

"Spying on me now?" Ace asked sharply.

"Nope. Just happened to be around here. I'd gone to check on the horses and happened to come back this way. I promise you, if anything that shouldn't have been was going on, I would have withdrawn discreetly." Chance paused. "Of course, that was pretty unlikely considering that she was with you."

"A stiff-necked boy, you mean?" Ace snapped, quoting Lorena.

"No, big brother. A man who's not in the habit of compromising what he believes in."

Ace frowned. Chance hardly ever called him *big brother*. Although they were twins, William "Ace" Jensen had been born several minutes before Benjamin "Chance" Jensen. Unlike a lot of boys, Ace had never tried to use that fact to his advantage while the two of them were growing up. He seldom even thought in terms of *big brother* and *little brother*.

Because of that, whenever Chance used the term, it was usually because Ace had done something to impress him.

Ace was touched by Chance's words. "Thanks. I appreciate that."

"Oh, I didn't say you weren't a damned fool. But I do admire a man with the courage of his convictions."

Ace laughed and aimed a half-hearted swipe at Chance, who ducked the lazy blow. Together, they walked back around the wagon to join the ladies.

The next morning, they took the trail to Cross Plains and spent the day traveling through rangeland criss-crossed by narrow creeks. They met several cowboys who tipped their hats and tried not to gawk at the ladies.

"Any trouble going on around here?" Ace asked one of the young men.

"Nope. You might want to steer clear of Brown County, though. It's off yonderways." The cowboy pointed to the south.

"Why's that?" Ace wanted to know.

"Some of the big ranchers have started fencin' off their range to keep the farmers and the little greasy sack outfits from comin' in and takin' over. And some of those fences have been gettin' cut on a pretty regular basis. It's made for a lot of hard feelin's and a considerable amount of gun smoke."

"What about Indian trouble?" Chance asked.

The cowboy shook his head. "Not around here. You got to go farther west for that. Haven't been any Indian fights in Callahan County for, oh, eight or ten years now, I'd say. I was just a sprout the last time the Comanch' done any raidin' in these parts."

As the young puncher rode away and Agnes got the wagon rolling again, she said. "Well, that's reassuring, I suppose. We don't have to worry about being scalped."

"He *did* say there might be Indian trouble farther

west," Ace pointed out. "The army established a post in San Angelo for a reason."

"But if there's an army post there, shouldn't the area around San Angelo be safer because of it?"

"You'd think so," Chance said, "but sometimes those war chiefs will go looking for a fight. If there's no war, there's no need for them."

"That makes sense, I suppose," Agnes said. She wasn't likely to argue too much with Chance, feeling about him the way she did.

Late in the afternoon they reached Cross Plains, most likely named for the terrain and the fact that two trails crossed there. Two large, wooded hills rose side by side a few miles west of the settlement, but other than that the landscape was gently rolling plains all around.

"It wouldn't hurt to pick up a few more supplies for the rest of the trip," Ace told Agnes. He pointed toward several cottonwoods and a store located near the crossroads. "You can park under those trees, and we'll stay there tonight."

Chance looked at a saloon they'd passed. "Might be a poker game going on in there. If Lorena would advance us a little of our wages, I could get us a bigger stake."

"This is a pretty small settlement," Ace pointed out. "I'm not sure how much money would be in a game around here."

"You never know until you try," Chance responded with a grin.

Agnes brought the wagon to a stop under the cottonwoods. Ace and Chance swung down from their saddles and helped the ladies out of the vehicle.

Several middle-aged, bonnet-wearing local women

were shopping in the store. They cast suspicious glances toward the newcomers and muttered among themselves at the sight of such attractive strangers.

The proprietor seemed happy to see them, though. He was a heavy-set man with thick jowls and graying red hair. As he stood behind the counter at the rear of the store, he called, "Howdy, folks! Come on in."

Agnes, who had taken charge of their supplies, went to the counter and began telling the man what they needed. The other four women looked around the store, seeing what merchandise was available.

Ace and Chance paused in front of a glass display case with several shiny new revolvers. Neither of them needed a new gun, but it didn't hurt anything to look.

The proprietor boxed up the supplies, then had a boy who worked in the store carry them out to the wagon. The youngster's eyes were mighty big as he looked at the mail-order brides, and his freckled face flushed a deep red when Jamie and Isabel smiled at him.

As Lorena settled the bill, Ace asked the man, "Is it all right if we camp out there under those trees tonight?"

"Why, sure, son. It's still a free country, ain't it?"

"The last time I checked," Ace replied with a smile.

Chance nodded toward the building across the road and asked, "What are the odds of there being a poker game going on over there?"

"In the Devil Horse Saloon?"

"Is that what it's called?" Ace said. "Strange name for a saloon."

"Yeah, but the fella who owns it, fella called O'Donnell, he bought it by racin' a horse he used to own. A devil horse, folks claimed, on account of it was black-hearted as Satan. Nobody could handle the brute 'cept O'Donnell. But fast? You never saw the like. He raced that devil horse against all comers, all over this part of the country, and never lost a match. Won a heap of money wagerin' on the critter and used it to buy the saloon from old man Elkins."

"You said he used to own the horse," Ace said. "What happened? Did he sell it?"

With a solemn expression on his jowly face, the storekeeper shook his head. "O'Donnell was on his way back here from Brownwood one day when a bunch of owlhoots jumped him. There was too many of 'em for him to put up a fight, so his only chance was to outrun 'em. He did it, all right, but just when he got back to town, that devil horse collapsed under him. He was the fastest anybody around here ever saw at racin' distances, but that long run plumb wore out his heart. He didn't stop until O'Donnell was safe, though."

All five of the women had been listening, enthralled by the story. Jamie said, "How sad."

"Yes'm," the storekeeper agreed. "Anyhow, mister, you asked about a poker game, and sure thing, some of the boys like to get together and play just about every night. It ain't a very high stakes game, though, and you look like the sort of fella who's used to bigger things."

"As long as it's a friendly game, I enjoy the competition," Chance said.

"Oh, it's friendly enough. Ain't been a shootin' over cards in six . . . no, eight months now. Nobody died, then, just limped around for a spell afterward. And that was less from bein' shot and more from bein' throwed through walls and such. Cross Plains boys get pretty rowdy when they go to scrappin'. Some of 'em are pure pizen."

Ace and Chance glanced at each other, not sure whether to laugh or take the man seriously.

Ace wound up nodding and saying, "Much obliged to you, sir."

As they followed the women out of the store, Ace said quietly to his brother, "Still think you ought to sit in on that game?"

"You heard the man. It's been eight months since there was a gunfight in there. What makes you think tonight would be any different?"

"Oh, maybe the way we seem to draw trouble like a lodestone attracts iron. How many run-ins with different hombres have we had over the past week?"

Chance shook his head. "I don't keep count. I've got better things to do."

"Like play poker in some small-town saloon."

"I've got a hunch the cards are going to be running my way tonight, Ace. I feel a lucky streak coming on."

CHAPTER TWENTY-NINE

Since they were spending the night in a settlement, they didn't have to prepare a meal and eat on the trail. They went to the local café. A set of deer antlers were mounted over the door, visible evidence of why the place was called the Staghorn.

They ate steaks, potatoes, greens, biscuits, and deep-dish apple pie. Ace and Chance were stuffed by the time they were finished with the meal, but the ladies had had enough sense not to eat so much.

"I'll go see what's happening at the Devil Horse," Chance said as he finished his second cup of coffee. "If things don't look too promising, I'll head on back to the wagon."

"I'll keep an eye on things," Ace said. "Don't play too late."

"And try not to lose all that money I advanced you," Lorena added. "Although I suppose it's not really any of my business if you do." She had given Chance two ten-dollar gold pieces, which was almost a fourth of the price they had agreed on for the Jensen brothers escorting the women to San Angelo.

Having Chance risk that much on the turn of some cards made Ace a little uneasy, but he knew in the long run it didn't really matter. He and Chance had fallen into a pattern of drifting for a while, working when they had to, and then moving on again. If they wound up flat broke in San Angelo, they would just look for other jobs.

As they stepped out of the café, Chance parted company with the others, strolling up the street toward the Devil Horse Saloon. Ace and the ladies headed toward the clump of cottonwoods where the wagon was parked.

Lorena glanced after Chance. "I sort of wish I was going with him. I've spent so much time in saloons I actually miss the smoke and the sawdust on the floor and the smells, even though some of them aren't what you'd call pretty."

"I suppose you can go if you wish," Isabel said.

"No," Lorena replied with a faintly sad smile. "I've put that part of my life behind me, or at least I'm trying to. It's better just to forget all of that."

Ace halfway expected Isabel to make some snide comment about Lorena's checkered past, but for once the half-Irish, half-Mexican beauty didn't say anything of the sort. Maybe the time they had spent together on the trail was starting to smooth off the edges of the friction between the two women.

While the ladies climbed into the wagon, Ace checked on the horses—the team and the saddle mounts. Then he spread his bedroll under the wagon but didn't crawl into it just yet.

He wasn't going to sleep until his brother got back and he found out whether that lucky streak Chance had mentioned had actually come to pass.

* * *

From a dark, narrow passage between two buildings, Ripley Kirkwood watched Isabel as she walked with the other women from the café to the wagon. It was the first time he had laid eyes on her in several weeks, and his insides were a roiling mass of emotions.

First and foremost was anger. How dare she turn her back on all that he could offer her? A life of leisure and comfort and wealth, and all she had to do in return was devote herself to him and be willing to accommodate his . . . appetites . . . every now and then. He was well aware that at times those appetites were somewhat outside of the norm, but was that his fault?

He also felt a longing for her that was disconcerting in its strength. The fact that any woman could have such an effect on him annoyed him. He was the one who had always been in control, not the other way around. From the day he had met Isabel, though, something had changed.

He wasn't sure anymore if he could live without her, and he didn't like that. Not one bit.

The better-dressed of the two young men accompanying the mail-order brides was walking toward the saloon.

Beside Kirkwood, Lew Shelby breathed, "That son of a bitch is Chance Jensen. I haven't forgotten what happened back in Fort Worth. He's mine." Shelby looked around at the other men in the alley. "Anybody want to argue about that?"

With a note of amusement in his voice, Henry Baylor said, "I don't believe you'll have any takers, Lew. Since you have a score to settle with the youngster, feel free to go about doing it."

"I'll come with you, Lew," Prewitt volunteered.

"You reckon I'm gonna need help with one man?" Shelby asked, bristling with resentment.

Prewitt said, "No, I just figured I'd take my rifle and keep an eye on everybody else in the place to make sure they don't interfere while you deal with Jensen."

"Oh. Well then, thanks, Prewitt."

In a flat voice, the Kiowa said, "I will kill the other one. I almost did, in their hotel room back in Fort Worth, and that failure tastes bitter in my mouth."

"An excellent idea as well," Baylor agreed. "Loomis, why don't you and I accompany our Indian friend? Those ladies will probably need firm hands to control them while their protector is taken care of."

Loomis laughed in the shadows. "I like the sound of that."

Kirkwood spoke up. "What about Leon and myself?"

"Leon's job is to keep you safe, Ripley," Baylor said. "And yours is to pay us the agreed-upon price when we deliver Miss Sheridan to you."

"You'll get your money, don't worry about that," Kirkwood snapped. "But I'm a part of this—"

"Let us do our job," Baylor insisted.

"And let's get on with it," Shelby said with a growling rumble of impatience in his voice. "Those Jensen boys have needed killing for a week now. It's past time we blow 'em both to hell."

After the general store, the Devil Horse Saloon was the second-largest building in Cross Plains. It was well-furnished for a saloon in a small crossroads settlement, with a genuine hardwood bar complete with brass foot rail and a big mirror behind the bar. Wagon-wheel chandeliers with oil lamps hung over the tables that filled most of the room.

Most of those tables were for customers to sit at while drinking, but a couple were topped with green felt. There were no roulette wheels or faro layouts. The only games would be played with cards. That was all right with Chance Jensen, since he was most comfortable with the pasteboards.

One of the poker tables had a game going, but Chance went to the bar first, figuring he would get a drink and feel out the situation. The establishment wasn't very busy, since it was a weeknight. Half a dozen cowboys stood at the bar nursing beers. Four of the tables were occupied by an assortment of hombres who looked like local businessmen. Chance pegged the three men playing a leisurely game of poker as a couple ranchers and maybe the local undertaker, judging by his black suit and sober demeanor.

The man behind the bar also wore a dark suit and had a thin black mustache. His hair was plastered down, except for a strand that had escaped and curled over his forehead. He gave Chance a non-committal nod and said. "Welcome to the Devil Horse Saloon."

Chance noticed something he hadn't seen in his first glance around the room. In addition to the mirror behind the bar was a painting of a magnificent black horse in full galloping stride. He knew that had to be the animal for whom the saloon was named.

"Fine-looking horse," he commented with a nod toward the painting.

"Thank you," the man behind the bar replied. "The best friend I ever had. If you've ever been fortunate enough to have a good horse, I'm sure you can understand the feeling."

Chance thought about his gelding. The two of them had been down a lot of trails together. He nodded. "I sure do."

"What can I do for you?"

"I'll have a beer. My name is Chance Jensen, by the way."

"John O'Donnell," the man said with another nod. He drew the beer and set the mug in front of Chance. "You're new to Cross Plains, so the first one is on the house."

"I'm obliged to you, Mr. O'Donnell." Chance sipped the beer. It was cool and tasted good, so he found it quite satisfactory.

"Are you just passing through or have you come to stay?"

"Passing through, although it looks like this is a nice little settlement."

One of the cowboys farther along the bar said, "I seen this fella when he rode in, Mr. O'Donnell. He's with that wagon full of women we was talkin' about earlier."

O'Donnell cocked a dark eyebrow and repeated, "A wagon full of women? Are you thinking about opening a sporting house somewhere in the vicinity, my friend?"

The question took Chance by surprise. He actually felt himself blushing a little, which didn't happen often, at the thought of the five ladies working in a sporting house. Lorena might have done such a thing in the past, but even she had put that behind her now.

He shook his head. "No, sir. Those ladies are, well, ladies. My brother and I are escorting them to San Angelo to deliver them to their prospective husbands."

"Mail-order brides? Well, what do you know?" O'Donnell laughed. "I'm not sure we've ever had such pass through Cross Plains before. I suppose it's true what they say about there being a first time for everything."

Chance drank some more of his beer and nodded. "Yes, sir, I expect you're right. But at the moment I'm interested in playing a little poker, and it *won't* be my first time for that."

O'Donnell chuckled again. "It just so happens there's a game going on. The man in the black suit is Jacob Dawson, the undertaker here in Cross Plains. Charles Patton and Tom Cameron both own spreads here in the area."

Chance was glad that his guesses about the men playing cards had been confirmed. Being able to read your opponents and tell something about them just by looking always helped when it came to poker. "They won't mind a stranger sitting in on their game?"

"They play each other so often, I'm sure they'll regard it as a welcome challenge." O'Donnell paused, then added, "You should be aware that games at the Devil Horse are friendly and honest."

"Wouldn't have it any other way." Chance picked up his beer and walked toward the table where the men had just concluded a hand.

The undertaker, Dawson, was raking in the pot. As Chance stopped at the table, the three men looked up and gave him friendly nods.

"Gentlemen. If you don't have any objection, I'd like to sit in on your game for a while. My name is Chance Jensen."

"Are you a tinhorn gambler, young Jensen?" Dawson asked bluntly.

"No, sir. Just a man who enjoys a friendly game of cards."

"In that case, I'd say sit down and join us." Dawson glanced at the two ranchers. "Is that all right with you?"

One of them, a white-haired man with a weathered, deeply tanned face, grinned. "Fresh blood's always good for a game, son." He waved at the empty chair. "Sit down and we'll deal you in."

"The game's five-card stud," the other cattleman said.

"Sounds fine to me," Chance said as he pulled out the chair. He was about to sit when he heard the batwings at the saloon's front door squeal slightly as someone came in. He glanced over his shoulder.

Lew Shelby and the dour hardcase called Prewitt had just stepped into the room. Shelby's hand, clawlike in readiness, hung over the butt of his gun, and it was obvious he was about to draw.

In the shadows under the cottonwoods, Ace sat down with his back against the wagon's left front wheel. From there he had a good view of the Devil Horse Saloon, which was located diagonally across the street from the general store. He figured he would sit there and wait for Chance to come back before he turned in.

Through the wheel, Ace felt the wagon shift a little as the women moved around inside it, getting ready for bed. He heard the small sounds that went with the movements but didn't allow himself to think about how the ladies were clothed, or unclothed as the case might be.

The wagon shifted some more, followed by the faint thumps of feet hitting the ground as one of the women stepped down from the tailgate. "Ace?" a familiar voice said softly.

"Over here, Miss Lorena," he told her.

She walked along beside the wagon until she reached the front wheels. Ace started to get to his feet, but she waved him back down. "Land's sake, you don't have to stand up for me. I don't have any interest in formal things like that."

"Doc Monday raised Chance and me to be gentlemen. He figured our mother would have wanted it that way."

Some light from the buildings filtered into the shadows underneath the cottonwoods, enough for Ace to see that Lorena wore a robe over whatever nightclothes she had on under it.

She gathered the robe around her legs and said, "I'm going to sit down next to you." She wasn't asking his permission, just informing him what she was about to do.

They hadn't been acquainted all that long, but he knew already it wouldn't do any good to argue with her. He reached up to help her as she settled herself on the ground beside him.

"What do you know about your mother?" she went on.

"Not much. I'm pretty sure her name was Lettie, but I don't know where she was from or what she was like. Or how she wound up with Doc."

"But he's not your father."

"Nope. Well, Chance and I have debated about it, but we both finally decided that he's not. We don't know if we're bastards, to be plain-spoken about it, or if our ma was really married to a man called Jensen.

But that's our name. We've never had any real doubt about that."

"For goodness' sake, why didn't this Doc Monday just *tell* you about your parents? It seems to me like you deserve to know."

"I reckon Doc's got his reasons. We used to pester him about it when we were younger, before we figured out that it didn't do any good."

They sat there in silence for a moment before Lorena said, "You called me Miss Lorena again. I thought we had talked about that."

"Sure. Just old habits are hard to break, I guess. I'll try not to do it again."

"Well, it's not like it's a big problem or anything." Without seeming to, she shifted closer to him. Her shoulder pressed lightly against his. It was more of a companionable touch than a passionate one. "Mighty nice night tonight."

"It is," Ace agreed. "I thought I'd sit up until Chance gets back from his poker game."

"You mind the company?"

Ace thought about it, but only for a second. "Nope. I'm happy to sit here with you."

"Well, hell, I guess being friends is better than being nothing at all."

They sat there quietly again, then Ace asked, "What do you know about the man you're supposed to marry?"

"He's a doctor. Lawrence Madison. I'll be Lorena Madison."

"A fine name. I hope the two of you are very happy."

"So do I. He's . . . an older man. We won't have any children."

"Because of his age?"

"I can't," she said bluntly. "So it seemed like a good match. I won't be depriving some younger man of a family."

"I don't reckon anybody could regard being married to you as deprived."

"That's a nice thing to say, but you'd be surprised. You're still pretty young, Ace."

"You're not that much older than me," he said.

"It's not the years, necessarily, that measure such things."

Ace might have continued the conversation, but at that moment, his and Chance's horses nickered softly and tossed their heads. Ace tensed immediately. He could tell from the horses' reaction that someone was probably sneaking around over there.

"Get back in the wagon," he snapped at Lorena as he started to his feet.

"What—"

Ace was up, hand reaching for his gun. He peered intently into the shadows where the horses were picketed but didn't see anything moving except the animals. He had just closed his fingers around the butt of his Colt when a scuff of boot leather on the ground behind him warned him.

Ace whirled and brought the gun out, but he was too late. Something whistled out of the darkness and crashed into his head, sending him spinning into an oblivion deeper than the shadows under any trees.

The last thing he was aware of as he spiraled into blackness was the sharp crack of a shot.

CHAPTER THIRTY

Chance's hair-trigger instincts took over as soon as he spotted Lew Shelby and recognized the threat the gunman represented. He threw himself away from the table where the three older men sat, hoping to draw any shots away from them. At the same time, his hand flashed toward the Smith & Wesson .38 under his coat.

He wasn't fast enough.

Shelby already had his feet set and his revolver came out smooth and fast.

Chance was moving fast as flame spurted from the muzzle of Shelby's gun. The slug smacked into the top of an empty table and gouged a long furrow in it.

Chance grabbed the edge of that table with his left hand and overturned it. He yanked his gun from its holster as he dropped into a crouch behind the meager cover.

Shelby fired again. The bullet thudded into the wood but didn't go all the way through. Chance thrust his gun around the table and snapped a return shot at the gunfighter.

Shelby wasn't standing still, either. He glided to his left as Chance fired. The bullet whipped past his ear and would have struck Prewitt if he hadn't already moved.

Prewitt had a rifle in his hands and swung it from side to side as he menaced everyone else in the saloon and yelled, "Nobody move!"

He hadn't counted on the sort of man John O'Donnell was. The saloonkeeper reached under the bar and came up with a long-barreled Remington revolver.

Prewitt saw the weapon and tried to bring his Winchester to bear on the saloon owner. O'Donnell's thumb was already on the Remington's hammer. Coolly, he pulled it back and squeezed the trigger. The Remington and the Winchester blasted at the same instant.

The rifle round blazed past O'Donnell and shattered the mirror behind him into a million pieces. O'Donnell's shot was more accurate. It slammed into the upper right side of Prewitt's chest and knocked the man back a step. He struggled to stay on his feet and hang on to the rifle.

It didn't matter. The next instant several more guns thundered out a deadly volley. The guns were in the hands of the cowboys who'd been drinking peacefully at the bar. All of them were armed, a fact that Shelby and Prewitt should have taken into consideration before charging in there with killing on their minds.

Across the room, Shelby had taken cover at one end of an old piano that no one had been playing. Nor was it likely that anyone ever would again, because two shots from Chance's gun struck it and raised a racket that could hardly be called melodic.

The two ranchers who'd been playing poker were packing irons as well, and like the punchers at the bar, they weren't the sort to stand by helplessly when trouble broke out. They pulled out their guns and opened fire on Shelby. Bullets slammed into the wall above his head.

With hot lead suddenly coming at him from more than one direction, Shelby realized how badly he had miscalculated. He threw one last shot in Chance's direction, then turned and lunged toward the saloon's front window to the right of the entrance.

Chance got one more shot off and saw Shelby's black hat fly into the air, but he didn't know if his bullet had knocked the headgear off. Shelby threw himself at the glass and crashed through it to land on the saloon's narrow porch.

Chance knew his gun was empty, but something else loomed even larger in his mind. If Shelby and Prewitt were in Cross Plains, Baylor, Loomis, and the Kiowa almost certainly were, too. Ace and the ladies were probably in danger right that very minute.

Chance leaped to his feet, abandoning the cover of the overturned table, and dashed toward the entrance, thumbing fresh cartridges into the .38 as he ran.

Because Ace had been moving, the blow that knocked him out was just a glancing one. He came to his senses quickly.

Pain roared in his head, but he ignored it as he forced himself to roll over and open his eyes. He saw a couple shadowy figures swaying back and forth as they struggled. One of them probably was Lorena, since she had been with him, but he couldn't make out who the other person was.

Then someone else leaped toward him. A stray beam of light reflected off a knife blade plunging at him.

Both of Ace's hands shot up. His left closed around the wrist of the hand wielding the knife and stopped it before the blade reached him. His right caught hold of a man's muscular neck.

With a convulsive effort, Ace rolled again and heaved the attacker to the side. The man crashed into the wagon wheel where Ace had been sitting only moments earlier.

Still somewhat muddled from the blow to the head, Ace had been fighting back mostly from instinct. He scrambled to his feet in time to see the man he had just thrown aside surge up and slash at him again with the knife.

Ace caught a glimpse of the man's face as he ducked under the blade. His attacker was the Kiowa, which meant Lew Shelby and the others had to be close by. It would be one of them who was struggling with Lorena.

Ace hooked a left into the Kiowa's midsection. The Indian grunted, but the punch didn't slow him down. He backhanded the knife at Ace, who jerked out of the way just in time to keep the blade from ripping open his chest. He had to give ground as the Kiowa continued slashing at him.

Fighting for his life, Ace was only vaguely aware of gunshots coming from somewhere in Cross Plains, not too far away. He thought of Chance in the saloon, but there was no time to check on him or go to his aid. It was all Ace could do to stay out of the way of that deadly, flashing blade in the Kiowa's hand.

"Enough!"

That sharp voice halted the Kiowa's attack, at least for the moment, but he stood ready to strike again.

Ace thought he knew who had spoken. A second later he saw that he was right as Henry Baylor stepped away from the wagon with his left arm around Isabel's throat. His right pressed a gun into her side.

She wore only a thin nightdress, and her long black hair was loose around her head and shoulders. Clearly, she had been asleep when the commotion broke out, and Baylor had either dragged her out of the wagon or more likely waited in the dark until Isabel jumped down from the tailgate and gave him a chance to grab her.

"Jack," Baylor went on. "do you have her?"

"Yeah," Loomis replied. "I've got this sweet little hellcat wrapped up."

Lorena unleashed a flood of profanity as she writhed in the grip of the beefy Loomis. His arms were looped around her, and he was too strong for her to break free.

"Bitch took a shot at me!" Loomis went on. "I've got a bullet burn on my cheek, thanks to her."

"You'll live," Baylor said dryly. He raised his voice. "You other women in the wagon, come on out now. Don't try anything, or I'll hurt your friend." He looked at Ace. "The same goes for you, Jensen. Reach for your gun and I'll kill her. Jack will snap the other one's neck, for good measure."

"Aw, Henry, we can't kill 'em before we have a little fun," Loomis protested.

Baylor ignored him. "Ladies, get out here! I won't tell you again."

At the front of the wagon, Agnes poked her head out. "Take it easy, mister. We're doing what you say. There's no need to hurt anybody." She started to climb down over the driver's box.

At the same time, Molly and Jamie emerged from the rear of the wagon, at the tailgate.

Ace saw instantly what was going on and figured that Agnes had come up with the idea. Baylor couldn't watch both ends of the wagon at once, and Loomis had his hands full—literally—with Lorena. Baylor had to turn one way or the other, and when he swung toward Agnes, the other two young women suddenly broke away, bolting toward the back of the general store.

"Henry!" Loomis cried. "They're gettin' away!"

Baylor snarled and pressed the gun even harder into Isabel's side. She let out a pained yelp as he said, "Let them go. This is the one we really want."

That was interesting, but Ace didn't have time to think about it. He was keeping an eye on the Kiowa, who still looked like he wanted to spring forward at any second and plunge that knife into Ace's chest.

Running footsteps sounded nearby. Lew Shelby raced up, gun in hand.

Baylor barked at him. "Did you get the other Jensen brother?"

"I don't know," Shelby answered. "What are you doing? Kill the bastard and let's get out of here!"

A group of horses surged around the corner. Two men were riding and leading five more saddle mounts.

One of the men shouted, "Isabel! Give her to me, Baylor!"

Isabel screamed, the sort of terrified shriek that Ace

never would have expected to come from the throat of the defiant, high-spirited beauty.

As the horses crowded in and added to the confusion, the Kiowa seized the opportunity to go after Ace again. Ace was ready. His hand dipped to his gun and brought it up. Colt flame bloomed in the darkness. The Kiowa was thrown backwards by the bullet ripping into his body.

"Over there in the trees by the store!" a new voice shouted.

Shelby whirled and started shooting. The group of men who had just emerged from the saloon returned the fire. A deadly storm of lead whirled around the wagon and the men and horses nearby.

The Kiowa made a weak swipe at Ace with the knife. Ace blocked it and hammered the gun in his hand against the Kiowa's head. Buffaloed, the Indian went down and stayed there.

"Hold your fire! Hold your fire! There are women over there!" That was Chance.

The sound of his voice made a surge of relief go through Ace. His brother was still alive, at least.

The man who had shouted at Baylor to hand over Isabel brought his horse closer and reached down for her. Baylor loosened his grip on her, and that gave her a chance to reach under her nightdress and produce her dagger from somewhere.

She drove it back into Baylor's thigh. He screeched and let go of her completely. She yanked the blade loose and slashed at the hand of the mounted man who was reaching for her. He cried out in pain and jerked his hand back.

Cursing, Baylor swung his gun toward Isabel and was about to blast her at almost point-blank range.

Ace shot the gambler in the head.

It was risky, trying to make a shot like that in bad light, but Ace knew if he drilled Baylor through the body, the man might still be able to squeeze off a shot at Isabel. The only way to put him down quickly and cleanly enough to save her life was to send a bullet through his brain.

Baylor dropped to the ground as suddenly as if a giant fist had hammered him into the earth.

Isabel wasn't out of danger. The other mounted man made a grab for her, but she twisted away lithely. The man didn't pursue her, instead catching the reins of his injured companion's horse and kicking his mount into a run. Both animals thundered off into the darkness.

Ace had lost track of Lew Shelby. He swiveled around, searching for the gunman, but didn't catch sight of him. Nor did Ace see Prewitt anywhere. Jack Loomis appeared to be the only one of the bunch still on his feet.

He backed away, still holding on to Lorena so that nobody could risk a shot at him. "Everybody stay back!" he yelled. "I'm gettin' outta here, and I'm takin' this gal with me!"

"No, you're not," Chance said as he stepped out into the open with the .38 in his hand.

"Give it up, Loomis," Ace added as he moved to flank the hardcase on the other side.

They had Loomis in a crossfire, but unfortunately, Lorena was right there in the middle as well.

"Let go of me, you big ox!" she cried. "If they don't shoot you, I'll claw your eyes out!"

A threat like that wasn't very likely to make Loomis surrender, but the odds stacked against him might. He looked around wildly, his head jerking back and forth.

Not only did he have the Jensen brothers covering him, but the men who had rushed out of the saloon to see what all the shooting was about were close by, too, all of them armed and apparently eager to burn more powder.

Agnes had reached into the wagon and brought out a rifle, too, and despite the fact that she was wearing a long, thick flannel nightgown, she looked pretty formidable as she pointed the repeater at Loomis.

Ace said, "Your friends are all dead or out of the fight, except for Shelby, and it looks like he ran out on you. No sense in you getting killed, too, Loomis."

Loomis looked like he wanted to continue his defiance, but his face twisted abruptly and he said bitterly, "The hell with it." He let go of Lorena and stepped back as he shoved his hands into the air above his head.

She whirled toward him and launched an attack of her own, striking out at him and forcing him to duck and flinch.

"Get this loco bitch away from me!" he exclaimed.

Jamie and Molly reappeared from wherever they had hidden behind the store. They hurried up to Lorena and took hold of her arms. Forcing her away from Loomis wasn't easy, but after a few moments her fury seemed to subside and she allowed them to steer her toward the wagon.

Blood oozed from a couple scratches on Loomis's face.

Chance stepped up behind him and plucked the gun from the holster on Loomis's hip.

Ace pouched his iron and moved over to Isabel. "Are you all right?"

She still clutched the dagger. Breathing hard was causing her breasts to rise and fall under the thin nightdress in a distracting manner, even under the circumstances. She nodded and said, "I'm fine. I just can't believe he found me!"

"Who?"

"Ripley Kirkwood," Isabel said with a savage gleam in her eyes. "The monster I almost married!"

CHAPTER THIRTY-ONE

Cross Plains was so small that it didn't have a jail or a marshal, but Jacob Dawson, the undertaker, had a room in his business where the townspeople could lock up anybody who caused too much trouble. It was used only rarely.

That was where Jack Loomis and the Kiowa ended up, once the wound in the Kiowa's side was patched up. Dawson took care of that, too, being the closest thing the settlement had to a doctor. The Kiowa's injury was minor, and he was expected to live, but there was no guarantee of that.

As Dawson sometimes wryly observed, if he didn't get a customer's money one way, sooner or later he would get it the other.

Henry Baylor and Prewitt were at the undertaking parlor as well, but they didn't need Dawson's medical services. He would be building their coffins and planting them in the ground. Ace's bullet to Baylor's head had killed the gambler instantly, and Prewitt had been shot to pieces in the Devil Horse Saloon.

None of the women were hurt. Lorena gently probed the lump on Ace's head with her fingertips, then announced, "You'll live. You're lucky you have a thick skull, Ace."

Chance grinned. "I knew his thick-headedness would come in handy one of these days."

They were gathered around a fire Agnes had built near the wagon so that she could boil a pot of coffee. It would be a while before any of them felt like sleeping.

As they sat and sipped from tin cups, Ace asked Lorena, "Did you see what happened? Was it Loomis who knocked me out?"

"That big bald son of a bitch? Yeah, it was him, all right. He came out of nowhere and walloped you with his gun butt. Thick skull or not, I'm a little surprised you weren't hurt worse than you are. He holstered the gun and made a grab for me, but he wasn't expecting me to have a pistol with me. I got a shot off before he knocked it out of my hand and wrapped me up in that bear hug."

"I heard the shot as I passed out," Ace said. "You're pretty quick on the draw."

"Thanks, but I think I'll leave the gunfighting to somebody else. Even that close to him, I didn't manage to kill the bastard."

"I came to my senses in time to keep the Kiowa from stabbing me. It's a good thing he didn't use a gun. He could have killed me while I was still stunned."

Chance said, "He must have believed there was more honor in killing you in hand-to-hand combat."

"I wasn't really thinking about honor when I shot the varmint," Ace said.

"You saved my life when you shot that other man," Isabel said as she cradled her cup in both hands.

"Maybe. But it sounded like you were worth a lot more to Baylor alive. I reckon he was a little out of his head after you stabbed him, though. It hurt too much for him to think straight."

Silence hung over the group around the fire for a minute or so.

Then Lorena said, "Don't you think you ought to tell us what really happened here, Isabel? You're the reason some of us almost got killed."

"You blame me for the actions of a madman?" Isabel shot back.

"You could have warned us somebody was after you," Lorena insisted. "They might not have taken us by surprise."

"There's some truth to that, but it was Chance and me that Shelby and the others had a grudge against. I'm not sure how they came to throw in with those other two fellas. It seems to me there's enough blame to spread around here."

"If you want to talk about blame," Chance said, "save most of it for Shelby and his pards. None of us forced them to be killers and hardcases."

That was certainly true. Ace still wanted to know the story behind the shocking statement Isabel had made earlier. "How about it, Isabel?"

She sighed and then slowly nodded her head. "I told you, the man's name is Ripley Kirkwood. He is from New Orleans, like me. Because his father is very wealthy, Ripley has always felt that he can do whatever he wants without anyone daring to deny him. Anyone foolish enough to try will be crushed, either by his father's money or Ripley's own cruelty."

"You knew that, and you agreed to marry him anyway?" Ace asked.

"I did *not* know," Isabel said forcefully. "Oh, I knew his father was rich and that Ripley had a reputation for being . . . colorful . . . and perhaps a bit dangerous. But he can also be quite charming when he wishes, and there are many young women from fine families who are eager for his attention. When he began pursuing me . . . it did not take him long to conquer any resistance I might have put up." She paused. "I was not just another conquest for him, though. He asked me to marry him. I was surprised, but I agreed. Then, as the date of our wedding drew near, I began to see"—she stopped again as a shudder went through her—"I began to see more clearly what he is really like. The way he treated me when we were alone together became less affectionate and more . . . violent."

"There are plenty of fellas who like it rough, honey," Lorena said. "Sorry to be so plain-spoken about it, but it's the truth."

Isabel shook her head. "This was more than that. I began to hear rumors that sometimes Ripley engaged the services of young women, and that some of these women . . . did not survive the encounter."

"How terrible," Jamie murmured. "I never heard of such a thing!"

"Count yourself lucky," Lorena said. "I've heard that and worse, plenty of times."

Chance said, "So once you found out what this fella Kirkwood is really like, you told him you weren't going to marry him after all?"

"That's right," Isabel said, nodding. "It angered him that I was breaking off our engagement, and then I saw that all the rumors were true. In his fury, he could have killed me right then and there. I had gone to his home to tell him, and I believed I might never get out of there alive. He grabbed my arm, threw me in a room, and locked the door."

She looked down as the terrible memory of her fear kept her from continuing for a moment. When she could speak again, she said, "Later, someone unlocked the door. One of his servants who took pity on me, I suspect. It was the middle of the night and the house was asleep. I was able to sneak out without being caught. I went back to my home, gathered up a few possessions and what money I had, and then I left New Orleans. That was months ago, and I've been fleeing ever since. I thought I had gotten far enough away, and enough time had passed, that Ripley would never find me." She laughed, but there was no humor in the sound. "Clearly, I was wrong."

With her story concluded, again the group was silent.

Finally Ace said, "I'm sorry you had to go through all of that."

"But you still should have warned us," Lorena added. "You couldn't be sure Kirkwood couldn't find you."

Isabel glared at her. "You of all people should understand that sometimes you just want to bury your past and never unearth it again."

Lorena shrugged but didn't say anything else.

Ace asked, "Who was that big hombre with Kirkwood, the one who hustled him away after you slashed his hand open?"

"Leon," Isabel replied. "That is the only name I ever heard him called. He takes care of Ripley. Cleans up his messes, I suppose you could say. He's a terrible man. I don't think he ever feels anything. Ripley mentioned once that he used to be a prizefighter, but that's all I know about him—other than that he frightens me a great deal."

"So he's alive," Chance said. "Kirkwood's alive, and as far as we know, so is Lew Shelby. The three of them are still out there, just like the three men who kidnapped Molly and the rest of that Fairweather bunch. Somebody's going to be dogging our trail all the way to San Angelo!"

Lorena looked at Jamie and Agnes. "Do you two have any old enemies who might be trailing us, too?"

"I swear, I don't have an enemy in the world," Agnes said.

"Neither do I," Jamie said. "And it's not Molly's fault those men carried her off before."

Molly just looked down into her coffee cup and didn't say anything. Ace figured the memories of that ordeal were bothering her, and he wished Jamie hadn't brought it up.

Isabel frowned at Lorena. "What about you?"

"What about me?" the honey-blonde snapped back.

"Is anyone seeking vengeance on you?"

"Not a damned soul, honey. I may not have lived the most righteous life anybody ever did, but I haven't cheated or robbed or killed anybody. I don't have to worry about any jilted lovers, either."

Isabel sniffed.

Before she could add anything, Ace said, "Why don't we all turn in and try to get some rest? I know probably nobody's that sleepy, but we need to cover some more ground tomorrow."

"That's right," Chance said. "With everything that's hanging fire, the sooner you ladies make it to San Angelo and get hitched to your new husbands, the better it'll be for everybody."

Lorena said, "You mean it'll be our husbands' problem, not yours."

"I mean that San Angelo's a good-sized town with an army post, and there's bound to be some local law, too. Anybody who's chasing any of you will have to think twice about bothering you there. That Kirkwood fella, for instance, will probably just give up and go back to New Orleans."

"I wish that were true," Isabel said, "but a madman seldom gives up. And I believe that Ripley Kirkwood is truly mad."

Kirkwood cursed bitterly as Leon tightened the makeshift bandage around his right hand. Isabel had laid the palm open to the bone when she slashed him, and it hurt like hell. The wound had also bled a great deal, and he was still a little lightheaded. Mostly, though, he was just angry. Lew Shelby and the others were supposed to be dangerous men, and yet they hadn't been able to deal with two youngsters and a handful of women.

Kirkwood and Leon were in the gap between the two hills so that the one to the east shielded their campfire from being spotted in the settlement. It probably wasn't a good idea to stop that close to town, but they had needed a place where Leon could patch up his employer's hand before Kirkwood lost even more blood.

On the other side of the fire, Lew Shelby hunkered on his heels and nipped at a flask of whiskey he had taken from his saddlebags. He had come running up as Leon was leading the horses out of town and grabbed one of the mounts.

Of the five gunmen, Shelby was the only one who had escaped from the unexpected gun battle. Leon had seen Henry Baylor killed, and Shelby claimed that Prewitt was dead, too, killed in the saloon when they confronted Chance Jensen. None of them knew what had happened to Jack Loomis and the Kiowa. It was possible Shelby was the only survivor.

"You could use a doctor," Leon told Kirkwood as he finished tying up the bandage he'd cut from one of Kirkwood's clean shirts. "That wound needs stitches."

Kirkwood moved his hand back and forth. It hurt like blazes. "You bandaged it so tightly it should be fine. I'll see a doctor once we have Isabel."

Shelby looked up from the flames. He had been glaring into them while he sipped the whiskey. "You're still going after that girl?"

"I set out to bring her to her senses or to see to it that she paid the price for turning her back on me. I don't intend to give up on that goal now."

"But there are only three of us left!" Shelby dragged the back of his free hand across his mouth. "Henry dead, Prewitt dead, Jack and the Kiowa, too, for all we know. I still don't know how the hell that happened."

"You were too confident and overplayed your hand," Kirkwood said coolly as he tried to ignore the pain in his hand. "Instead of splitting up, you should have stayed together and concentrated on the wagon. Ace Jensen wouldn't have been able to fight off all five of you."

Shelby grimaced. "If we'd all gone for Ace, Chance would have come running and hit us from behind. It was smarter to try to take care of both of them at the same time."

"Yes, well, we can all see just how well *that* worked out." Kirkwood held up his hand with the bloodstained strips of cloth tied around it and cocked an eyebrow mockingly. The loss of his shirt was also damned annoying.

"They'll be going south toward Coleman," Leon said. "It'll still take them at least two days to make it to San Angelo, maybe three. We'll have time to pick up their trail and try again."

Shelby said, "You'll have to do it without me."

"Lost your nerve, eh?" Kirkwood said.

The gunman's face darkened with rage as he uncoiled from his position by the fire. His hand moved toward his gun, but he stopped before his fingers curled around the Colt's ivory grips.

Leon had moved smoothly to put himself between Shelby and Kirkwood. The big man's hand was already inside his coat. He probably wasn't as slick on the draw as Shelby, but anything less than a perfect shot would leave him on his feet long enough to get lead into the gunfighter.

"All right, damn it," Shelby spat. "There's no point in us fighting among ourselves." He paused. "Come to think of it, the rest of the money you owed us won't have to be split five ways now."

"The money you'll receive only if we're successful in our mission," Kirkwood said. "Don't forget that."

"Yeah, yeah. Sure." Shelby put the cork back in the flask and shoved it into his pocket. "We'll pick up the trail tomorrow. We've still got time to get our hands on that girl for you—and to settle the score with those damned Jensen boys."

CHAPTER THIRTY-TWO

By the next morning, a rider had already been sent to Baird, the county seat of Callahan County, to ask that the sheriff send some deputies to collect the prisoners and charge them with attempted murder and kidnapping.

In the meantime, Jack Loomis and the Kiowa would remain locked up at Dawson's undertaking parlor. The money that the Kiowa had stolen from Ace and Chance back in Fort Worth was not in the saddlebags on any of the gang's horses that were recovered, so the Jensen brothers sadly figured that two hundred dollars was long gone.

Lew Shelby was still unaccounted for. Ace figured he had gotten away, along with Ripley Kirkwood and Leon, and his gut instinct told him they had not seen the last of any of those three.

After breakfast at the café, Ace and Chance were getting the team and the wagon ready to go when Dawson walked up. "I'm sorry your stay in Cross Plains wasn't more pleasant, folks."

"You don't have anything to apologize for, sir," Ace

told him. "We're grateful for the way everyone pitched in to help us."

"Well, I suppose we could have gotten up a posse and gone after the three who got away," Dawson mused. "But that seems more like a job for the sheriff. We're not really lawmen, just citizens trying to do the right thing."

"Folks like that are the most important ones in the country. Without them, we wouldn't even *have* a nation."

Dawson nodded. "You're probably right." He stuck out his hand. "Good luck to you."

Ace and Chance shook hands with the undertaker. He then tipped his hat to the ladies as they climbed into the wagon and Agnes took her usual seat on the driver's box. The Jensen brothers swung into their saddles, and a minute later the group was headed southwest out of the settlement.

The town of Coleman was about a day's travel in that direction. They would make it by evening, if nothing else happened to delay them.

If they were being honest with themselves, Ace and Chance would have had to admit they were surprised when the day passed peacefully. They didn't run into any ambushes, and despite Chance's frequent attempts to spot anyone on their trail, there didn't seem to be any pursuit behind them.

"If they're coming after us, they're hanging way back," he told Ace late that afternoon as they approached the settlement.

"Maybe they've gotten tired of banging their heads against a stone wall," Ace suggested. "That has to be what it feels like to them."

"Maybe. But if that Kirkwood gent is as loco as Isabel makes him out to be, it's hard to imagine him just turning around and going home. And we *know* that Lew Shelby, if he's still alive, is carrying a mighty big grudge against us."

Ace knew his brother was right. Ripley Kirkwood and Lew Shelby still represented a threat, and they would until the wagon and its passengers reached San Angelo.

Coleman was a little bigger than Cross Plains and had several saloons, but Chance wasn't tempted by them. After everything that had happened, he had decided to stick close to his brother and the ladies for the rest of the journey, and Ace was glad of that.

Nothing unusual happened that night, nor the next day as the wagon rolled on toward Hutchins City, the last settlement before they reached San Angelo. All the trouble they had encountered didn't exactly fade from anyone's memory, but at least those two days of uneventful, even monotonous, travel made the ladies relax a little.

"This is how I expected it to be when we set out from Fort Worth," Agnes commented from the driver's box as Ace and Chance rode alongside late that afternoon. "I never thought we would run into so much . . . excitement."

"And by excitement you mean folks trying to kill us . . . at least Ace and me," Chance responded with a grin.

"Well . . . yes."

"Don't worry, we're used to it."

"How in the world do you ever get used to people shooting at you?"

"You don't," Ace said. "Don't listen to him. There's nothing more nerve-wracking than hearing bullets zipping around your ears."

Chance said, "You just have to keep a cool, steady head. That's what gives you your best odds of surviving."

"I believe that," Agnes said. "I'd just as soon not be put in that position, though."

"Believe me, we feel the same way," Ace said.

The glance the Jensen brothers exchanged made it clear how unlikely they considered that possibility.

Neither of them saw the figure intently watching the wagon from behind a screen of mesquite on top of a ridge three hundred yards away. The copper-skinned, buckskin-clad young man had been keeping an eye on the wagon for the past couple hours. His keen eyesight allowed him to keep his distance so he wouldn't be noticed.

During that time he had seen the wagon stop and its occupants climb out to move around. The watcher expected to see men, but all the travelers appeared to be women except for the two outriders.

And not *old* women, either. Sunlight reflected on fair hair, red hair, glossy dark hair. They did not hide their glories under bonnets like so many of the settler women did. The graceful way they walked also testified to their youth. Even at that distance, the watcher found them very pleasant to look upon.

Up close—close enough to touch—they would be even better. He was certain of that.

The wagon was near the settlement and would reach it soon. If that was their final destination, there was nothing the watcher and his companions could do about it. They numbered only fifteen men, led by the war chief Swift Pony.

Three weeks earlier, in the dead of night, they had

ridden away from the despised reservation up in what the whites called Indian Territory. Swift Pony and his warriors called it a prison, and they had been happy to escape from it.

Since then they had made their way far south into Texas, lying low during the days, never showing themselves unless they came across some isolated farm or ranch where they could kill all the inhabitants and loot their belongings without being discovered.

The young man watching the wagon had been sent out by Swift Pony to see if he could find any more suitable targets for their wrath. The scout knew that Swift Pony longed for a real battle with the soldiers, but he was also wise enough not to throw away his life, and the lives of his men, on a fight they could not win.

Eventually they might raid all the way into Mexico. They might be killed along the way, but at least they would have known what it was like to ride free again, as their ancestors had done.

And maybe, if they could take those women with them and actually cross the border where they would be safe, they could find a new home. Could raise fine sons to carry on the war against the invaders. It was a happy thing to think about.

But first, the watcher told himself as he drifted back away from the crest and then turned to run to his horse, Swift Pony had to know about that lightly defended wagon full of women just ripe for the taking.

Riding through a gap with brushy, boulder-littered slopes on both sides, Earl Brock drew his lips drew back from his teeth as he grimaced at every jolt and sway of his horse's gait. The movements made pain stab through his wounded right arm, which was bandaged and tied against his body to keep it stable.

Cooper had done a pretty good job of cleaning up all the blood and then dousing the bullet holes with whiskey to make sure they didn't fester. The slug had gone clean through, tearing up muscle but luckily missing the bone.

The injury would heal in time, although that arm might not ever regain its full strength. It was Brock's gun arm, too, and that was bad. He could shoot fairly well with his left hand, but he was thinking about starting to carry a sawed-off shotgun, just to make the odds a little more on his side.

That was a worry for the future, he told himself. He had to concentrate on catching up to Molly and getting that fifty grand back.

"How you doin', Earl?" Hawthorne asked. He and Cooper flanked Brock, one on each side.

He figured they were worried he might pass out and topple from the saddle. Having them believe he was that weak annoyed the hell out of him. "I'm fine," he snapped, "but I'll be a hell of a lot better once we get that damned loot back."

"Yeah, we've come a long way on Molly's trail," Cooper said. "She's led us a merry chase."

"Nothing merry about it."

"Well, no, I reckon not. I just meant—"

"That's far enough!" a voice called from the left, taking the three outlaws by surprise. A second later a rifle cracked and a bullet kicked up dirt from the trail ten feet in front of them.

The men yanked their horses to a stop. Cooper and Hawthorne grabbed for their guns. Brock couldn't slap leather, and the frustration and anger he felt made him cuss a blue streak.

Before Cooper and Hawthorne could clear their holsters, another shot blasted, coming from the right. Cooper flinched as the slug sizzled past, inches from his ear.

"Next one goes right through your head," warned a voice as cold as the grave. "Leave those guns alone."

"Damn it!" Cooper exclaimed. "Those Jensen boys have ambushed us!"

Except for the fading echoes of the shots, silence hung over the gap for a long moment.

Then the rifleman on the left called out. "What did you say, mister?"

"Those aren't the Jensens," Brock said. "They sound like older men."

"Keep your hands away from your guns and don't get spooked," the cold-voiced hombre on the right warned again. "We're stepping out into the open."

Armed with Winchesters pointing at Brock, Cooper, and Hawthorne, one man on each slope stepped out of the brush. The man on the left was dressed all in black range clothes, and his lean, lantern-jawed face had an evil cast to it.

The one on the right wore a gray suit and bowler hat. Jug-handle ears stuck out from a blocky, expressionless face. He moved closer, the rifle rock-steady in his hands. "What's your connection to Ace and Chance Jensen?"

"I'd like to see both of those sons of bitches dead," Brock said.

"They ain't friends of ours," Cooper added. "I'm hopin' the same goes for you fellas, seein' as how you've got the drop on us and all."

"If you are working with the Jensens," Brock said. "you'd better go ahead and shoot us. But there's two of you and three of us, so don't go thinking it'll be easy, even with this wounded arm of mine. At least one of us will get lead in you."

The man in black laughed. "That's mighty big talk for a man with a busted gun arm."

"It's not busted. And I've got two arms."

The man in the suit said, "That's enough bravado from both of you. We're not friends of the Jensen brothers. In fact, we have scores to settle with them."

"So do we," Cooper said with a note of excitement in his voice.

"And they have something we want," Brock added flatly.

"Same here." The cold-voiced gent lowered the barrel of his rifle a little. "It sounds to me like you need to have a talk with my boss. It might be a good strategic move for us to join forces."

"What the hell, Leon," the man in black said. "What makes you think we can trust these hombres?"

For the first time, a trace of an expression appeared on the stony face of the man called Leon. It *might* have been a smile. Maybe.

"Because I know a killer when I see one," he said, "and we all want those Jensen boys dead."

CHAPTER THIRTY-THREE

Hutchins City was located on the Colorado River, but the citizens had built a bridge over the stream. Fording it with the wagon wasn't necessary. The settlement was hardly worthy of being called a city at the moment, but as the Jensen brothers and the ladies entered it at twilight, they saw that quite a few new lots had been staked out. Evidently the place was growing.

The garrulous proprietor of the livery stable where they put up their horses and parked the wagon was glad to explain what was going on. "Railroad's comin' through in the next year or so. They're talkin' people into movin' here. They got it in mind that they'll make Hutchins City the county seat, 'stead of over to Runnels. Of course, there ain't no tellin' how the folks in Runnels will feel about that. Chances are, they won't cotton to it. I'm hopin' it won't come down to a shootin' war. That happens sometimes, you know, when two towns commence to arguin' over which one should be the county seat."

"Really?" Agnes said in disbelief.

"Oh, yes, ma'am. Civic pride is a powerful thing."

Lorena said, "The two settlements aren't going to start shooting at each other tonight, are they?"

"Ain't likely. I reckon it'll be a spell before the fussin' gets too bad."

"Well, we'll be long gone by then, thank goodness."

"Where are you ladies headed?" The middle-aged man had cast quite a few admiring glances at the five young women, but at least he tried to be somewhat discreet about it.

"We're going to San Angelo," Jamie said.

"Oh." A worried-looking frown creased the stableman's forehead under his mostly bald pate.

Ace saw the reaction and asked, "Is that a problem?"

"No, probably not. It's just that we been hearin' rumors there might be some renegade Injuns in these parts. You couldn't prove it by me, mind you. There ain't been nothin' of the sort right here around town, but I heard that some fella was talkin' about how a few ranches had been hit northeast of here."

"Savage Indians," Jamie breathed. "My father warned me about that. He thought I was crazy to come here to start with, and that was one of the things he brought up."

The stableman waved a hand. "You shouldn't have to worry, missy. Might not be anything to those rumors. You know how folks like to talk, and what they gossip about ain't always true. Anyway, there are patrols from Fort Concho out and about, and that ought to keep those redskins spooked enough so they'll steer clear o' these parts. Assumin' there really are any redskins lookin' for trouble."

As they walked away from the stable, Isabel said, "If that man was trying to reassure us, he did not succeed very well."

"As if we didn't have enough to worry about already," Lorena said, "what with gunfighters and that madman from New Orleans and whoever those ruffians were who grabbed Molly."

"Don't forget the Fairweathers," Agnes said.

"Thanks," Lorena replied dryly. "Wouldn't want to forget about a family of crazy hillbillies."

"We've had a lot on our plate so far," Ace said, "but we've dealt with all of it."

"And we'll keep on dealing with it," Chance said. "That's what you hired us for."

"You've earned your money," Agnes told him. "We never would have made it this far without the two of you."

"That's right," Jamie added. "We owe you both so much."

"Save your thanks until we get to San Angelo," Ace said.

"One more day," Chance said.

Leaving the post oak country behind, the terrain was even flatter and covered with scrub brush, clumps of hardy grass, and an occasional stand of small, gnarled mesquite trees. There were fewer creeks. Here and there in the distance, mesas thrust up from the flats, punctuating the vast openness. The sky was incredibly blue overhead, and the drier air heated quickly as the sun rose into that blue vault.

Late in the morning of what Ace hoped would be their last day on the trail, he spotted a haze of dust hanging in the air ahead of them. He pointed it out to Chance, who was riding on the other side of the wagon. "What do you think of that?"

Before Chance could answer, Agnes asked, "Think of what?"

Chance said, "He's talking about that dust up in front of us."

"What dust? You mean . . . Oh, wait, I think I see it. Should we be worried about it?"

"It would take a herd of cattle on the move to raise that much dust . . . or a big group of riders," Chance said. "Cattle wouldn't bother me."

"But if it's a bunch of men on horseback, we need to find out who they are before we can tell what we need to do about it," Ace said. "Let's stop for a minute."

Agnes hauled back on the reins and brought the team to a halt. Ace reached into his saddlebags and brought out a pair of field glasses, which he lifted to his eyes and used to study the landscape in the distance.

After a couple minutes that seemed longer, he lowered the glasses and heaved a sigh of relief. "It's a cavalry patrol. I was able to make out the guidon and their uniforms, so I'm sure of it."

The women inside the wagon were looking out past Agnes.

Jamie said excitedly, "Soldiers?"

"Maybe they can give us an escort into San Angelo," Lorena suggested.

"I don't know," Ace said. "It looks like they're headed in this direction instead of back toward the post. They might not be able to turn around and return to San Angelo just yet, at least not without going against their orders."

"Well, at least we know it's not a bunch of outlaws or Comanches waiting to attack us," Chance said. "Maybe whoever's in command can tell us more about what to expect between here and the settlement."

Agnes slapped the reins and clucked to the team to get the horses moving again. The dust cloud in front of them grew bigger and more distinct, and it wasn't long until Ace and Chance could make out the dark shapes of the riders at the base of the cloud.

A short time after that, the blue uniforms became visible to the naked eye, as did the colorful guidon at the top of a staff carried by one of the soldiers. The regimental pennant fluttered a little as the hot wind tugged at it.

The sun was almost directly overhead. They needed to call a halt to rest the horses and eat a midday meal, which would be a bit on the sparse side because their supplies were getting pretty low.

With that in mind, when the troopers had closed to within a quarter of a mile, Ace signaled for Agnes to go ahead and stop. They would wait for the soldiers to come to them, which was obviously what they were doing. Ace was sure someone in the patrol had spotted them and pointed out the wagon to the commanding officer.

Three soldiers nudged their mounts ahead of the others and came on at a faster pace. A man wearing a black hat was in the lead, trailed on either side by two men in campaign caps. The man leading the way was probably the officer in charge of the patrol.

He was a young, fair-haired lieutenant, they saw as the man rode closer. Handsome and a little sunburned, he looked like he hadn't been out on the frontier for very long.

The troopers with him were both black. Buffalo soldiers, they had come to be called, because the Indians compared their hair to that of the buffalo. One was a stocky, middle-aged man with a lot of gray under his campaign cap and sergeant's stripes on his sleeve. The other was a private, much younger and leaner.

Ace and Chance had moved ahead of the wagon and thumbed their hats back. They sat easy in the saddle as the soldiers rode up to them. The lieutenant called a halt and said pleasantly. "Good morning, gentlemen. Or is it afternoon already? With the sun at its zenith, it's difficult to be certain."

"I think it may be afternoon," Ace said with a smile. Even though the officer hadn't asked their names, he introduced himself and his brother. "I'm Ace Jensen. This is my brother Chance."

"Lieutenant Benjamin Wingate, at your service." He looked past the Jensen brothers at the wagon, and his friendly smile got bigger and friendlier.

The ladies had that effect on just about everybody of the male persuasion.

Wingate took his hat off and held it over his heart. "Ladies."

Chance didn't say anything about his real name being Benjamin, just like the lieutenant. He hardly ever thought of himself that way anymore. "You and your men are out on patrol, Lieutenant?"

Wingate put his hat on again. "That's right. And you are . . . ?"

"Escorting these ladies to San Angelo," Ace said.

"You're opening some sort of, ah, establishment . . . ?"

From the wagon, Lorena asked sharply, "Do we look like a bunch of whores to you, Lieutenant?"

"N-no, ma'am. Of course not," Wingate stammered. "I merely meant . . . a group of ladies traveling together . . . in the company of two men—"

"At least he didn't call us whoremongers," Chance said to Ace.

"I reckon we can be glad for that," Ace replied dryly.

Jamie slipped past Agnes on the seat and climbed down from the wagon, gripping the wheel to help her down. Her feet hit the ground, and she turned toward the others.

"All of you, stop picking on the lieutenant! You're embarrassing him." She strolled boldly past Ace and Chance, stopped, and smiled up at Wingate. "My name is Jamie Gregory, Lieutenant, and I'm very pleased to meet you."

"The pleasure is all mine, Miss Gregory, I assure you. It is *Miss* Gregory?"

"That's right. None of us are married. Yet."

"Oh. You mean—"

"We're mail-order brides," Agnes said from the driver's box.

"I see." Wingate still looked a little flustered. "And you two gentlemen are escorting the ladies to meet their betrothed?"

"That's about the size of it," Ace said. "Are you out here from Fort Concho chasing renegades?"

Being reminded of his mission distracted Wingate from his obviously impressed inspection of the ladies. He looked at Ace and nodded. "You've heard rumors that there are hostiles abroad in the vicinity, I take it?"

"We've heard rumors," Ace confirmed, "but we haven't run into any of them, thank goodness."

Chance asked, "Where are you from, Lieutenant?"

"Rhode Island," Wingate answered. "What does that matter?"

"It doesn't. You just don't sound like any of the Texans we've run into down here."

"You didn't answer my question about scouting for Indians, Lieutenant," Ace pointed out.

Grimly, Wingate said, "The stories you've heard aren't just rumors, Mr. Jensen. Several weeks ago, a band of Comanche renegades led by a self-styled war chief called Swift Pony left the reservation in Indian Territory. They've managed to dodge all pursuit so far, and their depredations have been, ah, quite extreme."

"How extreme?" Chance asked.

Wingate looked at Jamie, who still stood nearby beaming up at him, and then at the other women. "I hesitate to go into the particulars . . ."

"Go ahead, Lieutenant," Lorena said. "We're all grown women, and speaking for myself, I'd like to know just how bad it is."

The others nodded and murmured agreement.

Wingate took a deep breath. "Very well. So far the renegades have murdered seventeen settlers—men, women, and children—and unless someone stops them, I've no doubt they plan to carry on with their bloody-handed rampage until they've spilled blood all the way across Texas!"

CHAPTER THIRTY-FOUR

Since it was the middle of the day anyway, Lieutenant Wingate told his sergeant to have the men fall out and prepare a meal then stood beside his horse and smiled at the women, all of whom had gotten out of the wagon after he'd made his chilling prediction.

"I'd invite you to share our rations, ladies, but we can't really spare any, and besides, I'm sure you'd find it very unappetizing fare. Hardtack and salt pork are hardly the sort of fine victuals that ladies such as yourselves must be accustomed to."

"You might be surprised what some of us have had to make do with, mister," Lorena told him. "But we have our own supplies, and they'll last us until we make it to San Angelo."

"I would advise you to proceed there as quickly as possible. A group of women, traveling by yourselves, would be a very tempting target should those renegades become aware of you."

Ace and Chance had been watering the horses, but they walked up in time to hear Wingate's comment.

Chance said, "Wait just a minute, Lieutenant. The

ladies aren't traveling alone. My brother and I are escorting them."

Wingate smiled rather smugly. "Of course, but there are only the two of you. Swift Pony has more than a dozen men with him. You'd hardly be any match for them."

"You might be surprised," Ace said.

"And we can fight, too," Agnes put in. "We have a couple rifles in the wagon."

"That's fine," Wingate said, "but your best defense is still to reach civilization as soon as possible. With the fort right there, the savages will never attack San Angelo."

Ace felt an instinctive dislike for Wingate. The lieutenant from Rhode Island was young and inexperienced, but that didn't stop him from being priggish and arrogant.

Despite that, Ace also knew that Wingate was right. The sooner they got to San Angelo, the better.

Ace built a small fire, then Agnes put a pot of coffee on to boil and broke out some biscuits left over from their breakfast that morning.

Jamie went up to Wingate. "Lieutenant, why don't *you* join *us* for lunch? We'd be very happy to have your company."

"I wouldn't want to impose . . ."

Lorena said, "We don't have that much extra food, Jamie."

The young blonde took the rebuke in stride, but the smile she turned on Wingate never lost any of its brilliance. "You could at least have a cup of coffee with us." She turned her head and her tone sharpened a little as she added, "We have plenty of coffee, don't we, Lorena?"

"We have plenty of coffee," Lorena replied, her own voice a bit tighter.

Wingate didn't seem to notice as he smiled. "In that case, I'd love to have a cup with you, Miss Gregory."

Chance blew out a breath, turned away, and walked around to the other side of the wagon. Ace trailed after him, and when they were out of sight of the others, Chance flung out his hands and said under his breath, "Did you see the way she's playing up to him? She's engaged to be married, and yet she's practically throwing herself at his feet!"

"You're talking about Jamie and Wingate."

"Of course. From the moment those soldiers rode up, she's been staring at him like a kid looking at a piece of candy, or a dog that wants a hambone." Chance grunted. "Hambone. There's a good name for the damned stuffed-shirt, eastern—"

"Take it easy," Ace advised his brother. He tried not to grin, which likely would have made things worse, but he couldn't resist saying, "Jamie's looking at Lieutenant Wingate pretty much the same way you've been looking at her ever since you first laid eyes on her in Fort Worth."

"What? That's not true! I've never been less than a gentleman—"

"A gentleman who's been licking his chops."

Chance's eyes narrowed. "Who the hell's side are you on here?"

"No side. Jamie's a mighty pretty girl, and nobody's going to blame you for thinking so. Agnes seems to think you're nice to look at, too, and Jamie feels that way about the lieutenant."

"Don't forget the way Lorena feels about you," Chance snapped.

"We seem to have gotten past that," Ace said. "I reckon we're just friends now."

Chance blew out another disgusted breath. "I'll just be glad when Wingate goes on his way and we can get on to San Angelo."

"If we run into any of those renegades, we might be wishing the lieutenant and the rest of those soldiers were still around," Ace pointed out. "Anyway, that rancher Jamie is supposed to marry is probably waiting for her in town. By the end of the day, she'll be with him. There was never going to be anything between the two of you."

Chance sighed. "I know that. I just hate to see her spending the rest of our time together mooning over that damn soldier boy." He laughed. "As for the Indians . . . you've seen him, Ace. How much good do you think a greenhorn like Wingate would be in a fight with the Comanches?"

"I don't know. That sergeant looks like he's been to see the elephant a time or two. And the rest of his troops seem pretty good."

"Wingate's probably a glory-hunter. I hope he doesn't get them all killed."

Ace scanned the seemingly empty landscape around them and thought about how many threats might be out there, unseen but still ready to strike. He hoped all of them made it through the rest of the day.

Chance glared at Lieutenant Wingate while the young officer drank some of the coffee Agnes had brewed and ate rations from his own pack. Jamie continued to be very attentive to him and questioned him about his army career, which as Ace suspected, hadn't been very extensive. Fort Concho was his first posting since graduating from West Point.

Not surprisingly, Wingate's father turned out to be a wealthy businessman with political influence back in Rhode Island. That was how he had gotten into West Point to start with.

Jamie hung on his every word, laughed whether what he said was amusing or not, and generally annoyed the hell out of Chance. Ace thought that was entertaining, and judging by the twinkle in her eyes, so did Agnes. She even smiled when she and Ace exchanged a glance, as if their amusement over Chance's discomfiture was a shared secret.

However, Ace wasn't sad to see the meal finished and the cavalry patrol ready to move out. It would take the rest of the day to reach San Angelo. Evening might fall before they got there.

While the sergeant was getting the rest of the men back into their saddles, Lieutenant Wingate stood holding his horse's reins. He took off his hat and told the women, "I truly wish I could accompany you and make sure you arrive safely at your destination. Unfortunately, to do so would be disregarding my orders, and I cannot do that."

"We understand, Lieutenant," Jamie said. "You have your duty, and you must do it." She stepped forward, put a hand on his arm, went up on her toes, and kissed his cheek. "Godspeed to you, and stay safe."

Wingate looked a little flustered but very pleased. "Thank you, Miss Gregory. I'll carry the memory of your beauty and graciousness with me, and I'm sure that will help me triumph over any adversity."

Mounted on his gelding near the front of the wagon team, Chance blew out a disgusted breath. He appeared to be on the verge of saying something, but Ace, mounted on the chestnut next to him, caught his brother's eye and shook his head.

Wingate put on his hat, swung into the saddle, and rode to the head of the column. He lifted a gauntleted hand and waved it forward in a signal to move out.

The soldiers rode off to the northeast. The wagon headed west toward San Angelo. Ace and Chance rode a hundred yards in front of the vehicle.

After a while, without looking over at Ace, Chance said, "Did I act like that? Has it really been that obvious?"

"The way you feel about Jamie, you mean?" Ace shrugged. "I noticed it, and I know Agnes did, too. Can't speak for the other ladies, but I wouldn't be surprised."

"So what you're saying is that I've been a damned fool."

"Because you think Jamie's mighty pretty and you let yourself get infatuated with her?" Ace laughed and shook his head. "Shoot, *I* think she's really pretty. I didn't fall for her or anything like that, but I've got eyes in my head, just like you do. And there's nothing wrong with being attracted to somebody. You haven't been *too* big a pest about it, I reckon."

Chance laughed, too, ruefully. "I guess it's a good thing we'll be there soon, and I won't have to worry about being tempted anymore. Right now I think I'll fall back and see how things look behind us."

Thinking about Ripley Kirkwood, Lew Shelby, the Fairweathers, and the mysterious trio that had abducted Molly, Ace nodded. "That's a good idea."

Chance turned his horse and peeled off, then rode back past the wagon with a wave for Agnes on the driver's seat and the other four ladies in the back with the canvas cover rolled up on the sides. They returned the wave.

Ace kept his eyes turned to the front, frowning slightly as he studied a narrow dark line that meandered in a zigzag fashion from north to south. That was probably a dry wash, he decided. They had crossed several such during the morning. They'd had to search for places where the banks had caved in and created slopes gentle enough for the wagon to handle. Sometimes that meant scouting back and forth for a while until a suitable spot was located.

Ace hoped this one wouldn't delay them too long.

Swift Pony lay against the bank, his head lifted just enough for him to peer over the edge at the rider coming toward him. Behind him, waiting tensely for his signal, were the rest of his men. They held their ponies and kept hands over the animals' noses so they wouldn't make any noise and alert the whites.

The wash was just deep enough to conceal the ponies. The war party had followed its twists and turns for more than a mile to get in position for the impending ambush. The wagon full of women and the two white men were almost there.

Swift Pony glanced over his shoulder. The young scout, Hornet, looked up with an eager expression. He had never known real battle before. He had been too young to fight when the soldiers came to Palo Duro Canyon and slaughtered the horse herd and broke the back of the Comanche people. Since then, he had known only the play fighting on the reservation, the struggles of the young men who hoped to one day use the skills to kill the enemy.

Hornet would finally get his chance to do that.

Swift Pony checked one more time to see how close the quarry had come then he slid back down the bank to join the others. "Get ready," he told them.

A few yards away the bank had washed out during one of the infrequent flash floods that roared through the arroyo. The men would be able to ride their ponies out of the wash there, three or four at a time.

"We are ready," Hornet said. "Soon the white men will be dead and the white women will be ours."

One of the other warriors, an older man known as Broken Branch, made a noise of disgust. "White women. Soft and ugly. They will bear weak sons."

"And we will make those sons strong," Swift Pony said. "Strong enough to come back someday and drive the intruders from all the land where the Comanche should roam free."

"You believe this?" Broken Branch said.

In truth, Swift Pony did not believe. But he also did not believe that his people should give up all hope and live in the way the white men commanded. So he nodded and held out his hand.

Hornet placed a rifle in it, an old Henry they had taken from one of the ranches they had raided.

"One of the white men has ridden back to check behind the wagon," Swift Pony said. "The other still rides in front. I will kill him, and that will be your signal to attack. Some of you surround the wagon while the rest kill the other white man. Be careful. The women may have guns. Do not let them shoot you."

"No white woman will ever shoot *me*!" Broken Branch declared.

Swift Pony hoped his old friend was right. But like all the others, Broken Branch would have to take his chances.

As the others got ready to mount and begin the attack, Swift Pony took the rifle and climbed back to the top of the bank. He found himself a good, stable spot where he could brace his feet and steady himself as he took aim. He worked the Henry's lever to throw a cartridge into the firing chamber and slid the barrel over the edge. He laid his cheek against the smooth wooden stock and settled his sights on the man riding in front of the wagon.

A young man, Swift Pony saw now that the rider was closer. Not much more than a boy in a buckskin shirt, with a brown hat cocked back casually on his head.

He would never get any older, Swift Pony thought as his finger tightened on the Henry's trigger.

CHAPTER THIRTY-FIVE

Ace was riding easy, his eyes constantly on the move as his gaze roved over the landscape ahead of him, when for the barest instant the sun glinted off something at the edge of that meandering wash. His instincts cried out for instant action, and finely honed nerves and muscles responded.

He jerked the chestnut hard to the right and leaned far to that side. The crack of a shot and the whine of a bullet passing close beside him sounded together less than a heartbeat later.

Off balance, his horse fought hard to keep from falling. Hauling hard on the reins to keep the chestnut's head up, Ace jabbed his heels into the animal's flanks. The horse leaped ahead, and that convulsive movement helped it regain its balance.

Ace grabbed his Winchester and yanked it from its sheath. He swung the horse back toward the dry wash as several riders burst out of it and were galloping toward him, firing rifles as they came.

By the time he recognized them as Indians and realized they had to be the band of renegades Lieutenant

Wingate's patrol was looking for, Ace had lifted the rifle to his shoulder in one smooth motion, drawn a bead, and pressed the trigger.

The Winchester cracked, and one of the attackers flew backwards off his horse with his arms flung out to the sides. He landed with a limp bounce like a rag doll carelessly tossed aside.

More riders were emerging from the wash as Ace fired three more rounds, jacking the Winchester's lever between shots as fast as he could.

Then he turned and raced back toward the wagon, glad to see that Agnes had brought it to a stop and scrambled over the seat into the back with the other ladies. The wagon's thick sideboards would stop most bullets. He just hoped they would stay low.

But he should have known better. Two of the women popped up—probably Lorena and Agnes—and rifle shots rang out from the wagon.

Now Ace hoped their aim was good enough that they wouldn't hit him as he galloped toward them.

A glance toward the rear told him that Chance had been drawn by the gunfire and was closing in from that direction. Ace looked over his shoulder. More than a dozen Comanche warriors were in pursuit, which matched what Wingate had said about the size of the war party.

If he and Chance could both reach the wagon and fort up there, they might have a chance. Sure, they were outnumbered, but they were good shots and had plenty of ammunition. Also, it was open ground around the wagon, so the renegades wouldn't have any cover and couldn't sneak up on them.

The Indians could, however, kill the horses in the

team and strand the Jensen brothers and the women, then keep them pinned down until nightfall came.

Once darkness cloaked the landscape, defending the wagon would be almost impossible.

One battle at a time, Ace told himself. Maybe they could inflict enough damage on the renegades to make them give up the attack. They might even be able to kill that war chief, Swift Pony, and take the heart out of the others . . .

That was what Ace was thinking when his horse went down with no warning. As it collapsed underneath him, he kicked his feet free of the stirrups. The next instant, he was sailing through the air as momentum carried him over the chestnut's head. He hit the ground so hard consciousness fled from him.

Chance's heart seemed to leap into his throat as he saw Ace's horse go down. Ace was thrown clear and after he landed and rolled over a couple times, he didn't move again. He was either knocked out . . .

Or the fall had broken his neck and killed him.

Chance didn't let himself believe that. He urged his horse to a faster pace, even though the gelding was already lunging forward with long, ground-eating strides.

From the corner of his eye as he flashed past the wagon, Chance saw Agnes and Lorena kneeling inside the vehicle and firing rifles toward the Indians. The other three women were all staying low, out of the line of fire. Chance was glad to see that. He hoped they could hold off the renegades while he grabbed Ace and then hurried back to the wagon.

It was a race, though, with life and death as the stakes. Some of the attackers charged directly toward Ace. Dirt flew in the air around his motionless form as the Indians fired at him. They wouldn't know if he was still alive or not, but they were willing to spend some bullets to make sure.

Shooting from the back of a galloping pony was difficult, but if they reached Ace first, they would be able to fill him with lead as they charged past. Even though it went against the grain for Chance to rein his horse to a sliding stop, he knew that was the only way to save his brother.

The cream-colored gelding trembled just a little but otherwise stood stock-still as Chance raised his rifle, aimed quickly, and fired. The whip-crack blast was followed an instant later by one of the renegades jerking around on the back of his pony and then sliding off. The man riding right behind him had to leap his horse over the fallen man to avoid trampling him.

Chance fired again, and that second man did a backflip as the slug blew a good-sized chunk of his head away. The other two renegades who had been heading for Ace veered off.

Chance kicked his horse into a run again, daring to hope that he could save his brother.

As he pounded up to Ace a couple heart-stopping moments later, he realized that the rest of the war party had skirted around him and was closing in on the wagon. Chance twisted his head around to look and saw that puffs of powder smoke still came from the vehicle.

"Hold out," he muttered as he threw himself from the saddle before the horse had even stopped moving. His hat flew off his head as his feet hit the ground. "Hold out for just a minute."

Ace lay facedown. Chance dropped to his knees beside him and grasped his shoulders. He rolled Ace onto his back. Ace's head was slack on his neck, but it wasn't bent at an unusual angle.

And he was breathing, Chance realized as he saw the steady rise and fall of his brother's chest. Ace had been knocked cold by the fall, but he was alive.

Chance pulled him up into a sitting position, got an arm around his shoulders, and slapped him lightly across the face. "Ace! Ace, wake up, damn it!"

Ace groaned and moved his head a little, but his eyes didn't open. Chance looked at the wagon. The Indians were circling it, but oddly enough, they didn't seem to be shooting.

Because they didn't want to kill the women, he realized.

They wanted to capture them.

That sudden knowledge was like a punch in the gut from a giant, ice-covered fist. Chance let Ace slump back to the ground and leaped for his saddle. Now that he knew Ace was alive, he could turn his attention back to defending the women.

The almost hopeless, overwhelmingly outnumbered task of protecting the women . . .

The shooting had stopped. Chance saw the wagon swaying back and forth and knew some of the renegades were in the wagon with the ladies. He was going to be too late.

Agnes struck out with the butt of the rifle she clutched, trying to ram it into the face of the warrior who had hold of Jamie, who shrieked and writhed but couldn't break free. The Comanche saw the blow coming and twisted out of its way. He lifted his foot in a brutal kick that sank into Agnes's belly and doubled her over.

At the other end of the wagon, Isabel slashed back and forth with her dagger at another of the renegades. He was one of four men who had leaped from their ponies into the vehicle. Face twisted in anger, he darted back, out of reach of the blade. In an instant, while Isabel was off balance, he leaped forward, knocked her arm up with his left arm, and cuffed her heavily across the face with his right hand.

Isabel's knees buckled and the dagger slipped from her fingers.

Lorena had dropped the rifle she had been using and pulled out her pistol, knowing it was better for close work. As one of the renegades leaped at her, she thrust the barrel against his belly and pulled the trigger. His body muffled the little pop of the gun going off so that it was almost inaudible.

His eyes widened in pain and shock, but he barreled into her anyway, catching hold of her by the neck and ramming her against one of the curved wooden struts that gave the wagon's canvas cover its shape. Even though he was gut shot, he kept choking her until she lost consciousness.

Molly was putting up a fight, too. She had no weapon, but she hammered her fists against the bare chest of the man who had grabbed hold of her. Unfortunately, the blows did no good. He was much too strong for her, and she cried out in horror as he swung her out of the wagon and into sinewy hands that were waiting for her.

After the kick to the belly, Agnes struggled to catch her breath and get back to her feet. She made it in time to see Jamie, Isabel, and Lorena passed out of the wagon to warriors on horseback. Molly was already held tightly on one of the ponies. Isabel and Lorena appeared to be unconscious—or worse. Jamie was still fighting, but to no avail.

Some of the men who had been in the wagon were abandoning it, leaping agilely from the vehicle to the backs of their ponies.

Agnes screamed, "No!" as the riders wheeled to gallop away with their captives. She made a grab for the rifle she had dropped a minute earlier.

One of the renegades backhanded her before she could pick up the gun. She slumped against the side-boards, too stunned to move. The man reached for a knife sheathed at his waist, and in that moment, Agnes knew she was about to die.

Another Indian grabbed that one by the arm and pulled him away. Both of them jumped from the wagon onto horseback. Shots roared somewhere nearby. The renegades returned the fire as their ponies lunged after the others.

Agnes found the strength to reach up, grab the top sideboard, and pull herself to her knees. As she looked out, something dripped into her eyes and blurred her vision. She lifted a hand, touched her face, saw the fingers come away smeared with blood.

"Agnes!"

A familiar voice bellowed her name. She looked over and saw Chance Jensen flinging himself out of the saddle with the Smith & Wesson held in his right hand. Smoke curled from the muzzle, telling her that he had fired the shots she just heard.

The bullets hadn't done any good. All the renegades who had swarmed around the wagon were still mounted and riding hell-bent toward the south.

Chance leaped into the wagon, caught hold of her shoulders, and pulled her around. A lot of times on the journey she would have loved for him to grab her like that—but that moment was not one of them.

"You're bleeding!" Chance said. "How bad are you hurt?"

Agnes found her voice. "I . . . I don't know. I don't think I was shot. One of them hit me . . . with his hand . . ."

"Looks like it just opened up a cut, and head wounds always bleed bad." Chance pulled a bandana from his pocket, wadded the cloth up, and pressed it to the wound. "Here, hold this. We need to stop that bleeding."

"Ace . . ." Agnes had seen him fall, and her heart had twisted inside her at the sight. They had become friends. "Is he—"

"He's alive." Chance looked toward the wash. "They didn't circle back to finish him off, thank God. They got what they were after and just wanted to get away with their prizes."

"The others," Agnes said hollowly. "The Indians took all of them."

"Yeah," Chance said, "and as soon as Ace comes to his senses, we're gonna go get them back."

CHAPTER THIRTY-SIX

The young warrior Hornet had his hands full with the woman whose hair was so pale it was almost like snow. Old women had hair that color, but this one was far from old. She was young and firm and rounded, especially the part that was pressed against his groin as he held her in front of him on the running pony. She twisted futilely, trying to get away.

Once they reached Mexico, one of the older warriors would probably claim the fair-haired woman, and Swift Pony would agree. Hornet, being young and having very little status in the band, would have to accept that decision, but for now, he was going to enjoy the closeness he felt with her. For the moment, she was his.

The tough, wiry Indian mounts could run all day, but after a while Swift Pony ordered his men to slow down. They rode for several more miles at that easier pace, then the war chief called a halt in another arroyo, much like the one where they had waited to ambush the wagon.

The two women who had been stunned during the

struggle had regained their senses. At first they had fought—all of them had fought—but as the miles passed, their efforts to break free had weakened. Both—the one with flaming red hair and the one with dark hair who looked like a Mexican—had given up, seemingly, and rode with their heads down and their shoulders slumped.

Despite that attitude, Hornet would not have trusted them. White women could never be trusted.

Swift Pony himself did not ride with any of the captives. That would have been beneath a war chief. But Hornet had seen him looking with considerable interest at the older woman with darker blond hair. She still struggled and spat white man's curses.

A woman with such a fiery spirit would be a good match for Swift Pony. Her sons might not be as weak as Broken Branch believed they would be.

Several of the men slid down from their mounts and took hold of the women, dragging them from horseback and throwing them to the sandy ground. Hornet hated to let go of his fair-haired captive, but he had no choice. He threw a leg over the pony's back and dropped to the ground.

The attack on the wagon had not gone exactly as Swift Pony had anticipated. Those two young men had been faster, more accurate, and deadlier shots than most white settlers were. Three members of the war party were dead, and another was wounded.

Worse still, at least one of the white men was still alive and probably galloping to Fort Concho to bring word of the attack. The cavalry would set out in pursuit of the renegades and their captives. Swift Pony had planned to be much farther away before anyone realized the women had been taken.

Angry, the war chief stalked back and forth with his face set in grim lines while the ponies and men rested.

"You should have let me kill the ugly woman," Broken Branch said as Swift Pony stalked past him. It wasn't a good time to be scolding Swift Pony, Hornet thought, but Broken Branch was stubborn and always believed he was right about everything.

Swift Pony swung around sharply, his lips curling in a snarl.

"There was no time, because we failed to kill both white men. It was more important for us to escape with our prisoners. Those women will bear us sons and ensure that our people continue."

Broken Branch spat. "Half-breeds," he said contemptuously. "Not white or red. We would do better taking Mexican women."

"We will need Mexican women, too," Swift Pony said, "but there was no reason to pass these up." He rested his hand on the knife at his waist. "I am still war chief here, Broken Branch. You would do well to remember that."

Broken Branch glared defiantly at him for a moment then looked away. He would push only so hard against Swift Pony's leadership.

"There would have been time to capture all the white women if both of the men were dead," Swift Pony went on, frowning all around the group. "But everyone went after the women, even though I said some of you should kill the men."

"You missed the first shot," Broken Branch muttered.

For an instant, Hornet thought Swift Pony was going to attack Broken Branch and kill him for his disrespect. However, they needed every warrior who could fight, if they were going to avoid capture themselves and reach the border.

They had been carrying on the conversation in the Comanche tongue, of course, when suddenly the darker blond woman said in English, "You. Big fella. Where in blazes are you taking us?"

Because of the time they had spent on the reservation, all the warriors spoke the white man's language, at least to some degree. Hornet was fairly good at it, having picked it up because he was young.

Swift Pony spoke it well, too. He glared at the blonde and said, "Be quiet, woman."

"Yeah, well, you can just go to hell," she responded. "If you're smart you'll let us go right now, before you get even deeper in trouble."

Swift Pony laughed scornfully. "Trouble? Do you believe my men and I fear women?"

"I'm not talking about us. I'm talking about Ace and Chance Jensen."

"The white men who were with you?" Swift Pony shook his head. "I am not afraid of these . . . *Jensen boys.* If they pursue us, they will die!"

The woman sounded strangely confident—confident enough to make Hornet frown in sudden worry—as she said, "You just keep on thinking that, mister, and in the end we'll see who lives . . . and who dies!"

Chance had dragged Ace to the wagon and propped him up against one of the front wheels. Agnes dipped a rag in one of the water barrels and wiped it over his face as he started to come around.

Ace's eyes fluttered open. For a moment he wasn't

able to focus, but then Agnes's face settled into familiar lines as she knelt in front of him and leaned close.

"You're hurt!" he said.

"What, this?" She gestured toward the strip of cloth tied around her forehead. "It's nothing, just a cut. Chance cleaned and bandaged it."

Chance walked around from the other side of the wagon, carrying a rifle. "He's awake?"

"Yes, he just came to. How do you feel, Ace? Can you see all right?"

"Yeah, things were a little fuzzy at first, but it's better now." He sat up straighter and winced. "What happened?" Something occurred to him and made him look around quickly, even though the movement caused fresh pain to pound inside his skull. "Where are the others?"

Agnes swallowed hard. "The Indians took them."

"All of them?" Ace said, his eyes widening in shock.

"Yeah." Chance's face and voice were grim. "I think all of them were all right when those renegades rode off with them, but God knows what's happened to them since."

Ace took hold of the wagon wheel and pulled himself to his feet. The world spun crazily for a second, but he braced himself on the wheel and his head settled down quickly. "How long ago was this?"

"Less than half an hour," Agnes said.

"I'd say twenty minutes," Chance added. "You were out for a while. You must've banged your head pretty hard when you fell off your horse."

Ace looked around again. Relief went through him when he spotted the chestnut standing not far off with Chance's gelding. The horse appeared to be all right.

"He's not hurt," Chance said, knowing what his

brother was thinking. "He must have stepped in a hole when he went down. Lucky he didn't bust a leg."

"Yeah, lucky," Ace repeated with a slightly hollow note in his voice. He was glad his horse was all right, but that was the only ray of light in an otherwise terrible situation. "We have to go after them."

"Damn right. Are you able to ride?"

"You bet I am," Ace said. "Where's my hat?"

"It's up on the driver's seat," Agnes told him. "I'll get it for you, and if you'll wait a minute I'll put together some supplies for you."

Ace started to tell her that they couldn't afford to wait, but considering that they didn't know how long they would be on the trail of the renegades, maybe taking some supplies with them wasn't such a bad idea.

Agnes climbed onto the box, tossed Ace's hat to him, and then disappeared into the wagon. The canvas cover had been lowered on the sides, so the Jensen brothers couldn't see what she was doing.

"I'm a little surprised you didn't go after them without me," Ace said.

"Believe me, I thought about it, but I knew how much you'd complain if you came to and I'd already had all the fun." Chance grew more solemn as he added, "Besides, I figure we'd stand a better chance of rescuing those ladies if we both go after them."

"You mean if all three of us go after them." Agnes jumped down from the driver's box.

Both brothers raised their eyebrows when they turned to look at her. She had taken off the simple traveling dress she'd been wearing and replaced it with a pair of overalls and a man's shirt. Work boots were on her feet, and she had a broad-brimmed hat on her head.

"This is what I wore back on the farm," she went on. "I thought it would be better for riding."

"Wait just a blasted minute," Chance said. "You're not coming with us, if that's what you're thinking."

"That's exactly what I'm thinking." Agnes picked up the rifle she had placed on the floorboards in front of the driver's seat. "I'm going to unhitch that bay horse from the team. He looks like he'll do the best for riding."

"We don't have an extra saddle," Ace pointed out.

"I rode all over my family's farm, almost from the time I could walk, and never saw a saddle. I'll put one of our blankets on him, and it'll be fine."

"You're going to fight Indians?" Chance said.

"What do you think I was doing just a little while ago? I burned plenty of powder, shooting at the varmints."

"How many of them did you hit?" Ace asked.

Agnes glared at him. "I don't know. Maybe I hit some of them and maybe I didn't. But the important thing is that you're not going to leave me here while you go off after those savages. I may not have known any of those ladies a couple weeks ago, but they've become friends of mine."

Ace thought about it for a moment and then said, "Having an extra gun along might not be a bad idea."

"But she might get hurt," Chance objected.

"Don't talk about me like I'm not right here," Agnes said. "I'm willing to run the risk. Besides, we may have trouble coming up on us from behind, too. What if I was here with the wagon by myself and those Fairweather brothers came along?"

"She has a point," Ace said. "It's not safe to take her with us, but it's not safe to leave her here, either. She might as well be where we can keep an eye on her."

Chance grimaced. "I suppose you're right. Let's get that horse unhitched."

"We need to take all of the horses with us," Ace said. "Once we've rescued the ladies, they'll need mounts to ride, too."

That made sense. They unhitched all the horses and rigged hackamores and lead ropes for them. Ace had considered taking the wagon along, then quickly discarded the idea. Even with the extra horses they could move a lot quicker than they would be able to with the wagon. They would have to leave the vehicle and all its contents. Somebody might come along and loot it, but that couldn't be helped, and anyway, it didn't really matter.

Everything the women had packed to bring along with them to their new lives wouldn't mean a blasted thing if they remained captives of the Comanche—or worse.

A few minutes later, Ace, Chance, and Agnes rode away from the wagon, leading the extra horses and heading south.

CHAPTER THIRTY-SEVEN

The six men reined their horses to a halt as they came in sight of what appeared to be an abandoned wagon.

"What's that?" Ripley Kirkwood asked as he lifted himself in his stirrups and peered across the scrubby wasteland.

"Might be just an immigrant wagon that some pilgrims went off and left," Lew Shelby said.

"No, it ain't," Seth Cooper spoke up excitedly. "That's the wagon them women were travelin' in, ain't it, Earl? We got a good look at it when we snatched Molly away from 'em."

Leon grunted. "Didn't do a very good job of keeping her, did you?"

Cooper's face flushed angrily, but Earl Brock lifted his good hand and motioned for Cooper to take it easy. They had come this far in their edgy alliance, and there was no point in letting it descend into argument.

"Let's just go see what that wagon can tell us," Brock suggested.

"Might be a trap," Shelby said.

"Not likely. The horses are gone. It looks like they went off and left the wagon there."

Kirkwood's voice showed the strain he was under as he asked, "What if the women are in there . . . dead?"

"They'd better not be," Brock said. "I've got too much riding on Molly still being alive. Nothing bad's going to happen to her . . . at least until I catch up to her again." He hadn't explained about the money Molly had stolen from him. There was no point in tempting their newfound allies into a double cross. All Kirkwood, Leon, and Shelby knew was that Molly was married to Brock and had run away from him, and that he was determined to find her and settle that grudge.

The men nudged their horses into motion again. They spread out so they could approach the wagon from slightly different directions. Kirkwood and the wounded Earl Brock hung back a little, letting Leon, Shelby, Cooper, and Hawthorne—all able-bodied fighting men—take the lead. Those four rode with their rifles ready.

Coming up to the wagon, it quickly became apparent that no lurking threat would be found. The vehicle was empty of human occupants—living or dead.

From the back of his horse, Shelby looked over the tailgate, spotted some bloodstains in the back of the wagon, and pointed them out to the others. "Something happened here, that's for sure."

Cooper poked at some marks on the outside of the wagon bed. "Bullet holes."

"Empty shells inside the wagon, too," Hawthorne added. "There was a fight here."

Kirkwood and Brock rode up.

Hearing the comments, Kirkwood quickly moved his horse over next to the driver's box. "Let me look through their things. If I can find something of Isabel's, that'll prove this is the right wagon." He stepped from the saddle onto the box and then climbed into the back of the wagon.

He was in there for only a few moments before he reappeared on the box clutching a gold necklace with an emerald dangling at the end of the chain. He waved it in the air and said, "This is hers! I should know since I gave it to her, the ungrateful bitch. This is the right wagon, all right."

"That's what we told you," Cooper said. "Question now is, where the hell are them women?"

Hawthorne pointed to a welter of tracks on the ground and said, "Looks like some unshod ponies were millin' around here. That means Indians."

"Savages," Kirkwood said. "I thought the Indian troubles in Texas were over."

"Mostly," Shelby said. "But that don't mean all the redskins are gone. Every now and then some of those bucks take it in their heads to go raiding again."

Kirkwood's face became more pale than usual as he asked, "They usually kill white captives, don't they? Often by torturing them to death?"

"Hey, you've got a grudge against that gal you've been chasing, don't you?" Shelby said with an ugly grin. "Maybe her winding up in the hands of some blood-thirsty Comanches will do the job for you."

A growl sounded deep in Leon's throat. He started to turn his horse toward Shelby's when Kirkwood shook his head in a signal for Leon to let the gibe pass.

Hawthorne said, "Any time redskins go to the trouble of carryin' off a woman, there's at least a chance they won't kill her. Could be they figure on makin' squaws out of those prisoners. That's happened plenty of times. After a few years, the only way you can tell a captive woman ain't an Injun is because she's got blond hair or blue eyes. Other than that, they talk Comanch', they dress Comanch', they have Comanch' babies and live like Comanch'. And some of 'em, even when they're rescued, don't want to go back to bein' white."

"That would never happen to Isabel," Kirkwood snapped. "She's too strong-willed for that. She'll force them to kill her before she would ever go along with such degradation."

Brock said, "You'd be surprised what some folks will do in order to survive."

Cooper had ridden off a short distance from the wagon. He called to the others and pointed to the ground. "Looks like they all headed south. Funny thing, though. There's this whole bunch of unshod Injun ponies, and then trailin' along behind them are the tracks of half a dozen horses wearin' shoes."

"That explains where the wagon team is," Brock said. "Those Jensen boys went after the Indians, and they unhitched the team and took the horses with them so the women will have something to ride once they've been rescued."

"There were more than a dozen renegades," Shelby said. "What are the chances those two youngsters can rescue those women?"

"More than likely they'll just get themselves and all the women killed. But they'd damned well better not do it before I get my hands on Molly!" With that, Brock set off on the trail of the Indians and their prisoners, following the tracks that were clearly visible in the sandy soil. Cooper and Hawthorne were right behind him, and after a moment, Kirkwood, Leon, and Shelby turned their horses and followed as well.

Ace had worried about Agnes's ability to keep up, but so far she had shown no signs of flagging. She rode well, just as she had claimed. Her face was etched with lines of determination. The bandage around her forehead just added to her grim appearance.

At the same time, it gave her a bit of a rakish look. Chance commented quietly on that while they were stopped to let the horses rest and Agnes had retreated into a stand of chaparral to tend to personal business.

"That bandage makes her look a little like a pirate, don't you think?" Chance said.

"Would you have noticed that if Jamie was still around?"

"I think I might have. Agnes is hard to ignore."

"You did a pretty good job of it starting out," Ace said.

Chance grimaced and waved a hand. "I was distracted. That doesn't mean I don't open my eyes sooner or later and see what's right in front of me."

"Maybe the way Jamie acted around Lieutenant Wingate helped open those eyes for you."

"Maybe," Chance admitted. "But I'd like to think I would have noticed her sooner or later."

Agnes came back from the brush then, so the brothers couldn't discuss the subject anymore. They all mounted up and resumed following the trail.

"How far behind them do you think we are?" Agnes asked. "Can we catch up to them before nightfall? Where are they headed?"

"That's three questions," Ace said with a smile. His

head still hurt from being knocked out, but the pain had faded to a dull ache. "Judging by the tracks they left, they were moving pretty fast when they rode away from the wagon. They've got a good lead on us. How big is hard to say. Can't really predict how long it'll take to catch up to them, either."

Chance said. "They're bound to be headed for Mexico. Across the border, they'll be safe from the cavalry, and there's plenty of rugged country down there where they can hole up. Comanches are Plains Indians, but Swift Pony probably knows that if they stay in Texas, they'll either be killed or captured and hanged. Hiding in the Mexican mountains is better than that."

"It's such a wild, uncivilized life," Agnes said. "I don't see how anyone can exist that way."

"It's all they've ever known," Ace said.

The terrain got even flatter and drier the farther south they went. The Jensen brothers hadn't visited that part of Texas before, but it struck them as pretty inhospitable. The only wildlife they saw were tarantulas, scorpions, long-tailed rats, big-eared jackrabbits, and rattlesnakes. And buzzards wheeling through the high, pale blue sky. Dry washes still cut through the landscape, rocky ridges reared here and there, and mesas thrust up in the distance. Prickly pear cactus seemed to be everywhere.

They moved at a fast, steady pace, resting the horses when necessary. All three of the pursuers were prepared to push themselves as hard as possible, but the horses had to be protected. Without their mounts, they stood no chance of rescuing the captives, and if they were set afoot, out there so far from anywhere, they might not make it out alive.

Ace felt his hopes sinking as the afternoon wore on

and the sun began to drop toward the horizon. As far as he could tell by studying the hoofprints they were following, they had cut into the renegades' lead to a certain extent, but the Indians were still well ahead.

The war party had been moving too fast for the women to be in danger of being assaulted, but once night fell, that vestige of safety might disappear along with the sun. The renegades would have to call a halt. They were traveling through unfamiliar country, just like the Jensens and Agnes, and the danger of riding right off a cliff into a canyon would be too great.

Then they would have time to start thinking about their prisoners as women, not just captives.

Ace wasn't going to bring up that subject. He knew Chance was probably aware of it already, and Agnes might well have her suspicions. All they could do was keep moving, keep searching.

And maybe pray a little, too.

By the time the sun touched the western horizon, they hadn't come in sight of the renegades.

Agnes said dispiritedly, "There's not much light left, is there?"

"Another half hour or so," Ace said.

"I really hoped we would find them."

"So did I, but their lead was too big and we're running out of time."

Chance pointed to a mesa that loomed several miles ahead of them. "We ought to be able to make it that far before it's too dark to go on. Might be a good place to camp. We can pick up the trail again first thing in the morning."

"It may be too late for my friends by then," Agnes said.

Gently, Ace said, "We don't have any choice. If we tried to track them at night and lost the trail, it would just delay things in the morning until we could find it again . . . if we were even able to."

"You tracked those men who kidnapped Molly," Agnes objected.

"There was more of a moon that night," Ace explained. "And honestly, I was really lucky, too."

Agnes didn't argue anymore, but her downcast expression spoke volumes.

Chance scraped a thumbnail along his jawline as he stared at the distant mesa and frowned in thought. After a while, he said, "You know, if I could get on top of that mesa and have a look around, I'll bet I could see for a long way. Miles, in fact."

"More than likely," Ace agreed. "But what good would that do us?"

"If those renegades built a fire, I might be able to spot it. That would tell us for sure how far ahead of us they are."

Ace thought about that for a moment and then nodded. "That's not a bad idea," he agreed. "Most of those mesas are rough enough on the sides that they can be climbed. Some even have game trails leading to the top."

"It'll be just about dark when we get there. By the time I can climb to the top, I ought to be able to see a fire if the Comanches have one."

They pushed on, the light turning gold and then orange and then beginning to fade. A darker blue, the hue of oncoming night, stole across the sky from the east. Ace looked in that direction, saw stars seemingly popping into existence here and there. The heat of the day still hung heavy over the land, but at least there was a hint of coolness in the breeze that stirred.

They came up to the base of the mesa and began

circling it, searching in the last of the light for a way up. The trail they found was steep but surprisingly wide. A man could lead a horse up it, if he was careful.

"Maybe we should make camp up there ourselves," Ace suggested when they had dismounted.

"Let me check it out first," Chance said.

"Be careful. That ledge might not go all the way to the top. It could end without any warning."

"I'll make sure of my footing with every step," Chance promised. He left his rifle on the saddle. He didn't expect to need it, since he was just having a looksee to the south.

Both of the Jensen brothers were naturally light on their feet and just as a matter of habit moved around without making much noise. As Chance climbed the trail, he kicked a rock loose every now and then and it rattled down behind him, but that was the only sound other than the sighing of the wind. From time to time he put out his left hand and rested it on the rock wall beside him, steadying himself as he climbed.

He was near the top, close to a hundred feet above the ground, when he heard something that made him stop in his tracks and listen intently. He couldn't be certain, but he thought it was the stamp of a horse's hoof.

For an instant, Chance believed the noise came from below him, but the more he thought about it, the more he believed that it had originated *on top of the mesa*. There was only one good explanation for horses being up there.

The renegades had made *their* camp on the mesa. The Jensen brothers and Agnes not only had caught up, they had almost blundered right into the camp of their enemies.

No matter how intently Chance listened, the sound didn't come again. A part of his brain tried to tell him he had imagined it, but he knew that wasn't true. He had to turn around and slip back down to the ground as quietly as possible so he and Ace could figure out what to do next.

The trail appeared to be the only way on or off the mesa. They could bottle up the renegades and keep them from fleeing any farther south, but as long as the Indians had the four young women as their prisoners, they still held the upper hand. They could bluff their way out by threatening to kill the hostages.

Considering their bloodthirsty recent history, they might go ahead and kill the prisoners anyway.

With that bleak thought in his mind, Chance backed away several steps and then turned around to head back down to where he had left Ace and Agnes.

As he turned, from the corner of his eye he saw a dark shape suddenly appear out of the gloom higher on the trail and leap at him.

CHAPTER THIRTY-EIGHT

Chance twisted and threw up his left arm as the attacker plunged at him. Acting by instinct alone, Chance struck the other man's arm and blocked it, and he knew he had just kept the renegade from planting a knife in him.

Figuring the man had been posted to guard the trail to the top of the mesa, Chance expected that any second now his attacker would open his mouth to yell a warning to the others.

Chance's right hand shot out, groping blindly for the renegade's throat. His fingers slid across sweat-slick skin and he clutched at it. The man rammed into him and knocked him back a step. The knife drew a fiery line across his shoulder as it slashed through his shirt but barely broke the skin.

Chance got a better grip on the man's throat and tried to swing him against the rock wall, but he didn't have his feet planted well enough, and they just staggered back and forth. A part of Chance's brain warned him that they had to be close to the edge of the trail, with a deadly drop beyond the brink.

Chance's boots scrabbled on the ground as he fought to maintain his balance. He blocked another thrust of the knife and caught hold of the Indian's wrist. Then a rock rolled under his foot and he felt himself falling. The renegade stumbled and fell, too.

They hit the trail hard. Gravity made them roll down the slanting surface. Chance went over twice, stopping as the back of his shoulders slammed against the ground for the second time. He sensed that his head was hanging out over a hundred feet of empty air. He writhed and threw the renegade to the side before the man could force him the rest of the way over the edge.

The renegade had hold of Chance's shirtfront with his left hand and dragged him along as they continued their wild tumble down the trail.

Chance recalled that it turned not far below them, where it followed the curving side of the mesa. If they kept going, both of them might fall off and plummet to their deaths.

Calling on all his strength, Chance timed his move and suddenly shoved downward with the hand clamped around the Indian's throat, causing the back of the renegade's head to slam with stunning force against the trail's rocky surface. The man went limp, but momentum sent the two of them rolling over one more time.

And just as abruptly, there was nothing underneath Chance. The trail was gone.

He let go of the renegade and flailed desperately in front of him with both hands as the man fell away. Chance's palms slapped the trail and slid for a couple inches before he clawed his fingers and clung to the rough ground for dear life. His weight hit his arms and he gasped at the pain that exploded in his shoulder joints, but for the moment, at least, he had stopped his fall.

The question was how long he could hang on. The toes of his boots pawed at the side of the mesa as he tried to find a foothold.

His right foot caught on something and took a little of the strain off his arms and hands. He pushed up, continued searching with his left foot, and found a place where the rock stuck out just enough to support some of his weight. With those two footholds, he hung there with his chest heaving as he tried to catch his breath.

He was far from safe. He had to find other footholds if he was going to climb off the almost sheer rock wall. By the sheer strength of his arms, he might be able to pull himself up far enough to throw a leg up onto the trail . . . but the odds were just as good that if he tried, he would fall off.

Because his pulse was pounding so furiously inside his head, he didn't hear the swift footsteps approaching on the trail. He didn't know anyone else was close by until a strong hand closed around his right wrist. Chance's head jerked back as he looked up. Another of the renegades . . . ?

"Hang on," Ace whispered as he knelt at the edge. "I'll pull you up."

"You . . . can't . . ." Chance grated.

"Sure I can."

Ace grunted with effort as he leaned back and hauled as hard as he could on his brother's wrist. At the same time, Chance tried to help lift himself. His body rose high enough for Ace to reach out and grab hold of Chance's shirt with his other hand and power himself backwards toward the wall.

Chance came with him, getting a knee over the edge and lunging forward. Both young man sprawled on the trail with their feet hanging over the edge.

When he was able to talk again, Chance said in a shaky voice, "Damn, that was close!"

"Too close," Ace agreed.

They sat up and scooted away from the brink.

After a moment, a still breathless Chance said, "Agnes?"

"She's down below. She's all right. She's the one who found the body of that Indian who fell from the top. I reckon you had something to do with that?"

"Yeah. You heard him land?"

"We did," Ace said. "It was a pretty ugly sound. But as soon as she found him, we knew the renegades had to be camped up on the mesa and that you'd likely run into trouble. I got up here as fast as I could."

"Fast enough," Chance said. "Barely. I'm obliged to you, big brother."

"Don't worry about that. We need to figure out what we're going to do next." Ace paused. "I'm surprised that fella didn't let out a yell on the way down."

"I had already knocked him out, just before we both went over the edge. He never had a chance to save himself. I did."

"Thank goodness for that." Ace got to his feet and held out a hand to his brother. "Let's get back down there."

Chance clasped Ace's wrist and let him help him up.

"Yeah, we don't have a lot of time. I figure that man was posted on guard duty at the head of the trail. He didn't get to raise the alarm, but there's no telling how long it'll be before the rest of them realize he's not there anymore."

They moved as quietly as possible back down the trail. When they reached the spot where they had left Agnes and the horses, she handed her rifle to Ace and threw her arms around Chance, hugging him tightly.

"When I heard that man land after falling off the mesa, I thought it was you," she said. "Then when I saw it was one of the Indians, I was afraid the rest of them had captured you. Thank God you're all right."

Chance didn't try to pull away from her or disengage her arms. Instead he returned the hug. "It was a pretty close call. I've got a little cut on my shoulder, but it's nothing to worry about. I'm still alive and kicking, and now we know the rest of the bunch is up there with our friends."

"Actually, we don't know that," Ace said. "Maybe they just left one man behind to watch their back trail."

Chance stepped away from Agnes and said, "Blast it! You're right. I never made it to the top. But I heard at least one horse up there. I think that's where they holed up for the night. With just that one trail, it would be easy to defend. Of course, the opposite is true, too. There's only one way out."

"We have to proceed as if they're there. That means we need to take them by surprise and maybe catch them in a crossfire so we can cut down the odds against us."

"How are we going to do that?" Chance asked. "I just said, there's only one way up there."

"But we don't know that, do we?"

Chance frowned in the darkness toward his brother. "What in blazes are you thinking about, Ace?"

"If I could find another way up, I could get on one side of them while you take a position at the head of that trail. Then while you draw them toward you, I could hit them from the other side."

"How do you plan on getting up there?"

"Well . . . I reckon I'd have to climb."

Chance didn't respond for a moment. Then he said, "And folks seem to think I'm the reckless, loco Jensen brother! Do you have any idea how hard it's going to be to climb up there, Ace? Especially in the dark?"

"I've got a pretty good idea. I didn't say it would be easy. But I think we should at least take a look around on the other side to see if we can find a place I might be able to climb it."

Chance didn't argue. He knew Ace was right. There were at least ten of the renegades left alive, maybe one or two more than that. Taking them by surprise was the only way to rescue the prisoners.

"I'm coming with you," Agnes said.

"That's a good idea," Ace said, "but only as far as the place where I climb. If I can make it to the top, I'll signal you. Then you can signal Chance and let him know to start the ball. Better give me a few minutes to look around first, though, so I'll have an idea where the other ladies are."

As they were walking around the mesa, they worked out the details of the plan. When Ace was at the top, he would strike one of the several matches he had in his pocket, holding it below the rim where it wouldn't be seen, and drop it toward Agnes.

That would be her signal to hurry back around to the other side, where she, in turn, would strike a match so that Chance could see it where he lay in wait at the head of the trail. He would then start shooting and hollering to draw the renegades toward him while Ace moved in behind them.

It was a pretty desperate plan, and even if everything went off perfectly, the odds would still be against them.

They might not survive—and if they didn't, the five women were doomed, too.

"They're not going to take me alive," Agnes said. "I'll put up such a fight that they'll have to kill me."

"Let's hope it doesn't ever come to that." Chance put a hand on her shoulder and squeezed reassuringly.

When they judged they were on the opposite side of the mesa from where the trail came out, Ace began closely examining the rock face. As Chance had commented earlier when they first spotted it, the sides of the mesa were pretty rugged. There were a lot of cracks and crevices and places where the rock jutted out to form knobs.

In the dark, they had no way to know what Ace might run into farther up, but he was confident he could climb part of the way to the top. He would have to trust to luck that he could find a route to take him all the way.

"All right. Head back around and go up the trail," he told Chance. "Be careful. They could have discovered that their guard is gone."

"I think they would have raised a howl if they had," Chance said. "They're probably all asleep."

Agnes said, "I don't see how they can sleep after all the atrocities they've committed."

"They'll pay for what they've done," Ace promised. He had rigged a sling for his rifle and draped it around his neck and shoulder, so the weapon rode across his back. He reached up, closed his hand around one of the rocks, and added, "Good luck, Chance."

"You, too, brother." Chance stole away, heading for the trail on the other side of the mesa.

Ace found a foothold, pulled himself up, and felt

around for more places he could grasp with his hands or cracks where he could wedge a toe.

Since they had been raised by a gambler, the Jensen brothers hadn't spent as much time outside while they were growing up as most boys, but they had climbed rocks now and then. Ace had at least some experience doing that.

Not under such desperate circumstances, however.

Since he had to work by feel, he couldn't get in any hurry. The urgency of knowing what the captives might be going through prodded him, but he quickly suppressed that feeling and concentrated on what he was doing. Slowly but surely, he rose up the side of the mesa, detouring slightly from side to side when he reached smoother stretches and had to find a new way.

His pulse pounded. The muscles in his arms and legs began to quiver slightly from supporting his weight. But his grip never slipped, and he remained calm.

Finally, after what seemed like an hour but surely was much less than that, he could tell that the rim was right above him. He made sure both feet had secure holds, tightened his grip with his right hand, and fished in his shirt pocket with his left hand.

Finding one of the lucifers he had made sure was there before he started to climb, he took it out and held it a little to the side, so his body wouldn't block Agnes's view of it. He used his thumbnail to snap it to life. Flame shot up from the match head. It was small, but in the thick darkness, Agnes would be able to see it, especially after Ace let go of the match and it fell, still burning, toward the ground.

The flame winked out before it got there, but its brief flight had been enough. Ace knew Agnes would be hurrying around the mesa to pass along the signal to Chance.

He found a hold with his left hand, pulled himself up again, and less than a minute later rolled over the edge onto the top of the mesa. He lay there on some short grass, catching his breath and listening intently.

The night was quiet for the most part, but after a few moments, Ace heard sounds he identified as horses shifting around.

Then a faint murmur came to his ears. Someone was talking quietly. He couldn't make out any of the words, but he was sure what he heard was human voices.

The mesa top was approximately a quarter of a mile in diameter. The renegades were probably camped somewhere near its center, so they would be less likely to be spotted from the ground.

Ace rolled onto his belly, pushed himself to hands and knees, and then got to his feet. He pulled the rifle around in front of him and lifted its sling over his head. With the weapon held ready, he moved warily toward the middle of the mesa.

A few scrubby bushes grew here and there, as well as clumps of grass, but for the most part the ground was bare. Ace's steps were silent on the rocky surface. He tested each place carefully before he put his full weight on it.

He hadn't gone very far before he spotted some dark shapes ahead of him. From their size, he knew he was looking at the Indian ponies. Off to the left were other, smaller shapes, two of them standing upright. Those would be the two renegades he had heard talking.

Near them were other dark patches on the ground. People sleeping, renegades and prisoners alike. The ladies had to be exhausted after their ordeal.

With any luck, soon they would be free. Ace lifted the rifle to his shoulder and waited. The tranquility of the scene told him no one had discovered that the guard who had fallen from the mesa was no longer at his post.

Chance ought to be in position, and any minute he would put their plan into action.

That thought had just gone through Ace's mind when the crack of a shot split the night's stillness and orange flame spurted from a rifle barrel on the other side of the mesa.

CHAPTER THIRTY-NINE

Chance had felt the tension growing inside him as he crouched beside a rock just below the head of the trail and waited for Ace's signal to be relayed by Agnes. It was probably where the guard had been hiding earlier, when Chance came slipping up the trail the first time.

His second foray to the top of the mesa had gone a lot smoother. He hadn't run into any more sentries. The renegade camp was quiet. He'd heard horses moving around a little, as horses did at night, but that was all. He didn't take a look because he didn't want to risk exposing himself, and also because he had to wait for the sudden flare of a match down below, telling him to start the ball.

He didn't even want to blink, for fear he would miss the signal. Minutes dragged past while he thought about Ace trying to climb the mesa's rugged face on the opposite side.

In the shadows below, a miniature red star was born and moved back and forth three times. Chance's hands tightened on the Winchester he held. That was the sign he'd been waiting for. It meant Ace was at the top of the mesa and would be stealing up on the Comanche camp.

Chance began to count silently in his head, keeping a steady rhythm. Counting to five hundred would give Ace time to move into position and get ready.

Assuming, of course, that nothing went wrong . . .

Four ninety-seven, four ninety-eight, four ninety-nine.

Chance drew in a deep breath, let it out quietly.

Five hundred.

He straightened, moved four steps to the head of the trail, dropped to a knee behind another rock, and brought the rifle to his shoulder. He had already worked the lever to put a cartridge in the firing chamber before he ever went up there. All he had to do was squeeze the trigger, aiming a little high just to make sure he didn't hit Ace or one of the prisoners.

The *whipcrack* as the Winchester went off was startlingly loud.

As he worked the lever, Chance shouted, "Come on, boys! Bugler, blow the charge!" He threw that in just to make any of the renegades who spoke English think the cavalry was there. He wanted to spook them and make them charge right toward him. Yeah, a dozen kill-crazy Comanches against one man.

Maybe he *was* the loco Jensen brother after all.

He fired three more times as fast as he could work the rifle's lever, spraying lead across the mesa as he whooped and hollered. Shots blasted back at him, blooming redly in the darkness. A slug whined off the boulder next to him. Angry screeches came from the renegades.

Chance hoped that Ace would be getting into action

soon, because he had a whole heap of hell bearing
down on him.

As gun-thunder filled the night, Ace raced toward
the camp. The moon hadn't risen yet, but there was
enough starlight for him see men leaping to their feet
as the shots jolted them out of their sleep. They ran
toward the muzzle blasts from Chance's Winchester
and started shooting back at him.

With that much racket going on, Ace thought they
might not notice a few more shots coming from
behind them. He just had to be sure that none of the
women were in the way. As he came up to the area
where everyone had been sleeping, he saw four figures
still on the ground, writhing around as if they were tied
up and trying to free themselves.

"Stay down, ladies!" he called to them, then opened
fire. He swept the rifle from left to right, cranking off
half a dozen rounds, then tracked the Winchester back
the other way, firing four more shots.

The lead tore into the renegades like a scythe mowing
down wheat. Several of them went down right away,
the slugs hammering them off their feet, while others
stumbled but remained upright. A few of them even
managed to turn around and try to meet the unexpected threat.

Chance had lowered his sights, and the renegades
were close enough to the edge where he knelt behind
the boulder that they were good targets. Ace heard
the cracks from his brother's rifle and saw more of the
Indians fall.

But some of the renegades hadn't been hit, and they
weren't giving up without a fight. Ace emptied the rifle

as two of the warriors charged at him. One man went down with a couple bullets in his chest, but the other bounded on without slowing. Either Ace had missed him, or his battle frenzy allowed him to ignore his wounds.

Ace dropped the Winchester and drew his Colt. He got off one shot before the Comanche launched himself into the air with a shrill war cry and crashed into the young man.

The collision drove Ace over backwards. The Indian's weight came down on him, driving all the air from his lungs and putting a painful strain on his ribs. The man tried to thrust a knee into Ace's groin, but Ace twisted aside and smashed his gun against the man's head.

That should have knocked the renegade out cold or even fractured his skull and killed him, but somehow he kept fighting. His fingers closed around Ace's throat and squeezed. Ace was already caught without much breath, and he couldn't get any more as the man's brutal grip closed off his windpipe.

A red haze swam up from the bottom of Ace's vision and threatened to swallow him whole. On the verge of passing out, he had no doubt the Indian would choke him to death if he lost consciousness.

Ace thrust the Colt's barrel underneath the renegade's chin and pulled the trigger again. The gun's boom was muffled, but he felt the hot shower of gore on his face as the top of the man's head blew off. Gagging, Ace shoved the corpse to the side and rolled the other way.

As he came up on his knees, he heard a scream from where he had seen the women a few moments earlier. In the dim starlight it was difficult to be sure, but he thought he saw one of the renegades looming over a figure lying on the ground. The man raised his arm as starlight winked on a knife blade.

Ace shot him, the Colt roaring again. The figure groaned and toppled sideways. Ace breathed a swift prayer that he had not made a mistake and shot one of the prisoners.

That worry was soon put to rest.

The intended victim reached over to the fallen man and picked up the knife. She sat up and started sawing at the bindings around her ankles. "Ace! Ace, is that you?"

He recognized Lorena's voice. Springing to his feet, he dashed over to her as she finished cutting her feet free. He holstered the gun, knelt beside her, and took the knife from her hands, which were tied in front of her. A few quick slashes of the blade, and the bonds fell away.

"Is everybody all right?" he asked.

"We're fine," Lorena said. "Give me that knife, and I'll cut the others loose. Is that Chance over there on the other side of the mesa?"

"Yeah."

Shots still rang out from that area.

"It sounds like they have him pinned down."

"Not for long. When you get the others free, all of you stay here. We'll be back for you." Ace jumped up and hurried toward the battle that was still going on. Working by feel, he thumbed fresh cartridges into the Colt's empty chambers. The darkness didn't matter. He could load a gun in his sleep.

He couldn't tell exactly where the trail came out on top of the mesa, but when he saw a couple muzzle flashes he knew where Chance was. Three tongues of flame licked out from the rifles wielded by the renegades as they returned Chance's fire. Ace headed for the nearest one.

Spotting a figure crouching behind one of the small bushes that dotted the top of the mesa, he called, "Hey!"

The renegade spun toward him. Ace fired first. The Comanche's rifle went off harmlessly into the air as he toppled over backwards with Ace's bullet in his chest.

The exchange drew the attention of one of the other surviving members of the war party. A rifle cracked and sent a bullet whipping past Ace's ear. He dived forward and landed on his belly. The Colt roared and bucked in his hand as he triggered twice. The renegade howled in pain, spun around, and pitched to the ground.

That left just one. As Ace leaped to his feet again, the Comanche ran toward him, screeching in insane hatred as he charged.

Chance's rifle cracked again. The renegade arched his back as lead smashed into it. He stumbled a few more steps and then fell face-first, almost at Ace's feet.

Echoes from the gunshots rolled across the flatland around the mesa and gradually faded, leaving hollow silence in their place.

"Ace?" Chance called into that hush. "Are you all right?"

"Yeah," Ace replied. "How about you?"

"I'm fine." Chance stood up from behind the rock where he had taken cover and trotted toward his brother. "Where are the women?"

"We're over here," Lorena called.

Together, the Jensen brothers hurried to join them. The ladies were getting shakily to their feet. Their tight bonds and awkward positions had caused their feet and legs to go to sleep. Despite that, they stumbled forward to meet Ace and Chance and hug them in relief and gratitude. Jamie was sobbing, but Lorena, Isabel, and Molly were all dry-eyed.

"Are any of you hurt?" Ace asked when the happy reunion had calmed down a little.

"Not enough to worry about," Lorena replied. "We got roughed up some during the fight at the wagon, but nothing serious."

"And they hadn't gotten around to doing anything since we camped," Isabel added.

Lorena went on. "The boss man—the one called Swift Pony, I guess—he seemed to give them orders to stay away from us. I reckon he didn't want to try to divvy us up until they got to where they were going. Figured it might cause too much jealousy and friction."

"You were lucky," Chance said.

"I know. Where's Agnes?"

The others echoed that question, worried over the fifth member of their group now that they had been freed from captivity.

"She's down below," Ace said.

"You brought her with you to chase those renegades?" Lorena sounded surprised.

Chance laughed. "You didn't think she'd willingly be left behind, did you?"

"We didn't think it would be safe to leave her with the wagon, either," Ace added.

Isabel said, "She is a very strong-willed girl. It will be good to see her again."

"No reason you can't do that right now," Chance said. "You'll just need to be careful going down that trail in the dark. You wouldn't want to slip and fall."

"You go ahead and take the ladies on down," Ace told his brother.

"What about you?" Lorena asked.

"I have something to do up here," Ace said.

Chance nodded, knowing that Ace meant he needed to check the bodies of the renegades and make sure all of them were dead. He had been keeping a close eye on them, even during the reunion with the ladies, to make sure none of them were stirring.

Chance herded the ladies over to the trail and started them down single file. Lorena led the way, then Jamie, Molly, and Isabel. Chance brought up the rear. Ace reloaded his Colt again and began the grim chore of looking over the bodies. He had to light matches to make sure some of them were dead.

A couple of the lifeless faces revealed by the glare of a lucifer were so young that Ace's jaw tightened. Two members of the war party had been little more than kids, only a few years younger than him and Chance. But despite their youth, they had decided to go on the war path, probably because they dreamed of glory following their chief, Swift Pony.

They had taken part in slaughtering a number of innocent settlers, Ace recalled. He wasn't going to lose any sleep over his part in putting an end to their murderous rampage.

Satisfied that they didn't have to worry about any of the renegades posing a threat in the future, he turned his attention to the ponies. He and Chance could lead them down off the mesa in the morning, Ace decided. He didn't want to risk doing it in the dark.

He was about to start down from the mesa, ready to rejoin his brother and the ladies, when a figure appeared in front of him at the top of the trail.

"Chance? Something wrong?"

A harsh voice said, "Something's wrong, all right, Jensen. You're about to die."

The shape split into two as one person was pushed to the ground by the other. Ace recognized the one who had stumbled and fallen to her knees as Agnes.

Stepping up behind her, putting a gun to her head, was the man who had spoken.

Lew Shelby.

CHAPTER FORTY

Ace's hand started toward his gun, but Shelby went on. "Don't do it, Jensen. I'll blow this bitch's head off if you touch that Colt."

Ace lifted both hands slightly. "Take it easy, Shelby. Don't get nervous and pull that trigger."

"I won't unless you give me a reason to. Believe me, I don't mind killing a woman, but I'd just as soon not have to. Now back up and don't try anything funny."

With no other choice for the moment, Ace backed away from the trail. Shelby reached down with his free hand, caught hold of Agnes's shoulder, and dragged her roughly to her feet again.

Keeping a tight grip on her, he forced her forward. More shapes appeared at the top of the trail behind him and filed onto the mesa. Ace didn't know who was with Shelby, since most of his allies had been killed or captured back in Cross Plains, but it was obvious the gunman wasn't working alone.

"I'm sorry, Ace," Agnes said. "I guess I'm not cut out to be a frontier woman after all. I didn't hear them sneaking up on me."

"That's all right," he told her. "We'll figure this out."

Shelby laughed. "There's nothing to figure out. I'm gonna kill you two Jensen boys, and my new friends are going to get what they want, too."

One of the newcomers said, "We need some light. Cooper, get a fire started."

The voice was vaguely familiar to Ace, and when he heard the man mention the name Cooper, he knew why. It was one of the men who had kidnapped Molly, way back there on the other side of that escarpment west of Weatherford. That explained who three of the men were.

The others would be Hawthorne, Ripley Kirkwood, and his man Leon. The groups had joined forces.

All Ace needed to make things complete was for the Fairweathers to show up.

The renegades might have had a fire back in the center of the mesa where they had camped, but the man called Cooper didn't try to stir up its embers and rekindle the blaze. He gathered some dry brush near the edge, piled it up, and lit it. As the flames caught and began to grow, the flickering yellow light they cast spread over the thirteen people clustered near it.

Ace saw that his guess about the identities of their enemies was correct. The six men all had guns out. Some of them covered the women, who were huddled together, while the others kept their revolvers pointed at Ace and Chance.

Shelby told Ace, "Get over there with your brother, you little bastard."

Chance appeared to have been disarmed. His face was pale, not from fear but from anger. "I'm sorry. They met us when we weren't even halfway down the trail. Shelby had a gun to Agnes's head, so there was nothing I could do."

"I know. He had me in the same fix."

Shelby said, "All right, Jensen . . . you, Ace . . . take that gun out with your left hand and toss it down."

Ace's jaw tightened. He hated to give up his gun. But if he forced a fight, outnumbered as they were, he and Chance would almost certainly wind up dead, and the ladies would be in the hands of these varmints. Still, he hesitated.

Molly provided a distraction by saying, "Have you told your new friends what you're really after, Earl?"

"Shut up, you little—"

"Fifty thousand dollars!" Molly's voice rose as she interrupted him. "That's what he wants. He's just a no-good outlaw, and he wants his loot."

"Loot that you stole from me!" Brock roared at her.

Lew Shelby glanced over at him. "What the hell? Fifty grand?"

"All the money my gang and I had cached," Brock said as he glared at Molly. "And she stole it and ran away, the hussy!"

Tight-lipped, Molly said, "I reckon I earned it, being married to you."

So it hadn't been a random kidnapping after all, Ace thought. Brock and his companions had a reason for what they had done. But they hadn't shared that with Shelby, Kirkwood, and Leon, probably because they were worried about a double cross.

From the look of avarice that had appeared suddenly on Shelby's face, that concern was justified. Molly was trying to drive a wedge between their captors, and she might just succeed.

Kirkwood had eyes only for Isabel, though, and Leon was as impassive as always.

"Where's the money?" Brock went on.

Molly shook her head and laughed coldly. "Miles from here. You'll never find it."

"I'll make you tell me. I've heard about how the redskins torture their prisoners. I'll make you wish those damn Comanches still had you, girl."

"Go to hell," Molly snarled at him.

In a voice sharp with impatience, Ripley Kirkwood said, "I've had enough of this. Brock, you and the others can settle your own affairs. Fifty thousand dollars means nothing to me. I came for Isabel. I'm taking her and leaving."

She jutted out her chin defiantly. "I'll never go with you, Ripley. You're a madman. You'll have to kill me."

"Well . . ." Kirkwood smiled. "I always said that if I couldn't have you, no one else could." He raised the gun in his hand.

"No," Leon said.

Kirkwood glanced over at him and frowned. "What did you say?"

"No," Leon repeated. "You're not going to hurt that girl or even *try* to hurt her, ever again."

Anger flushed Kirkwood's face an even darker red in the firelight. "I think you're forgetting that you work for me. You do whatever I tell you, damn it. Now go over there, get Isabel, and bring her to me."

Slowly, Leon shook his head. "I didn't help her get away from you back in New Orleans and then come all this way just so you could get your hands on her again."

Isabel gasped. "That was you who unlocked my door? Why?"

"I figured you deserved better than this piece of scum."

Kirkwood's eyes widened. Rage made his voice tremble as he said, "How dare you! I won't stand for this!" He jerked his gun away from the women, pointed it toward Leon, and pulled the trigger.

Leon was already moving, but he didn't try to avoid the bullet. He grunted as the slug punched into him, dropped his own gun, and spread his arms wide as he lunged at Kirkwood.

The young man fired twice more, but the shots didn't seem to have any effect. Leon caught him up in a crushing grip and lifted him off his feet.

Kirkwood screamed in pain and horror as Leon bore him backwards toward the brink.

The big man said, "There's only one way . . . to make sure you never hurt anybody else . . . and I never help you . . . again!"

Kirkwood's shriek rose as they both went over the edge. It continued for a couple seconds before it stopped with an abrupt finality.

Everyone was staring in shock at the spot where the two men had disappeared. Everyone except the Jensen brothers.

Chance leaped toward Shelby. From the corner of his eye, the gunman saw Chance coming and swung his gun around, but before he could fire, Chance tackled him and drove him off his feet. The revolver boomed, but the bullet went high in the air.

At the same instant Chance went into action, Ace's hand dipped to the Colt still in his holster. The gun came up spitting flame and lead.

One of the men with Brock went down with a bullet in his heart before he could pull the trigger. The other got a shot off, and Ace felt the wind-rip of the slug as it passed his ear. He triggered again and saw the man's head snap back as the .45 round bored between his eyes. His knees buckled and pitched him forward.

Despite being wounded, Earl Brock had his gun out, but it was in his left hand and he was slow bringing it to bear on Ace. Before he could pull the trigger, Molly leaped forward and grabbed his arm, forcing it up and throwing off his aim. He snarled and slashed at her, raking the barrel and the front sight across her face.

She had given Ace time to draw a bead, and when his Colt boomed again, Brock staggered as the bullet drove into his chest. The gun slipped from his fingers.

Molly scooped it from the ground, raised it in both hands, and fired it directly into Brock's face from close range. The outlaw's features disappeared in a bloody smear as he went over backwards.

While the shooting was going on, Chance and Lew Shelby rolled across the rough ground, wrestling over Shelby's gun. Chance had his left hand locked around Shelby's right wrist to keep the muzzle pointed away from him. He used his right to hammer punches into the gunman's head and body.

They rolled into a clump of grass next to some rocks along the mesa's edge. Chance heard a sinister buzzing sound, then Shelby suddenly screamed and jerked away from him. The killer leaped to his feet and fired down at the ground, blowing a thick, writhing shape into bloody pieces. Chance scooted away and looked around for something he could use as a weapon.

Shelby turned toward him, and Chance saw the angry red fang marks on the man's cheek where the rattlesnake that had been coiled up against the rocks had struck him. Shelby screamed as he stumbled around, no doubt feeling the venom coursing through his veins. The way Shelby's heart was pounding, the poison spread through most of his body quickly.

Chance surged up from the ground and launched himself at Shelby again. His shoulder rammed into the gunman's belly and knocked him backwards. His knees hit the rock behind him, and in the blink of an eye, he flipped over it and was gone. Chance heard him hit the trail somewhere below, then Shelby screamed again. He'd bounced off and fallen the rest of the way to the ground.

Chance leaned on the rock for a second to catch his breath, then backed hurriedly away from it. Where there was one rattler, there might be another.

Ace came up beside him and grasped his shoulder. "Are you all right?"

With his pulse still hammering in his head, Chance nodded. "Yeah. How about you and the ladies?"

"We're alive—and all the rest are dead."

It was true. Corpses littered the mesa and the area around it. Despite the grim death that surrounded them, Chance laughed.

"What in the world is funny?" Ace asked.

"This is when . . . the rest of those damned Fairweathers ought to show up."

"Don't even think it," Ace said, but he started reloading his Colt just in case.

By the light of the campfire Ace and Agnes built at the base of the mesa, Lorena cleaned and bandaged the wound on Molly's face. It was probably going to leave a scar, but at least she was alive, which had looked pretty doubtful when they were prisoners.

* * *

The Fairweathers didn't show up. Ace and Chance were both grateful for that.

The next morning, after the group had spent the rest of the night at the base of the mesa, Lieutenant Wingate and his patrol of buffalo soldiers did.

Ace saw the dust rising first and alerted Chance. Quickly, they got the ladies started up the trail, so they could take shelter on top of the mesa. The Jensen brothers intended to hold the trail against any attackers.

Ace used his field glasses and was able to make out the blue uniforms and the guidon, as had happened with the previous encounter, and he called them back down.

Wingate had his pistol in hand as he reined in. He looked around and exclaimed, "Good Lord! Are you ladies all right?"

"Molly and Agnes each have an ugly cut," Lorena said, "but the rest of us are fine."

Jamie said, "We're a lot better now that you're here, Lieutenant Wingate!" Her relief was obvious and heartfelt.

Chance gave Ace a wry smile. They had saved the women, but neither brother had any doubt that Jamie was going to carry on as if Wingate was responsible for their rescue. Chance no longer appeared to care what her attitude was, though, so that was an improvement, thought Ace.

In fact, Chance and Agnes had been talking together quietly and seemed to be enjoying each other's company quite a bit.

Wingate dismounted. Jamie hugged him, but he looked around. "Are those bodies I see?"

"Yeah," Ace said. He and Chance had dragged the bodies of Kirkwood, Leon, Shelby, and the Comanche guard into a crevice in the rock face. The other dead Comanches, along with Brock, Cooper, and Hawthorne, were still atop the mesa.

Wingate could bury them all if he wanted to. Ace and Chance weren't going to that much trouble when there were plenty of coyotes and buzzards around.

"What are you doing here, Lieutenant?" Chance asked.

"Yesterday after we parted company from you, we heard shooting in the distance," Wingate explained. "We doubled back and found the empty wagon, then followed the tracks from there. I'm afraid we, uh, lost our way for a time or we would have arrived before now. I'm relieved to see that we weren't too late."

"Well . . . too late to do any real good," Chance pointed out, which earned him a quick glare from Jamie.

"I take it you encountered Swift Pony's war party?"

Ace nodded. "Those Comanche renegades are all dead, Lieutenant. You can go back to the fort." Thinking about the Fairweathers, he added, "In fact, if you'd care to give us and the ladies an escort to San Angelo . . ."

"Of course. I'll have to make a report on the incident, and that will give me plenty of time to find out all the details." Wingate pinched the brim of his cavalry hat. "By tonight, ladies, you'll all be safe in San Angelo. I give you my word on that!"

"I don't reckon we ever really doubted it," Lorena said with a smile, "since we'll still be traveling with those Jensen boys!"

The smiles from the other ladies, even Jamie, made it clear that they felt the same way.

CHAPTER FORTY-ONE

Since the mesa was considerably south of the route they had been following, the group had to backtrack some to retrieve the wagon before heading west again.

It was after dark before they rolled into San Angelo, accompanied by Lieutenant Wingate's patrol. The lieutenant had to take his men on to Fort Concho, but he lingered long enough to say good-bye to Jamie and promise that he would come back to check on her the next day.

Agnes commented to Ace and Chance. "I think that rancher who was supposed to marry Jamie is going to be disappointed. She's set her cap for a dashing young cavalry officer, and I have a feeling she's going to get what she wants!"

"I wouldn't be a bit surprised," Chance agreed.

Molly stood nearby. She put a hand to the bandage on her cheek and said, "I doubt if Jonas Blosser will want to marry me now. Not as ugly as I'll be with this terrible scar."

"That's crazy," Lorena said. "If he's got any sense, he won't let that bother him."

Isabel said, "The fact that you have fifty thousand dollars of stolen money might put a crimp in your plans."

Molly sighed. "I've already said I'd return the money. I didn't steal any of it, you know. Earl and his men did that. I kind of . . . took it with me . . . when I ran away from him, but I'd just as soon it go back to where it belongs."

"Easy to say, now that your secret has been revealed," Isabel pointed out.

"Well, at least I didn't have a lunatic chasing me." Molly paused. "Well, maybe Earl *was* a little bit loco. But it's not really the same thing."

Lorena put a hand on her arm. "Come on, honey. Let's go find the doctor's office so he can take a look at that cut. I'm engaged to him, you know—"

"Molly!" bellowed a big man with a large voice.

Everyone turned sharply toward the sound. Ace and Chance moved their hands toward their guns.

Three men were walking quickly toward the wagon. One was tall and brawny, dressed in rough work clothes. The other two were smaller and wore suits. None of the trio appeared to be armed.

One of the men took his hat off and said, "Miss Hutton?"

"That's me," Lorena told him.

He smiled as he said, "I'm Lawrence Madison. Dr. Lawrence Madison. We've exchanged letters—"

"Larry!" Lorena threw her arms around him. "It's so good to finally meet you." She planted her lips on the startled medico's lips in a big kiss.

Madison was surprised, but he got over it quickly.

"Isabel?" said the other well-dressed man.

"Mr. Gilpin?" she replied. "I mean . . . Abner?" She held out a hand, and he took it.

"You're even more beautiful than I expected. We were all commiserating with each other over coffee at the café, wondering if the ladies we'd pledged our troth to were ever going to arrive, when someone came in talking excitedly about a cavalry patrol riding in with a wagon full of women, and we just knew it had to be the ladies we'd been waiting for!"

Smiling, Isabel said, "Do you always talk so much, Abner?" She leaned her head toward Lorena and the doctor. "You're being given a good example to follow right there."

Abner Gilpin took her into his arms.

A few feet away, the big man who had to be blacksmith Jonas Blosser had both hands wrapped around one of Molly's. "I can't believe a gal as little and pretty as you would want to marry a big ol' ox like me—"

"Wait, Jonas," she said.

Blosser's expression plummeted. "I knew it. You've changed your mind."

"No, but there are some things you need to know. There are some . . . legal matters . . . that will have to be cleared up before we can be married." Molly turned her head to look at Ace. "The money's hidden under the wagon, you know, in that storage area."

"*That's* what you were doing messing around the wagon that night!" Ace exclaimed. "The night that I—"

He had started to say *grabbed you when you were mostly naked* then decided that might not be the best thing to talk about in front of Molly's future husband. She could decide what she wanted to tell Jonas about her past and everything that had happened on the trip between Fort Worth and San Angelo.

Molly, Lorena, Isabel, and their prospective bride-grooms drifted off down the street toward Dr. Madison's office. Jamie went into the hotel, saying something about getting word to the rancher she was supposed to marry, but Ace wasn't sure she would get around to doing that. Not with Lieutenant Wingate having promised to come see her the next day.

Chance said, "We need to get that money and see about having the sheriff lock it up until everything is settled."

"Yeah, we may have brought it this far, but I don't want the responsibility for it," Ace agreed.

Chance turned to Agnes and went on with a trace of reluctance, "You'll have to get in touch with your fella, too, and let him know you made it."

"Well . . ." Agnes cocked her head to the side and frowned. "That's going to be a little difficult to do, since I don't, uh, don't actually *have* a fella who was supposed to meet me here."

That revelation took both the Jensen brothers by surprise.

Ace said, "What are you talking about? You're a mail-order bride."

"Actually, I'm the one who paid Mr. Keegan to arrange for my trip out here. I let him believe the money came from one of his clients, but that fellow never wrote back to me. I wanted to come anyway, so I used the money I had saved to start a new life. I thought it could pay for an adventure instead." She smiled in the light that came from the nearby buildings. "And it was an adventure, there's no doubt about that."

"So you don't have a husband waiting for you," Chance said.

Agnes shook her head and smiled. "Not a husband in sight, prospective or otherwise."

That was certainly true, Ace thought—but he had a hunch his brother and Agnes might enjoy getting to know each other better before the day came when the Jensen brothers went on the drift again.

TURN THE PAGE FOR AN EXCITING PREVIEW!

*National bestselling authors William W. Johnstone and
J. A. Johnstone spin a breakneck tale about a heroic
chuckwagon cook who knows just what to do
when cowboys get hungry—for revenge . . .*

THE CHUCKWAGON TRAIL

Framed for murder, Dewey "Mac" McKenzie is
running for his life. Though Mac's never even made
a pot of coffee, he talks his way onto a cattle drive
heading west—as a chuckwagon cook. Turns out he
has a natural talent for turning salt pork and dried
beans into culinary gold. He's as good with a pot and
pan as he is with a gun—which comes in handy on a
dangerous trail drive beset with rustlers, hostile
Indians, ornery weather, and deadly stampedes.
Mac can hold his own with any cowboy twice his age.
At least until the real showdown begins . . .

Mac's trail boss, Deke Northrup, is one mean spit in
the eye. Before long, he's made enemies of all his
men. Mac learns that Northrup is planning to
double-cross the herd's owner, Mac stands up to
the trail boss and his henchman. He might be
outgunned and outnumbered, but Mac's ready to
serve up some blazing frontier justice—
with a healthy helping of vengeance . . .

THE CHUCKWAGON TRAIL
by WILLIAM W. JOHNSTONE
with J. A. Johnstone

On sale now, wherever Pinnacle Books are sold.

LIVE FREE. READ HARD.

CHAPTER ONE

Dewey Mackenzie shivered as he pressed against the wet stone wall and blinked moisture from his eyes. Whether it came from the chilly rain that had fallen in New Orleans earlier this evening or from his own fear-fueled sweat—or both—he didn't know. He supposed it didn't matter.

Right now, he just wanted to avoid the two men standing guard across the street. Both were twice his size, and one had the battered look of a boxer. Even in the dim light cast by the gas lamp far down Royal Street, Mac saw the flattened nose, the cauliflower ears, and the way the man continually ducked and dodged imaginary punches.

At some time in the past, those punches hadn't been imaginary, and there had been a lot of them.

A medium-sized young man with longish dark hair and what had been described by more than one young woman as a roguish smile, Mac rubbed his hands against the sides of his fancy dress trousers and settled his Sunday go-to-meeting coat around his shoulders.

Carrying a gun on an errand like this was out of the

question, but he missed the comforting feel of his Smith & Wesson Model 3 resting on his hip. He closed his eyes, licked his lips, and then sidled back along the wall until he reached the cross street. Like a cat, he slid around the corner to safety and heaved a huge sigh.

Getting in to see Evangeline Holdstock was always a chore, but after her pa had threatened him with death—or worse—if he caught him nosing around their mansion again, Mac had come to the only possible conclusion. He had been seeing Evangeline on the sly for more than two months, reveling in the stolen moments they shared. Even, if he cared to admit it to himself, enjoying the risks he was running.

He was little more than a drifter in the eyes of Micah Holdstock, owner of the second biggest bank in New Orleans. Holdstock measured his wealth in millions. The best the twenty-one-year-old could come up with was a bright, shiny silver cartwheel and a sweat-stained wad of Union greenbacks, but he had earned the money honestly at a restaurant in the French Quarter.

Mac held his hands in front of him and balled them into fists. He had worked as a farmhand and a half dozen jobs on riverboats before he washed ashore in the Crescent City three months earlier. Every bit of that work was honest, even if it didn't pay as well as sitting behind a bank desk and denying people loans.

He tried to erase such thoughts from his mind. Holdstock's bank served a purpose, and the man made his money honestly, too. It just wasn't the way Mac earned his. It wasn't the way anyone else he'd ever known in his young life had earned their money, either.

If he wanted to carry out his mission tonight, he had to concentrate on that. He had gotten himself cleaned up for a simple reason.

Looking his best was a necessity when he asked Evie to marry him.

"Mrs. Dewey Mackenzie," he said softly. He liked the sound of that. "My wife. Mrs. Evangeline Mackenzie."

A quick peek around the corner down Royal Street dampened his spirits a mite. The two guards still stood in front of the door leading into the Holdstock house. Shifting his eyes from the street to the second story revealed a better way to get in without being caught and given a thrashing.

More than likely, Evie's pa had told those bruisers they could toss him into the river if they caught him snooping around. This time of year, the Mississippi River roiled with undertow and mysterious currents known only to the best of the riverboat pilots. It wasn't safe to swim anywhere near the port.

"Besides," he said softly to himself, "I don't want to muddy up my fancy duds." He smoothed wrinkles out of his coat, then boldly walked across the street without so much as a glance in the guards' direction.

He stopped and looked up when he was hidden by the wall. A black iron decoration drooped down from the railing around the second-story veranda just enough for him to grab. He stepped back a couple paces, got a running start, and made a grand leap. His fingers closed on the ornate wrought iron. With a powerful heave, he pulled himself up and got a leg over the railing.

Moving carefully to keep from tearing his trousers or getting his coat dirty, he dropped to the balcony floor and looked down to see if he had drawn any unwanted attention. Mac caught his breath when the guard who must have been a boxer came around the corner, scratched his head, and looked down the street. Moving quickly, Mac leaned back out of sight before the man looked up.

Senses acute with fear, he heard the guard shuffle away, heading back toward the door where his partner waited. Mac sank into a chair and used a handkerchief to wipe sweat from his forehead.

If this had been a couple of months later, he would have been drenched in sweat and for a good reason. Summer in New Orleans wore a man down with stifling heat and oppressive humidity, but now, late April, the sweat came from a different cause.

"Buck up," he whispered to himself. "Her pa can't stop you. You're going to marry the most wonderful girl in all New Orleans, and tonight's the night you ask for her hand."

Mac knew he had things backward, but considering how Mr. Holdstock acted, he wanted to be sure Evie loved him as much as he did her. Best to find out if she would marry him, *then* ask her pa for her hand in marriage. If Evie agreed, then to hell with whatever her pa thought.

He took a deep breath, reflecting on what she would be giving up. She claimed not to like the social whirl of a young debutante, but he had to wonder if some part of her didn't enjoy the endless attention, the fancy clothing, the rush of a cotillion followed by a soirée and whatever else they called a good old hoedown in New Orleans society.

A quick look over the railing convinced him the guard had returned to his post. Stepping carefully, knowing from prior experience where every creaky board was, he made his way along the balcony to a closed window. The curtains had been pulled. He pressed his hand against the windowpane, then peered into Evie's bedroom. Squinting, he tried to make out if she stood in the shadows. The coal-oil lamp had been extinguished, but if she was expecting him, she wouldn't advertise her presence.

He tried the door handle. Locked. Using his knife blade, he slipped it between the French doors and lifted slowly. When he felt resistance, he applied a bit more pressure. The latch opened to him, as it had so many times before. Evie liked to playact that he was a burglar come to rob her of her jewels, then ravish her.

The thought of that made him blush because he enjoyed it as much as she did. More than once, he had sneaked into her room and gone through the elaborate ritual of demanding her jewels, then forcing her to disrobe slowly to prove she had not hidden anything on her body. Both of them got too excited to ever carry on with the charade for more than a few minutes. He went to the bed now and pressed down on it with his fingers, remembering the times they had made love here.

Mac swung around and sat, wondering how long he should wait before he went hunting for her.

For all he knew, her ma and pa were out for the night. Their social life mingled with Holdstock's banking business and caused them to attend parties and meetings throughout the week to maintain their standing in the community. Mac got antsy after less than a minute and went to the bedroom door. Carefully opening it, he looked down the hallway. Evie's room was at the back of the house, while her parents had the room at the front, at the far end of the hallway lined with fancy paintings and marble sculptures. The Persian rug muffled his footfalls as he made his way to the head of the stairs.

The broad fan of steps swept down to the foyer. He ducked back when he heard Holdstock speaking with someone at the door. From the guest's accent, he was French. That meant little in a town filled with Frenchmen and Acadians. French Creole was almost as widely spoken as English or Spanish.

"I am glad we could meet, Monsieur Leclerc. Come into the study. I have a fine cigar from Cuba that you will find delightful."

"*Bon*, good, Mr. Holdstock. And brandy?"

"Only the finest French brandy."

The two laughed and disappeared from sight. Mac cursed his bad luck. It would have been better if Holdstock were out of the house rather than entertaining— or conducting business, judging by the formality the two showed one another. Some high-powered deal was being struck not fifty feet away. That deal would undoubtedly make the banker rich. Or richer than he already was.

But Mac didn't care about that. His riches were wrapped in crinoline and lace, with flowing blond hair and eyes as green as jade. He stepped back and wondered where she might be.

Then he heard her soft voice below as she greeted Monsieur Leclerc and exchanged a few mumbled pleasantries. The sound of her slippers moving against the foyer floor set his heart racing. He hastily retreated to her bedroom and closed the door behind him. From past times here, he knew the exact spot to stand.

Beside her wardrobe, hidden in shadow when she lit the oil lamp, he could cherish her for a few seconds before she realized she was not alone. Mac pressed into the niche just as the door opened. He closed his eyes and took a deep whiff. Jasmine perfume made his nostrils flare. This was her favorite perfume, but he told her often she did not need it, not with him. Just being around her intoxicated his senses more than enough.

He opened his eyes and squinted as he stared directly into the burning wick of Evie's bedside lamp. She bent over slightly, hands on the bed, her bustle wiggling delightfully.

"I have never seen any woman so lovely," he said. "If I live to be a thousand, I never will forget this moment, this sight, this beautiful—"

She straightened and spun. Her eyes went wide. His heart almost skipped a beat when he realized it wasn't surprise that caused her face to contort. It was fear.

"What's wrong, my dear?" He went to her, but she pushed him back.

"Go, Mac. Get out of here now. Please. Don't slow down. He knows we've been seeing each other."

"I don't care. I love you. Do you love me?"

"Yes, yes," she said, flustered. She brushed back a wayward strand of lustrous, honey blond hair and looked up at him. True fear twisted her face. "I love you with all my heart and soul, Mac. That's why you have to leave."

"Then let's go together. Let's elope. We can find a justice of the peace. We don't have to get married in the St. Louis Basilica."

"Mac, you don't understand. I—"

"I can't give you a fancy house or fine clothing or jewelry like this." He touched the pearl necklace around her slender throat, then moved to caress her cheek. "Not now. Someday I will. Together we can—"

"You have to go before he catches you!"

"I'll go down and beard the old lion in his den. We'll

have it out, man to man. I won't let him chase me off from the love of my life." He moved her around so he could go to the door.

Before he could get there, the door slammed open, reverberating as it smashed into the wall. Silhouetted against the light from downstairs, Micah Holdstock filled the frame.

"I should have known you would come, especially on a night like this!"

Mac began, "Mr. Holdstock, I—"

"Papa, please, you can't do this. Don't hurt him." Evie tried to interpose herself between the men, but Mac wouldn't have it. No woman he loved sacrificed herself for him, especially with her father.

"Evie and I love each other, sir. We're getting married!"

Micah Holdstock let out a roar like a charging bull. The attack took Mac by surprise. Strong arms encircled his body and lifted him off his feet. He tried to get his arms free but couldn't with them pinned at his sides. Still roaring, Holdstock went directly for the French doors and smashed through them. Shards of glass sprayed in the air and tumbled to the balcony as he used Mac as a battering ram.

The collision robbed Mac of breath. He went limp in the man's death grip. This saved him from being driven against the iron railing and having his back broken. He dropped to his knees as Holdstock crashed into the wrought-iron railing and fought to keep from tumbling into the street below.

"Papa," he heard Evie pleading, trying to stop the attack.

Mac got to shaky feet to face her pa.

"This is no way for future in-laws to act," he gasped out. "My intentions are honorable."

"She's betrothed. As of this very evening!" Again Holdstock charged.

Mac saw the expression of resignation on Evie's face an instant before her father's hard fist caught him on the side of the head and sent him reeling. He grabbed the iron railing and went over, dangled a moment, then fell heavily to the cobblestone street and sprawled onto his back. He stared up to see Evie sobbing bitterly as her father grabbed her by the arm and pulled her out of sight.

"You can't do this. I won't let you!" He got to his feet in time to see the two guards round the corner. From the way they were hurrying, he knew what they had been ordered to do.

Shameful though it might be, he turned and ran.

The guards' bulk meant they were slower on their feet than Mac was. Three blocks later, he finally evaded them by ducking into a saloon in Pirate's Alley. He leaned against the wall for a moment, catching his breath. The smoke in the dive formed a fog so thick it wasn't possible to see more than a few feet. He coughed, then went to the bar and collapsed against it. "I say this to damned near ever'body what comes into this place," the barkeep said, "but in your case I mean it. You look like you could use a drink."

CHAPTER TWO

The bartender poured a shot of whiskey.

Mac knocked it back, and it almost knocked him down. He wasn't much of a drinker, but this had to be the most potent popskull he had ever encountered. He choked, swallowed, then said, "Another."

"The first was on the house. The next one you pay for."

"I just had a run-in with my lady friend's pa." He sucked in a breath and endured the pain in his ribs. Micah Holdstock had a grip like a bear. The powerful liquor went a ways toward easing the pain. He fumbled out a greenback for another drink. He needed all the deadening he could pour down his gullet.

The bartender picked up the bill, examined it, and tucked it away. "Don't usually take Yankee bills, but seeing's as how you're in pain, I will this time." He splashed more whiskey into Mac's empty glass.

Mac started to protest at not getting change. As the second shot hit his gut and set his head spinning, he forgot about it. What difference did it make anyway?

He had to find a way to sneak Evie out of the house and get her to a judge for a proper marrying.

"Do tell."

Mac blinked and frowned. He hadn't realized he had been talking out loud, but obviously the bartender knew what he'd been thinking. He ran a shaky finger around the rim of his empty shot glass and captured the last amber drop. He licked it off his fingertip. The astringent burn on his tongue warned him that another drink might make him pass out.

"I'll find a way," he said, with more assurance than he felt. He needed both hands on the bar to support himself.

As he considered a third drink, he noticed how the sound in the saloon went away. All he heard was the pounding of his pulse in his ears. Thinking the drink had turned him deaf, he started to shout out for another, then saw the frightened expression on the barkeep's face. Looking over his shoulder, he saw the reason.

The two guards who had been stationed outside Micah Holdstock's front door now stood just inside the saloon, arms crossed over their chests. Those arms bulged with muscles. The men fixed steely gazes on him. Out of habit—or maybe desperation—Mac patted his right hip but found no revolver hanging there. He had dressed up for the occasion of asking Evie to marry him. There hadn't been any call for him to go armed.

He knew now that was a big mistake. He turned and had to brace himself against the bar with both elbows. He blinked hard, as much from the smoke as the tarantula juice he had swilled. Hoping he saw double and only one guard faced him, he quickly realized how wrong that was. There were two of them, and they had blood in their eyes.

"You gonna stand there all night or you gonna come for me?" He tried to hold back the taunt but failed. The liquor had loosened his tongue and done away with his common sense. Somewhere deep down in his brain, he knew he was inviting them to kill him, but he couldn't stop himself. "Well? Come on!" He balanced precariously, one foot in front of the other, fists balled and raised.

The one who looked like a boxer stirred, but the other held him back.

"Waiting for the bell to ring? Come on. Let's mix it up." He took a couple of tentative punches at thin air.

"Mister, that's Hiram Higgins," the bartender said, reaching across the bar to tug at his sleeve. "He lost to Gypsy Jem Mace over in Kennerville."

"So that just means he can lose to me just east of Jackson Square."

"Mister, Gypsy Jem whupped Tom Allen the next day for the heavyweight championship."

"So? You said this man Higgins lost."

"He lost after eighteen rounds. Ain't nobody stayed with the Gypsy longer 'n that. The man's a killer with those fists."

Mac wasn't drunk enough to tangle with Holdstock's guard, not after hearing that. But the boxer stepped away deferentially when a nattily dressed man stepped into the saloon. The newcomer carefully pulled off gloves and clutched them in his right hand. He took off a tall top hat and disdainfully tossed it to the boxer. Walking slowly, the man advanced on Mac.

"You are the one? *You?*" He stopped two paces away from Mac, slapping the gloves he held in his right hand across his left palm.

"I'm your worst nightmare, mister." Still emboldened by the booze, Mac flipped the frilled front of the man's bleached white shirt. A diamond stud popped free. The man made no effort to retrieve it from the sawdust on the floor. He stared hard at Mac.

"You are drunk. But of course you are. Do you know who I am?"

"Not a clue. Some rich snake in the grass from the cut of your clothes." Mac tried to flip his finger against the man's prominent nose this time. A small turn of the man's head prevented him from delivering the insulting gesture.

"I am Pierre Leclerc, the son of Antoine Leclerc."

"I've heard the name. Somewhere." Mac tried to work out why the name was familiar. His head buzzed with a million bees inside it, and he was definitely seeing double now. Two of the annoying men filled his field of vision. He tried to decide which one to punch.

"He owns the largest shipping company in New Orleans. It is one of the largest in North America."

"So? You're rich. What of it?"

"You will leave Miss Evangeline Holdstock alone. You will never try to see her again. She wants nothing to do with you."

"Why's that, Mister Fancy Pants?"

"Because she and I are to be married. This very night my father arranged for her hand in marriage to unite her father's bank and our shipping company."

"Your pa's gonna marry her?"

"You fool!" Leclerc exploded. "You imbecile. *I* am to marry Miss Holdstock. You have given me the last insult that will ever cross your lips." He reared back and slapped Mac with the gloves. A gunshot would have been quieter as cloth struck flesh.

Mac stumbled and caught himself against the bar. He rubbed his burning cheek.

"Why, you—"

"You may choose your weapons. At the Dueling Oaks, tomorrow at sunrise. Be there promptly or show the world—and Miss Holdstock—the true depth of your cowardice." Leclerc slapped his gloves across his left palm for emphasis, spun, and walked from the saloon. The two guards followed him.

"What happened?" Mac said into the hollow silence that hung in the air when Leclerc was gone. He was stunned into sobriety.

"You're going to duel for this hussy's favor at sunrise," the bartender said.

"With guns?"

"You'd be wise to choose pistols. Leclerc is a champion fencer. He can cut a man to ribbons with a saber and walk away untouched."

"Heard tell he's a crack shot, too," piped up someone across the saloon.

"Eight men he's kilt in duels," another man said. "The fella's a fightin' machine—a killin' machine. I don't envy you, boy. Not at all."

Mac found himself pushed away from the bar by men rooting around in the sawdust looking for the diamond stud that had popped off Leclerc's shirt. He watched numbly, wondering if he ought to join the hunt. That tiny gemstone could pay for passage up the river.

Then he worked through what that meant. Evie would call him a coward for the rest of her life. And running would show how little her love meant to him. He loved her with all his heart and soul.

If it meant he laid down his life for her, so be it. He would be north of town at the Dueling Oaks at dawn.

After another drink.

Or two.